Caught In Their Own Explosion

"Ships have set out from Dielaan, Garth." Finally she looked at him, her delicate features backlit within. "I think Rex wants a war. . . . He will lead soldiers from our lands into war, and they will all die. Especially if Rex seizes the Atare's wife—Sheel Atare will move mountains to find her. The last war was less than fifteen years ago!" This was ragged; intense. "Do you think the clans will tolerate this? What if Atare decides to wipe us from the planet?"

Garth knew he was staring at her, but he couldn't help himself. First murder, and now war. *Lucy is right; I am going to die.*

"Lucy . . . do you realize what you're saying?" It sounded stupid to his ears, but he desperately needed time to think.

"We have been used," she said steadily. "My honor is stained."

"Screw honor, woman! We're talking about our lives!"

☆   ☆

"The intricacies of the well-controlled plot are far too great to go into here—there is much upheaval, much intrigue, and much romance . . . a particularly fine mix."

—*Locus* on *Fire Sanctuary*

*

Also by Katharine Eliska Kimbriel

FIRE SANCTUARY
FIRES OF NUALA

HIDDEN FIRES

KATHERINE ELISKA KIMBRIEL

WARNER BOOKS

A Time Warner Company

This story is a work of fiction. All characters are fictitious, and any resemblance to actual persons, living or dead, is purely coincidental.

WARNER BOOKS EDITION

Questar® is a registered trademark of Warner Books, Inc.

Cover design by Don Puckey
Cover illustration by Don Dixon

Warner Books, Inc.
666 Fifth Avenue
New York, NY 10103

W A Time Warner Company

Printed in the United States of America

First Printing: February, 1991

10 9 8 7 6 5 4 3 2 1

For my parents, and my grandparents, with love:

Katharine Layman Schell Kimbriel
who has taught me patience;
William Donald Kimbriel
who has taught me prudence;
Frances Eliska Stricklin Kimbriel
who has taught me graciousness;
Harry Augustus Kimbriel
who taught me generosity;
Mary Katharine Turman Schell
who taught me honesty;
James Layman Schell
who has taught me endurance.

Thank you all

Acknowledgments

There are always people who contribute to the birth of a book. Most of them are never named, even if they are thanked. They are people like the Chicago gang [Thomas, Guy, Diane, Mark, Lynn, Jeff, Penny, Shannon, John, Kathy, John, Marcia, etc., etc.] who encourage and question and are always ready with sympathy and/or a kick in the pants as needed. There are people like the Greater Chicago gang, i.e. the rest of the country—people like sibs Beth and Karen, Wanada, Terry, Bob Asprin, Ru Emerson, Ardath Mayhar, Elizabeth Moon, Warren Norwood, Patricia C. Wrede, Kathleen, Jean and Bob, etc. etc. There are the internationals, like Al and Amy and troops and Guy Kay. And there are the locals—in Texas that means a long day's drive, by the way—like Deborah and Michael, Nancy and Liten, Susan and Robert, John and Julie, Todd and M.J., Tom, Liz, Larry and Darla, Della and Steve, Scott and Sandi, Becky, Paul, Willie, Robert, Teresa and Scott, Fred and Karen, and—well, you know who you are. . . . Of course, there are the business folks—Valerie Smith, my agent, and Brian Thomsen, my editor, who are patient and supportive, even when they're not quite sure what I'm doing!

But this time there are people who have given more than encouragement and a place to prop an elbow, and they deserve special thanks. When I wrote geologist Ann Palen and miner Al Mosch of the Independent Mining Association, I hoped for a few suggested references. I did not expect an invitation to see their mine and their work through their eyes—everything from the Phoenix Mine in Idaho Springs, Colorado to the Buffalo Bar and Grill! They said: "You must see it to understand it." At the least, I know what they meant, and I hope I have conveyed a bit of the wonder and terror the hardrock mines inspire. Their tireless efforts on my behalf led to one of the most incredible experiences of my fledgling career—a tour of the AMAX Inc. Henderson Molybdenum Mine in Empire, Colorado. Thanks to their work with AMAX public relations manager Terry Fitzsimmons, I spent the better part of a morning 2,000 feet beneath the earth. Kudos to general manager William R. Hinken for graciously allowing the tour, and enthusiastic thanks to chief engineer William G. Doepken and industrial engineer Eivind B. Jensen. Bill gave me the bird's eye-view, while Eivind took me to the depths, giving me a solid base on which to build a trinium mine. If this book even hints at the realities of mining, it is greatly due to their efforts. All errors and wild flights of fancy are my own.

The search for Element 110 was long and tiring, and Mike Inbody helped ferret out articles I simply didn't have access to—thanks, Mike! Last, but certainly not least, heartfelt thanks to Jack Crain, Weatherford, Texas, designer and maker of fine knives. His love of his craft comes through in every word he speaks, and I hope the antique Crain cat knife is worthy of him.

A Note About the Nualan Language

Down through the centuries, the various colonies of Earth each evolved their own language. If the founding group was homogeneous in background, its primary language generally derived from the culture; if it was heterogeneous, the favorite language of choice eventually dominated. At the time of the first launches, the languages of choice for the myriad peoples who chose the stars were Chinese, English, and Spanish. These three langages formed the pidgin tongue which was the basis of Axis Standard.

The colony of Nuala was one of the few founded involuntarily, and its linguistic progression was radically different. Due to the high number of scientists among the original settlers, English, Latin, and German predominated, with a sprinkling of Gaelic and several African dialects thrown into the language stew. Since the pronunciation of several commonly-used Nualan words do not translate easily, assistance is offered below.

ä   — used in:

     Ragäree
     ragäree
     Ciedär
     the ciedär
     Ciedärlien

This "ä" is pronounced as American speakers say "o" in *bother* and "a" in *father*. The first "a" in *ragäree* is pronounced as in *rah*.

aa   — guaard

This double vowel is the long exhalation *ah*. It is almost identical to the first "a" in *ragäree*, and in most parts of Nuala and on the planet Niamh has become identical. Only tradition leaves the spelling of ragäree unchanged.

ē   — sini

This vowel is the old usage for the "e" sound in *beat*, *bleed*, and *sleepy*. Both "i" 's are pronounced the same way.

ü   — used in:

>   Mendülay
>   Mendülarion

This "ü" is pronounced as the "ue" in *cue* and the "ew" in *few*.

A bracketing effect is used by the Nualans in their written language, mostly in titles and in proper names. In the first example below, the second and third words are pronounced differently when linked; in the second, the written usage is merely traditional. A few very strict septs of clans use this bracket only when a child is the heir of its mother (eldest daughter or son) but this is not a general interpretation.

^   — used in:

>   Mendülarion S^Atare
>   Nadine reb^Ursel Kilgore

ATARE LINE—2401 A.R.

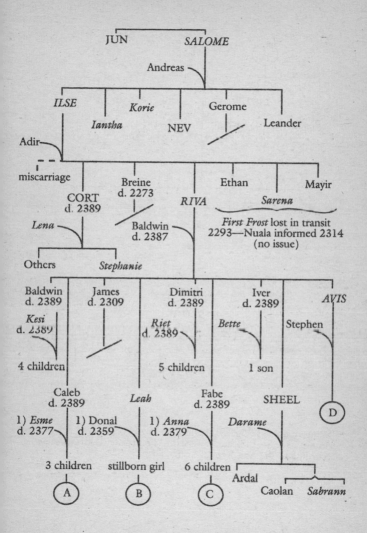

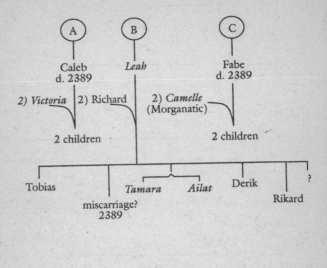

| A | | B | | C |

Caleb
d. 2389

Leah

Fabe
d. 2389

2) *Victoria* | 2) Richard | 2) *Camelle*
(Morganatic)

2 children

2 children

Tobias — | *Tamara* ⌒ *Ailat* | Derik | ?

miscarriage?
2389

Rikard

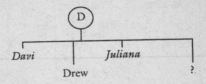

| D |

Davi | Drew | *Juliana* | ?

Ruling Atare and Ragäree are indicated by CAPITALS; lines that end
without issue are indicated by a slash. Premature deaths are dated
according to the Axis Republic calendar.

DIELAAN LINE—2401 A.R.

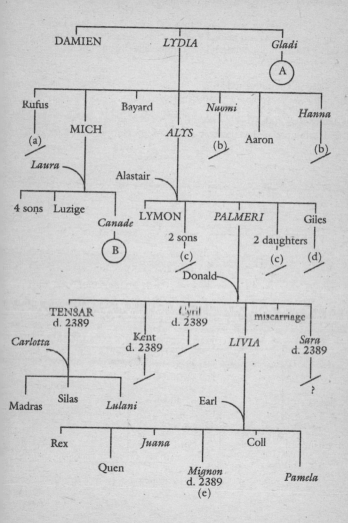

Dielaan and Ragäree are indicated by CAPITALS; lines that end without issue are indicated by a slash. Premature deaths are dated according to the Axis Republic calendar.

NOTE: Names can and do repeat in the royal Dielaan line. Only reigning Dielaans and named Ragärees have names reserved to them alone. Accordingly, children in the immediate throne line are usually named uniquely.

a) Died in a hunting accident.
b) All legal issue died of Wasting Sleep.
c) Died without legal issue.
d) Killed in a duel.
e) Death unrelated to poisoning of Palmeri's heirs at Yule, 2389 A.R.

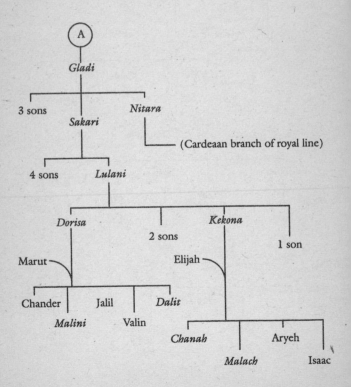

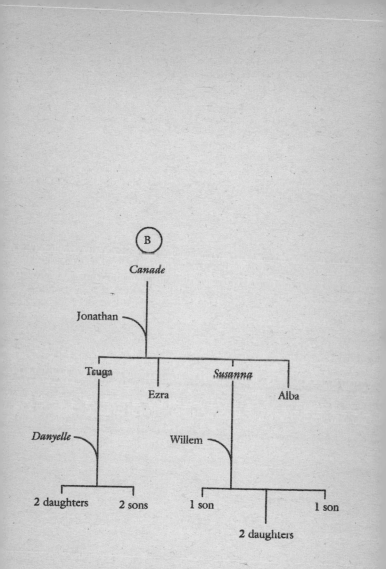

Nualan Time

The planet Nuala has a twenty-five-hour day, retaining the ancient sixty-minute hour and sixty-second minute, although Nualan time-keeping appears hazy to off-worlders. It can be extremely difficult for planet visitors to keep track of time, since moonrise and moonset can vary enormously. In Amura-By-The-Sea, the hours are canonical. Elsewhere, however, the moon cycles are closely watched, and it is possible for second bell to precede first bell—or follow third bell, depending on moonset. The same situation applies to moonrise.

Matins	—	First bell and the deepest point of night.
Lauds	—	Second bell, moonset (firstmoon)
Canonical	—	Between matins and starrise
Prime	—	Third bell, starrise (Kee)
Tierce	—	Fourth bell, midmorning
Sext	—	Fifth bell, high noon
None	—	Sixth bell, mid-afternoon
Vespers	—	Seventh bell, starset (Kee)
Compline	—	Eighth bell, moonrise (firstmoon)
Canonical	—	Between starset and matins

The Nualans' sequence also changes fractionally with the seasons. Compline and Lauds are rung at their median points during the dark of the moons.

Nualan Calendar

The Nualan year is an ecliptic orbit of 432 Nualan days, based on a twenty-five-hour day. Ancient Terran hours are used as the base measurement. Nualans divide the calendar into four seasons of 108 days each. These divisions are based on the rainy seasons; it rains almost thirty-six days straight at the beginning of spring and autumn. A Nualan month is thirty-six days. Nualans do not use any smaller fraction of the calendar between month and day; they refer to the passage of time according to festivals and religious feast days.

New Year	Firstday (first day of fall)
Festival of Masks	Thirtyfiveday
Feast of Souls	Thirtysixday
Yule	Onehundred Twentysevenday (midwinter)
Feast of Atonement and Anointing	Onehundred Eightyoneday (first day of spring)
Ascension Day	Twohundred Fortysixday
Midsummer's	Threehundred Fortythreeday
Feast of Adel	Fourhundred Twentyfiveday
High Festival	Fourhundred Twentysixday through Fourhundred Thirtytwoday

Lebanon
Canaan
Tyner
Caraddyn
Boone
Cambria

Atare

Tolis

Starrise
Mountains

1 | 2

Tribal
Region

Starrise →
(to Dielaan
and
Andersen)

Ciedar

The
Lakes

Wadeyo
Forest

Sonoma
Mountains

Painting
Rock

← Starset

Amura
By-The-
Sea

Sonoma Valley

Bloodsand

Stone
Ring

Evermind

Dragoche
Region

N
W ✦ E
S

Alameda
Sea

Ciedar

The 200 Kilon

Dragoche
Mountains

Monterey

*Wasuu
Land*

Seedar

To
Montspirtt →

Legend
< Time Zones >
1 — Coastal
2 — Dragoche
3 — Ciedar
4 — Andersen
* Free Well
X Mare Imbrium Mine

Stormside
(No Humans
Dwell Here)

Kilgore

1 | 2

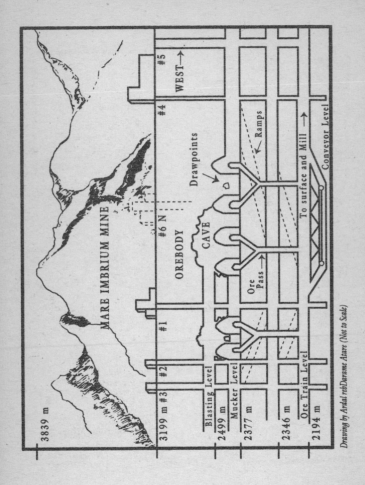

MARE IMBRIUM MINE

3839 m

3199 m #3   #2   #1   OREBODY   #6 N   #4   #5   WEST→

Blasting Level

2499 m   Mucker Level

2377 m

CAVE   Drawpoints

Ore Pass→   Ramps

To surface and Mill→

2346 m

Ore Train Level

2194 m   Conveyor Level

Drawing by Ardal rebDerome Atare (Not to Scale)

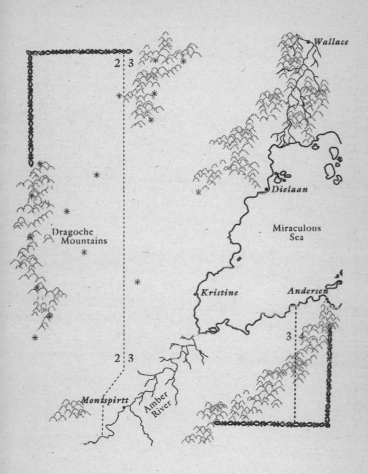

Enemy: One who desires to harm or destroy a person or thing to which he is opposed. SYN *Enemy* and *Foe* both indicate a person, group, thing, etc. that is hostile to one.

CHAPTER ONE

CAESAREA STATION   2389 A.R.

He had spent a hundred years seeking the woman called Silver; he still didn't know if he was going to kill her.

It was an idle thought, floating through a haze of weariness to the front of his mind. Garth slowed, his eyes focusing on the gaudy calendar filling the display window to his left. Tiny white lights framed the safety glass, clustered like wild grapes at the tops and sides where the curve was pronounced, trickling off like fireflies through the blazing dates. Had he lost track . . . ? No—there was the Axis year, in the corner. It was the last month of 2389, and his parents had died in 2288. A hundred years of searching, and the prize was as elusive as ever.

Damn Hobbs and his penchant for gambling! Damn the Caesarean port authorities for discovering his smuggling operation and demanding reciprocity when they did. *A few hours, I only needed a few hours.* . . . But the port authorities at Norwood had sealed off the ship, seizing the cargo. No money for the crew, no money for fuel—no way off Norwood Station, or even *onto* Norwood, as in Garth's case. Bundled back into Sleep and returned to Caesarea Station for questioning. Damn, damn, damn! How many years lost?

No one had seen any of Silver's recent partners since a trip made to Norwood, so the people to question would be on Norwood. No sense in asking other free-traders. No one in "the business" talked about anyone else . . . it was a marvel they got any work done at all.

Without really noticing, Garth had started moving again. If he had thought about it, he would have simply said the area in front of that display window was stuffy. In truth, the vacuum beneath the alloy grills below his feet had been defective; the lack of air movement around his legs had made him nervous. It was only a sectional breakdown—the familiar sucking motion now pulling at his soles soothed the uneasiness within. A spacer reaction, an instinctive reaction . . . the type of knowledge that could save a life. Only those who learned it in their bones lasted more than a few years at this trade.

"Garth! Garth Kristinsson!" The voice was low and almost furry; Garth turned his head in response. A dark, slender man appeared to his right, his personal gear still stored in his bakit. "They sprung you?"

"No reason not to," Garth replied, fixing the speaker with a steely eye. Jamar could be very good company, but his tongue tended to wander too freely when he was among friends. A dangerous habit on a wheel. . . .

"Of course." Jamar flinched back into his shoulder pack as he took the hint. "Now what?"

Garth knew that he meant work. Idiot. "I'm hungry," he answered. "What's good right now?"

Since Jamar had been on Caesarea Station before transferring to Hobbs's ship at Norwood, the deportation had given him a quick round trip. "Blue Diamond and Lowe's are still good, and Rest has been good lately, I heard."

Studying reflections in the polished aluminum walls, Garth said: "Let's try Lowe's." Was that the same man he had seen outside the Protectorate offices? Undistinguished, the type Caesarea preferred as police. . . .

"Turn here," Jamar prompted, nudging Garth slightly to the left. The wiry little man with long years of practice led the way into the maze of the wheel.

How did they keep it so clean? Most geosynchronous wheels quickly acquired the grimy, beaten look of the stations circling Gavriel and Emerson, but Caesarea was different. It must have something to do with their image, Garth decided, keeping one eye on the deep green pack strapped to Jamar's back and the other on the man following them. "Commerce" was every Caesarean's middle name, and "gold" was their lifeblood. The face presented to potential clients and customers must be immaculate.

A sharp left turn took them off the rim and onto a spoke of the wheel. Sweet Jesu, he hated spokes—the soundproofing wasn't as good as the rim, and the echoes of voices made his head ache. Why a wheel entirely of steel, aluminum, and chrome? Norwood System's discovery of petroleum meant plastic was cheap again. They could replace a few interior panels for variety. . . . Although what glass there was faced away from the star, it was still darkened, and lent little relief to the scenery. In this row, glass was almost non-existent. Most of the free-trader bars were along this strip, as well as a few eating places popular with Axis Forces. Free-traders were much pickier than military personnel or pirates; food and liquor had to be good, and the establishment had to have a few quiet, private areas. Word of mouth kept these places going, much to Caesarea's chagrin. The military served a purpose, and pirates could be boarded, their cargo confiscated—but free-traders usually managed to slip through cracks in the floor. Their favorite haunts were much like they were—destructive in their own way, like rats, for instance, but not dangerous unless approached.

Lowe's was a perfect example of why authorities disliked free-trader hangouts. It looked like a dive from the outside; walls and dark glass smudged and dirty, the metallic paint over the door flaking, making the place "I owe" to the uninitiated. If Lowe still owned it, Garth imagined it was purposely left in poor condition; it would be Lowe's idea of a joke. To Caesareans either outbound or meeting for business on the wheel, the facade was a clear warning: This place is not for you. Stay out.

Inside was another story. Lowe's was licensed for food, liquor,

and gambling—the sex outlet was upstairs, and considered to
be separate from the main operation by regulars. A cousin of
Lowe's handled that end . . . Garth suspected Lowe didn't like
the cousin. Lowe himself was in the "passive entertainment
business," as he called it. Good food, strong drinks, and a
pleasant place to hide out; it was clean, but not fancy. If you
wanted music, or something else, you went elsewhere. At
Lowe's, you were getting the extended family treatment. It was
a good enough combination that he actually made profits Caesarea knew about. If the police knew Lowe also sold information,
they couldn't do anything about it.

Slipping in the front door, Garth followed Jamar's lead, hoping
Lowe was out on business. Lowe was one of the few who remembered his father, Kristin Arnason, and therefore was certain
to remember Garth. After six hours of questioning, Garth was
in no mood for the old man's subtle prying.

Someone was cooking fresh pea pods and tofu, and the smell
was heavenly. Jamar found a small table to his liking and placed
his bakit on a chair. While he went to the bar—liquor service
was from the bar only, or had been the last time Garth was on
the wheel—Garth settled in the chair facing the door. As he had
hoped, the undistinguished man had disappeared. Or had he?
Garth glanced up at the screens lining the top of the aisle wall.
Only one was an omni, broadcasting news; a few showed the
gambling activities in back, or the formal dining room behind
the bar, but most showed current scenes from the wheel. The
central arboretum, the landing bays, the administrative sector
. . . the spoke outside the door. Framing screens on opposite
sides of the wall showed both sides of the aisle. And there was
his pursuer, loitering at a push vendor hooked a meter or so
down the way. Dumb. All push vendors were assumed to be
administrative spies. Definitely not a free-trader, then. Probably
police.

"Wheel activity fascinating tonight?" came a soft voice.
Growing still, Garth mentally cursed Jamar. True, the authorities
would not dare follow him in here—legally they might enter,
but whether someone followed them back out and cut their throat
was anyone's guess—but Garth really did not want to talk to
Lowe. He had the lecture memorized. Besides, he was angry
with the old man. One of Kristin Arnason's best friends, and he
kept saying he knew nothing about a woman called Silver.

Horseshit on that—there was nothing worth knowing about free-trading that Lowe didn't know. If it was nothing else, Silver's elusive career was the stuff of which legends were made.

"Just one spoke," he decided to answer, keeping his voice casual. A drink appeared in front of him. Lowe must have brought it himself; the waits did not truck liquor around. Knowing it was safe, Garth nodded his thanks and sipped the sweet drink. It would have been rude to refuse, even though it implied a slight debt to accept it. If Jamar would just—

Damn. He'd spotted a woman he'd obviously known his previous jump here, and was trying to turn their recent problems into a humorous story. Not funny to the police, who had received an entire shipload of workers ignorant of the smuggling . . . and obviously didn't believe in their innocence.

"Will you dine with me in back?"

This required facing the old man. Lord, what had he done to deserve this? All he wanted to do was relax, fill his stomach, and get a line on cargo ships going to Norwood. Now he'd be tied up an entire evening. Slowly Garth angled his body toward Lowe.

This time Lowe actually looked older; the FOY treatments must have reached their limit. That bothered Garth. Lowe might have been a pain the last few times they'd spoken, but the man was one of the pillars of the station. Too bad there wasn't really a Fountain of Youth, despite the company's claims. Only Sleep gave extended life, and even *it* had its price. Lowe's hair was still dark, but lines were beginning to show in his face. *He's lost weight,* Garth thought. *He looks tired, not like Lowe.* Thoughts of using Jamar as an excuse withered. This might be the last time; Garth could stand the lecture if only Lowe would spare him any questions.

"I'll have to make my excuses to Jamar," Garth started, his fingers entwining around the delicate, fluted glass.

"I've already spoken to Jamar. It's better that Hobbs' crew see very little of each other in the next few days . . . and take separate ships out, if possible." Slowly turning, the man moved with stately grace toward the stairs and the casino. What with a noticeable weight drop—Garth estimated he'd lost at least fifty kilos—Lowe looked more than ever like his establishment. The silvery suit and dark, high-collared shirt made him resemble his own front door. But then Lowe was taller than most men, and

could draw attention accordingly. Pushing two meters, Lowe
was hard to miss in a crowd. Yet he had been a famous free-
trader . . . it took many different links to form the chain.

Finally the words sunk in, and Garth stood to follow. Better
they not see each other? Damn! Worse than he'd thought. All
this shit and only standard wage? He was tempted to tell Lowe
he wanted storm pay, and let him negotiate it with Hobbs for
his usual fee. First the dinner; it was an honor to be asked to
dine in the club area, one Garth had never had without his father
present. There had to be a reason. If he was patient, Lowe would
tell it to him.

Dinner was impressive; fresh, chopped salad made of vege-
tables native to three worlds, followed by real meat, delicately
roasted and seasoned, a crumbly, white cheese melted on top.
Fine brandy and whipped chocolate finished the meal, filling the
few remaining empty spaces in Garth's stomach. Not wishing
to borrow trouble, Garth neither calculated the value of such a
spread nor tried to guess what Lowe wanted in return for such
generosity. Instead he politely inquired about current wheel gossip, and listened as the secrets of half a dozen worlds strolled
across his ears.

At last Lowe gestured for the wait to leave the brandy. In the
stillness that followed, the old man slowly turned his glass stem
between a strong finger and thumb, watching the reflections
thrown by the fluid within. "And what of you, Garth?" he said
finally. "It has been a while since you graced my establishment."

"Here and there," Garth replied, hazarding a grin. "Norwood
most recently."

"A very quick trip. You intend to find another ship heading
that way?" Keen, gray eyes raised to meet icy blue innocence.
"I can save you some looking. A transport left a few days
back—there won't be another until next month, at least."

Probably true . . . it was too easy to check the story. Was
Lowe actually going to hire him for something? But the old man
preferred experienced free-traders—Garth knew his own training
was still too meager to satisfy Lowe.

"Let us dispense with fencing. I take it you are still searching
for Hank Edmonton and Silver Meath?" Lowe's voice was very
quiet; Garth did not remember it as so quiet.

"Silver Meath. Hank Edmonton is dead." He tried to keep

the reply simple as he concentrated on the heady vapor of the brandy.

"People die," Lowe said conversationally, almost as if agreeing with something.

Garth acknowledged the unasked question. "Natural causes, apparently. He pushed FOY as far as it would go, and his heart finally gave out. I think he left free-trading not long after dad died." Tell only the truth; Lowe had a nose for ragged tales, and it was said he could smell a lie at ten paces.

"I noticed during your absence that a century had passed since the unfortunate demise of your parents. A hundred years is a long time to follow someone merely to ascertain your father's last emotions before death claimed him." Lowe's eyes had not swerved from his face.

That was essentially what Garth had told Lowe. No one knew the entire story—good luck and a glib tongue had kept all secrets safe. But an uneasy feeling traced his spine; Garth had a feeling his luck with secrets was about to run out.

"Rumors still surface about that job . . . about the aftermath. Almost five hundred bars of gold vanished from that vault. Must have been, oh, 150, 160 a piece for them. You certainly don't need to work. Is your only goal in life to find this woman?"

"Yes."

Lowe's eyebrows lifted slightly at his emphatic tone of voice. "A hundred years, and only a few months for you. . . . Any chance you might tell me the entire story this time?"

"Are you calling me a liar?" Very soft; Garth felt muscles starting to bunch and fought it.

Lowe's expression softened. "No, you're not lying. You're simply not telling me all you know or suspect—it's quite a different thing." His gaze dropped to his brandy snifter. "I can't help you unless you tell me what is going on. And this is probably my last chance to help you. Information is my lifeblood, Garth—why have you never used the best source at your disposal?"

"Because you always tell me to give it up!" The return to normal volume sounded like shouting, but Garth couldn't help it. Old resentment mingled with new pain, as the old man obliquely confirmed earlier guesses. Time was running out for Lowe . . . there would be a new pillar of information on Caesarea

Station the next time Garth passed through. "I'm going to find this woman if it takes a *thousand* years! All your meddling to keep me on false trails has only made it harder—it hasn't changed my mind."

"You think I've tried to stop you?" Lowe looked up once again. His face was intent—then Garth thought he saw a trace of humor. "I haven't done anything more than keep a vague eye on your travels." Lowe reached absently for a piece of the cheese the wait had slipped onto the table. "Do you really think someone has muddied the waters? Beyond what Hank, Silver, and your father did after the job," he added.

Garth remained silent. He had been so sure Lowe was trying to stop him. . . . So. Was there someone else planting false clues, or was he merely paranoid about the whole thing?

"Are you going to kill her, Garth?" Lowe asked pleasantly.

Like a conversation about the latest live band, or interactive show . . . Garth thought deeply. "What makes you think that?" he said finally.

"I can't think of any other reason why you wouldn't question me about that job," Lowe answered.

"Why would you know anything?"

"It's my business to know things. I know what the Prime Minister of Caesarea has for breakfast before it's digested. I have heard every rumor ever attached to any free-trader, any job. Yet you have never questioned me. It seems I will have to question you."

Garth felt his thin face tighten. Before he could speak, however, Lowe added: "I know where Silver is."

As his fingers curled, Garth released the snifter in his hand for fear of fracturing it. "Now?"

Lowe smiled. It was odd, seeing that smile . . . Lowe hardly ever smiled. "If she still lives, right this moment. And if you tell me what I wish to know, I will tell you where she is. You are . . . twenty-five years behind her, what with this added delay? I can put you one trip behind her."

"Why?" What he really wanted to ask was: *What do you want in return?* But Garth knew Lowe would get around to that eventually.

"I was very fond of your parents. They did me many . . . services. I feel I owe them what little I can do for their only son." Lowe refilled the brandy snifters. "Now. Your father was involved in his latest scam. It was with two other people, neither of them your mother. . . ."

Sweet saints, guide me. Garth picked up the tale at that point. "I still don't know exactly what the scam was, but I think you're right—the goal was that big gold shipment going to Kiel. Did you ever hear what was taken?"

"Four hundred eighty bars of gold," Lowe told him.

"Well, 160 bars of gold were deposited in my parents' account at Traders the day after my father died." Lowe nodded at this statement. Traders' Trust was the bank used by almost all free-traders, and was considered one of the few institutions off-limits to scams. Traders handled only precious metals—the currencies of six planets were mere promissory notes to Traders, and were redeemed with high penalties. It was also the only existing reserve which never surrendered accounts to heirs without instructions left by the depositor. A trip of a hundred years was nothing to Traders—when a free-trader returned, his or her metal wealth would be waiting. It had survived recession, war, and political upheaval; Traders was more solvent than many countries.

"Possibly one-third of the take, then. No one demanded a planning fee?" Lowe asked.

Garth shrugged. "He didn't tell mother much, when they talked. From the little she said, I think the group planned it together. At any rate, we knew how things would finish. His partners would leave in a hurry, drawing off any pursuit, while dad deposited the money in Traders."

"What went wrong?"

After a long pause filled by the taste of brandy on his tongue, Garth said: "I don't know. So much was going on then . . . Lise had just married, and was shipping out to Gavriel the day after Dad was due back. She already had new citizenship papers. We were watching, and waiting . . . and then the police arrived, to say that Dad's body had been found in an abandoned transpo tunnel."

"No one saw anything?"

"No one admitted to seeing anything. No one spoke." This was harsh; the memories rising to the surface were recent in Garth's timeframe. "Lise was frantic, and Mom was in shock. After pacing the floor all night, Mom insisted that Lise take the ship as scheduled. *Insisted* on it—said it was what Dad would have wanted. I went with Lise up to Caesarea Station to see her on board her ship. By the . . . by the time I returned, Mom had slashed her wrists."

"You have no idea why?" Lowe's voice seemed to come from far away.

"No. Unless it was grief . . . but I can't accept that. Mom adored him, but she didn't live for him, if you know what I mean." Garth realized he was drawing patterns in the air with his fingers, and gripped his hands tightly together. "There was no message, except—except she had given one of her favorite holos of the family to Lise, before Lise left. I found the copy sitting on my pillow when I got back, along with 250 cubiz Caesarean. Everything after that is fuzzy . . . was fuzzy for a long time. I didn't find out about the gold deposit and withdrawal until several days later."

"Withdrawal?" Lowe said suddenly.

"Yes." Garth finally looked up, catching the glint of Lowe's eyes with his own gaze. "The deposit was made that afternoon, probably while Mom was killing herself—certainly while I was returning from station. I don't know if she saw it or not, it didn't occur to me then to check whether anyone had accessed the file from our home. The account was emptied that evening—everything, the new gold and everything else my family had as assets."

"But . . . how? Traders is inviolate if anything is. . . ." Lowe had tilted his head to one side and was staring hard at Garth.

From Lowe's expression, Garth knew he was going to have to supply the final puzzle piece. "Oh, whoever cleaned us out had the proper codes. They even left a message: 'Aesir considers the debt to be paid.' " He kept his eyes on Lowe's face as he spoke.

There was no flicker of change. Lowe repeated the last words, his tone almost a whisper: "Aesir considers the debt to be paid." Then a sip of brandy, and silence.

Instinct told Garth to remain silent; minutes passed. Abruptly, Lowe demanded: "Tell me everything your mother said, from when your father died until she took her life."

Puzzled, Garth did his best to reconstruct the last clear day within memory. Lowe asked questions; he wanted nuance, tone of voice, any messages or mail received. "Is this leading anywhere except into your private mental vault?" Garth asked abruptly.

"Will you never learn patience?" Almost testy. Garth was

surprised; it was as close to losing his temper as he had ever seen Lowe approach. "Do you want certainties or supposition? Very well—did the police investigate the possibility of murder? In your mother's case," he added, as Garth's eyes narrowed in irritation.

It struck him dumb. Never, even for a moment, had he considered that possibility. "But—the coroner said—"

"They knew your mother was in the business?"

A pause. "I think so. They didn't seem to think it odd that she'd done it right after dad was killed . . . or that I knew nothing about it." He did not add that they'd wired him, just to be sure. He held no anger over it—it was all part of the business.

"They are trained to see anomalies—I know, you children have only contempt for them, but trust me, the Caesarean Forces are among the best. They find out what is needful without trampling everyone's rights underfoot. A great skill. On another world, they would have locked up Hobbs' crew just to be certain they'd covered all exits. Here, they merely watch and wait—a blessing you obviously do not appreciate." Lowe shrugged in dismissal. "If they saw nothing to make them suspicious, it was either suicide, or done on such a level that they could have proved nothing even if they'd suspected." Lowe fixed Garth with a hard stare. "Your mother would not have killed herself unless there was something to be gained by it."

"What could possibly be gained by it?"

"There are things," he said vaguely. "But that doesn't matter, now. I have heard of Aesir, but I can no more tell you what it means than I can change the rotation of this station. Secret and deadly, that is what it means. I don't know if Silver can tell you any more, but it would not hurt to ask. If you ask politely, you might be amazed what she'd tell you. A generous woman." He sipped at his brandy.

"You'll tell me where she is?" Garth finally said.

"I can tell you where she went, last time she was here, ten years ago Terran. She was finishing up a job, and about to start something with her old mentor, Halsey."

That name caused Garth to straighten. He had heard of Halsey. Probably the richest free-trader still living, he was older than memory. Most people in the business could trace their line of learning back to him. So Silver was one of his own students . . . no wonder she left such a sketchy trail.

"They were heading to Nuala." Lowe's voice was ridiculously calm, considering what he'd just said.

For a moment Garth was blank—Nuala? A country on Emerson? Then the name gathered meaning. *Nuala?* Holy Virgin, was he cursed? She'd gone to that radioactive slag heap? "Why?" he heard himself whisper.

Lowe allowed amusement to slide across his face. "Because she's a free-trader, Garth. Nuala is the wealthiest planet in the Axis Republic. Between the myths surrounding it and the dangers threading it, it's the biggest challenge imaginable short of charting a new star yourself." Lowe reached for the plate again, and nibbled at another piece of cheese. "She's a gypsy, the best of our breed. The scam is half the fun."

You call this fun? Garth kept the words to himself, wondering if his face gave him away. He began to despair of learning this game. What could be worth going to Nuala?

An unreadable expression crossed Lowe's face. "I *do* remember one thing about Aesir . . . but it may not apply in this case. Weren't the Aesir the warrior gods of ancient Norse mythology?"

This thought gave Garth pause. "Maybe," he said at last. "My people remember them only in story and song—their worship was dust long before we left Mother Earth."

"I don't see a connection—not a direct one. But Silver was born on Gavriel . . . perhaps she can find a link. Surely it cannot be coincidence." Lowe pushed his empty glass to one side. "The ship you seek is one of the Tiger fleet, called *Crowned Tiger.* It leaves for Nuala in about three days. They need crew, and pay profit-sharing as an incentive. I'll send word to the captain that you're interested. It's a safe ship; no need to have someone timelock your Freeze tube."

The last words were brisk, but well-meant—they would save him inadvertently offending the captain of the long-hauler. In them Garth also sensed dismissal, and realized it was time for good-byes.

"Thank you," he said aloud, unable to comprehend that he finally had what he wanted—Silver's direction. Lowe had turned out to be a better friend than he had hoped.

"You may pass in transit, you know."

"But I'll only be a trip behind, and that's worth anything."

A strange combination of excitement and dread began to knot beneath his sternum.

"Almost anything," Lowe said gently.

Garth found his response puzzling, and knew his own expression had changed.

Lowe was watching his face. Something he saw there did not comfort him. Shaking his head slightly, Lowe said: "Be careful out there. And always think through your actions to their ultimate conclusion. You'll live longer." Pausing, he finally added: "I hope I have done the right thing."

There was nothing to say to such fatherly concern, so Garth gravely extended his hand. Lowe touched his wrist lightly in farewell and remained at the table as Garth moved off into shadows, heading into the bowels of the restaurant.

Hesitating at the elbow of the corridor, Garth turned back toward Lowe, prompted by a moment of unease. He saw the man pull a small device out of his pocket and point it at the blank wall beyond the table. A huge screen flared into life, flickering in communiqué mode.

"2618ABD," Lowe said quietly. In moments the line was connected, and Lowe said: "Yes, this is Lowe for Captain Morse of *Crowned Tiger*. Tell him I've found him crew."

Even an introduction . . . Garth considered waiting, but decided to move on; it was not courteous to eavesdrop on a friend, and Lowe was merely doing as he had promised, insuring Garth a smooth transition onto *Crowned Tiger*. Long strides carried him through the bar; Garth headed out toward the bag drop to retrieve his bakit. This time he could feel it, the closeness, the *rightness*. Lowe had finally told him the truth, and he was going to find Silver. Any thoughts about the mysterious planet Nuala were kept firmly in the back of his mind.

His people called it wergild, the price owed to blood kin upon the death of a valued relative. Garth suspected Silver owed him wergild, a large one—now there would be a reckoning.

In the meantime, Captain Morse had finally answered Lowe's call. "Morse, I'm not the only one who needs to get to Nuala —I found you that last hold man I promised you." Lowe was not smiling . . . but then, he rarely did.

Blood Feud: A war of revenge or rivalry between families, clans, factions, et cetera. It is almost always born out of an act of violence perpetrated by one member of a group against a member of an opposing group, and results in a continuing and often escalating series of alternating retaliations of "equal value" i.e., An eye for an eye. SYN *vendetta*. Compare *BLOODWITE* and *WERGILD*

CHAPTER TWO

AMURA-BY-THE-SEA, NUALA
    ONEHUNDRED EIGHTYTWODAY   TIERCE
ATARE WINTER PALACE   2401 A.R.

Syluan had strength and durability rivaling silk; it took color as readily, and its sheen practically glowed in the dark. But it had one great advantage—syluan came from the flower of the same name. No expensive import, this wondrous fiber . . . and on Nuala, at least, syluan was priced within reach of everyone. As the foremost supporters of both inter-clan and interstellar trade, the rulers of Atare always wore syluan before silk. At least that was the public reasoning.

Sounds reasonable to me, Darame thought to herself as she tossed the cloud of flaming red syluan over her head and felt for the armholes. Toki stilled this fumbling with a hiss of dismay, and Darame felt her swift, competent hands take over. Darame inhaled deeply, her full breasts rising to strain slightly at the material. "Are you sure I have not eaten my way out of this?" she asked aloud, using the Ciedärlien dialect of Nualan that Toki had taught her.

"Stop that breathing," was the even reply—in coastal Nualan; Toki was determined to learn the language as well as Darame had learned Cied.

"I suspect I will be the talk of the town . . . unfortunately," Darame went on dryly in coastal Nualan.

"You will be magnificent," Toki replied calmly. "And many foolish women who do not have your body will be demanding similar garments. *I* am the one who must dissuade them."

"Dissuade?" Darame could not resist teasing her. "To advise or persuade them to make another choice?"

Cornered by the word's precise meaning, Toki's hands slowed only momentarily. "I will not put fat women in this dress," she said succinctly.

"You would be rich if you did," Darame pointed out, turning slightly as Toki poked her shoulder.

"I do not want to be rich." As Darame prepared her next sally, her friend continued: "Beside," and now Toki's smile was sly, "They come back. First they find fools who will make them what they want. After they see themselves like pregnant hazelles, they come back. Then I make *them* beautiful—in another way." Tossing back her mane of black hair, Toki stepped away from the pedestal before the half-circle of mirrors. "*Now* look."

"Besides," Darame said absently, pirouetting slowly from windows to mirrors. The tiny whirlwind that was Toki rarely revealed temper, but language provoked her ire like nothing else. Those who spent time with her learned to correct her immediately when she made a mistake . . . or they heard about it later, when she repeated her mistake in company that caused "loss of face." At Toki's puzzled expression, Darame added: "*Beside* the stream. *Besides* means . . . in addition to what was previously said—sometimes over and above what was said." Then her eyes finally lit on the dress.

"Magnificent," Toki stated.

"The *dress* certainly is," Darame started, but the jest faded in her throat. So much material . . . Backless, and essentially frontless, except for the sleeves and the material which both covered and held her breasts and ribs . . . the magic was in Toki's use of draping and weight.

"Is this quite the . . . thing . . . for the Atarae of Atare, mother of three?" she said doubtfully, even as something started to smolder deep within her breast. *Sweet saints, I'm still beautiful*. The silent quip was in Caesarean, which Toki spoke little of, but still Darame kept the thought within, amused at her own vanity.

A rustle at the door alerted her. Glancing up, Darame smiled and asked her ten-years-Terran son: "What do you think?"

Gravely Ardal entered the room and stood behind and slightly to one side of Toki. His thin, fine features made him seem taller next to the tiny, dark Cied woman. Experimentally the right eye closed, hiding the intense black iris and leaving the left eye with its pale green iris to make the decision. Finally, he announced: "I think Da will like it."

"I hope so. Court tongues will wag over this one," she murmured, turning around again and examining the back of the skirt.

"So?" Ardal said in his blunt way.

"If people criticize me it reflects badly on your father."

Ardal grinned cheerfully. "The Wallace loves your clothes."

"And what do you know about it, big ears?" she countered, referring not to his physique but to his habit of always hearing things not meant to be overheard.

"His voice changes when he talks about you." The humor vanished, and Ardal was very serious.

"Perhaps," she answered vaguely. Ardal was not quite old enough to have the game of flattery explained to him—not the game of flattering a male ego, at any rate. Her black gaze shifted in the mirror, settling on her favorite of the multitude of merchants who sought her favor.

Toki smiled faintly, in that mysterious way of hers, which meant she knew Darame loved the dress. "Red and black and trinium . . . it will be perfect."

"Silver, not trinium," Darame said, the fingers of her right hand reaching up to touch a long curl of shimmering hair which had slipped loose from its clasp. Hesitating only a moment, she freed the rest of it, letting the silver curtain fall over her shoulders and down her back and breasts.

"Trinium is more valuable," Toki stated.

"Yes, but silver was discovered first, which is why the color is called silver . . . polished silver," she added, studying the pale woman with the black eyes who stared out of the mirror. *Ah, to Sleep again!* But that was vanity talking, a vanity she had not known she had until recently . . . but then she had spent nearly a hundred-and-fifty Terran years slipping in and out of Cold Sleep. Aging was a new experience. *There was only one prerequisite to a lifetime of loving Sheel . . . knowing that sometime it had to end.*

Reverie ended abruptly when she realized still another had joined their group. So silently . . . but then he was a master of *elkita*, that art which was prayer and dance and weapon all in one, and so Sheel moved without sound when he chose. Catching his eye, Darame waited for some comment; although Sheel's idea of fashion was comfort first, he valued understated elegance.

Darame waited . . . and waited some more. Toki's smile widened, and she began to pack up her markers and hot needles. If the Atare was reduced to speechlessness over one of her creations, there would be no alterations.

"That good, eh?" Darame finally said, the Caesarean colloquialism sounding odd in Nualan. "I thought school started at tierce?" she directed toward Ardal, glancing out of the floor-to-ceiling windows as she spoke. The yellow star of Nuala System, called Kee by the natives, was well up in the sky.

Wrinkling his nose, Ardal turned and started back down the hall.

"Finish your history assignment, Red, and you can come to the party for a time," Sheel said easily, striding into the room. These words caused the fading footsteps to hasten.

"Trinium does not grow dull," Toki pointed out. "You remember how to hang that?" At Darame's easy nod, Toki rearranged her long, leaf-green skirt and moved toward the entryway. "Do not crease it," she said cryptically as she passed Sheel.

Again motionless, Sheel merely smiled.

Lifting her eyes beyond him to the black-suited shadow that followed in his wake, Darame studied the *guaard's* expressionless features.

"Mailan, you might as well let it show in your face. That woman is simply too familiar for your tastes," Darame suggested, stepping down from the pedestal.

Mischievous thoughts sparkled through her, but Darame subdued them. She knew better than to tease a *guaard*, especially one to whom she owed so much. The *guaard* existed for one purpose only: to protect the royal line of Atare. A mere smile, a word of conversation; those were dangers, things that might

distract a *guaard* at a crucial moment. Hence the silent, statu-
esque appearance of these guardians of her new family. Like
janissaries of old, their entire allegiance was to the rulers of
Atare. In this generation that was Sheel and his youngest sister,
Avis, called The Ragäree, the mother of the heir. Funny how
that had never bothered her, that her children would never rule
Atare. . . .

With both Ardal and Toki several rooms away, Sheel relaxed
his own guarded stance, reaching for his delicate wife as she
walked past him toward the sanitation. Pausing in his arms,
Darame knew why her own drive for control halted short of the
throne. Sheel Atare had never regained the weight lost that terrible winter ten years and more ago, when a conspiracy among
the most trusted folk of the land had meant the deaths of the
previous Atare and almost all his heirs.

Which was where I came in, Darame thought idly, leaning
into his tall form, all bone and muscle in contrast to her soft
curves. Well, not exactly where she came in—her part at that
time had been frantically covering up her own tracks in a trinium
scam gone hopelessly awry. As for learning to love Nuala and
its people . . . as for severing almost every tie she had ever
acknowledged in order to help those people . . . that came later,
in a jumbling whirlwind that caught up all before it. But that
episode had left scars, both physical and mental, on her enigmatic
lover. And had kept her constantly alert, juggling movements
and motives among friends and enemies alike as she had woven
her own line of defense around the clan of Atare.

"The Atare retinue would probably think her 'familiar,' "
Sheel said quietly, breaking into her thoughts.

"She is Ciedärlien, for all her repudiation, and that means
she recognizes no law but that of the holy Dragoche. Good thing
the old fellow does not mettle in secular Cied matters, or she
would cast him off, too."

"Do you think she is loyal to Atare?" Sheel asked, amusement
lighting up his eyes.

"Toki is loyal to herself. Those she trusted destroyed everything else," Darame growled into his shoulder. Toki was not
what she wanted to talk about, not with Sheel so near. What
kept attraction so strong, so long? Who would have thought she
would have stayed, had children even—

"Someday you must tell me her story," was all Sheel said.

"Are you coming to court today?" His fingers had moved to trace the side slits in the skirt of her gown.

Darame tickled him, effectively halting his movements. "Behave, you must go work. Do you need me there?" Although she had no official power, Sheel relied on his wife's "tricky brain," as he put it, to notice things that he and Avis sometimes missed.

"I think not. It is slow today, the petitions are not unusual." Tilting his head down, he added softly: "Perhaps you should wait for me in the sauna?"

An intense gaze met hers, the right iris, cool sea green, the other capable of stopping people in mid-step—the iris half-green, half topaz-brown, the horizontal Sheel Split which was his and his alone. Some had been relieved none of his children were "marred" by it, but Darame's relief had had a different origin . . . it was Sheel's alone, and he was hers alone, despite the dozens of women lying in wait for him. "You are worse than I am," she muttered.

"You were the one who placed the holograms in the corridor of the palace."

Darame merely smiled and pulled away. "You have court, and I need to see how the twins are feeling." Their younger children had managed to contract a virus of some type, and had been confined to bed for several days.

"They are stronger I just came from there. But they are not ready to get up, no matter what they try to tell you!"

A sweet chiming broke in on their conversation. "Duty calls," Darame said lightly, moving in the direction of the vid. Touching the control membrane, she lit up the screen. Today a man in a fuchsia uniform was controlling vid access to restricted areas. Darame did not recognize him. "Yes?"

"A satellite call, serae," he said politely, using the term of respect for a woman of high rank. "From Dielaan Palace. It is The Ragäree's assistant who calls; she asked for you."

Raising her eyebrows, Darame nodded once, to show she would take the call. Usually the assistant contacted Donn, the person who kept track of Darame's schedule . . . unless she called on behalf of her employer, Livia.

The screen switched abruptly to a courtyard in the ciedär, that relentless desert of the northern continent which was home to the great Dielaan clan. Seated upon a stone bench was the current

regent of Dielaan, Livia Ragäree, the mother of the future ruler
of Dielaan. Law was different among Dielaan; The Dielaan ruled
alone, his sister merely caretaker of the future ruler and *his* sister
. . . unless the Dielaan died. Tensar Dielaan had fallen in the
same plot which had killed Cort Atare a decade previously. With
but the sweep of an assassin's hand, Livia had abruptly gained
unlimited power over twenty percent of the planet's population.

"Bright morning to you, Livia," Darame said easily, nodding
farewell to Sheel as he took his leave, Mailan following at a
calculated distance. "You are up early." Like most desert cultures, the city of Dielaan was liveliest in darkness, its vigor
rarely fading before starrise.

"The rule begins long before Kee rises," Livia replied, a tiny
flick of her right index and second fingers dismissing the subject
of starrise. As Livia leaned forward, her hair fell in a polished
copper blanket down her right shoulder, blending pleasantly with
her tea and cream complexion and the dark sandstone walls
behind her. "I have called—" Then the famous emerald eyes
of the distaff line widened slightly, the arched black brows lifting. "My, my—you are going to give those foolish men heart
failure."

The woman sounded genuinely amused. Livia Ragäree had
found a soulmate in the wife of The Atare—who, whatever her
secret past, had learned both patience and cunning before reaching Nuala.

"It will be a wonderful party, Livia. Are you sure you cannot
come west?"

A fleeting expression crossed the Dielaaner's face—rueful?
Bored? It passed so quickly—and Livia shook her head. "I am
trapped here," she said candidly. "Some of the youngbloods
have been kicking up their heels, and the injured parties *want*
blood. I must contrive penalties which will satisfy the merchants,
yet not enrage the nobles. But I need you to do something for
me." This was so breezy Darame had no time for surprise;
Dielaaners did not ask for assistance, not until they were desperate.

Like and respect Livia she might—but Dielaan was Atare's
traditional enemy, and the last war was still fresh in the memories
of both armies and most citizens. "If I can," Darame said, her
expression placid.

"Today I am sending a special ambassador to the coast. It

would be politic if an individual invitation was waiting for him upon his arrival at our embassy. An uncle of Tsuga, he is high in our government—and on special assignment." Livia's eyes actually darkened a bit as her gaze wandered past her own vid screen.

Ah—what she could not say, she still found a way to communicate. A *high-ranking* member of the house—one who held by ancient Dielaan codes; one who would allow his name to be known in his own time, or perhaps not at all. One sent to deal with the "little" problem of Rex reb^Livia Dielaan, the future Dielaan of Nuala. . . .

"I will personally attend to it, Livia," Darame said deliberately, and saw relief slip across the woman's face. She knew Livia would even forgive her friend's own curiosity, as long as she was careful in her questions. "You are not recalling Quen, are you? I must confess I enjoy having him in Synod meetings. When tempers run hot, he has a talent for calming ambassadors . . . even when they do not wish to calm themselves."

Livia tried not to let her pride show, but it glittered in her eyes. Her second son was turning out very, very well—a credit to her own efforts, Darame knew. Too bad the heir was so caught up in his pleasures that his responsibilities had totally slipped his mind.

"No, Quen will not return to Dielaan until he himself wishes it. I have heard that a young off-worlder has caught his eye."

There was question in this statement; Darame considered how much she could say without betraying Quen's privacy. "I have met her," she started. "Not a beauty, certainly, but a warm, lush personality—a comfortable person to have around. She understands respect without dangling on sleeves. I think she would bear intelligent children." An odd testimony to a fun-loving and friendly girl, Darame reflected, but very Nualan—Livia visibly relaxed her spine. No doubt her spies had reported on Rebekah. Darame could imagine what they had said: *Neither looks nor wealth to recommend her*. Not true, actually—Rebekah was quite pretty, but she was tall and bosomy, as unlike the classic Dielaan women as could be imagined. In only one thing did she fit in . . . Rebekah was a flaming redhead. Masses of freckles, however, indicated a very different homeland for her ancestors.

"She is . . . connected to an embassy?" Livia pursued.

Dear woman, are you worried? Those who trailed Quen through his daily activities must have dismissed Rebekah out of hand. "No," Darame said aloud. "She is a cousin of a merchant family from the confederacy on Gavriel, controlling her father's offices in Amura. They sell various types of fuels—methane, liquid hydrogen, and of course antimatter."

Livia relaxed still further. What with the cost of creating, transporting, and storing antimatter, it currently cost 500,000 cubiz per milligram—per Axis cubiz, which was equal to one pennyweight of gold. It was the only substance remotely approaching the value of trinium. Rebekah's family was not running a third-rate pawn shop.

"I like her," Darame added, knowing her words would endear the girl to Livia . . . who knew Darame did not suffer fools gladly.

"Well, I must not keep you with idle chatter," Livia said briskly. "It is good to see you; you must come east before the star begins to melt the day! Try to make room in your schedule."

"As soon as I can get away," Darame promised. "By the Festival of Masks, if not before then."

"That is next year, Darame," Livia pointed out. "I had hopes you would visit before *Midsummer's*." Livia stretched the word to four syllables.

"It depends on how much attention Tsuga's uncle needs," was the wry answer, her eyes twinkling.

"Hummph." It was Livia's most matronly sound, but she was not offended. In the game of wits played by every clan of Nuala, the premier rule was to attend to one's own house first. Livia knew Darame would trace this new turn of affairs down to the last iota.

"Take care, Livia. I will call you soon." With that farewell, Darame disconnected her vid.

Reaching carefully around her left hip, Darame released the pressure seams holding the new dress in place. A special ambassador . . . of course Dielaan could not ignore Rex's behavior much longer. All of twenty-two-years Terran, Rex was preparing to take ship in the fall, bound for The Brethren, which was what the Nualans called the six stars closest to their own. There he would learn firsthand of their neighbors' cultures, and seek a fertile bride to bring back to his homeland. A long trip, to The

Brethren . . . the closest star was Caesarea, and that was ten
years Terran one way.

Even though he had shown no interest in the duties attached
to his position as heir apparent, and had in Livia a fine regent
protecting his interests, Darame wondered if Rex would leave.
Because Quen had (apparently) genuinely fallen in love with
smiling Rebekah, and, for him, the trip would be unnecessary?
Could Rex fear a coup in his absence? For all his talents, Quen
had shown no desire for his brother's throne, not even in his
least guarded moments.

Rex wanted the rule, but not the responsibility . . . at least
not the responsibility of day-in, day-out ruling. Wine and women
were more to Rex's taste; even supervising the group representing
Dielaan at the trade Synod was more work than he was prepared
to perform. Somehow that had ended up on Quen's shoulders.
A mistake on Rex's part; Quen was proving himself an able
administrator and counselor, despite his tender nineteen years.
Was that giving fringe factions ideas? Something was brewing,
or Livia would not be worried.

Sliding the dress off and carefully slipping it over its padded
hanger, Darame paused in mid-step, considering . . . considering
the obvious problem, if common sense was set aside. Rex was
twenty-two; technically, he was now The Dielaan—all that remained was a formal announcement and the anointing ceremony.
Why hadn't Livia made the announcement?

Damn Livia's cousins! Unlike Atare, Dielaan currently had
no close kin—plague had wiped out almost an entire generation
of the throneline. Livia's second cousins were the most numerous
and vocal of her extended family, as Darame remembered it.
Tsuga was the worst—an eldest son, himself, and an advisor
Livia depended on . . . used to depend on, until he had declared
The Synod no longer useful. Thanks to the trade negotiated by
the ten great clans together, Sheel Atare at their head, Dielaan
was now not only populous but wealthy. Convinced of a need
for The Synod, as the clans called their joint venture, Livia had
turned from Tsuga's counsel to that of others.

What had Livia said, the last time they were together . . . "If
only Tsuga will leave him alone," "him" being her eldest son.
Hanging up the dress, Darame started off into the depths of her
private quarters. Behind her the main door slid closed; glancing

up, she saw her morning *guaard*, Jude, moving deliberately in the same direction. Doorway duty was never good enough for Jude, not when she watched The Atarae. *You have a habit of disappearing on us, serae,* Jude had casually mentioned once as she was going off duty.

Have you been stressing his rights, and not his duties, Tsuga? Darame wondered as she dipped a tentative toe into the swirling water of the huge, sunken whirlpool. What did Livia want to confide . . . and could not?

Seating herself on the bench lining the inside of the tub, Darame reached over to a nearby membrane and selected the RAM bank. A request for the royal Dielaan genealogy brought up a many-branched tree.

"With most of the twigs missing," she murmured aloud, skimming the information to refresh her memory. It was as she remembered it; Livia was the only surviving throneline Dielaaner . . . and of the previous generation, only her mother and ruling uncle had survived "The Wasting Sleep." Plague had killed all descendants of the two sisters of Ragäree Alys, Livia's grandmother—the non-ruling brothers had had few children survive, as well. . . .

Her head whirling, Darame turned from the screen, sinking up to her neck in the churning hot water. To find surviving female descent beyond Livia's line required going back *three* generations, to her mother's mother's mother, a ragäree named Lydia. Lydia's sister, Gladi, had founded a healthy line. *Especially healthy, since it is so far from the throne,* Darame thought drily.

From the eldest daughter alone of that line, the descent included two women and three men who were Livia's age, and nine children among the two sisters. A mass of out-kin; no wonder Dielaan had nearly exploded into battle at Tensar Dielaan's death. *Livia's two sons are the only clear choice to rule.* Tsuga had said that, a long time ago. Three sons, now—Livia was taking no chances with the peace of her land.

What of her peace of mind? *No confidants. Few . . . any? . . . she calls friend.* Tired of genealogies, Darame touched the communiqué square on her membrane, connecting the vid.

"Yes, serae?" asked Donn's soft voice.

"Do you have any extra invitations for the fête tonight?" Darame said without preamble. "A special ambassador from Dielaan is coming in, and I want to take him an invitation."

Donn knew better than to point out anything she felt might be beneath The Atarae's touch. Skilled at holding her tongue when necessary, Donn merely replied: ''I can have one for you in moments. Should it be addressed?''

''No. I will need it in . . . when is the Synod meeting?''

''None, serae. It is early, because of your party.''

Mid-afternoon. What with delivery, and being here when Sheel was finished with court. . . . ''Two hours?''

''Shall I use the office printer, and bring it tô you?'' Donn went on.

''That would be fine. Make a few extras, in case he brings subordinates.''

''As you wish, serae. Do not concern yourself with anything; it will be the event of the season.'' With this assurance, Donn's heart-shaped face vanished from the screen.

''We are always *the* event of the season, Donn,'' she murmured to the blank vid. ''I created the season.'' It was only within the last ten years that any type of cultural or social life existed in Amura-By-The-Sea. Before, it had been merely a port, neutral ground where all clans could meet. Now, what with the founding of the Synod, embassies had been built in Amura, complementing the solitary Atare winter palace. Darame had taken things a step further; for the first time in memory, the various tribes actually had begun to socialize with one another. Remembering the first inter tribal event she had held, a smile crept across Darame's lips. At least no one had been stabbed.

No one to tell except me, Livia? Then what am I to do? In the past you have used me as a sounding board, but can The Ragáree of Dielaan speak to The Atarae about family matters? At the core of all things, wasn't that what Nuala was all about —family? And loyalties. . . .

Darame reached for a towel.

AMURA-BY-THE-SEA, NUALA
      ONEHUNDRED EIGHTYTWODAY   SEXT
                                   . 2401 A.R.

It was a hot planet, all right. Radioactive? Well, it didn't glow—at least not outside the medical center where they revived Cold Sleep travelers. But it definitely had a hot climate. And now it was Restricted, as well. Peter's Keys! He had no luck! After some assassination ten Terran ago, the Nualans had confined all off-worlders to the port city of Amura-By-The-Sea. Ten years . . . Silver might be considered a native by now—she could be anywhere. Acquiring a visa for travel was almost impossible; he would need to appeal to each regional embassy, and wait while the request was processed through the home city—

Enough. He'd worry about it later. Adjusting to the midday heat was his immediate priority. The packet they had given him included a seasonal calendar. It *claimed* that the spring equinox was only yesterday, but the star was blazing brightly. Removing his jacket, Garth stuffed it in his bakit. Where was . . . ah. A tube of UV block. Smearing some of the stuff on his face and hands, Garth tossed the soft container back into his packet and dug for a map.

Most of this stuff would be useless—advertising probably paid for this courtesy info, which meant that they would try to sell him things. Or give him things . . . the omni information he had been shown mentioned land incentives for relocating to Nuala. A bonus for marrying a native . . . Sweet Saints. They had to bribe people to keep the population up?

Where were the landing bays? How did the med techs transport Sleep tubes from the space station proper to the planet? Not that it was much of a station—perhaps a dozen off-world ships at one time could tie up to the orbiting wheel. Small vessels had to land somewhere around here. . . . Another day for solving that mystery; Garth had located the map.

It was a simple affair, a thin plastic sheet color-coded in symbols. Even people who didn't speak Caesarean could get along on Nuala—signs were both written and oral, and in four languages. He needed a hostel of some kind, so he could get his bearings and examine all the things in the packet. Then off to find Halsey, who with luck would lead him to Silver. . . .

There was a moderately-priced hostel in the next block of buildings, if the visitor's guide was accurate. He had only to follow the signs through the business and embassy districts. Shouldering his bakit, Garth left customs and the medical center behind and started walking. Slowly; coming out of Sleep had been harder this time—they had kept him an extra three hours, just to monitor his body's return to normal.

Been pushing it a bit, haven't you? the technician had asked in crisp, unaccented Caesarean. In fact, everyone had been much too concerned about his health and history. Fortunately Sleep tags only went back three trips; if they knew how much he had really jumped, they might have kept him overnight.

As he walked, Garth examined his personal copy of the medical tests the Nualan authorities had run on him. They had wanted to see every medical disk he possessed, and since he had to declare everything on his person (to avoid having it taxed when he left) they knew all he knew. His history, a bit of blood, a bit of saliva, X-rays, PET and CAT scans—*I doubt anything gets by them.* Maybe they didn't want immigrants as much as they said they did. . . .

Tired, his mind wandering, surrounded by sound after hours of solitude, Garth was unprepared for surprises. Certainly the last thing he expected was to see the object of his quest walking casually toward him down the street. As he focused on her, his brain registering what he saw, Garth frantically tried to think of what he was going to do.

Smaller than he'd expected . . . a tiny, delicate woman, her figure worth looking at, even covered by dark slacks and a flowing blouse. The holo he had seen was taken at twilight, the scene washed of color . . . she really had silver-colored hair. *I didn't remember she'd be beautiful.* . . .

Two people dressed in black uniforms walked behind and slightly to either side of her; hiring bodyguards, are we? Who else is looking for you? Or are you just cautious?

He had to hide. Or did he? How foolish, she didn't know him from Adam himself—

Huge black eyes flicked past his face; paused—flicked back again. In the middle of a busy thoroughfare with at least a hundred witnesses, his lawful prey addressed him in the Reykjavik dialect of Gavriel.

"Be you kin to Lisbet Bjornsdottir of Reykjavik, on Gavriel?"

Garth's mind froze. *Sweet Sebastian's Arrows, I have no luck!* Finally her actual words sunk into his head. Controlling his face was difficult; exultation swelled in his breast. His fair, wild resemblance to his mother had saved him. Did this woman even know Lisbet had married? *They were both free-traders from the same planet—I should have guessed they had met!*

"She be my mother before." Garth knew only this version of Gavrielian, and was not strong in it—he trusted his careful speech would mask the emotion trembling within him.

A thousand years of viking strength gazed at him through black irises. "She be my friend before," the woman said gently, acknowledging the implication of death. Continuing in Caesarean, she told him: "I was Darame Daviddottir in that life. Are you here in trade or immigrating?"

"Trade," he said hastily. What name had his father used, in that scam? Not his own— Ah, by Nicholas's Golden Balls, all life was a chance. "I'm Garth Kristinsson." Hooking his left thumb firmly through the straps of his bakit, he used the maps and guidebook he was holding as an excuse not to offer his hand to her.

"Welcome to Nuala. You must come and tell me how Lisbet's life went on," she said graciously. "I lost track of her, oh, over a hundred years ago, when she left Gavriel for good—or such was her intent."

"She never went back," he offered, nodding.

"Do you have someplace to stay?"

"Yes," he lied pleasantly. "The Black Hazelle." Amazing! But one did not violate guest laws by possibly plotting the host's demise—and he had not yet made up his mind about this Silver, called Darame Daviddottir in still another time and place.

"A comfortable hostel," she responded easily. "You may not feel like socializing this evening, but if you do, there will be a big party up on the hill." She gestured vaguely off in the direction from which she had come. Reaching into a pressure pocket, she withdrew a small square of what looked like real paper. It was printed in both Caesarean and another language, and said simply: "Present this invitation to the door warden of 7 Dragonhold after compline on the second day of spring." Beneath it was written: *Formal attire*.

Garth was startled by the stiff, stationer's card; he never knew if her response was from simple courtesy, or from misreading him.

"Interpretations of 'formal attire' vary enormously," Silver said dryly. "However, there are places to rent clothing, if you feel like dressing up and don't own ceremonials." Smiling, she started walking again. "I hope to see you there."

Managing a slight smile, Garth remained where he was until

the trio had entered a wide stone portal at the street's end. It took several moments for him to realize that he was the subject of general envy.

"Guard it with your life," a passing merchant said with a smile. "The Atares throw quite a party, and invitations are highly prized."

The Atares? Garth looked down at the invitation once again. What did "after compline" mean? He had to get to a unit quickly, he needed to figure out how to load these "rings," as the Nualans called their flimsy storage units. A Read-Only Module would do—he did not need to access data. Not yet. Unless, of course, the rings the spaceport had supplied did not explain the mystery. Glancing back down the street, Garth saw an individual in a black uniform reappear at the stone gate, and quickly continued on down the boulevard.

Who said he wasn't lucky?

AMURA-BY-THE-SEA, NUALA
ONEHUNDRED EIGHTYTWODAY   SEXT
ATARE WINTER PALACE

"My Atare, it is nearly time for The Synod meeting."

Startled, Sheel flicked his eyes away from the RAM. Glancing over at the elderly man, Sheel said. "Elek?"

"The Synod meeting?" Elek prompted gently.

"So soon?" Sheel murmured, his gaze wandering past the remains of his lunch to an outside window.

"It approaches none, my Atare," Elek told him. Reaching to remove the plate and utensils stacked neatly before the membrane, Elek added: "It will be a short meeting, will it not?"

"As short as court today?" Sheel suggested.

Elek shook his head slowly. "A bad business, Atare, a very bad business. Let us hope that more bloodshed has been averted." Moving the dishes over to a dumbwaiter, Elek touched a small panel, sliding the doors shut to hide the view. "Will you change for this meeting?"

Mentally still in court, Sheel did not answer. Dear Mendülay, they had worked so hard to avoid that problem, and it had followed them to Amura. Months ago he and Avis, his sister and fellow high judge, had made a ruling concerning a piece of land claimed by two families of Tarn clan, a sept group of Atare. Title to the acreage was nebulous, and there was a history of joint use. However, an heir had been promoted through his uncle's death—and he no longer wished to share the pasture with his assorted relatives. It would make a good vineyard, true, but. . . . Sheel shook his head. After evaluating all the available information, Sheel and Avis had ruled in favor of the clan council. That meant a majority of the twelve people who advised The Tarn had to agree to the change—and, as he would personally benefit from that change, The Tarn could not break a tie vote.

It should have been a solution; most land cases never even reached the high court. Perhaps it would have been, except that the elders of the council were completely split on the subject. Then a few youngsters had taken matters into their own hands, and tried frightening one ancient woman into changing her vote.

"Atare?"

"Just my boots, Elek, thank you," Sheel murmured, smiling faintly. The one humorous portion of the entire episode . . . languidly Sheel reached to save the notes he had been entering. Not only had that old woman refused to buckle under, she had set a trap—a physical trap—for those who had tried to terrify her into voting for the change. Two prime young men of the blood had landed in her pit—and she had pressed charges.

Sorting it out had been a nightmare. Since the youths were closely related to the council, the council could not try them— so they were immediately packed off to Amura. Friends and foes alike had poured into the court. The seneschal had tacked them onto the end of the court session, which had meant privately interviewing everyone involved, which had meant—

Idly glancing down, Sheel noticed blood on his wrist and cuff. Staring, he tried to remember. . . . "Elek," he said easily. "It seems I must change my mind."

"Atare! How did we miss that?" Appalled, Elek immediately rushed off to start the shower.

Sheel started chuckling. A simple touch-up with a wet rag would not do, not for Elek. Laughing out loud, Sheel stood up and peeled off his shirt. "For now it is settled." Amazing how much that boy's nose bled . . . of course the fight had spread about the courtroom. "Elek, be sure and tell the seneschal to check the throne for blood. The Ragäree would be distressed at the idea of citizens petitioning before a bloody throne."

Unamused, the creases in his cheeks more pronounced than ever, Elek offered Sheel a robe. Accepting (because Zara was now on duty, and Elek was always nervous when one of the *guaard* was a woman) Sheel secured the soft robe around his waist and started into the sanitation. *I should appreciate you more, Elek,* Sheel thought ruefully, wondering what they were going to do with that huge pasture the crown had confiscated. Maybe wait a moon or so, then divide it in half, giving The Tarn the hilly part for his vineyard and leaving the rest as common grazing . . . maybe a public access between them, so there would be no encroachments either way. . . .

Hot water was shooting vigorously from the vertical row of nozzles. Eyelids drooping, Sheel leaned into the spray, his sandy hair darkening from the steam. How long he stood there he did not know, but when he finally opened his eyes, he saw a red light glowing. What— *I did ask for them to be installed,* he reminded himself. Red meant a visitor waiting—one who could not be scheduled later in the day. Allowing himself one good rinse all over, Sheel turned off the water and reached for a wipe. It had been warmed and was thick and fluffy. A few of the most exclusive hostels had installed shower vacuums, but Sheel was not interested; in their hot climate, vacuums caused the skin to flake. Wipes, on the other hand, constructed of heavy, looped cotton, were both absorbent and stimulating.

But enough of pleasures . . . few and infrequent as they were. Late court had meant no chance to even speak with Darame today, much less anything else. "Who is it, Elek?" Sheel asked, pushing his thoughts aside and stepping into the dressing room. How tired was he, that his mind was wandering so? Too many late hours spent going over petitions. They would have to delegate more work to the seneschal . . . perhaps even create a prime minister—

"It is Halsey, my Atare," was the response. "I have placed your clothing on the rack, and have ordered saffra and scones for the two gentlemen." Knowing Sheel really preferred to dress himself, Elek started backing out of the dressing room.

"Two gentlemen?"

Sheel's stare caused the old man to pause in mid-step. "The name of the second was not volunteered, Atare."

Blotting at a bead of moisture, Sheel did not respond. Interesting . . . and just who had Halsey brought along today?

"Thank you, Elek," he said aloud. "Could you turn off the RAM for me, please?"

"It is already done, Atare." With that, the elderly retainer slipped out between the sliding doors.

Quickly pulling on a dark, long-sleeved wool shirt and tight pants, Sheel tossed a loosely-woven tunic over his clothing and belted it close to his body. Without thought he slid his signet ring of heavy trine gold onto his right index finger. As usual, he almost forgot the chain of office; ten years he had worn it, and still it did not rest comfortably upon his chest.

Slender fingers closed on the heavy chain, lifting it from a velvet-lined box. One of his ancestors, acting on half-formed instinct rather than any proven facts, had decided that a crown created a tyrant. And was not the throne of Atare a double throne, when all was said and done? So, The Atare wore a heavy chain of trinium links around his neck, studded at regular intervals with faceted rubies. If she chose, The Ragäree wore a matching delicate chain. Perhaps it was because Avis rarely wore The Ragäree's chain that he felt so uncomfortable wearing Cort's—

No, Cort was dead ten years. And there was no one else to wear it.

Placing the lengthy chain around his neck, Sheel moved silently into the adjoining room. The two men waiting for him rose as he entered; their very lack of expression set off warning bells in Sheel's head.

One of them was familiar; Halsey, too, had never regained the weight lost during his ordeal in the ciedär, but his round face, wide eyes, and fringed topknot of remaining hair always echoed the huge man he had once been. Rav had been his downfall, the ingested radiation which often had lingering effects. Still possessed of an accelerated metabolism, Halsey inadvertently had had his most private dream come true—he could eat as much as he wanted, and never gain weight. Was keeping up with such a calorie burn dimming his pleasure in food? Sheel had never asked.

"Introductions?" Sheel asked pleasantly, as Halsey nodded his fealty. The other bore wrist marks indicating he had just arrived on a transport. Tall, extremely tall, the man had a sad face, reminding Sheel of an elderly hound. How old Sheel could not guess—although lines gave his face character, the man's hair was still mostly dark. Intent gray eyes took him in at a glance; the man lowered his head briefly, graciously, in a variant manner not seen in generations.

"You are the . . . grandson . . . of Salome?" His voice was soft, pleasant, a vibrant tenor laced with dark tones.

"Great-grandson," Sheel replied, recognizing the accent. "You have been gone a long time," he ventured.

"Almost two hundred years," the man agreed.

Eyes twinkling, Halsey said smoothly: "I did not burst in on your afternoon simply to bring you a relic of the past."

"Relic?" This was both bemused and calculating; this man kept score, whether he chose to use the knowledge or not.

Halsey's merry laugh rang out. Smiling, Sheel sat down in his stiff-backed chair and gestured for the others to regain their seats. "I trust you will explain why you have burst in upon my afternoon—after you introduce your guest," Sheel added, reaching for the pot of saffra sent up by housekeeping. Still warm, good. . . .

"The Atare pursues an anomaly like a cat pursues a mouse," Halsey replied. "You are almost impossible to sidetrack." Gesturing to his right, Halsey said: "May I present Eduard reb^ Katerina Alexeiovich, most recently known as Lowe of Caesarea Station. A man of many talents, the foremost being he is an absolute sponge where information is concerned. I have few secrets from him, and consider him my friend."

Ten years in Halsey's wake had taught Sheel that those words were never uttered lightly. "I am pleased to make the acquaintance of such a legendary free-trader," Sheel offered in return.

"The pleasure is mine, Atare. It is good to be home again, and to know that despite many changes, the hospitality of Atare never varies."

As "Lowe" paused for a sip of saffra, Halsey jumped into the conversation. "Lowe has finally retired from his base of operations. Shortly before he took Cold Sleep here, he stumbled upon some information of which I think someone here should be apprised."

"Which is why I am here, Atare," came a low murmur behind him.

Even as he recognized the voice, it took willpower not to flinch. Ten years back the *guaard's* highest ranking warrior had betrayed Cort Atare. Even though the woman standing behind him had been instrumental in rooting out the traitors with a minimum of trouble, the damage had been done, and sometimes, late at night. . . . His sister Leah's son, Tobias, was still leery about his *guaard*.

"Welcome, Mailan," Sheel said aloud, knowing Zara and Leo were still on duty, leaving Mailan free to study the men before them. "What information?"

"In the course of my work, I often kept tabs on certain free-traders. One was the son of two friends who died mysteriously over a hundred terran years ago. I kept an eye on him, partly out of a sense of duty and partly out of curiosity." The words were rusty, the pronunciation on one or two of them oddly stressed, but Lowe spoke quite adequate Nualan. "Garth was not yet trained as a free-trader when his parents died. He has supported himself mostly with dock work—a bit of low-level trading on the side—but that was not what was so interesting about him. What I found fascinating was that everywhere he traveled, he asked for news of a free-trader he called Silver."

Sheel did not miss the implication. "Darame used that name?"

"On occasion," Halsey confirmed.

"Do you know why he was looking for her?"

Lowe spread out his hands and studied the backs of them. "I know why he claims he is looking for her. Garth wants to know about his father's death—and his mother's. After a hundred years, Darame is the only person left alive who was actually involved with the scam. The logical person to ask . . . but his search has gone on too long."

"That seems . . . a bit single-minded," Sheel said softly, unease touching him.

"Obsessed," Mailan said dryly. "He has no other family, no spouse?"

"None, except the descendants of his sister. All of them still live on Gavriel, as of ten years ago Terran." Lowe glanced up; his gray eyes were so keen Sheel momentarily wondered if Mailan was his descendant. "I cannot betray a trust, Atare, yet I have a great deal of respect for your wife. At the least, she should know that this lad has spent his entire life looking for her . . . and that he arrived on Nuala today."

One eyebrow arched in response; Lowe's eyes flickered, but he did not comment on such body control. Hot healers were famous for tremendous physical and mental acrobatics, and clearly Halsey had already told his friend that Sheel was not only Atare, but both doctor *and* healer.

"Better to catch him in the act, if he is up to something," Mailan said in her low, alto voice. "Can you tell us more, free-trader?"

"I imagine what I can tell is in his file, but for the record—"

Sheel kept his eyes on Halsey while Lowe gave Mailan what information he felt he could. *Only last night I dreamed of her in darkness, bruised and bleeding. . . .* What good were fitful visions of a bleak future if they gave no hints that could lead to prevention?

It had been too much to hope for, that Darame's past would never come back to haunt her. Had she not warned him? *I expected blackmail . . . some off-world fool who thought I would care if my people knew of her previous life.* An inward smile traced his mind's eye. *We are stronger than that, we Nualans, and when we say your past disappears once you pass the pillars, we speak truth.* In fact, a few people knew she had been a free-trader; their response had been to ask for archival stories or business advice.

A strange, detached mood had taken hold of Sheel, making it hard to concentrate on Lowe's words. No matter; Mailan would insist on going over this before he left for The Synod meeting. So, he had spent his entire life seeking the free-trader called Silver. *She is not Silver, she is Darame Daviddottir . . . who is also the wife of Sheel Atare. You probably do not know what that means. But if you try to harm her, you may be surprised how long my arm truly is . . . and how heavy my hand can fall.*

Dupe: 1.) A sentient that is easily deceived because
it lacks either the ability or the training to be
selective. 2.) A sentient who becomes a tool or
puppet, especially to a powerful person or idea.
SYN *gull; fool; cull.*

CHAPTER THREE

AMURA-BY-THE-SEA, NUALA
    ONEHUNDRED EIGHTYTWODAY   COMPLINE

It was a small room, full of light and warmth by day—but the
star had left them hours before, and now the cubicle held only
shadows. At least Garth assumed the star had set hours ago; he
had yet to find any conversion of Nualan time into Caesarean
time. *It has to be here somewhere*, he thought irritably as he
whipped through the introductory material.

Hand straying to his plate for the remains of his "noneing,"
as the innkeeper called it (and why was he called an innkeeper
when he ran a hostel?) Garth ripped his last roll into tiny pieces,
his eyes never leaving the screen of the Random Access Module.
Out of habit he left off the oral narration; until he had checked
the soundproofing, he wanted to be sure no one overheard his
business.

His purchase of a late afternoon snack had told him that food
imports were incredibly high, and that locally-processed items
prepared for off-world stomachs were almost as expensive. There
was one other alternative . . . Garth currently did not consider
it an option. Nualans made something they called rav pills,

which, over a period of time, produced permanent immunity to rav poisoning. Rav was the locals' name for Dielaan Poisoning caused by ingestion of untreated Nualan water or food. Natives needed no such protection; born to the planet, their systems had adapted to the higher-than-Terran radioactivity.

Granted, untreated food cost a fraction of the import price, except for real meat, which was rare. Cost, however, was not enough of a factor for Garth. Just the idea of taking those pills made him feel ill. He had saved his wages over the years, aiming for this day; what with Sleep cost usually thrown in by the cargo haulers, Garth's purse was well-lined. First he had to decide how long he was going to stay . . . then he'd face a decision about rav pills.

Glancing to one side, Garth let his pale eyes flick over the rented white wool pants and long-sleeved shirtcoat of ice blue syluan. He couldn't resist it—just once, he had to wear syluan, even if the damage deposit could have bought him a silk shirt. Fortunately syluan was as tough as silk.

Echoing bells snapped him out of his concentration. Five, six, seven—eight bells. What was . . . jumping back to the time and calendar sequence, he saw that eight bells was compline, the time the party began. Switching off the RAM and popping the ring, Garth stood and moved quickly into the sanitation. It was scrupulously clean, yet primitive—Garth had spent a long time trying to locate the moisture vacuum for the sink before he figured out there *was* no vacuum, not even for the shower. Instead, thick, absorbent pieces of cloth were hanging at convenient intervals. Fortunately, Garth vaguely remembered something about using cloth to remove water from skin. Damned inefficient—he still felt damp. Would a more expensive hostel have a vacuum . . . was it worth the money. . . .

Quickly rinsing his teeth, Garth stripped off his outer clothes and carefully pulled on the tight crêpe wool pants. Lined with silk—good, sometimes wool was a bit itchy. His fingers reached to carefully caress the syluan shirt. Surely syluan was cheaper on this planet? Garth checked the collar for markings, but the script was indecipherable. Shrugging minutely, he slipped on the shirt and crossed the front panels purposefully. One thing he *had* discovered in the last few hours was a cheap library access. If he wanted to locate the city of origin, he'd find it eventually.

Garth allowed himself to pause before the full length mirror in the sanitation. Finding a shirt which matched his eye color had been a stroke of luck. Not a hair out of place.

"You'll do," he told the image in the mirror. Looking closely, he saw an unfamiliar glint in his eye. "Don't get over-confident," Garth warned the reflected youth. How long since he'd had time to be happy about anything? "Lise's wedding," he murmured, his thoughts flicking to his sister. "I never did make it to your farm, did I?"

It was like cold water in the face. *This is not pleasure, it's business. Pay attention to detail—detail can make or break your plan.*

The fact that he did not yet have a plan was immaterial. He would.

ATARE WINTER PALACE   COMPLINE

"I do not wish to argue anymore." Darame's voice was still level, but the tone could have frozen raindrops.

"We are not arguing, we are discussing," was Sheel's calm reply.

Darame continued to face the mirrors, carefully sliding a curved wire of trinium behind and over the top of one ear. A blood-red, one-karat ruby mounted in trinium winked at her through her loose hair. "We are not arguing because I promised your mother I would always try to hold on to my temper when you start doing this."

"This?" Now it was Sheel's turn to stiffen; the word sounded as if it was clamped in a vise.

Inhaling deeply, Darame slowly turned to face him. Dressed simply in a laced tunic and pants of pale topaz syluan, Sheel's bronzed face and sun-tipped sienna hair radiated health. Only his expression was at odds with the image; lips compressed, features remote and still except for the slight tension that lined his body.

"Riva told me that hot healers were overly protective. I promised I would try to remember that whenever you tried to pad me with down."

"I am not—"

Darame did not let him finish. "You will not call this boy in for questioning," she began, stepping down from the pedestal.

Walking right up to him, she lifted her face and waited until his wandering gaze met her eyes before continuing to speak. "Most of all, you will not assign people to follow me—not *guaard*, not Halsey or his crew, not even a free-lancer. Are we agreed?"

A tiny twitch at the corner of Sheel's eye caused the slightest lift of the opposite eyebrow. Darame reached with gentle fingers to smooth the front panels of his tunic. "I am not going to do anything foolish, like wander off down a private drive with him. And this is not Dielaan—you cannot tie Lowe up and pump him full of truth serum in your search for solutions."

A glimmer of a smile. . . . "Livia would not have hesitated."

"Lowe would not have warned Livia." Smiling, Darame turned and moved over to her jewel box. "We have enough information to take precautions. It may be quite simple, you know. The boy's life was destroyed with one blow—he wants to know if I can tell him anything about the incident."

"If only I believed that," came her husband's soft, weary voice. "I would be happier if you knew of *which* scam he needs knowledge of. You have no holos of this woman?"

"I have one holo, taken when we were young. His resemblance to her is startling." Pulling out the last trinium necklace for her ensemble, she gestured for his aid. "His parents' demise may be totally unrelated to whatever scam I was involved with at the time."

"You have no idea who his fa—"

"Sheel, free-traders do not use their names!" Darame concealed her scorn under amusement. "I had worked more than a hundred-and-fifty terran years before I came here, and Nuala was the *first* place I ever used my real name!"

"And why was that?" Taking either end of the clasp, Sheel fastened the trinium collar with its burgundy-colored stone carefully around her neck.

"Because Nuala is known throughout the Seven Systems for its interrogation system," she replied, turning and throwing her arms around him. "I had to give authorities no reason to doubt the foundation of my story. When you concoct an elaborate lie, my love, you must wrap it deep in truth—otherwise it will trip you. And you know it is said that Nualans do not lie, and therefore can sniff out untruths."

"Wicked woman," he murmured, his arms tightening around her.

"Hummm," was her reply. When he finally freed her lips, Darame said: "This boy is nothing to me but the son of Lisbet. We will have to be content with that, for now." Reaching to her neck, she made sure that the huge, faceted oval was centered snugly in the hollow of her throat.

"You need not wear that on every occasion, you know," Sheel told her as he gently pulled away. "A serae stone is not a wedding ring."

"The red tones in its depths compliment my dress," was her mockingly prim answer. "And it does what your ancestor intended it to do when she started the tradition—it tells all who look upon it that the bearer is beloved by an Atare." A slow wink, and she whirled away from him, letting the long, full skirt billow out in a circle. "That should reassure you—no one in his right mind would lay a hand on me."

"Are my enemies sane?" came the voice behind her.

"Most of them," she said quickly, grateful his tone was so light. After his older sister Leah's breakdown ten years before, "sanity" was often a delicate subject. "Come, our guests arrive."

Usually Darame went before Sheel down the narrow corridor leading to the front room, their *guaard* silently bringing up the rear, but tonight he caught up with her, sliding an arm behind her bare back. Perfectly willing to push aside their quarrel, Darame laid her fingers on top of his. Incredible warmth crept through her hand, easing the cold in her joints. Despite Sheel's endless work in the hospices and his occasional bouts of protectiveness, having a hot healer in residence was very convenient. Darame had to constantly remind herself that what she now took for granted was a very rare talent, even among Nualans. It was not to be abused.

Was it abuse to ease your stretch marks during pregnancy? a voice within teased. Darame gave the voice a quick shove back into the nether reaches of her mind. No, it had *not* been vanity—not when the marks began to split and bleed, when her tiny body could not keep up with the growth of the children.

Sheel's sudden laughter brought her back from her reverie. "I had not noticed," he got out between chuckles. "Obviously my eyes are always on you, even if my mind is elsewhere."

What—Tilting her head, Darame followed his line of sight to the wall at their right. Numerous holos formed a lovely grouping running the length of the sculpted wall. It was an exact copy of the display in the private corridor that lead to the Atare city throne room. They had been here *months* and he was just noticing—

"You work too hard," Darame growled at him.

Shaking his head, Sheel pulled away and paused at the door, waiting for his two evening *guaard* to move up behind him. As the group slowly proceeded through the heavy, wood archway, Darame hesitated, sparing a glance for the wall beside her.

One of her better notions, that display. Its center was a holo of Sheel and herself, ringed by their three children; the depth of the wall cases and the recessed lighting gave it especially good presentation. At the heart of Nuala's concerns was fertility—or the lack thereof. Those who were fertile were expected to do their part to keep up the population, since off-world gene packets required lab work before they were useful. In a world where eighty percent of the population was sterile, fertility was power.

Of course Sheel had fathered children before Darame ever met him; his progeny now totaled twenty-four in all. Eight had been conceived before Sheel left on his trip to Emerson. Those children were all physically older than Sheel, grown with families of their own. Many of them were grandparents, for Cold Sleep to Emerson was thirty-four years Terran round-trip. These festival children (for many of them were undoubtedly conceived during the Festival of Masks) were in special frames circling the central holo. *Their* children and grandchildren radiated outward in ever-increasing circles.

Nualans had no word for illegitimacy. Only children born of marriage could inherit mining stock and use their father's clan name—otherwise, there was no difference.

Well and good—but you have done your part, Darame announced to the holo of Sheel, reaching to touch the unattainable image. Women never stopped trying to attract Sheel's attention, much to his embarrassment. For Sheel was a hot healer, the ultimate adaptation to Nuala's radiation, able to draw fevers and mend broken bones by mere touch alone. And healers were always very fertile people. Occasionally he felt guilty about his reserve . . . as if he thought he was keeping clean gene stock to himself. Darame knew he hated the attention, hated wondering if the woman knew or cared anything about him as a person.

This display was her compromise, her way to free Sheel of

his odd racial guilt and keep his attention directed toward herself. "Any man who has fathered twenty-four children has done his duty," she murmured aloud. Smoothing the flaming syluan down one leg, Darame turned toward the end of the hallway.

Mailan was waiting. The captain of the *guaard* had served earlier, as well as attended several meetings, she should be with her family—Darame's eyes narrowed. She noticed Mailan was wearing her formal black uniform, but her stance was relaxed. Glancing over one shoulder, she saw Ayers' blond, burly form. So, Ayers was on duty . . . Mailan was making a social appearance.

"I thought I might run interference for you," Mailan suggested, her tone almost offhanded. "The Wallace is lying in wait at the foot of the grand staircase."

Tonight, Sheel reb´Riva Atare. Tonight. In a sudden flush of both anger and humor, Darame was unable to decide among numerous punishments, including a cold shoulder, a cold shower, or an attack upon strategic places with a feather. Meeting Mailan's eyes, Darame said: "Now he is in trouble."

"But not in public."

"Of course not," Darame responded, wondering just how she was going to get around this "unofficial" increase in the number of her *guaard*. Smiling brilliantly, deceptively, Darame said: "Come, Ayers." Knowing that actually addressing him had clearly expressed her displeasure, Darame did not trouble herself to look over her shoulder. With a nod, she waited for Mailan's tall, slender form to precede her into the Alameda Room.

As he walked up to the entrance, Garth was surprised at how *comfortable* the place looked. It was not at all what he thought a palace would look like. No high wall, no guards (at least no visible guards) and a minimum of ceremony. From the road, the building appeared low and secluded, with beautiful gardens accented by walkway lamps. Its walls were not stone, and yet . . . they were seamless, their neutral shade soft in the subdued white lights of the landscaping. Undulant roofing tiles were lost in near-darkness; only one of Nuala's three moons was visible, and it was old and crooked.

A tall, white-haired man of indeterminate years was greeting the guests. After inquiring whether or not Garth had taken the rav series, the door warden requested his right hand. Producing an odd pocket device, he gravely marked a damp streak across the back of Garth's hand. Smiling once more, the man gestured toward the inside.

Slightly bemused, Garth nodded and walked into the hall. A divided staircase immediately curved down into the depths of the house. The high, beamed ceiling above supported a heavy, many-tiered, antique chandelier lit by an unknown power source. Laughter and garbled conversation caught his ears. Walking down toward the noise, Garth decided that although the wall sconces might be reproductions, the chandelier itself was authentic—dull, matte gleam hinted at wrought iron, bent and twisted into fantastical shapes. *Older than the governments of The Brethern,* he thought.

Reaching the bottom of the stairs, Garth's attention was caught by the room itself, which must have traced the backside of the building. It was easily six meters wide and twice that in length, and the long wall opposite him was clear. The window looked out over a huge expanse of water and sky. To the right, slivers of color glittered, lining the coast, while to the left there was only the sea, glimmering in starlight and thin moonlight.

Drawn by the scene, Garth moved like a ghost through the brilliant, swirling crowd. A few boats remained upon the water, their running lights outlining their sails. Enchanted, Garth settled upon the back of a huge, low couch.

"It *is* beautiful, is it not?" murmured a delicate voice, its Caesarean oddly accented.

"I have never seen its like anywhere," Garth responded without turning his head. "Caesarca boasts of its many bodies of water, but . . . this is incredible!"

"It has always been a comfort to this world," the voice continued. "When our ancestors first were trapped here, its . . . familiarity . . . was all that kept some of them sane. It is a . . . a monstrously beautiful world, with its hints of the Homeland. Superficial similarities, at least," she added at the last.

"Homeland?" This caused Garth to turn his head.

"One of our many names for Earth, that place the Caesareans call Terra," the woman said smoothly.

Garth realized he was staring. The creature before him—woman was too ordinary a word for her—was swathed in either green syluan or silk. Both necklace and earrings were fabricated of dozens of tiny trinium crescents, asymmetrically balanced in a waterfall of metal that rippled like tinkling bells and shimmered like the pricks of starlight dotting the lush Nualan sky. In contrast to this sea of silver and green was her hair, which was the color of burnished copper. It was twisted into a coil near the top of her head, the bulk of it falling down her back like a curtain. Shorter around her face, copper shavings curled softly in counterpoint to her tiny, elegant features. Only her hair cut through the soft vision—and, of course, her eyes and brows.

They were black, glossy black, as deep as anything Garth had ever imagined. It seemed impossible for such a tiny, red-haired creature to have such black eyes and brows, and such a golden bronze complexion. Could it be natural? *You can't ask if she's lab get, boy, don't even think about it.*

His subconscious had another explanation. "You're a huldre," Garth heard himself whisper, and immediately felt a blush rising.

"I hope that is a compliment," was the response, her smile intact even as her eyes narrowed slightly.

"It . . . is," he managed to say. "It's an old, old tale, told by the grannies of Gavriel. It is said that on old Earth there was another people who lived among my ancestors. In Scandinavia they were named huldre by the peasants. They were also called . . . elves?"

Her laughter was like a chiming bell. "Yes, I am tiny! It runs in my family." Her eyes were still creased, and Garth realized it was caused by amusement. "We have no elves here," she said gently. "They had no ships to bear them hence across the airless sea." Her words had the rhythm of poetry, but Garth did not recognize them. Another grin popped out, and the woman said: "I think this is your first visit to Amura-By-The-Sea."

"It is my first visit to Nuala," Garth admitted.

"Then we must be sure your impression of us is favorable! Are you in need of refreshment? If you do not care for alcohol, there are several other beverages offered," she began, gesturing toward one wall.

As he started to assure her that he did, indeed, drink alcohol, something within him paused. "Not tonight, at least not yet," Garth heard himself say. "Alcohol dulls the faculties. There's too much to see and do to waste time—" *Getting drunk* sounded a bit blunt. . . .

"I agree. Come, I will find you saffra." As she started toward one wall she suddenly hesitated and looked back at him.

Taking a guess, Garth said: "I just arrived today; I haven't taken the series." It was a good piece of mind reading. Smiling sunnily at him, she continued toward the sumptuous spread of food.

Before he could say yea or nay, the elf had seized a plate and was heaping food upon it. A simple shrug of her shoulder in his direction brought an attendant to Garth's side.

"Your hand, sir?" the youth asked politely. Wordlessly Garth offered up the appropriate hand. "*This* is your refreshment table; if you see something being served at the opposite buffet which you would like to try, speak to me. I will see if an equivalent dish is possible." With a slight nod of courtesy, the youth faded into the background.

"All those pretty words meant that some Nualan dishes have no off-world counterpart. Stevos, for example—we can grow tomatoes and the various peppers in purified soil, but most visitors find stevos too spicy for their taste."

"The ambassadors don't eat any native foods?" Garth asked, accepting the plate she pushed into his hands.

"Some of them—and Amura has been smart enough to arrange for off-world equivalents. But they are pale copies of Kilgore or Dielaan delicacies. I am certain, I have tried them," she added at his expression.

"You sure have the staff hopping. Are you a . . . relative of The Atare?"

An odd smile crossed her face. "Hardly. What do you know of us?"

"Of Nualans?" Uncertain of what she meant, Garth searched for an appropriate reply. A tall glass of an iced reddish beverage nudged his hand; taking it from her, he finally said: "You have a . . . a clan system, don't you? A dozen or so major clans, and many minor ones, all interlocking in various trade and protection treaties."

"You have some wits," she said easily. Her Caesarcan was accented in strange places, and Garth wasn't sure how she had stressed that last sentence. "Yes, we are many tribes, each with a ruling clan. My tribe is Dielaan. We have battled Atare for a thousand years," she added casually. "Be grateful you said that to me and not to my cousin. She probably would have slapped you and stalked off.''

"Leaving me wondering what I had said wrong," Garth said ruefully. "Thank you for your patience."

"One cannot deal with off-worlders without patience." Removing a cube of cheese from the pile on his plate, she told him: "You may call me Lucy."

"I am called Garth Kristinsson." Belatedly, Garth realized he was standing with a plate in one hand and a glass in the other; in a sense he was trapped.

Chuckling, Lucy took him by the sleeve. "Come; I noticed untenanted seats at the far end."

Scarcely an hour past compline and already it is packed, Sheel thought idly, pausing where the two spirals joined into one grand tier of steps. Amazing how much body heat could be generated by a crowd; Darame's dress had been a good choice, after all. Not like several ambassadors, stiff in their formal uniforms . . . poor souls had to be melting.

"Atare always draws a crowd," came a deep voice behind him.

Glancing over his shoulder, Sheel saw his seneschal, Zaide. The slight, dark-haired man scarcely reached his Atare's shoulder in height, yet Zaide always walked as if he were taller. *How were you raised, to have such pride and yet such modesty?* Sheel felt lucky to have such a person serving Atare; Zaide was the strongest personalty in a dozen provinces.

Except for Darame, of course.

"What are you doing here? I thought these things bored you," Sheel asked.

"They do," Zaide replied without a hint of discomfort. "But I helped Donn plan this occasion; the least I can do is make sure it starts well." A wide smile crossed his sharp, narrow features. Leaning over, Zaide confided: "I have a few new rings, fresh off *The Crowned Tiger.* Before matins sounds I plan to be well into the histories of the seven great republics of Emerson."

Nodding, Sheel let his eyes stray over the crowd. *Guaard* were stationed at various points around the room, but so far there had been no trouble. Not even an argument loud enough to turn heads . . . .

"It *is* odd, however, how our parties are packed, while the other houses can scarcely draw representatives of each clan," Zaide continued. "Our food is similar, and this band played at Kilgore for Yule—"

"Wallace serves cheaper wine late at night, when they think everyone has lost their discrimination?" Sheel suggested.

Zaide gave Sheel a look worthy of Elek's most severe reproaches. "No one stays that late, my Atare," Zaide announced, loftily overlooking the comment. "No, I have my suspicions why they come."

"Looking for ways to knife me in the back?" Sheel asked, only half in jest.

Zaide seemed to consider the idea, even as his gaze wandered to see how close strangers were to their side. "Figuratively, perhaps. Not literally . . . few of them, at any rate. And the reasons of those who would might surprise you. I think Wallace would cheerfully slit your throat, if he thought he could convince your wife to marry him."

"She would be on the next ship outbound," Sheel said without hesitation.

"That is why Wallace will never be a part of a plot against your person. This way, at least he can dream, and worship from afar." Encouraged by Sheel's thin smile, Zaide continued. "They come, Atare, because you want them here."

Sheel lifted an eyebrow.

"*Want* them here," Zaide stressed. "Not need, not expect . . . not hope—you genuinely want them as your guests. Though you do not think of all of them as friends, or even potential friends, there is not a man or woman in this room whom you hate, and they know it. They are welcome here, in this curiously neutral place of gathering, this heart of Atare. Your Synod allies, they may host parties . . . but it is because they think they are expected to host them. Or because they hope to gain useful information. You merely create an atmosphere that inspires trust."

"Darame thinks it cools down tempers when The Synod heats up," Sheel said quietly. "It helps, but I suspect the 'cooling' is in her efforts. Have you ever watched her work a crowd? It is fascinating." His voice faded as he caught sight of his wife in the press. A streak of red, her hair shimmering in the warm light, Darame wandered at will, greeting embassy members, making sure drinks were filled and strangers welcomed—

Strangers. Where was . . . ah. By the window; occupied with one of the young Dielaan outkin, it appeared. What sort of problem would this youngster be? A fledgling free-trader, with few of the skills needed to survive the games people like Halsey and Darame played. *You admit it . . . she still plays those games. But now she plays them for the gain of Atare.*

"My cousin is successful, as usual," came a soft voice.

Sheel was very conscious of the *guaard* at his back. "Your cousin is a lovely young woman," he replied. "I doubt she leaves these things unaccompanied, unless she so chooses." Turning slightly, Sheel's eyes flicked down to meet those of Rex reb^Livia Dielaan, heir to the Dielaan throne. "It is a family trait, Dielaan," he added, glancing meaningfully at the fair young merchanter who dawdled at the foot of the wide staircase.

"A Nualan trait, seri," Rex said, chuckling, his firm stance relaxing slightly. Almost alone among the clans, Sheel had called Rex "Dielaan" ever since he arrived in Amura as Synod representative for his tribe. It made it difficult for Rex to remain remote, even hostile, in Sheel's presence. Still, Sheel never deceived himself about Rex. Quen, the second son, respected his ancient enemies even if he could not bring himself to like them. Rex could never find a worthy enemy.

"True. I imagine my nieces and nephews are equally busy this evening." Sheel studied the dusky face dispassionately, trying to read Rex's mood. Immaculate as always, his red-tinged sable hair a smooth cap upon his head, Rex was one of the few people Sheel knew who never perspired. He had body control rivaling a healer's, although Rex was certainly not a healer.

"Tell me, Atare. Is it true you do not avail yourself of this meadow full of flowers because your wife would probably stick a knife in your ribs if you did?" Black eyes gleamed merrily as Rex asked the question.

Anyone short of a ruling clansman would have been snubbed for such a question. Then Holy Mendülay gave Sheel inspiration.

"Is that how Livia keeps your father in line?" Sheel asked curiously.

Rex burst out laughing. "It would not surprise me," he finally got out, his eyes narrowing slightly as he chuckled. "She always has several knives secreted about her person . . . and she knows how to use them." Glancing down the steps, Rex said: "My friend grows impatient. Good evening to you, seri."

"Dielaan," Sheel responded formally. Although his gaze drifted over the crowd, his mind followed Rex Dielaan down to the floor and off toward the buffet, his little merchanter in tow.

"Does he call you 'seri' to annoy you, or because he feels that political equals should be intimate?" Zaide said suddenly.

Surprised, Sheel glanced to his right. "I thought you had left."

"I am very good at invisibility, my Atare—especially around Dielaaners. They do not see their own underlings, much less anyone else's." This was spoken with a polite nod in The Dielaan's direction. It was as Zaide had said: Rex was oblivious to the courtiers floundering after him through the press of people. "To be honest, Dielaan *may* have seen me—but he does not care for me, and cuts me whenever our paths cross. I did not wish to force his hand, should you feel obligated to introduce me. Either he would snub me, which would annoy you—or he would greet me, which would annoy him."

"I remember his retainers; he should remember mine."

"I suspect he forgets only what he chooses to forget, Atare," Zaide said gently, his gaze scanning the crowd. He stopped moving and tilted his head in concentration. Tracing the path with his eyes, Sheel looked in the same direction. Off by the window were Quen of Dielaan and his tall, bosomy redhead. They were nearly of a height, and aware of little else as they talked. "He has not forgotten that young woman. But she is too strong for him, I suspect . . . he will not drive her off."

"Has he tried?" Sheel normally did not pay much attention to Amuran gossip, since Darame enjoyed sifting it for valuable information. But he liked Quen, for what it was worth, and he did not care for Rex.

"Oh, yes, he has tried ridicule, and has hinted that Quen toys with her. She hears, but she stays. I think she loves young Dielaan. He will be fortunate if he can win her."

"Would she turn down a prince of the land? Gavrielian merchants usually do not serve on Nuala unless they are willing to consider Nualan spouses," Sheel pointed out. "Especially the women."

"Would you like to have Rex as a brother-in-law? If it was reversed, and Quen was eldest, I do not think she would hesitate. But Rex can call Quen—and his family—to court. I can well understand her hesitation." Glancing at Sheel out of one eye, he said: "You missed most of the politicking of your uncle's reign, my Atare, but your brother Caleb enjoyed mentally abusing your uncle's retinue. Since they served The Atare, they could not slip away to their own lands . . . and who would speak against an heir?''

"A point," Sheel conceded. "I would not stand for such a thing."

"It is commonly believed that you are uncomfortably aware of the atmosphere of your court. Your lords play their little games far from your knowledge, or so they think."

"So they think?"

"The Atarae always finds out eventually." As a chuckle escaped Sheel, Zaide added: "You are a very good team, my Atare."

"So it appears," Sheel murmured. "I think I could do with some cold saffra. Coming?" Glancing to the side, Sheel started down the stairs.

"I think I shall speak to Donn one more time before departing," Zaide responded, matching Sheel's stride. "Good evening, Atare." With a nod of fealty, Zaide slipped off toward the back of the great room.

Sheel was able to reach the buffet with a minimum of fuss. Accepting a glass of chilled saffra from one of the caterers, he sent his compliments to the chef in charge, then wandered in search of another vantage point. With no particular purpose in mind, Sheel chose to walk on the window side as he made his way through the crowd. This allowed him to pass quite close to the newcomer Garth and his Dielaan acquaintance, but other than making brief eye contact with the youth, Sheel continued on without stopping.

As he was concentrating on lovely Lucy, Garth was not really paying attention to the press around them. This caused him to startle visibly when a lathe-thin Nualan briefly caught his eye.

"Garth?" Lucy had paused, noticing his change of expression.

Standing swiftly to avoid spilling his drink, Garth swallowed immediate unease. Oh, lord, the white pants—

"Do not worry, I caught the drops with my napkin," came Lucy's voice at his side. "What is wrong? You look as if you have seen an emissary!"

"Emissary?"

Lucy dimpled. "You . . . would call it an angel, I believe. A messenger of Mendülay, the One God."

"More like a demon," he muttered. Whoever he was, that look had intent behind it. Had that woman set a tail upon him already?

Lucy's gaze was following his line of sight. "Oh!" She chuckled. "You have never seen The Atare before? How did you get in here, anyway?" Inquiring black eyes settled upon him.

"I met one of my mother's old friends in the streets. She gave me an invitation. The silver-haired one over . . . there." Her dress momentarily set Garth back. *Sweet Peter, why did she have to be young and beautiful?*

Shifting her flimsy green stole from her shoulders to the crooks of her arms, Lucy said: "The Atarae? That is what their clan calls her. She is the wife of The Atare. So you do not know Sheel . . . shall I introduce you? He can be very approachable." Her look was almost mischievous.

Remembering those strange, penetrating eyes, Garth quickly said: "No! No, thank you . . . not just now."

"He *is* unnerving, is he not? Those Atare eyes can look right through you, and his see more than most. Too bad, really. Otherwise, he is an attractive man." Her gaze flicked toward the window. "The moon is already low, it must be nearly matins. I have questioned you all evening! Thank you," she added, touching his wrist gently. "I will go off-world soon, and I have been nervous about it."

If you can face this place without qualms, you can face The Brethren, Garth thought. Those odd eyes had reminded him of what he had conveniently shoved into the background—that these people weren't quite normal.

Suddenly Lucy's face changed radically to an expression of distaste. "This way." Seizing his sleeve, she guided him along the glass wall.

"I left that plate—"

"The staff will see to it."

"Lucy?" Garth got out before she abruptly stopped, causing him to crash into her. Fortunately his glass of saffra was almost empty. "What's wrong?"

She was already grabbing the arm of a young woman moving past them. Unknown words flowed briskly; brilliant green eyes

flicked past him, looking down the path they had just traced.
Then the newcomer looked back at Garth.

"Introductions?" she suggested in Caesarean.

"This is my cousin Malini. Garth Kristinsson, from Caesarea," Lucy said quickly. The look she was giving her cousin
was a clear warning.

"Cousin?" They were both petite women, scarcely reaching
his shoulder, but other than that they looked nothing alike. Malini
had dusky skin, as if she was powdered with spice, and her hair
was as black as Lucy's eyes. Now that he looked at them both,
Garth could see a teasing resemblance in the shape of their faces;
they had the same delicate bone structure.

"Distant cousins," Malini corrected. "We are . . . fourth
tier?" she asked Lucy. "All Dielaan cousins are distant cousins,
since the plague."

"Generations ago," Lucy added. "You need not worry about
that kind of illness. I wanted to get away from *that*—" A quick
jerk of her chin indicated a tall, fair-haired man who was standing
near the window.

That was wearing some sort of environmentally-controlled
suit. It was not heavy, but it clearly had its own atmosphere.
The man wore a brilliant, yellow skinsuit beneath it; in his gloved
hand he held a cane of polished wood, which he was leaning
on. As if aware of Garth's scrutiny, the individual looked up.
Eyes like polished amber focused on him. A knowing smile
crossed the man's face, setting well on the strong, tanned planes.
Not a young man, but far from feeble.

"You need not be rude, Lucy. After all, he is mock sini. The
suit is just to relieve the fears of the nervous," Malini said easily.

Garth noticed that however casual Malini wanted to appear,
she made sure to keep several people between the suited man
and herself.

"Why was he invited?" Lucy muttered, sipping her drink.
"You do not know, do you?" At the slow shake of Garth's
head, she continued: "You have heard that eighty percent of the
population is sterile? We keep fighting the planet, we humans,
and we adapt in odd ways. That creature is a mock sini. Sinis
were once human, but the radiation changed their genes."

"Hot humans," Malini said simply. "Some are so hot we
could not approach without becoming ill—headaches, vomiting,

and such. Some are *mock* sinis; we can be around them for several hours without damage.''

"So scientists say. Scientists are sometimes wrong," Lucy stated.

"Then there are sinishur. . . ." Malini's pretty mouth twisted. "Now *those* I cannot call human, though they claim the name. Hope that you never see one; the sight would haunt your dreams." Flicking a glance at her cousin, she said: "I hope Rex has not seen him; we do not need a scene."

"A scene about what?"

Both women jumped at the soft voice. Garth looked beyond them, and saw a slender man who looked about his own age. His hair was as dark as Malini's, but with a halo of red reflecting from it; like Lucy, his eyes were black, but these held no warmth. A dark, burly man in a black, red, and gold uniform was close on his heels; on his arm was a young, full-figured blond.

Turning to Lucy, Garth saw her visibly relax; the reflections in the window told him that the mock sini had disappeared from view.

"The Atare has a few of his pet sinis roaming the party," Lucy said easily. "I hope you will refrain from baiting them."

"There is easier sport to be found," the man responded. "Have you two reached an accommodation, or is there a clear victor?"

"Rex!" Malini said, laughing. "You make us sound so predatory!"

"Do you prefer brunettes or redheads?" the newcomer continued.

"Is this the cousin?" Garth asked instead, gesturing at Malini. All three Nualans stared oddly at him for a moment; then Lucy laughed.

"Yes, I was thinking of Malini." Still chuckling, she turned dancing eyes on her kin. "Garth asked me if I was one of the hostesses."

Malini visibly stiffened, her green eyes blazing; then she flexed her shoulders to relax them. "You *are* new," she said dryly.

"Redheads," Garth said courteously to the young man. "At least until I know a bit more about this planet."

The other smiled slightly. It was an expression full of capri-

cious pleasure. "You should stick to redheads. Malini may not
have the hair, but she has the temper. Lucy is the kindest of us
all."

"Except to sinis?" He said it teasingly, but as he spoke, Garth
realized that might not be a joking matter.

"Even to sinis," the Nualan said smoothly. "I prefer her
open fear and dislike to Malini's progressive piousness." Beside him, the dark woman stiffened again, but she did not respond.

"Garth, we are very lax in our manners tonight," Lucy said
quickly. "This is another of my cousins. Rex, this is Garth
Kristinsson. He just slipped in the door, it seems—his mother
knew The Atarae."

"Indeed?" Some life actually flickered in Rex's black eyes.

"We were schoolgirls together," came a low, vibrant voice.
Turning slightly, Garth found "Silver" at his elbow. "You
have come a long way since then," Garth said neutrally.

"A long way," the woman agreed. "I wish we had stayed
together; Nuala would have amused her. Lisbet had a wonderful
sense of the absurd."

"Have you been on Nuala long?" Garth hadn't intended to
risk much conversation with her—someone might remember that
they had talked, after it was all over—but she drew him like
metal to a magnet.

"Not long, really," was the murmured reply. Facing toward
the others, she said: "Good to see you all. Have you found
things to your liking?"

"You have the best whiskey in town," Malini assured her.

"I imagine your embassy uses the same importer."

"But we do not share it quite so freely," Rex responded with
a smile. Nodding graciously to the women, he said: "A pleasure,
Garth. Come see me; I am sure our conversation would be en-
lightening to both of us." And with that, he disappeared back
into the crowd.

"Did I meet that blond earlier?" Garth asked Lucy.

"Not since I met you; Rex has a new one every few days,
we usually do not bother to learn their names. What do you think
of our special ambassador, Atarae? I saw you speaking with
him," Lucy said politely.

"He is quite a charmer; I shall have to warn the ladies of my
court," the silver-haired woman said easily. "I look forward to

bettering my acquaintance with him.'' Her perfect features lifted;
a swirl of silver hair revealed a huge, burgundy stone set in a
trinium oval, suspended between triads of chains. ''Nadine
reb^Ursel Kilgore has arrived. If you will excuse me? Come see
me, Kristinsson.'' A gracious nod, and the pale woman backed
into the press, her flanking, black-suited shadows close to her
heels.

''I would kill to look like that after three children,'' Malini
said flatly. ''If only the timing had been different, and she had
married a Dielaan.''

''Why?'' Garth asked.

Malini looked amused. ''She is an enemy, my dear. Scarcely
thirteen years ago we were at war with them; we are on speaking
terms now only because we found an enemy more dangerous
than Atare.''

''Who?'' If Atare was, as he understood, the enemy of a
thousand years, who could be a larger threat?

''Why, you, my dear. It was an off-worlder who nearly destroyed the royal lines of three clans.'' Glancing at her cousin,
she added: ''One can never be too careful.'' Nodding easily,
she moved off up the window corridor.

Bewildered, Garth turned to Lucy. ''Did I offend her somehow?''

''Not really,'' Lucy said soothingly. ''You *did* say you preferred redheads.''

''I was just—''

''I know.'' Lucy glanced away for a moment, then looked
him in the eyes. ''It is nearly matins; I have had enough of
partying. Would you like company for the night, or shall I say
good-bye?''

The abruptness of it startled him. ''But . . . you don't know
anything about me,'' Garth said slowly.

''I know that you have no communicable diseases, are attractive, and good company. You have no criminal record, or
you would have been detained. I doubt you would be foolish
enough to commit murder within a half-day of your arrival.''
She gave him a brilliant smile.

''How do *you* know I have no disease? Do you work at the
medical center?'' Garth said, genuinely surprised.

''It is posted.'' Seeing his confusion, Lucy reached for his
wrist. ''You said you arrived today; these marks confirm that,

they fade within a few days. *Crowned Tiger* is the first to arrive
in a moon. I checked the listing, and no one was listed black
except a man who was quarantined—that means all the men and
women who arrived today are fertile and healthy.''

"You're kidding."

Her eyes widened appealingly. "Would I tease you?"

"Probably." Garth did not know whether to be flattered or
insulted. "When did you have time to check this 'posting?' ''

"Oh, I checked before the party. If there had been a few black
listings, I would have memorized their names, so I did *not* leave
with any of them. Our fertility is too fragile to risk it for a bit
of fun." Her eyes were twinkling, now. "I will show you the
listing, if you wish . . . I am even in there, somewhere, if you
want to check *my* rating."

"I imagine The Atarae would have dragged me off if you
were a secret sini." At her puzzlement, he amplified: "A sini
pretending to be normal."

Nodding, Lucy seized his sleeve once again and drew him
toward the stairs. "I am about as far from a sini as you will
find," she promised him.

Somehow those words seemed carefully chosen, but Garth
had no idea why.

traitor: 1.) A sentient that violates his allegiance to a government, group, or cause. 2.) A sentient that violates a subject oath to a government, monarch, or country. 3.) A sentient that betrays another's trust. 4.) A sentient that is false to a contract, binding promise, or responsibility. Compare *APOSTATE* and *SUBVERSIVE*.

CHAPTER FOUR

AMURA-BY-THE-SEA, NUALA
      ONEHUNDRED EIGHTYTHREEDAY   LAUDS
ATARE WINTER PALACE

Silence reigned in the household; the lack of sound was so marked Darame could hear the blood pounding in her ears. Usually a party wore her out, but not this party . . . not this time. Tossing and dozing for hours, she had finally surrendered to the mood. A warm robe of red velour now cradled her body and covered her feet. In her hands, a mug of hot cocoa; it was simply too early for food and saffra. Seating herself on a cedar chest next to a window, Darame let her gaze wander out toward the restless water.

It was the darkness before the dawn, and neither stars nor moons marred the blanket of velvet where sky met sea. A deep rumble reached her, vibrating along the tiny bones of her ears. Was it an electrical storm, warning, yet denying them the life-giving monsoons? Or had the rains finally come? It was early yet—the onehundred eightieth day was merely the average time of their arrival. But the western coast of this continent depended on that thirtysixday of rain which came in the spring . . . the far side of the mountains lived or died by it.

Darame did not deceive herself; pressure changes had not awakened her. No, it was something seemingly innocuous . . . or was it innocuous? Had her instincts been dulled through years of living on Nuala? Surely not. But on Nuala she was more than a free-trader, fleecing criminals with their own greed. Here, she was the wife of a powerful man, the mother of heirs to wealth . . . and guarded by a legendary troop, the Atare family's *guaard*. Had privilege made her careless? Could she no longer recognize threat, no matter what its guise?

You have come a long way since then. . . . Simple words, in and of themselves. Darame set her empty mug on the ledge, her mind weary with the machinations. By Peter's Keys, if only she had sensed threat in those words! Threat would be simple—they would pick him up and lock him away.

But threat was not what the youth Garth Kristinsson radiated. No . . . what echoed and re-echoed in those words was *indecision*. The gaze, the posture was confident, decisive . . . but not the words. *Like a farmer eyeing a snake, trying to decide whether to ignore it or kill it.*

So, am I a threat to him? Or is he a threat to me? Does it matter? Perhaps I should ask instead if he thinks it matters? Even as questions flitted through her brain, Darame stood and moved toward the other room. Something soft and warm brushed against her ankles, and she controlled her swift intake of breath. Reaching down, Darame bundled the exotic cat into her arms and walked past the *guaard* out of the room. A gesture at a control stopped the panels from sliding closed behind her; they were used to each other's nocturnal wanderings, but Sheel would wake at the sound of a door or window changing position.

Ribs pumping vigorously with her purring, the Somali rubbed her face trustingly into Darame's robe. Running her fingers through the shaggy hair, toying with the delicate ear tufts, the woman walked up to her RAM screen. Tapping the "read" mode, she simultaneously pulled up the data banks. Settling the cat in her lap, Darame requested access to the passenger and crew lists of *The Crowned Tiger*.

That had been Mailan's gift—an unrestricted access code. As

far as Darame knew, nothing on this infonet was barred to her. It had taken several years to acquire that code, and Darame still was not certain what had prompted the gift. What had assured Mailan of her total loyalty to Sheel? None of the other spouses had such freedom—she had checked. Did Sheel know? Not necessarily . . . there was no need for him to know.

"Kristinsson, Garth," she murmured to the panel. Data blurred before her eyes, finally crystallizing into a personnel entry. The picture looked younger than she had expected, but it was the same man. *He is an adult*, she reminded herself, *no matter how young he seems to you*.

Born on Caesarea, a second-level education with high marks. . . . Her eyes focused on the family entry. One sister, an emigrant to Gavriel in 2288 . . . the same year their parents died. No images of parents or sister, but the parents' place of origin, birth, and death dates were given. Lisbet had found herself a man of Gavrielian heritage, although he was listed as having been born on Caesarea. Still, that registration hall . . . it had burned down a good dozen decades ago, destroying the storage facility. A lot of free-traders, wishing to hide their antecedents, created fictional birth certificates issued from that city.

What was I doing in 2288?

Although Darame had fairly good recall of every job she had ever worked, dates were always hazy . . . and keeping records was dangerous. Setting the cat down on the other side of the bench, Darame moved to her clothes dresser. The top drawer slid silently from the wall at her gesture. Reaching underneath it, her fingers touched a pressure-sensitive latch and paused for the print to be read. A momentary twitching sensation, then a teardrop-shaped slice of reddish quartz dropped into her hand, the tarnished silver chain falling between digits to form a loop. The drawer closed before Darame had time to coil the links.

Returning to her seat, Darame carefully positioned her thumbs on the quartz teardrop, supporting the back with index and second fingers. Even her meager body heat could eventually infuse the mineral—after a while, the pendant warmed to her touch. Stray thoughts began to filter into her mind . . . the pentimento was responding, giving her back her past.

It was a *very* expensive toy, a pentimento . . . and much more than a pretty trinket. A former free-trader had discovered this particular type of quartz, and had also discovered its strange properties. But now was not the time to think about that—not unless she wanted the pendant to record her musings. As soon as the date in her thoughts was perceived, the chip of quartz would begin its backward search, peeling away its own layers of memory like the skin of an onion.

A permanent form of memory, with an immense appetite for data . . . but a pentimento was aptly named. Although read like a film ring, it was capable of input only—once an incident was recorded, it could never be changed.

Finally, the proper date was reached. Had she had so many jobs since then? Two different scams that year, both of them on Caesarea. She had fled the planet following the second. Memory rose up within her, and she nearly lost her grip on the pendant. *That* job . . . that year. What could possibly interest Garth Kristinsson in that job?

Last month, 2288 . . . Darame had been working with two other free-traders, at a job that went hopelessly wrong before it came about right. Reviewing what she had recorded concerning those days, Darame found she had forgotten a great deal. Surely Hank had killed Kurt? That was not what she had recorded . . . in fact, she had actually quoted Hank—*He's dead; I don't know why. We'll leave his cut of the gold at Traders*.

Darame released the slice of quartz, letting the chain glide through her fingers. A hundred years was a long time . . . and she had tried to forget that job. It was a difficult thing to forget—Hank had contributed to her education almost as much as Halsey. Lessons threaded every scam they had ever worked together. Still, it had been her last job with Hank; her first job to be betrayed by a partner. Had Kurt actually stolen the gold? Had Hank killed him? Or had someone else shadowed them, twisted their scam. . . . Had Hank meant that Kurt was dead, but that Hank knew nothing of the details? Could Kurt have died without active intervention on someone else's part?

I left Caesarea too quickly. Yet Hank had split the gold three ways. That was important—free-trader law said that if a partner totally betrayed the company, all rules became void, and the traitor's cut of the profits was forfeit. Hank had left Kurt's account his share of the profits.

"You should have told me what you knew or suspected, Hank," Darame murmured aloud. She glanced over at the RAM . . . yes, Garth's parents had died at the same time she was packing to flee Caesarea. *Did I see something?* Touching the pentimento once again, she meticulously examined the year, this time checking both Caesarean jobs.

Darame always recorded situations in detail, in case casual introductions or gossip might prove valuable later. This time there was nothing; nothing that seemed to matter . . . unless there was an actual connection to one of the jobs.

Hank Edmonton, Kurt Eriksson, Tina Lockheart, Douglass Doyle, Natane, and Donhassen . . . was one of them connected with Garth in some way?

"How?" she asked the Somali cat sitting next to her. Nyani responded by yawning at her preferred person and stretching across Darame's lap. "As if you could know, lover," Darame murmured to the animal, rubbing her ribs and stomach. Delicately she traced the rim of the pentimento, grateful again for an old friend's advice. How does one keep records that no one else suspects exist? What a marvelous device, worth every scrap of gold she had paid for it. Attractive, yet not valuable enough to attract a pinch thief's eye . . . it needed a touch of polish. *I have been so busy with big things, little things have been pushed aside.*

How long she drifted Darame did not know, but the sound of the bells startled her. Three bells—prime. The star was rising.

Warmth crept up her spine, but Darame did not jump. Leaning back into him, Darame lifted her chin and gave Sheel a soft smile.

"You are up early," she told him.

"You were up very early," Sheel responded, warm fingers tracing the line of her throat. "Catching up on your reading?"

Darame did not miss the tone of voice. Reaching to disconnect her tap into the infonet, she said: "Just being cautious."

His hand seized hers. "Is that from *The Crowned Tiger*?" At her nod, he continued: "How did you call it up?"

"I pressed 'read,' then requested information on Garth Kristinsson," she responded. Seeing the eyebrow shoot up, Darame added: "There is another way to do it?"

If he had pressed the point, she would have elaborated. But

old habits died hard; Darame still rarely volunteered information, even to the people she loved most. What they did not know could not hurt them.

"Can I coax you to the breakfast table?" Sheel finally said.

"I suspect you could coax me anywhere."

AMURA-BY-THE-SEA   TIERCE

Tumbling clouds and brilliant starshine struggled to control the skies; for Garth it was an appropriate backdrop. Confusion above and below, this morning, and he was trapped somewhere in-between. It was hard to admit that an old friend might have been right, but Garth was beginning to wonder . . . maybe he should have acquired some training as a free-trader. True, his quest might have been in vain if he had waited—Edmonton was already dead, and Silver no longer had the stretch of Cold Sleep—but now that he was here, what was the next step? Riding around on these rails was getting him nowhere; he had started looking for signs of a free-trader haunt before the second bell, and the third had just rung.

Preliminary dips into the visitor information during the dark hours before dawn had revealed an ancient, complex culture. Contacts were needed—to get more data on Silver, to provide allies should he decide against her—yet he was already stymied. The simple history provided in an overview of the clans indicated that Silver had managed to bewitch one of the wealthiest and most powerful people on the planet.

Just thinking about it made him angry. His parents had died in their pursuit of wealth and security, while this woman practically had stumbled into a vault at Traders, with title to the contents. . . .

A voice intruded into his dark thoughts. "I thought this was your first visit to Nuala."

"It is," Garth replied, his eyes on the crowd. "Why do you ask?"

"Because you are obviously looking for someone," Lucy said, shoving a long, copper curl out of her eyes and leaning across him to look out the window. "If you want to talk to someone you met last night, I imagine I can find them for you."

"Faster than this rail car?" Garth pressed his lips together; surely his impatience showed.

If it did, Lucy did not refer to it. "Tram," she corrected. "Possibly . . . but if we knew *which* tram we should be on, it would go faster." Glancing around the crowded passenger car, she added: "We might be able to see more from the top."

"No, I need to see faces," Garth told her, looking back out the window once again. Maybe this wasn't such a good idea . . . or maybe he should have gone without Lucy. But it didn't seem right to take a woman back to your room, then not invite her to breakfast.

It had surprised him when she agreed to accompany him to breakfast; had surprised him even more when she called someone to bring her street clothing. Her current attire was a long-sleeved work shirt of pale blue and white stripes, with close-fitting pale blue pants woven of the same plant fiber. A simple belt of braided hemp and white thongs finished off her outfit. It seemed appropriate for the heat, if a bit rustic. *For all you know, it may be the height of fashion,* Garth told himself. It was hard to guess how much family connections meant here . . . and if they meant money.

Early prowling through his Random Access Module had given Garth more than basic clan information about Nuala. The colony was over two thousand years Terran in age, the result of a scientific expedition that was abruptly abandoned during the final years of the first republic. Nuala's excessive radiation caused genetic mutation, which had led to the sinis, the hot Nualans, that Lucy and her cousins avoided. It also caused local life forms to change; one irradiated organism was capable of reducing the hull of a spaceship to rust in less than thirty-six days, the length of a Nualan month. These two massive problems had nearly destroyed the original colony. It had taken the group over a thousand years to figure out how to protect their metals . . . how to escape their planet.

Genetic mutation was still a problem. Eighty percent of the population was sterile—accordingly, children were highly prized, and fertility was a major issue with all Nualans. The laws were quite specific about pregnancy—it was the business of the woman and her family, although the father was usually identified for genetic records. *At least we're good for something.*

All this thought was not going to put Lucy off—eventually, she'd find out what she wanted to know. So how to tell her. . . .

"I'm looking for anyone else who might have known my parents," Garth said simply.

Lucy rolled her eyes, her perfect chest heaving with her sigh. "All the spies and pirates eat over by the wharf! Let us disembark at the next stop." Seizing his wrist, she pulled him to his feet.

"Spies and pirates?" Garth said, staring at her.

"Shuhh! Would 'thieves' have been a better choice of words?" As the tram slowed, the doors folded open before them.

"Free-traders are not thieves," Garth told her tartly. Then: "What makes you think I will find who I'm looking for . . . by the wharf?"

"Did you not say your mother and The Atarae were friends?" Lucy asked, glancing up at him as she led him down a cobbled alley.

"When they were younger." Garth eyed her a moment. Salt and fish odor threatened to distract him, but he kept his concentration on Lucy.

Lucy grinned guilelessly at him. " 'Free-trader,' that is the word. What few there are in Amura usually eat at Limpin' Lobster."

"The Atarae was a free-trader?" Garth felt his nerves tightening. This was an unexpected turn of events. Motion to one side of them caught his eye; was that the same man he had noticed on the tram?

"So you said." Lucy twinkled at him for a few moments, her eyes creasing in her amusement, then said: "So rumor goes . . . it is said she was what people here call a wheedling wizard, someone skilled enough to cheat a cardsharp at his own game. Of course I *know* not—" Lucy paused, waiting for a tram to go by. "I have met her but a few times; Rex is invited to Synod functions, you see, and so our presence is also requested."

"Huh." That had been embarrassing, finding out that her cousin was *the* Rex mentioned in the world overview as the ruler of Dielaan. Perhaps they were all third or fourth cousins, but any connection to a royal line a thousand years old was pretty impressive. A quick glance in a shop window told him the man was now behind them, but still in sight.

It is all show at my end, she had told him with a chuckle. *No chance for me to get my hands on any power! I must settle for being ornamental.*

"Limpin' Lobster has a very good breakfast," Lucy promised,

drawing him back to the moment. "If I have been reading things into the situation, you can explain to me who your parents really were, and we will look after we eat." Rounding a wooden building, she led him onto a boardwalk. "Is it not wonderful?" Lucy dropped his wrist and waved her arms expansively.

Garth was too overwhelmed to speak. Before them was the western sea, and it was even more impressive by day. Salt and spray mingled on a southwest wind, seasoned with the promise of rain. Brilliant starshine played games with towering thunderheads, rays of light winking in and out of cloud banks. Overhead strange birds spiraled, screaming unintelligibly at winged companions and landbound creatures alike. Tree branches whipped in a gust, but they were trees unlike any Garth had ever seen, gnarled and barely showing green.

"I hope the Lobster has food you can eat," Lucy continued slowly. "I had not thought of that. . . ."

"I grew up far from the coast," Garth said finally, turning reluctantly from the water to face Lucy. "Most of Caesarea's lakes are man-made; we had nothing like this. It's so blue!"

"Not as blue as further out," she replied, taking hold of his cuff and tugging him along. "More turquoise green, here, and a softer shade at that. Sand churns within it by the beach. A bit farther it becomes a very dark blue-green, and then at the points almost blackish, just for a moment . . . then the water is the color of the sky." Pointing off to their left, Lucy cut across his path and pulled him down a row of small, stone buildings. "At home the Miraculous Sea is much darker in color, a deep turquoise blue . . . but some say the sky is also a deeper hue." Reaching an open door, Lucy dragged him inside. "Finally! I am so hungry!"

A wait gestured for them to sit where they pleased, which Lucy was already doing. She chose the only table left on the waterfront, a tiny folding board which was perched on the wall like a tree burl. Pulling the rectangle down between them, Lucy quickly ran her hand along the short edge. Words appeared upon the table; they were written in what Garth had come to recognize as Nualan.

"That will not do," she murmured, moving her hand once again. The print vanished. Two quick passes along the edge, and menus printed in Caesarean appeared on the tabletop, one facing each bench. "Here—anything marked with an asterisk

can be prepared for off-worlders . . . at three times the price!''
Lucy winced visibly.

"It's all right.'' Even as the words left his lips, Garth realized
they were indiscreet for a public place. "I budgeted for the
food—why do you think I'm in such a small hostel?"

Shrugging, Lucy turned her attention to the menu. "I like
their omelets, and the baker makes wonderful scones and muffins.''

"What's an omelet?" This question earned Garth an incredulous look from Lucy. The look was followed by a spirited
explanation which included eggs and milk cooked flat but not
really, with almost anything imaginable tossed into the concoc-
tion and cheese placed between when the pan-shaped eggs were
folded in half upon themselves. "I think I get the idea," Garth
finally said, cutting off any further attempt to describe the food
items. "They have one with shredded crab and jack cheese, I
think I'll try that.''

"And a bread basket," Lucy insisted.

When an actual wait came to take their order, she insisted on
several other things, including fruit juice and hot saffra. Garth
had trouble controlling a smile, and of course Lucy noticed. Her
black brows rose slightly as her black eyes widened, and Garth
took the hint.

"How do you stay so skinny when you eat like a long-hauler?"

"Skinny?" she responded, running delicate fingers down her
exquisite waistline.

"Slender," Garth substituted hastily.

"I get a great deal of exercise," she responded, "and that
takes care of it. I also eat well . . . for example, I do not care
for sweets.''

"Lucky you. I love chocolate." Garth was happy to keep
talking about food, if it kept Lucy's mind off Garth's reasons
for seeking a free-trader haunt. It also kept his own anger and
unease under control. Yes, it *was* the same man from the tram.
Did Silver have a tail upon him already?

"Well, *chocolate*," Lucy agreed feelingly, then gave him a
sharp glance. "Why do I feel as if I have only half your attention?"

"I have a few things on my mind," Garth admitted.

Her gaze swept around the room, and lighted upon a corner.

"Ah-ha! I told you this was a free-trader restaurant!" This was a whisper; leaning across the table conspiratorially, Lucy continued: "Do you see the thin, bald man over in the corner—the one with the beaming smile? He is called Halsey. He is a trader of some kind, a wealthy one; he has a beautiful estate north of town." Lucy's voice dropped another notch in volume. "Rumor has it that he was a famous free-trader in his youth!"

Halsey? He was still on Nuala? Garth flicked a glance at the corner in question. Another piece of luck—it was too soon to tell if it was good or bad. But it was a name, the name of a previously powerful free-trader. Could he be the head of the Nualan net? That was the one thing he had forgotten to ask Lowe—who was running the Nualan free-trader network.

Did Nuala have a head of their net? Rumors had said that the Nualan authorities were very good at identifying potential organizers and deporting or otherwise eliminating them. The only name anyone on Caesarea gave him was "Brant," a Caesarean who had headed for Nuala twenty years ago Terran. Wheel traders had expected him currently to be at, or near, the top of the pecking order—if he had not already returned to Caesarea Station.

But no one "ran" the net—it was not like the underground, where underlings paid heed (and a tithe) to a superior. Net was more of a communications network than anything else. Finding the head and introducing oneself was part courtesy, part self-defense. Otherwise, there was no way to know if a new scam would blunder into something currently in the works.

Brant had been a dead end—literally. According to Nualan records, he had been an ambassador who had meddled in local politics, and had caused the deaths of several aristocrats. Undoubtedly, Brant was the "enemy" Malini had referred to the night before. The man had been executed after killing the captain of the Atare *guaard*.

"If he is *the* Halsey, he was a *very* famous free-trader," Garth said in answer to Lucy's comment. "I heard he was a fat man, though."

"You are not a free-trader, are you?" Lucy said suddenly.

After a moment of thought, Garth answered, "Not really. I've had some training, but my parents died before they could bring me into the business. And I've been . . . busy, since then. But

I know enough that I could probably be hired for an entry position—and you simply can't wander in and be accepted in a free-trader group without *some* useful experience.''

Lucy inclined her head slowly, her gaze intent. "So 'entry level' is not actually the bottom."

Garth nodded simply.

"I need to visit the sanitation," she told him offhandedly. "I might as well do it before the food arrives."

"Good idea," Garth agreed. "An omelet sounds involved— you should have enough time." He waited until she had disappeared around a partition before jumping up and moving toward the exit. Surely that was a RAM he had spotted when they entered the restaurant—ah. A RAM, and it had a vid module.

It took only a few moments to find a communiqué listing for a "Halsey." After thought, Garth decided to send a RAM letter instead of calling. Either way he would be leaving a message, since Halsey was in the restaurant. He kept the wording simple, saying he was the son of free-traders and was looking for introduction to the local network.

Signing off politely with his own name and the name of his hostel, Garth managed to settle himself and pry open one of the hot rolls left for them before Lucy returned. "They set them in front of me, so they must be all right for both of us," he explained. "Wouldn't you think?"

"Oh, yes," she agreed, reaching to take one of them for herself. "It is you who must be careful—I can eat anything served on this planet."

Since their omelets had arrived, he was spared from making any comments about the heavy rolls flicked with dried fruit that he found so tasty. There was little he could do until Halsey responded.

Shadows beyond their window grew visibly shorter as they devoured their meal. Lucy had been right; omelets *were* good, and Garth made room for several more varieties of scones and muffins. Stress and relief combined oddly, leaving Garth ravenous, then suddenly satisfied. Last night had been much the same; he hoped Lucy hadn't been disappointed in his real desire for *some* sleep, at least. Apparently not—though she had not let him out of bed come morning until they had continued their experiments of the night before. And she *had* accompanied him to breakfast. . . .

"Garth Kristinsson?" The tones were tenor, both brisk and cheerful. Lucy's face showed surprise, swiftly masked. Turning his head, Garth saw a slender, balding man with delicate eyebrows and a beaming countenance. His round face and fringed hair were almost comical, until one met his eyes—they were clear, like starlight on water, and there were more layers to them than in any slice of rock.

"I am called Garth Kristinsson," Garth replied formally in Caesarean, rising to his feet as he spoke.

A spark of amusement glinted in those clear eyes. "I am called Halsey," he said gravely. "I understand that you left a message at my office."

It would not do to ask how the man knew what he looked like; Garth merely nodded affirmatively.

"Shall we walk and talk? We have some time before the rain comes."

Halsey was looking directly at him as he spoke; at any rate, Garth had never intended to take Lucy into *this* confidence. The next move would require all his untrained skill   because this man had trained Silver.

"I really should be going," Lucy interjected. "If you will loan me your codekey I shall remove my things stored in your room. The desk staff will keep it for you. You can reach me through the Dielaan embassy."

Garth had a split second of indecision. But why not? He had no valuables; no records other than his medical card, which was in his thigh pouch. Most of his clothing was old and worn—the evening wear had been returned first thing that morning. Why not trust her with his codekey?

"Remember to lock it," he said with a grin, extending the metal card. "I don't want to find anyone unfamiliar in there when I get back."

"Of course," she said reprovingly. "Thank you for breakfast, it was lovely. Later?" Although she gave it the inflection of a question, Lucy spoke with confidence. Accepting the card, she turned and strode easily from the restaurant, followed by admiring glances from several patrons.

Garth himself was the recipient of several admiring glances. *It seems that my taste in women is approved.* He found that the price of the meal had already been calculated, and glowed where the menu had once been. Remembering that there had been

service, Garth carefully estimated a gratuity and tapped in his
personal file number. Since the total vanished soon afterward,
Garth concluded he had remembered it correctly.

The free-trader was waiting for him outside. There were decks
attached to the walkway; all of them had clusters of benches.
Halsey had appropriated a small grouping, and was seated facing
the sea, sipping a hot beverage. As the odor reached him, Garth
recognized the smell of kona.

Halsey noticed his surprise. "I import the beans; they are
fresh-frozen on Kiel. It is considered a stimulant, but the tariff
on them is not too stiff. Old habits die hard," he added, almost
musing. "I suspect the beans would grow well in the southern
hemisphere, but I doubt I could find a large enough market to
justify the experiment."

It was not necessary for Halsey to explain the problem. No
one would buy imported foodstuffs from Nuala; the very idea
was ludicrous. And if it was necessary to import kona, the internal demand was small.

"You said in your message that your parents were free-traders,
and that you would like to enter the network here. Have you
received much instruction?" Halsey's voice was pleasant, but
his eyes were very bright.

So. How to give—and get—information. Free-traders volunteered so little. . . . "I had just begun to receive instruction
when they died. Since I was left with nothing but a debt, I
turned to long-haulers for work," Garth said easily, sitting
gracefully on the empty bench nearby. "I did some entry
work with Martinez of Kiel, and did leg work for Spadden on
Norwood."

"I knew your parents' reputation, and I heard from Lowe that
you were coming," Halsey replied, his smile rivaling starlight
on a mirror. "If the opportunity presents itself, would you consider apprenticeship?"

Garth had already felt a bit off-center, facing this cheerful
extrovert; this pushed him completely out of the ring. Halsey
was definitely the head of whatever net existed. It was almost
too good to be true. . . . "Surely that is unlikely."

"Youngsters interested in our business tend to head for Caesarea Station—to their grief and ours. The competition increases
a hundredfold there, of course, and we have too few to handle
the lower level work. It is quite possible you could rise to journey

level in only one job." Halsey's chuckle was infectious; Garth felt himself smiling in response.

Sebastian's Arrows, why now? But a job offering that kind of reward in status—never mind material potential—would definitely be full-time. Would he be able to give an assignment the concentration it needed? Or would his mind be filled with research on Silver?

"I'm . . . flattered, sir," he said sincerely. "But I am involved with a debt. Therefore, I'd like to be posted on the net for basic entry work. If you see such an unusual opening, I'd love to talk to the sponsor . . . but I would feel obligated to explain my prior interest."

"As you should," Halsey agreed, nodding his approval. Another sip of kona, and his gaze drifted out toward sea once again. "Be wary of anything not advertised on the net, young Kristinsson; the clans do not allow meddling in their corporations and institutions. Fortunately for us, Nualans still have our basic weaknesses."

That was clear enough; gypsy cons were perfectly all right. Cheat a man with his own greed, and he is unlikely to run to authorities. But major scams involving politics or corporations were dangerous.

"The last free-trader who toyed with localized treason ended up with his head on a pike before Dielaan's royal courtyard," Halsey added mildly. "It was merely chance that he was dead before they removed it."

Correction: Politics and corporations were fatal. Messing with planetary politics could invoke "localized treason." In other words, if they stated that the penalty for your offense was death, your own world couldn't help you. Free-traders still attempted major scams, Garth was sure, but only the best of them . . . or those tired of living.

Well, he had no plans to follow the lead of one Brant of Caesarea, who was now nothing but bleached bones. He had a debt he was dealing with, and—

Debt. *I am here because of a debt I owe my parents.* Garth's gaze flicked toward the windows of the restaurant behind them. Reflected there was the strange man called Halsey and a fair-haired child of the north, a Gavrielian no matter what citizenship his passport claimed. *And my tail is gone—because I'm with Halsey? Does he report back to that Gavrielian witch?*

Gavrielian. Two words slid seamlessly together; debt, Gavrielian. A debt to a Gavrielian was a wergild. . . .

One hundred sixty bars of gold, Caesarean issue. A fortune on any world—expect maybe Nuala. Wergild. *"Aesir considers the debt to be paid."* Lowe had been right—she was Gavrielian, and she did know about Aesir . . . was Aesir? How long had Aesir existed. . . . So, the goddess considered the debt paid? What debt did you think my father owed you? A debt so great his life and 160 bars of gold was needed to repay it? His life wasn't enough—you came back for the gold? Or your partner did. . . .

Garth realized that Halsey was speaking to him, and snapped his head back toward the man. Something about leaving word if he changed hostels . . . to be careful around the high house women, that their notions of behavior, honor and responsibility were quite different than he was used to. . . . He heard it with half an ear. If a free-trader betrayed his partners, he was dead within the scam; he no longer had a claim on the reward. Yet it was paid—his father left his associates honorably, whatever they did afterward. Paid, and then taken . . . taken back?

Of course his father would have seen to automatic deposit, which meant they would have had to return for it. Did Silver kill him, or did Edmonton?

No matter. Edmonton is beyond me. You are not.

subterfuge: 1) A scheme by skill or stratagem to conceal, evade, or escape. It has no true synonyms—the closest would be *deception*, which implies actual fraud as opposed to simply misleading.

CHAPTER FIVE

Standing at the top of the winding pathway with two *guaard* at his back, Sheel looked down into the courtyard behind his home. A breeze both warm and biting curled past his face, bringing the shouts of children to his ears.

"Is that Drew on that white pony?" he murmured, picking out the white-blond hair of the future Atare. Yesterday the child was demanding a horse instead of his usual animal. . . . A quick survey noted the mounted presence of dark-haired Davi, the future ragäree, his own son Ardal, their cousin Denis, and two more youngsters who looked familiar.

"Darame let him try every horse in the stable until she convinced him that his legs needed some length," came Avis's lilting voice.

Glancing back over his shoulder, Sheel saw the tousled golden curls and voluminous azure dress that heralded his younger sister. Extending an arm to her, he ran an experienced gaze over Avis's taut, round belly and slightly swollen feet, even as his fingertips gauged the pulse and chemistry of the flesh against his own. "I thought you were going to rest this afternoon."

"We thought we would watch you keep peace at The Synod meeting. It should be an amusing change from court." Her blue eye sparkled with mischief, the green glinting slyly.

"We?" There was movement at the corner of Sheel's field of vision; ponderous, not the floating grace of a *guaard*.

"I see all chance of surprising you is past."

Her voice was low, as great a contrast to Avis's as her height, dark curtain of hair, and green-brown eye combination. Smiling, Sheel reached carefully to embrace his elder sister's full figure. "You look ready to burst. Pray you both do not deliver at the same time!"

Chuckling, Leah said: "You would manage."

"Then those other two are your girls?" Sheel asked, turning back toward the courtyard. A blaze of silver announced the arrival of his wife, mounted on her long-legged Arabian stallion.

"Very good, at this distance," Avis said admiringly.

Darame's clear voice carried above the murmur of the waves beyond. "Is everyone ready? Heads up, heels down—Drew, ball of the foot on the stirrup, not the arch. To the beach!"

In the flush of a beautiful spring afternoon, Sheel could forgive her anything . . . even her latest scheme. Rushing off to teach "riding lessons," Darame had mentioned in passing that she had invited Kristinsson to the palace for dessert and drinks. Only Ardal's presence had kept him from pursuing the subject then and there. Obviously, Darame had known Leah had arrived, her family in tow—

"An amusing change from court?" Sheel glanced back from the retreating flash of silver toward his sisters. Just what had Darame? . . .

"Yes," Leah said, as if reading his mind. Her nod was slight, eyes narrowing briefly, and Sheel thought he caught a hint of a wink, her brown iris momentarily obscured.

Sheel eyed her in silence. Although she still could not piece together the events leading to her breakdown, Leah was otherwise recovered from the demons which drove her to condone treason and murder over ten years before. A calmer and happier woman, she was no less intelligent—and she had an eye for a rogue that rivaled Darame's.

The Synod delegates were often careful around his wife, knowing her reputation. But many thought Leah had thrown over all her power and influence when she relinquished her hold on the throne. Not at all; she had merely changed goals. What they were Sheel had no real idea, but they no longer included ruling Atare. How strange that otherwise intelligent people would think that a woman who was breeding had stopped thinking.

"I suppose this means that you had better come with me and do your part for her current scheme," Sheel announced, his voice slightly aggrieved. *More than one scheme, I am sure,* he added privately, wondering which *guaard* would be on duty tonight for Darame. Even as he spoke, the bell rang announcing vespers. "We are going to be late."

THE SYNOD   VESPERS

It was a crowded room, barely large enough for the representatives and their honor guards, but it had served as their neutral territory for almost nine years. Settling himself comfortably at the oval table, Sheel placed his receiver into his right ear. A touch to the panel before him brought up the Amuran infonet, giving him immediate access to any general information he needed. Since the others were present and his sisters were seated against the wall to his right, Sheel was free to call the meeting to order.

"Good afternoon," he said simply. "The notes of the last meeting were placed on the net within two days of adjournment, and have been reviewed by any who were so inclined. If there is no objection from The Synod, I would like to declare the notes accepted and open the new meeting of our group." A double row of bright, green lights beneath the screen of his RAM told him that all present agreed to his request. "Please enter your codes."

This was something Halsey had suggested. With the clan peace so fragile, there was no room for error—or impostors. The rulers of the great clans had given special codes to their senior ambassadors alone, and only the senior ambassadors could vote on critical issues. Diclaan's strange delegation initially had caused a few problems; since Rex rarely attended the meetings, his brother had been forced to nag the heir in order to get voting instructions. Livia had put a stop to that several months ago by simply giving second son Quen the identical code. Had Rex noticed that there had been no votes since Yule—at least none that he was consulted about? Possibly . . . today he was present, as well as his new ambassador.

All the codes were in order. . . . "The Synod welcomes the ambassador from Dielaan," Sheel said formally.

Standing, the tall, grave Dielaaner proceeded to give his opening remarks to the others present. At no time did he offer the group his name, which was not unusual. Dielaaners usually announced their titles, however; this one said only that he was an "advisor" to the embassy.

To the heirs, you mean, Sheel thought to himself, studying the older man's clothing. It was black silk trickled with bright threads of red, green, and yellow—the sign of both wealth and mourning. Darame could work on that aspect of this arrival, perhaps pick up some clues to his identity. Now, Sheel's only concern was whether this man would work for or against the existence of The Synod.

At least the man could keep his comments brief. With a courteous nod, the ambassador returned to his seat.

"Atare, Kilgore would like to introduce some new business into the old business of inter-tribal trade." It was the lowest-ranking Kilgorian. "It concerns agricultural exchange between Kilgore and Dielaan."

"Objection," came Rex Dielaan's smooth voice. "The buying and selling of any item produced planetside is the province of individual clan ministers. Let us not entangle domestic concerns with our far-flung enterprises."

"Kilgore believes that the results of this discussion will impact upon both domestic and interstellar trade. We have spent the last year attempting to resolve this through ministry channels," the young Kilgorian continued, a spot of color tracing each cheekbone. "If it is not resolved now, negotiations will be broken off and another grain substituted for KTL-83."

"There is no substitute for KTL-83," Rex pointed out gently. "Unless someone has stolen the swatch."

The young Kilgore aide swallowed the words reflected in his eyes and said: "I did not mean to suggest that there was a substitute. Although we desire KTL-83, there are others, nearly as versatile, which could be used instead. If Dielaan is not prepared to set reasonable terms for their licensing, they must expect buyers to go elsewhere."

While others divided their attention between the newest member of the Kilgore delegation and Rex Dielaan, Sheel concentrated on his RAM screen and Nadine reb^Ursel Kilgore. The piercing amethyst eyes were half-lidded; she sat almost at profile, gazing across the table and over the left shoulder of the ambassador from the clan Yang. This was not a new strategy—Nadine usually let one of her subordinates start things off. Too many of the ambassadors either feared her intellect or disliked her biting humor. Introducing her own topics was the quickest way imaginable to have them tabled for discussion "later."

Another ambassador might have grown insulting or intractable; Nadine merely grew subtle.

"Their privilege to set the terms, boy," came the gruff voice of Alasdair of Wallace. "If you find them too tight, go elsewhere."

"It is not a question of too tight, ambassador," Kilgore responded, gracefully overlooking the "boy." "Rather it is a question of vagueness, of setting a standard so loose as to be impossible to enforce."

"Come now, there is nothing vague about the specification," Rex said, flicking his fingers in dismissal in an unconscious imitation of his mother. "We set only three requirements—that you do not wholesale the seed grain to any other buyers, that you do not sell the grain or its by-products or finished products outside of Kilgore province, and that you mark any item which uses KTL-83 with its registration number. Surely that is reasonable?"

"Of course Dielaan finds it reasonable," Nadine said suddenly. "Dielaan would find it quite amusing if Kilgore's wheat trade suddenly ground to a halt. Or had you hoped we would not realize the full impact of your demands until after the bargain was struck?"

Sheel felt his body growing tense, responding to the danger in the words. Clans had gone to war over less than a tricky trade agreement. His fingers were pulling up Atare's intelligence files on "KTL-83" even as the new Dielaan ambassador began smoothing over the scene.

Now that he examined the actual wording of the agreement, Sheel could understand Kilgore's concern. Nadine was not exaggerating by much—not if the problem had gone unnoticed until some time had passed. Wheat was used in *everything*, of course. It was even used in pastes and paints, in animal feed and binders. If the agreement had slipped through, it would have either completely negated KTL-83's value to Kilgore by destroying their trade, or it would have placed tremendous strain on Kilgore-Dielaan relations, since Kilgore would have refused to halt their exports.

Nadine was in the process of ticking off the pertinent points, tapping her strong fingers one against another to emphasize each item. As understanding percolated through the group (or as other, previously briefed ambassadors decided it was time to react) a low murmuring drifted down the length of the table.

"I can understand the desire of the Dielaan labs to limit the spread of KTL-83 seed—although we all know that exclusive control of a genetic swatch is a situation that lasts a few years, at most," Sheel began slowly. As if it was necessary to remind any of them that cracking a genetics code took their lab people little time. Nadine's husband was a geneticist—who no doubt knew to the hour how long it would take to duplicate the sterile seed in Kilgore labs. "And it seems quite reasonable for Dielaan to want 'Contains KTL-83 wheat' somewhere on each package. But I must admit that the second condition gives one pause."

Kilgore, Yang, and Seedar, with their low rainfall, would want that seed—Andersen would pay a fortune for it. Would they take it with such binding restrictions? Sheel's gaze wandered over toward the man whom Nadine had been carefully overlooking.

His dark face still, its ochre tinge pronounced, the ambassador from Yang said evenly: "Yang will not accept those terms." As he spoke, his fingers were tapping something into his RAM membrane.

Since he could not be entering the entire conversation, Sheel assumed that Yang Chen, like many others of their group, had a private listening device hidden somewhere in the room. Apparently Yang's ambassador had enough status to negate negotiations by the trade minister of his government.

From the set expressions on the Dielaan ambassadors' faces, this had to be the case. Many buyers for KTL-83 could rapidly diminish to none . . . if Dielaan did not drop their second requirement.

"I do not think our minister understood the depths of your objection," the new Dielaan ambassador said courteously. "I will personally give him the details of this discussion. Are we not in agreement on two of the points?''

Nadine smiled her broad, closed-lip smile . . . which was not her friendly expression. ''We are indeed.'' Her meaning was plain: Kilgore will concede the first and third points; strike the second, or you will have no market.

How succinct, Sheel thought.

''Looks as if that can die, now,'' Alasdair of Wallace mumbled into his thick, gray beard. ''Since we are speaking of things that . . . can . . . effect all the clans, I would like to ask the assembled ambassadors their opinion on a . . . problem . . . we are having in Wallace.'' His face florid, Alasdair continued: ''I am looking for . . . precedence, if you will.''

Not the smoothest of transitions, but he had succeeded in grabbing their attentions. ''Objections?'' Sheel asked. The light board before him remained untouched . . . then several green lights appeared. No reds, and several were curious enough actually to express interest. Wallace consulting the other clans?

''Continue, ambassador,'' Sheel said formally.

''Well, we have had something occur which has never—to my knowledge—happened before. After some very . . . serious . . . charges were made against a private lab right outside Wallace city—''

''Which lab?'' Rex Dielaan said quickly.

''It is not necessary to the story,'' Wallace said neutrally, his bluff voice as even as Sheel had ever heard. ''At any rate, we made a surprise visit to the lab and gained entry into their coded system. With it we had access to the inner labs, of course. We . . . found a problem. Not a large one,'' he said hastily, when he saw the changing expressions of the others. ''I need not ask that you descend en masse to wipe a sept of Wallace from the face of Nuala. They were not trying to breed super-humans. Not exactly.'' Alasdair's color heightened.

''Alasdair, we are dying of curiosity,'' Nadine said dryly. ''Spit it out, man. I promise I will not laugh.''

A slight tightening of the lips; Nadine had anticipated the problem. ''One of the young geneticists had taken a contract from an out-clan seri. He used some general bank material with import swatches from Gavriel and Kiel, and produced some lab babies. Only they rushed things a bit.''

Sheel knew what was coming. Not from any espionage, but

from personal experience. A glance at Avis revealed their uncanny ability to think alike; there was an amused blush across
her cheeks.

An Anderson aide suggested: "Black market babies?"

"Worse." Alasdair looked gloomy. "He was producing adult
blank rings, intending to program them as . . . sexual toys, I
suppose. A bunch of pretty faces without background or
education—"

Rex Dielaan burst out laughing.

"Using stock noted for placid temperament, I suppose? Or
were they tampering beyond that?" Sheel said quickly.

"Not sure yet." This was gruff. "But we have twenty of
them, Atare! Twenty of them, with no more education than a
toddler! Training had gotten as far as hygiene and table manners.
Since we do not allow sub-classification of *Homo Sapiens*, we
have no . . . no materials for socialization of physically mature
humans, like on Caesarea. We may have to put them in Freeze
until we can get training material for them."

"So you do not have to mindwipe any socially unacceptable
bedroom traits?" Rex asked, his eyes brimming with humor.

Wallace's ambassador actually pretended he had not heard the
question. "Well, what we do with them is our problem. They
have minds and can breathe on their own—by definition they
qualify as newborns, and we must make provision for them. But
the question is, how do we treat a case like this?"

"Slavery, of course," Nadine said without hesitation.

"I wish," Wallace replied, glowering. Penalties for enslaving
a sentient were severe, no matter which clan had jurisdiction.
"But they were clever—no documents exist indicating what
Ca—the seri was going to do with them. We suspect he was
going to keep one of the women, and sell the others on Kiel.
But there is no proof—we have yet to find out how he was going
to get them off-planet," Alasdair added, anticipating the next
question from the group. "Even now we are tracing all leads."

"There is precedent in Dielaan," Quen of Dielaan said quietly. He glanced at the new ambassador as if asking for permission to speak. When the older man nodded his graying head,
Quen continued: "About twohundredyear ago, a seri commis-
sioned a breeding scheme."

"Why did we never hear of it?" Nadine asked, no trace of
humor in her chiseled face.

"Because it was considered an internal problem," Quen answered easily, his composure unruffled. "In this case, we did not feel it was encompassed by the guidelines the tribes set down after the Eugenics War. There was no attempt to deviate from the Nualan goal of natural adaptation. This family was merely trying to vastly increase their number of warriors. The intent was overthrowing the throne, of course, and it was dealt with as treason. Fortunately it was discovered before the fetuses could be pushed beyond their first year of growth. We placed all the children with 80s families, mindwiped the seri and his war leaders, and made an example of the geneticist in charge. It was the last known incident of its type."

Sheel had let his gaze wander. In the mirrors lining the left wall, he could see that Leah looked a bit pale; this talk of treason had disturbed her surface calm. Some things never healed. . . .

"Mindwipes could be tricky right now," Alasdair said evasively. "And this is not treason, merely a proven contract between a sept leader and the head of a lab to create humans without intent to implant, foster, or adopt."

Now was the time to volunteer Atare's experience. "Do what we did," Sheel said easily, "when something like this happened about six years ago." Nadine turned her intense gaze to the end of the table. "As in this case, there was no treason, and intent to enslave was difficult to prove, since programming had yet to be accomplished. It involved the heir of a sept," he continued, ignoring Nadine's expression, "and the request was for normal swatches." Nadine let her glare become unfocused. Interesting . . . did this mean that Kilgore had stumbled into another serious breeding scheme, and suspected that it had spread beyond their own tribe? Something to mention to intelligence. . . .

"He was creating 'gifts,' if you will . . . pretties for some of his friends, and himself. I suspect he intended to take them along when he finally went off-planet, to use as barter material in his search for a wife." Sheel shook his head slightly. "Of course he would have had to go to just the right place to make it worthwhile, and I do not think he would have liked that part of Emerson. Being taxed as a slaver on Kiel, or an indentor on Gavriel, would have probably shocked him." A slight smile which had no humor at all touched his lips. "He kept swearing he had no intent to create 'mockeries' of humans. So we held him to his so-called word.

"We had papers processed for all six of the young women. After they were officially adopted by him, my sister and I declared him an unfit parent and made the women wards of the court. The estimate to make them independent citizens of Atare, educated and socialized to take their place in our society, was set at ten years Terran." With the slightest of pauses for effect, Sheel added: "Of course he was expected to pay for all this education and socialization—at a level befitting heirs of the Name. We made sure it would be coming out of *his* accounts, not his family's fortune." His eyes roamed idly, taking in the red faces of several assistants struggling for control.

"Does this sept still have a dowry system?" Nadine inquired innocently.

"As it happens, it does," Sheel said blandly. "But the manager of his estates need not worry about dowries for, oh, another two years at least. Fortunately for his accounts . . . Avis insisted upon *generous* dowries."

It was too much. Several ambassadors burst out laughing. Freed by this informal reaction, their aides lost their own battle and collapsed over their RAM screens, smothering their humor in their arms. Even Rex Dielaan allowed himself to smile at someone else's joke.

"We confiscated his entire personal fortune," Sheel went on. "After his peers had had a few days of thoroughly enjoying his predicament and pretending to his face that they knew nothing about it, we had him shipped off to Caesarea to find himself a wife . . . who did not mind marrying a bankrupt man with six 'adult dependents.' "

"And the geneticist?" Alasdair asked when his laughter had finally tapered off into wheezing.

"Since he was not in a position to assist financially in this judgment, he was required to 'donate' a certain number of hours of service to the Stargazer Lab—the free lab established by Adel Atare Stargazer and his consort Kathleen Atarae." Allowing his face to remain deadpan, Sheel added: "He should finish his service in the third moon of 2036 Nualan."

This time everyone started laughing, even Yang Chen, who had spent much of the last twenty minutes in silent withdrawal. This was rare for The Synod, so Sheel let it run its course. As the laughter and comments slowly began to recede, Sheel spoke above the noise: "I hope these suggestions will be useful to you, ambassador. Incidentally, there *are* Caesarean acclimation tapes in Amura's libraries—the university's Psychology Department has them. They might help your socialization attempts.''

"Yes, indeed," Alasdair chuckled. "Yes, indeed. I shall pass on your information, and we of Wallace appreciate the time of The Synod. Perhaps we should call a special session someday, and pound out a few planetwide solutions to such problems. But today the schedule called for addressing the subject of a joint passenger ship for our children on spouse search?''

Sheel was not sure if he should send Alasdair a bottle of fine wine or kick him under the table. An inter-tribal council on law was a very touchy subject for several of the tribes. But he had passed it by smoothly, and no one seemed willing to draw attention to the idea by returning to it—not even Rex Dielaan, who had grown silent and remote at Alasdair's words.

But no one walked out, like the first time it was suggested. No one even entered a formal protest, as Valdez and Andersen had the last time the topic appeared. *Someday, someday . . . maybe the grandchildren of Avis can pull off that trick, and even make it hold the center.* It had been literally years since he had felt this good at a synod meeting.

As the ambassador of Boone presented a plan for a joint travel venture, thus reducing costs and security problems, Sheel glanced at the mirrors. Avis gave him a merry wink, obviously amused by the proceedings; there was also amusement in Leah's face, but her eyes held something more. A mere flick of her gaze toward the Dielaan faction. . . .

What do you see, Leah? What do you fear?

He should have known better than to feel confident about The Synod.

ATARE WINTER PALACE   COMPLINE

Pawn or queen? Pawn or queen? Words, mere words, rumbling through her brain, trying to distract her from the conversation at hand. But behind those words Darame could hear her father's voice, whispering the eternal question. Are you a pawn, to be pushed and pulled by the will of another, or will you be a queen, and cover the board with your schemes?

It had not really surprised her that there were Nualans who still enjoyed chess, *shal mat*, The King is Dead. It was one of the last things her father had taught his ten-years-Terran daughter, before he overplayed his final game. Long ago she had surpassed him, at least at the game of free-trading; the talent always seemed to skip a generation, the child either vanishing in the mists of time or erasing the parent's fame. Was that why Halsey never spoke of the children she knew he had fathered? Had they vanished in the mists?

Is it my will that he is here, or his that I called him to me? A ride on the beach with the children had calmed the storms within, but only momentarily; Halsey's call had thrown Darame back into silent reflection.

He is like a labyrinth, Halsey had stated without hesitation. *Full of twists and turns and dead ends.* Ah, to have a few less scruples. . . .

"Only sixty-three people!" came Kristinsson's voice. "I can't understand that—how can you have a *war*, and only sixty-three people die?"

So. Back to Nualan history. Sighing inwardly, Darame said aloud: "By Nualan standards, that is a lot. The previous clan war claimed only two lives. And that was Kilgore and Andersen, who are always at each other's throats. They boast of it, in their sly manner—that they had only two fatalities, while Atare and Dielaan let their anger overcome them." She was acutely conscious of the presence of her *guaard*, Jude.

Garth Kristinsson shifted in his chair, his pale, restless gaze searching the water stretched before them. Although they had talked for little less than an hour, Darame felt as if it had been years. Now she was sure—this young man was avoiding talking about Lisbet, except in the most general terms. It was as if the subject was painful. He kept his face tranquil, but there was something in his eyes and voice that said otherwise.

"If not to kill their enemy, then why do they fight?" he said suddenly.

Darame considered the question. "For prestige and power," she said finally. "To erode the power and prestige of the other. Sometimes you can win and still lose—or lose, yet ultimately win. Back in the Eugenics War, clans Cantrel and Saunder were decimating the opposition, but in the end, the other clans joined and wiped out their royal lines. For all intents and purposes, clans Cantrel and Saunder no longer exist. As for winning and still losing. . . ." Darame considered the safety of mentioning her best example . . . ah, he could find out for himself without too much trouble. "Cort Atare won that last war with Dielaan, yet he handled it badly. Both his own people *and* Dielaan felt the losers hadn't been punished enough. This made Cort Atare —and by inference, Atare itself—seem weak. I think his actions, or lack thereof, led to the attack on the royal line by off-worlders . . . and to some Nualans helping that plan along."

"Nualans will work with off-worlders?" That seemed to surprise Kristinsson. He shook his head negatively at her offer of more cocoa.

"Nualans are still *Homo sapiens,*" was her mild reply. "The best of them may have evolved into something superior to the average off-worlder, but there are still many, many average and—defective—examples."

"You would think they'd splice out anything they couldn't control," the youth suggested, removing a cookie from the heaped dessert tray. "Since the royal lines are the government, and the government controls the labs."

Darame frowned into the dusky light. The closest of the solar lights rimming the patio was behind her, to keep direct light from her face, but the Caesarean seemed to sense her reaction.

"I don't mean to—"

"No insult taken," she responded, cutting him off. "*Most* of the labs. You must remember that the Nualans are the descendants of a scientific force which was stranded, then abandoned to its fate. I've never probed too deeply into the histories, but I suspect that in the first few hundred years the Nualans were more humanoid than human. Fortunately they did not lose their knowledge when they lost their refined metals. Genetics work continued, even as each generation became stronger, better able to deal with the radiation of the planet. A few groups tried to control and direct the patterns, but it didn't work—the mutation rate was incredible. There was an obvious choice—turn to the labs, and raise their fetuses in glass and plastic forevermore, or keep trying to bear their own. The Nualans decided that 'life must be viable in its own environment, and survive without extraordinary measures. It must be as nature decreed, and any changes must be transmittable through genetic code.' That's actually spelled out in the agreement that binds all the tribes. It's one of the things that can destroy the peace—more than one tribe has taken it upon themselves to decide what will be used for breeding, and

what will not." A faint smile traced her lips. "One of the reasons
Atare and Seedar are so large is because many of Cantrel and
Saunder fled to other tribes—Atare and Seedar foremost—before
the final confrontation took place."

"Fleeing their own governments?"

"Yes," Darame answered. "In Cantrel, becoming pregnant
from the wrong source was punishable by 'therapeutic abortion'.
No true Nualan would stand for that; only twenty percent of the
population is fertile. The '80s' would gladly go to war to protect
fertile family and friends. Later, the winners divided up the tribes
and moved the survivors. Today the capitals of those provinces
are tumbled stone."

"Must 'survive without extraordinary measures,' " Kristinsson repeated quietly. "My aunt had Rh blood problems . . . she
could only have one child."

"That is one of the odd exceptions they have," Darame said.
"Since there is nothing wrong with either mother or child—only
the problem of the link between them—the fetus is placed in an
external unit until birth." Sighing, Darame added: "They don't
do surgery in the womb, though . . . the fetus has to make it to
birth on its own. Of course, Nualan women have changed
slightly, in the centuries since they arrived. The same thing which
protects mother and child from inherent Nualan radiation in one
or the other prevents most probes and *in utero* scans from suc-
ceeding. To attempt to see what's going on aborts the embryo
or fetus."

"But once it has a life of its own, that life is sacrosanct? I
mean, what with war being fought without fatalities." Kristinsson's voice was intent.

"From the first moment of brain activity, it is a person, with
the right to life. If a mother doesn't want it, for some odd reason,
or simply doesn't want the stress of carrying it to term, it is
brought to term in a 'bottle'. But bearing children is something
every Nualan desires. Even the men—there is status in fathering
children which grow to term within a womb." Darame decided
it was time to try the subject of Lisbet again. "Your mother
would have appreciated such a value on life. There was nothing
of the coward in her, but she hated fighting. In her opinion, it
was a waste of valuable time and energy."

"One thing mother never wasted was time," Kristinsson said
idly, twisting his body so he was facing the sea.

"I think she would have understood the Nualan concept of honor," Darame murmured. "It is more complex than it seems."

"Loss of face or position is everything . . . but its importance varies, depending on how others respond to that loss," Kristinsson said under his breath. Raising his voice, he asked: "Are you Nualan—in that sense?"

"In some ways, I suppose . . . in other ways, I am free-trader to the bone." After a while she added: "But I have learned to love these people. I care about their tragedies and triumphs . . . I wish them health and peace."

"And what do they wish for you?" Very soft, and not quite a question.

Darame chose not to answer.

conspiracy: 1) An illegal and/or treacherous plan by two or more sentients (manifesting itself in either words or deeds) to injure or destroy a sentient being or recognizable group. This includes utilizing unlawful means to do something which in and of itself is lawful. SYN *stratagem*, where the means of gaining an end are carefully contrived. Compare *MACHINATION* or *PLOT*, which imply subtle maneuvering intended to accomplish an end.

CHAPTER SIX

AMURA-BY-THE-SEA, NUALA
 ONEHUNDRED EIGHTYSEVENDAY COMPLINE
THE BLACK HAZELLE HOSTEL

I don't know whether to be frantic or angry, Garth realized, as he flicked through the Caesarean version of a Dielaan periodical.

I'm an idiot. So the people seem provincial and the trade ships are few and far between—what made me think that meant the culture was simple? Sighing, Garth punched up the editorial section and glanced over it.

Boring. Dielaan's press was not censored, exactly . . . rather it was careful. It was very easy to forget that the city-states of Nuala were, for the most part, absolute monarchies. Only the hot cities of the north varied—the curse of the hot gene made all citizens equal. Yet the Nualan clans were not hasty or abusive . . . not since the death of Tensar Dielaan ten years earlier. True, his sister seemed just as bloodthirsty as he had been, but she chose her "examples" carefully. All other clans of Nuala appeared subtle in their rule.

Something Lucy had said was finally beginning to make sense. In a world where eighty percent of the population was permanently sterile, the rules were very different. *Everyone* worked; accordingly, automation was not used for very many things. Where merchandise made by hand was rare in most parts of The Brethren, on Nuala those who chose to pay for, say, handmade furniture, could find it. Clan wealth varied from the unbelievably wealthy Atares to poor Boone, who had scarcely a name site and the surrounding countryside to call its own . . . and a sister hot city to sum up its problems. Kilgore was also wealthy, thanks to syluan fiber.

No one in Atare paid for utilities or communications . . . the trust from the mines paid for it. Few paid rent or worried about a mortgage. Those who owned tremendous amounts of mining stock lived in magnificent stone houses; those less fortunate lived in simple, single-family dwellings, or supplemented their dividends. But no one was hungry in Atare; no one lived without a roof over heart and head. No wonder other forms of government had made little inroad. With free press and no sustenance problems, with free lab help for the genetically troubled, Atare had created a strange and wondrous state.

Things were poorer in the deserts. Most of Dielaan herded sheep and hazelles, the latter a genetic construct of horses and native tazelles, or grew low-moisture items like olives and adapted grapevines and grains. Seedar lived almost exclusively on the bounty of land and sea, while Andersen exported all manner of luxuries—perfumes, dyes, fine dessert items, and a fledgling silk industry. Next to Amura-By-The-Sea, Atare actually had the greatest variety of industry—animal husbandry, cloth, ship-building, jewelry, and finally specialized hazelle/horse genetics and breeding filled out their extensive mining operations.

Where to put in his wedge? The city-states were amazingly separate, much more so than the entwined economics of the Emerson nations. Genetics and foreign trade . . . they were the only things he could find that overlapped. Anything else skirted localized treason, and Garth had decided long ago that he wasn't looking for his own death. Not yet.

Certain possibilities he had dismissed out of hand. He would not simply kill Silver—what would that prove? Threaten her children? No—Nualans were fanatical about their children. Quite apart from Silver's reaction, Garth suspected that Sheel Atare could keep an assassin looking for *him* for a hundred years—a *thousand* years. *I want to show skill—verve, even. I'm not sure I want this wergild in hard currency.*

Garth had a suspicion he could not embarrass Silver—Darame, he had to start thinking of her as Darame—by revealing her free-trader origins. As best as he could make out, the royal families of Nuala had intermarried with everything from concubines to pirates, from illiterate Gavrielian farmers to erudite Caesareans under suspicion of second degree murder. Free-trading (which was, after all, merely fleecing someone with his or her own greed) lit this place like an interlocking puzzle piece.

If he could make it look as if she had turned against Atare? Had found a scam she simply couldn't pass up? He would concentrate on either genetics or foreign trade; surely they had potential. The Synod was a touchy subject—the press handled it carefully, as if an explosion was imminent. *Is The Synod that important to you?*

Important to Nuala . . . to Atare. Sheel Atare, ruler of his clan, clearly wanted this synod to succeed—his actions of the past ten years bore that out. And it was fragile, so fragile, this thing called The Synod . . . and perhaps easier to erode than the many genetic labs? A false message here, information volunteered to the wrong people, and . . .

"Poof," Garth whispered aloud.

A chime interrupted him. Clearing the RAM function, Garth brought up the outside call. Lucy's sweet face filled the screen. "Ready to surface?" Apparently his face looked blank, because she immediately continued: "You have been working for *days*, Garth—I begin to feel neglected."

Maybe something would occur to him if he didn't press quite so hard. "What did you have in mind?"

"We are having a small gathering at Dielaan House," she replied, leaning forward on the console of her unit. "A mixture of people—friends, artistic types, political malcontents . . . anyone Rex thinks will be amusing. Our uncle is not present," she added hastily, seeing his reaction.

Her last words brought the invitation into the realm of possibility. He had seen the uncle only from a distance, but the man's neutral, forbidding gaze had warned him off. Garth was not sure he was an approved "suitor," as the Nualans seemed to name all new opposite-sex friends.

"The liquor is imported, and there will be food you can eat. Please?"

After all, it *had* been two days since he'd seen her—Political malcontents? "Sure. How do I get there?"

"Take the shuttle to Embassy Row and wait at Dielaan," she replied. "I will come get you in a meth'." Twinkling, she added: "Dress is casual. I will be right there!" The screen went blank.

"Hell's Bells," Garth muttered. One thing about Lucy; she was prompt. If she said "right there," that meant she was walking to wherever they stored their ground transportation even as the thoughts passed through his brain. Quickly pulling on his newest shirt and sealing the pressure points at the cuffs, Garth pocketed his codekey and hurried to the elevator.

Rushing through the cozy lobby to the outside curb and waving his arms wildly produced the proper response—the shuttle, which had been pulling away from the closest pickup point, ground to a halt.

The vehicle moved handily, and he reached Embassy Row before Lucy. Disembarking at Customs, Garth chose to walk the last few steps. He still couldn't shake the feeling that he was being watched—

"Right on time!" Startled, Garth turned at the familiar voice. A sunny smile flashed at him through tinted glass. Rounded, winged doors lifted before him, rising above his head, and a delicate hand beckoned.

"Fast," Garth said, sliding in next to her and nodding to the dark, uniformed man at the wheel.

"We are missing a good party, and you have been practically hooked into that RAM," Lucy replied, her tone almost—but not quite—scolding. "All that politics and history will give you indigestion."

"I find it fascinating," Garth admitted. "You have more variety than Emerson or Gavriel, and they're pretty diverse people. I can't figure out why you have so many monarchies—they're not very common anymore."

Lucy wrinkled her nose. "You prefer social states? Dictatorships? Theocracies? Corporation facades? The only true democracy left in the Seven Systems is the Sini Alliance." The vehicle quietly began to move.

"Caesarea is a democracy," Garth replied.

"It is not. It is a modified republic. People elect representatives, do they not? They do not vote directly upon every issue that is presented to or by them?"

"Of course n—"

"And only certain people can vote—reaching an age of majority on Caesarea does not guarantee the right to vote? And, even stranger—your prime minister is elected for six years, and cannot be removed from office! What if the prime minister turns out to be incompetent, or a crook?" She shook her head. "We call that a modified republic. Caesareans are no more interested in politics than the average Nualan, or Gavrielian. Your people are interested in making money and acquiring power—mine are interested in heirs and the quality of life. And all the clans vary, you know. We even have elements of a social state on Nuala—after all, everyone who is born an Atare or gives birth to an Atare has mining stock, and that means free utilities and infonet service—omni, RAM, communications, everything."

"All the monarchies differ?" Garth said slowly. *He* was not eligible to vote back home, owning no property on Caesarea. . . .

"Very much so. I cannot tell you all the differences—there are many clans! I do not know all the variations. When The Synod began, ten or so years ago, Atare started teaching its young everything it knew about each tribal system. Well, Dielaan would not stand for that!"

"You didn't like others knowing about your ways?"

Lucy chuckled. "No, silly, we did not want Atare to seem more generous when discussing other clans! And we wanted to be sure no erroneous information was taught simply because we could not be bothered to place it on a ring. So *all* the tribes began teaching about all the other clans—for the first time! Every major city has a net link to the library in Amura, as well, so no one can truly censor anything. If Seedar, say, or Dielaan *really* wish to keep something about their government structure from the other clans—or something about the other tribes from their own people—they must leave the library net.''

"But that would imply they had something to hide, or to be ashamed of—"

"Exactly!" Seizing his arm, Lucy turned and pointed out the back window. "Oh, we have reached the hills! Is not the view wonderful?" Looking back over his shoulder, Garth saw the Alameda Sea, now a strip of darkness beyond the chain of lights rimming the shore. One slender, new moon glittered low in the sky. White street lights twinkled like diamonds, tracing the trail they had followed. "I do love living in the mountains here." Sighing, she leaned against him slightly. "I never tire of water—here I have real mountains and a real sea!"

"At home you have pretend mountains and a pretend sea?" Garth could not resist asking.

Another chuckle. "Our sea is small, compared to this one— and our mountains very small! The ceaseless wind grinds them away," she murmured sadly. "Did I answer your question?"

"I think I forgot my question."

"Different monarchies," she reminded him, her tone slightly pedantic. Something that sounded suspiciously like a snort came from the young woman. "I said once that if I was not royal Dielaan, just a common, I would want to live in Atare or Kilgore. Rex was *so* mad when I said it!"

"Why did you say that?"

"Because being a common in Dielaan would not be . . . pleasant." The last word was emphasized oddly. "In Atare, if the people feel a judge has handled a case 'with prejudice'— letting family or personal feelings interfere—they can appeal to The Atare and The Ragäree. The case then is reviewed on its merits. Although all the judges are Atares, and can serve for life, they must have training and intelligence to reach the bench—not all Atares do, you know. And they can be removed at any time by The Atare or Ragäree, if reason is found to do so.

"Law is made by The Atare and Ragäree, but the judges frame decisions from precedent, or something like that. They have a bill of rights and responsibilities for their citizens, too—you would have to look it up."

"Then Atare takes the law seriously?"

"Indeed. Now, in Dielaan, The Dielaan not only makes the laws, he enforces them—he is the final and sole authority, able to suspend law at will. He also appoints judges, but he can appoint anyone—Rex could place me on the high court if he chose, just because he wanted to . . . without training, without inclination—even against my will. I could do nothing but serve, or retire to my father's estates. In Dielaan, a royal's main purpose is to produce heirs and to administer any hereditary lands— anything else is at the discretion of The Dielaan. If The Dielaan wanted to appoint a hazelle —or no one—to a post, he could do so! In Dielaan, judges may have many other responsibilities, while in Atare, the heads of sept clans, for example, resign judgeships, in case of conflicts of interest. Am I losing you?" Lucy asked abruptly.

His gaze drifting out the window, Garth wondered if she *was* losing him. Interesting, the road was a switchback—the ocean was now before them. "Are you saying that in Atare there are limits to power, while in Dielaan, there may not be?"

"Yes! Thank you. If Rex wanted to make Uncle Tsuga not only the head of his immediate family, not only advisor to the throne, not only administrator of his lands, but a judge as well —simultaneously—he could do it. In Atare, The Atare and Ragäree avoid that. One must put ones's inheritance in another's hands while one serves Atare— that I do know. For us, it is a tricky system, because if The Dielaan is conscientious, the judges are very good. But if The Dielaan is lazy, or playing favorites, the judgeships can become a disaster."

"Your people stand for it?"

"They are Dielaan—they do not want to be anything else. But when we have a good Dielaan, his shadow falls for generations, and that helps in bad times. In *very* bad times. . . ." A tight chuckle reached his ears. "A knife in the back takes care of all ills."

"What?" Garth turned back from the setting moon. "Are you saying someone simply kills The Dielaan?"

"Well, not *kills*. Incapacitates, shall we say," she said candidly. "That is always in the back of a ruler's mind. Even now, our regent wonders when someone will put a stop to her work. To balance the needs of the people with the wants of the aristocracy—that is the trick. Atare and Kilgore do it better."

Garth waited, watching an outer stone wall with mounted lights flash by. "In Kilgore," she said finally, "once every three years, the province is closed to outsiders. In the center of their beautiful city, on a platform of stone and precious wood, erected for the purpose . . . a forge, a kiln, and a casting machine are set up. There, starting at dawn, The Kilgore and The Ragäree melt down the crowns of clan Kilgore, and make them once again, fabricating and casting, adding fresh gold as needed. No barriers . . . no guard. During that time, should any citizen have a grievance, they present it to the archpriest or archpriestess of Kilgore. The archpriest and archpriestess then formally offer the grievance to the crowd. If the crowd agrees it merits a new regime, then the succession is proclaimed." Garth scarcely caught the final words. "If the crowd agrees it merits the death of one or both of the rulers, then the succession is proclaimed."

A pale, dome light flickered on, and serious black eyes met his. "I do not think I would have the courage to do that . . . to go among my people totally exposed."

"You walk in Amura alone," Garth pointed out gently.

"I walk in Amura with a bodyguard—and Amura is not Dielaan. There are some villages on the fringes of Dielaan I would not dare even enter, and I am both powerless and blameless, merely my father's daughter."

"Bodyguard?" Garth felt puzzlement slipping across his face, even as a solution occurred to him.

"Churr." Lucy gestured toward the driver as they pulled up before the red stone walls of Dielaan House. "He, or another guard, is always somewhere nearby . . . closer, if he is suspicious of the crowd." Barely dimpling, she added: "He does not think you a threat to me."

Movement ceased; the doors lifted, and the driver stepped out and turned to offer his hand to Lucy. Staring, Garth realized it was the man who had followed them to the restaurant.

"Did you not notice we were being followed?" she giggled.

"Of course, but I thought—" He cut himself off abruptly.

After a moment: "Why would someone want to follow you, Garth?"

This time she expected an answer. "My family is a bit like your family," he said finally, feeling a touch of cold air against the nape of his neck. "You can never be sure who might be at your back . . . and why."

Lucy smiled faintly, the expression pulling slightly at one corner of her mouth and promising a dimple. "Indeed. Then you should be right at home." With that enigmatic statement, she swept off toward the front door.

Everything about Dielaan House was slightly skewed, off-center from what he had seen at the Atare home. The house itself was flopped—instead of long, low, windowed levels, this huge edifice had no windows at all on the first level. It was but three floors, and rambling, traveling up and down the hillside with the dexterity of a mountain goat. Everywhere, one saw dusty, red stone, blunted with black basalt and a creamy sandstone. But the surprise was the color—it was everywhere. The people of Dielaan worshipped color.

No wonder Lucy prefers vivid green clothes, Garth thought wryly as he followed her up the heavy, stone steps. *Don't these people pay their utility bill?* A good place for an assassin to hang out . . .

"I apologize for the lighting—one must become accustomed. It is partly habit; at home the star is always so bright, we need no indoor lighting, except at night. Also, Rex prefers it this way," Lucy said over her shoulder as she loosened the reddish fur jacket she was wearing. Handing it to a young woman in uniform at the top of the stairs, Lucy turned and indicated with a gesture that they would go to the left.

Blinking rapidly at Lucy's skinsuit of shocking green and yellow, Garth fell into step at her side. They moved swiftly down a corridor lined with bold, abstract tapestries and all too few lights, entering a large room.

Swirling smoke and babbling voices overwhelmed him. Incense stabbed sharply at his sense of smell, cloaking the odor of several other burning items. Tobacco, cannabis, krystal—"Aren't depressants and stimulants controlled here?" he murmured into Lucy's ear.

"Yes, but the artistic types use all of them, except for the Purists—they never do anything Rex thinks of as fun, so you will not meet any tonight. This house is protected by the embassy laws, and Dielaan allows unregulated use of these items—prop-

erly taxed, of course,'' she replied, tilting her head back to lend
privacy to her words.

Tall ceilings, once again, and tiled floors covered by an occasional woven rug of brilliant red, black and white—''Where
are we going?'' he asked, surveying the crowded room. All kinds
of clothes and hairstyles, or lack thereof; the tall, bald woman
in nothing but a linked-metal loincloth could not help but catch
his eye. He smelled a familiar odor beneath the eye-level haze
. . . kona? If this group was any indication, Halsey should re-
consider that farming scheme.

''Here,'' she responded, pushing past several men leaning up
against the lintels of a doorway. The second, smaller room had
little smoke in it. Garth did not have to ask—Lucy went straight
to the open doors leading out to the balcony. ''Hooo!'' was her
first word. ''I can see why Sheel Atare forbids that stuff in his
home!''

''I hate the way it makes my mouth taste,'' Garth offered.

Laughing, Lucy seized two vials off a passing tray and pressed
one into his hand. ''This will change the taste, I promise you!''
Sipping at the tall, narrow, etched glass, Lucy started moving
toward an intimate group at the edge of the stone balcony.

The thought of assassins lingered . . . Garth hesitated, until
he saw an empty tray tucked into a dumbwaiter of some type
and a·fresh tray of drinks lifted from it. *We are being served
separately from the other rooms.* Heartened, Garth sipped his
drink.

Sweetness and anise shocked both his tongue and ‘his brain
into silence. *Maybe I* have *been poisoned,* was his first coherent
thought. His feet had continued moving; Lucy had led him up
to Rex Dielaan. Meeting amused, black eyes, Garth realized that
his face was an open book. Glancing around quickly, he took
note of the others seated at the metal mesh table. A tiny, fair-
skinned female with curly black hair, whose manner was retiring
. . . Rex had a new woman. Malini was seated to her left, and
on Rex's right was an unfamiliar young man whose hooded
features proclaimed a possible family link—a lock of red hair
curled out along his jawline. An ever-familiar soldier of Dielaan
hovered in the background.

''Too sweet for you?'' Rex asked, amusement thick in his soft
voice. ''Ouzo is definitely an acquired taste.'' Waving a hand

negligently, The Dielaan indicated that Garth should sit. "Have you met everyone here?"

"Not Silas," Lucy said quickly, gently wrestling the ouzo away from Garth and offering him a glass of white wine. "Silas reb´Carlotta Dielaan, my brother—hiding in his hood, over there," she added, her voice poking gently at him. "This is Garth Kristinsson."

"I do not hide, exactly," came the response, as the man shifted back the cowl. "There is a breeze tickling my neck." Ignoring Lucy's chuckle and Rex's amusement, Silas gravely rearranged the cowl into a collar.

"Admit it, you hide from our nanny," Rex said, chortling aloud. "Uncle has retired, rather . . . miffed. It is the height of decadence to be seen at one of my parties, is it not?" This last was addressed to Malini.

"Only if one is present past matins," Malini replied, her expression deadpan.

Rex roared with laughter. Taking advantage of the moment, Garth glanced over at Lucy, and saw she seemed amused. So, Malini had intended to poke fun at Rex—and he had allowed it.

"What would you like to eat?" Lucy murmured into his ear.

"Anything except ouzo—thank you," he added. Throwing him a saucy grin, Lucy leaned back and caught the sleeve of a young wait scurrying past.

"You do not care for the local cheese?" came Rex's voice.

Did he hear everything? Garth glanced down at the potentially deadly cheese and crackers artistically arranged around the candles.

"Garth has yet to take the series," Lucy said easily.

"There is never a better time than the present," Rex responded.

Lucy chuckled, shaking a finger at him, but Garth felt his spine stiffen. Didn't Lucy sense the edge to Rex's voice?

"You must be careful to avoid offending the natives by implying there is something disgusting about their food," Rex added, and Lucy's hand tightened on her glass.

"I like saffra," Garth offered smoothly. "And I think Caesarea needs a revival of scones and muffins."

Rex smiled, and Lucy's grip on her drink loosened. "Imagine

paying three times its worth just to sample local delicacies," he
mused. An arriving soldier bent down to speak by his ear.
"Please, continue," Rex added, standing and moving off into
the restless crowd.

It was as if a storm had passed. "Well done," Malini said.
"Most people swallow their teeth at that tone."

"I seem to have offended him," Garth said tentatively. "I
didn't mean to. It's just that . . . I'm not sure how long I'll be
staying, and—"

"You owe us no explanation," Silas said, brushing away
protests with a typically Dielaan wave of hand. "And you did
not offend him—you would know for certain if you had! No, I
think you pleased him . . . you have wits and the nerve to use
them. Few people speak freely before Rex Dielaan."

"Come," Lucy said suddenly, "there is someone I want you
to meet, before Rex returns." Standing, she seized his wrist in
a familiar grasp and tugged him toward the opposite side of the
balcony.

Connected balconies, it turned out—they were linked, like
pearls on a string. The deck Lucy led him to was cozier than
either walkway. This gathering had five people grouped around
a centered table, and they were all drinking various forms of
kona. Garth recognized a tall, striking redhead from the party
—not pretty, really, but humor lit her freckled countenance—
while the others were unfamiliar.

"I want you to meet my cousin Quen," she murmured as he
moved up behind her. "I think you will like him—he is my
favorite of all my cousins."

"Different tastes . . . in conversation and in women?" Garth
asked.

Lucy shot him a sharp glance. "What brothers share those
tastes?" Letting her fingers slide into his hand, she drew him
over near the tall, bosomy redhead. Reaching with her other
hand, Lucy clasped the shoulder of still another youth with hair
as burnished as her own.

"—I still think Hansun's intent was to illustrate the state of
mind of his protagonist," someone was saying.

"He could have used a better image," responded a distinctly
Dielaan—and feminine—voice.

"But—"

"Quen," Lucy murmured, so as to not distract the others. "This is Garth—the one I told you about."

A turn of the head, and Garth was startled. This young man had eyes as brilliantly green as Malini's—like chips of emerald. Placed in a slender face of polished bronze, they could be part of a statue. But Quen had warmer eyes than Malini, and his smile seemed genuine. He actually offered his hand, palm-up, as Caesarean natives did. "Welcome to Dielaan House."

Grateful his hands were dry, Garth accepted the handshake. "Thank you. I'm sorry if I looked surprised, but—"

"The eyes?" Quen laughed. "In my house it is normally the women who have it, but Juana and Pamela had to share with me! I am the first man in generations to have them . . . my father's fault, undoubtedly, if we cared to trace it." Winking carefully with the eye farthest from the bosomy redhead, he added: "I think they set Rebekah on my trail at the first."

"Quen," she protested, her expression almost comic in its dismay. Garth noticed that she had huge, dark eyes and thick lashes, a pleasing compliment to her flaming red hair.

"You know redheads avoid other redheads," Quen went on quickly. "My eyes were all that kept her from running the other way."

This time she knew she was being teased, and tossed a piece of some fresh vegetable at him.

"Broccoli, now. Does this mean I am a dip?" Quen asked seriously, offering her back the floret.

"Quen!"

Well, it is obvious how things stand with them. Glancing at Lucy, Garth knew she was thinking the same thing. Her smile was wistful.

"We must get back—Rex needs an audience," she murmured.

"Come see me," Quen said simply, his expression including Garth in the invitation.

"Seri, tell her I am right!" suddenly drew Quen back into the conversation at the table.

"Tell him he is right, so we can talk about something else," Quen suggested, and the gathering started laughing.

Silently Garth followed Lucy back down the narrow pathway to the main balcony. "I can see why Quen is your favorite," he said quietly. "I am surprised you do not spend more time with him."

"What I can," she responded artlessly. "He understands."

"Does Rex merely need the audience, or is he jealous of Quen's . . ." What? *The difference of star and moon.*

Lucy threw him a startled look. "Be careful," she murmured, slowing to a halt. "Rex is The Dielaan, and his power is absolute . . . he has 'the right'. I am Dielaan, and would remain so. I am wise enough to keep a foot in each camp. Even Malini knows better than to snub Rex, and she would dearly love to see Livia's line fall."

Garth merely tilted a head at her.

"Despite the hopes of the sword side, the distaff side is strong in Dielaan, if one goes back far enough . . . and Malini has three brothers." Her look a definite warning, Lucy turned and marched toward the smaller balcony.

Resuming his seat, Garth tried to pay attention to the running conversation, but found it full of Silas and Malini's plans to go off-world.

"If you could choose an interesting planet to visit, which of The Brethren would you choose?" Malini asked abruptly. "But only one."

"Yes, Garth, give us some words of wisdom," came Rex's smooth tones as the man approached once more.

"It depends on what you find interesting," Garth answered. At their puzzled looks, he amplified. "If you want historical ruins, go to Emerson. If you want varied social life, go to Caesarea; they have the most performing arts, too. If you want things a bit spicier, go to Kiel—but be careful. Slavery is legal there, because their genetic labs produce human stock for certain kinds of labor classes. Some merchants don't ask questions when they're offered healthy, attractive, unconscious material. It could take your people years to find you, much less redeem you."

Rex smiled. "Our personal guards would leave a trail of broken bodies right up to the embassy door, should we be so foolish as to elude them."

"Fertility and intellect," Malini said caustically. "We need healthy livestock with brains."

"I don't know about fertility," he murmured, "but Caesarea and Kiel are usually thought to have the most progressive universities in the region. Unless you want to go a lot further—CSSI system, or even to Terra.''

"Ha!" was Silas's response. "If *that* is required, I will doom my legal line! A few hundred years in Sleep does not appeal. Kiel sounds interesting—all proper and stuffy on top, and a cesspool beneath. Tell us more.''

It was thirsty work, trying to satisfy their desire for firsthand knowledge of The Brethren. Garth kept his wine intake down to sips, but he lost count of how many times his glass was refilled. Somewhere along the line Lucy had a sandwich brought for him, but he didn't remember what it tasted like . . . Rex's earlier comment made his nibbles few and far between.

A waiter was bringing fresh candles for the centerpiece when Garth noticed that his audience was smaller . . . Rex's new woman had left. The few unnamed individuals sitting near but not at the table had also disappeared. How late was it?

"You have seen everything," Rex said simply. "Been to every world. Why did you choose to come here? Since you could not have known we had restricted access when you left Caesarea." The slightest of pauses, and he added: "Lucy says you are looking for someone?"

"I'm alone," Garth started slowly, "for the most part. My parents raised me in a rather exclusive living class. They left me with a few things . . . unresolved, shall we say. I have been simply tidying up.''

"Free-traders." Rex said it as fact.

Surely Lucy knew. . . . "Yes, my parents were free-traders."

"Your mother worked with The Atarae?"

Lucy had asked that before . . . hadn't she? *How much wine.* . . . Forcing his mind to focus, Garth said: "My mother knew The Atarae long before either of them left Gavriel, back when they were *very* young. Both of their parents died early on, and they were raised in the major city by non-relatives—" Sweet Saint Peter, *Halsey* must have been the old man who raised her!

"Yes?" Rex prompted.

"I think The Atarae left after both finished their required education . . . mother left with my dad, a few years later. I don't know whether they ever worked together." Garth managed a smile. "Being raised by free-traders means having absolutely no idea what your parents are doing from one moment to the next! And it's usually better not to know.''

"Often," Rex agreed mildly. "What are you, Garth? A child of wealth at loose ends with yourself? You obviously are not an immigrant. You imply you are not a free-trader, although you take time to find out where free-traders congregate. You make a strange merchant—you have nothing visible to buy or sell. You arrived here as crew on one of our own ships."

A hollow, sick feeling was beginning to form about the location of Garth's breastbone . . . was his discomfort visible?

"Maybe I should leave—" Silas began, starting to rise.

"Why?" Rex asked, pinning him with a glance. "You have no intention of babbling Garth's business to the world, do you?"

"Of course not!"

"I am genuinely interested, Garth," Rex went on, turning his dark gaze back toward his guest. "You see, I noticed something during the party at Dragonhold. Sheel Atare's wife frightens you. You hate that . . . and perhaps her?" Before Garth could say anything, Rex added: "You see, I am not fond of the House of Atare, either."

This is why you came here. . . . Excitement was burning away any lingering fumes of alcohol. *But is this something I can use?* "No, I gathered that Dielaan and Atare have been . . . competitors . . . for a long time."

Rex smiled. "An apt choice of words. Yes, we are competitors. Our foremost means of keeping score involves power. I understand that you have delved deeply into our history, both ancient and recent. So you know that a catastrophe happened here, oh, a dozen years ago Terran. An outsider infiltrated our greatest clans and wreaked havoc among us. More than two dozen died directly from his efforts, and a coup was attempted in Dielaan following my uncle's death—several more deaths resulted from the riots." Rex shook his head. "An incredible occurrence, far beyond our comprehension. We dealt with it, finally. The skull of the man responsible still rattles on a pole before my gate. But that was not enough. We had to take measures to insure it would never happen again."

"The Synod."

Rex's nostrils flared, as if something rotting had moved into range. "Yes, The Synod. We closed down all the embassies, and confined them in one city—this one. We created embassies among the clans, something we had never had before. Then we created The Synod, to negotiate foreign trade agreements for the great clans.''

''But The Synod has gone beyond its original boundaries,'' Silas continued, rearranging his cowl back into a hood. ''Its purpose was to be a breakwater against the corruption of the outside, to protect our people and to improve our bargaining power. But it has had another effect . . . it erodes clan power when dealing with off-world principalities.''

''What was supposed to be foreign trade *only* has become everything dealing with off-worlders,'' Lucy added. ''And most of the clans do not like that.''

''The clans, or their governments?'' Garth asked slowly.

''It is the same thing,'' Rex stated flatly. ''We cannot deny there have been benefits to this system. But the system now erodes the sovereignty of our individual governments.'' Rex's expression seemed to grow momentarily unfocused. ''I should be doing as Silas and Lucy and Malini do—looking forward to my trip off-world. But my mother, as Regent, has already weakened the base of my power. If I leave, even for a year, that is twenty-one-years Terran when Sleep is considered! I may not have a throne to return to. . . .''

''You see a republic of some—'' Rex's laughter stopped Garth in mid-sentence.

''No, no—our people have the habit of obedience, and they struggle for mere survival. They have little time for politics. But I could become a puppet king under Atare . . . or have a branch of my house decide that my mother was damaging Dielaan, and wrest my regency from her.''

''And then refuse to return it to you?'' Garth finished.

''You begin to see,'' Rex said simply.

Garth shuffled subtlety and bluntness in his hands . . . the sum suggested laying a card face up on the table. ''What has all this to do with me?''

''I suppose you could say that I wish to hire a . . . consultant.''

''Consultant?''

''I know you have been all over the Seven Systems, Garth. You have been studying us. Your choices from the library indicate that you have concentrated a great deal on the last ten years of our existence . . . and always, you return to the clan of Atare. Now I will add up all that I know of you, Garth

Kristinsson, and I will suggest that you came here to find the wife of The Atare. And that you wish to do her a . . . 'mischief,' shall we say?''

Garth remained silent. *Carefully, son. This place could be wired to the eaves.*

"Well, I, too, have need to do a mischief to Atare.'' Once again, Rex emphasized that word in his velvet voice. ''I can take my throne now, if necessary. I can pull out of The Synod. But if I leave The Synod otherwise intact, I will damage Dielaan's ability to gain top price for its interstellar goods. The existence of The Synod might depress domestic prices as well. Perhaps I can draw other clans with me . . . perhaps not. Some are more extreme than I—they wish to return to individual clans negotiating alone, but from the safety of Amura.'' Rex gestured dismissingly. ''That would be acceptable, although it would bring about a dip in our finances which might spark dissension in our citizenry. The operative concept is 'intact,' Garth. We cannot leave The Synod intact, not in its current form. Sheel Atare and his woman have invested a great deal of time, energy, and personal prestige into this assembly. It would be a blow, to say the least, if it should suddenly fall apart.''

Silas's voice came once more from his hood. ''But it must fall apart with no hope of resurrection, not for many, many years. Not until we can assure it is but an information network and mouthpiece, with no power building beneath it.''

"Yet we have no thoughts of war, no thoughts of toying with any other clan structure,'' Lucy said earnestly. ''We want only to place Rex squarely upon his throne with no erosion from a synod. So we must discredit The Synod.''

"To discredit The Synod is to discredit Atare,'' Rex reiterated.

They hope to offer you what you want while getting what they want, Garth reminded himself. Well . . . could they? Silas was crazy if he thought that The Synod could be revived as "merely" an information network. Obviously these people did not bother with their own tribal nets, much less any other group's. The increase in the past decade of sheer global awareness was astonishing. *Do you seek a united confederation of city-states, Sheel Atare? You may get it from the ground up, if your people begin to see themselves as Nualans first and clan second.*

"Why do you think I would be interested in this?'' Garth began slowly.

"I realize I do not have the free-trader mentality, but I assume the best way to accomplish what you wish to do is to minimize your risks, then go forth with your plan," Rex said smoothly. "What we seek to accomplish is perfectly legal, as seen from clan law. But surely we will have to cross a line or two . . . in our quest, if you will. The greatest dangers to an off-worlder are charges of murder and localized treason. We will violate neither of those things." Pausing for effect, Rex added: "I am The Dielaan, and I can protect you from anything else, should our group be exposed."

But will you? Of course there really wasn't any way to ask that question. Garth thought about what he had just heard . . . and what he had learned that was not volunteered. Anger started to rise. Then he thought about whether or not he wanted The Atarae to know what he had chosen for his wergild. Possibly . . . but there was plenty of time for that. This way, he could keep a distance for a time, even keep his name out of it completely. *First things first.* Anger could give strength, when controlled . . .

Turning slightly toward Lucy, Garth said coolly: "You were quite good. I never guessed you picked me for a purpose." Aristocrat that she was, Lucy did not blink—but she did glance at Rex.

"My cousin chose you for her own reasons, Garth, as we always choose," Rex purred. "I was the one who suspected that your reaction to Darame Atare could be useful to us. I was the one who persuaded her to find out if I was correct in my surmise. Please do not be angry with Lucy. After all . . . this partnership may be just what we both need to accomplish our goals."

Already you assume I will do it. Well . . . any reason not to? "As you pointed out, I can have nothing to do with murder or localized treason. All I am interested in is discrediting Darame Daviddottir. If that serves your extended purpose, then good— but even in name, I can have nothing to do with any political actions. My goal is to get everyone in The Synod so angry and mistrustful of each other that the summit falls apart. Sort of a . . . dare." At their blank expressions, Garth continued: "On Caesarea, students have been known to arrange collapses within organizations on their campus—just to prove it can be done. Planting false information or rumors on the infonet, gaining access to secrets and publicizing them at the right—or wrong—

moments . . . that sort of thing. On Caesarea, a well-played scam can be so structured that no proof of wrong-doing can be made—privacy laws are different for information stored on net."
Glancing at Rex, Garth decided it was time for *him* to offer something. "I understand that an oath made on your god's name is binding. So tell me—do you swear that you are indeed the rightful ruler of Dielaan, merely hastening your accession of your throne because you honestly believe the policies of the current regency will otherwise cause the downfall of your clan? Do you swear that you intend no death in this matter?"

"I am The Dielaan, as of my twenty-first birthday, which is past," Rex replied somberly. "I am the supreme authority of my people. As I am scheduled to go off-world to seek a spouse, I have not taken up the reins of my office—but in this time of threat, I see no choice but to do so. I intend to murder no one. Mendülay is my witness."

"In that case, I suggest you examine any contacts you have in the transportation industry . . . off-world transportation. If The Synod is your goal, the quickest way to upset it is to disrupt the path between your trade goods and their planned departure. And the swiftest way to hurt Atare is to discredit what they have offered to The Synod—the services of the *guaard*." Garth decided to smile—after all, they were now allies.

"How? We have considered trade as a pressure point," Silas offered when no one else spoke. "But we have many shipping families who charter for the tribes. We cannot stop them all— some are not . . . cosmopolitan, shall we say? They would spit in the eye of a Dielaan who asked them to hold off their trade."

"And we cannot damage the Wheel," Lucy said firmly. "It is like Amura-By-The-Sea, a neutral thing. To damage it would set back interstellar travel by many years."

"The source, woman, you need the source," Garth told her, shaking his head at their obtuseness. "Steal the fuel, hold it hostage—then you call the shots. The *guaard* patrols the warehouse district. Do you see?"

"How can we steal all the methane or liquid hydrogen—" Lucy began.

"Not the reaction mass! Take the source of the propulsion energy. Steal the antimatter."

Silence greeted Garth's words. Only Rex responded . . . a slight nod.

"Steal *antimatter*? How?" Lucy sounded genuinely appalled.

"Do you produce it on Nuala?" Garth asked patiently. When the group made various negative gestures, he continued: "It can travel, in the right kind of container—they call it a trap. How did you think it arrived here?"

"I never thought about it," Lucy admitted.

"For our purposes, Nualan storage is perfect. Your people are so paranoid they don't even trust other Nualans! Years ago, a desperate crew who arrived with no cargo tried to steal antimatter from the wheel. It was a mess—berths gutted, station seals blown, several people killed—" Garth shrugged. "At any rate, the stationmaster said: 'Get it off the wheel!' So now it's all stored in Amura-By-The-Sea. Ships try to avoid transportation costs by buying before it's sent downworld. Of course, if their trading isn't complete. . . ." He rubbed his fingers together to illustrate the added costs.

"Antimatter is essential to *all* our off-world trade?" Lucy asked.

"There *is* no off-world without it," Silas told her. "It takes ten years Terra to get from here to Caesarea right now, and that is at one-tenth the speed of light. Antimatter is too expensive to think of going faster. But without it? The stars are but lights in the sky."

"But does not the antimatter arrive at regular intervals?"

"Of course. You cannot corner the trade indefinitely—only slow down or temporarily blackmail the people chartering the starships. I know for a fact that antimatter arrived on the ship I came in on. Determine when a shipment comes in, then take it. You not only make the Atare *guaard* look ineffective, you have control for as many days as exist until the next shipment arrives. There is *no* way for them to call for more, remember," Garth added, his light eyes watching Rex's face.

"Could we make them do what we wanted?" Lucy asked slowly.

"You must decide what you want in return for the antimatter. You may have to give back part of it, say, if they agree to certain demands, then wait to return the rest. Or . . . pretend you are a reactionary group." *Pretend?* "You have stolen the antimatter, and if they don't disband The Synod, or confine its activities to foreign trade only, you'll destroy the shipment. That would destroy all trade for however long the next shipment takes to arrive.

Of course, that is a last measure decision—once you destroy the antimatter, you have lost your hold over the people you're attempting to control."

"The power to destroy something is to hold absolute control over it," Rex said briefly. "You have made a good point."

"We could take it and simply keep silent," Silas suggested. "The Synod will be tearing its hair out trying to decide what is going on. But the antimatter is well-guarded . . . everyone knows that."

"No one said it would be easy," Rex said mildly. "But there is plenty of time to decide upon the details. Others aid the *guaard* in their vigil, and *they* may be susceptible to bribery." He smiled slightly at Garth. "Already you have been very useful to our group, Garth Kristinsson. I hope you find our little intrigues useful."

"Not so little," Garth responded carefully. "My parents' vengeance is a small thing next to your throne and the trade agreements of dozens of clans, but together we may accomplish much."

"Conspiracies weary me," Malini murmured. "Can we not close for now?"

"An excellent suggestion, Malini. We can do little more this evening." As Rex spoke, the clear echo of a bell reached their ears. "You must hurry to bed, cousin—that was matins, I believe." Standing, Rex moved languidly toward the inner doors. "I will call you, Garth, when we need to speak further. Good evening to you."

The balance of the party had risen when Rex did—now Malini and Silas followed him into the depths of Dielaan House. Remembering his previous irritation, Garth considered ignoring Lucy, then discarded the idea. Why her little game of spy and counterspy should bother him, he didn't know. When the relationship had appeared to be based simply on pleasure, it had felt . . . more equal?

Apparently little had changed on her side; Lucy seized his shirt sleeve and led him back through the smoky maze. Once they reached the antechamber below, she turned to face him. "I did not actually pursue you because Rex needed a free-trader," she began without preamble.

"But it *was* convenient, wasn't it?" Garth suggested easily.

"Well . . . yes." Her voice lowered slightly. "It is so important to us, Garth! And we have had months of waiting, of *nothing* to base our decisions upon . . . we could not risk contacting any criminal element, you see. We needed people who work independently of all that—"

"The net is always intertwined," Garth pointed out. An old memory popped out of some obscure synapse, surprising him. "I thought Nualans don't lie."

"Not to each other," she agreed. "We are very sensitive to nuance. You must remember a lie, you see, and that can become complicated—"

"You searched my bag, didn't you? Even checked my laundry labels, eh?" When she did not speak, he went on: "And reported our outings down to the last crumb on the table. Did you tell him preferred sexual positions, too?" Garth tried to keep heat from his words, but he could hear an edge to them.

"Now you are being silly," she said firmly. "Of course I did not. When I suspected you might be useful, I introduced you to Rex. When he decided I was correct, he asked me to . . . investigate certain things. Would you offer such a job to someone you were unsure of?"

Now it was Garth's turn to be silent.

"I like you, Garth," Lucy said seriously, her intense, black eyes meeting his hooded ones. "I am glad you will be helping us. And we will help you, will we not? Surely it is easier to do this type of thing with friends."

But you are not free-traders. You do not know the code, the rules . . . we are not being paid in the same coin, are we? Usually monetary gain stood at the end of a free-trader scam, but this was an elusive reward. *I guess we each want justice, and are seeking it in the best way open to us. But I think I will study Dielaan a bit more, just to be sure.* After all—the mark of a good politician was often the ability to lie convincingly. And if he was nothing else, Garth suspected Rex of being a good politician. And Lucy?

Ah, well. He was warned.

isolate: 1) To set apart from others: to place alone.
2) To separate or keep apart from others by some
sort of intervention (barrier, space, or verbal
demarcation) so as to minimize any effect on/
interaction with others. SYN *segregate*, although this
word often implies isolation for a specific, perceived
reason—economic class, religion, species, culture,
political affiliations. Compare *QUARANTINE*, where
isolation is imposed to prevent the spread of disease.

CHAPTER SEVEN

AMURA-BY-THE-SEA
ONEHUNDRED NINETYONEDAY   MATINS
ATARE WINTER PALACE

It was very late; only two waxing moons were visible in the
cloudy western sky. In the hills beyond Amura, Darame could
hear the echo of a bell. Only one toll . . . matins. Sighing, she
considered retiring. How long had she been waiting in the whirlpool bath for Sheel, anyway?

"The ox of Sainted Luke was faster than the wits of The
Synod," she muttered to herself. It had to be Synod business.
Anything else required Avis, and The Ragäree had no strength
for late nights without need. *Ah, well, Sheel's mother warned
me about days like this.*

The previous ragäree had been a soft-spoken woman of in-
cising intelligence—sharp as a faceted diamond, but never cruel.

While Darame's memories of her own mother were nebulous, Riva stood fast as the older confidant Darame could never have imagined finding. A pity they had had so little time to know one another—Riva had lived scarcely five years after the murder of her sons and brother Cort.

He is a healer, Darame, and healers must be healing—or protecting. Always trying to shelter what they loved, even to the point of suffocation. Riva had warned her . . . had still been living the one time a rousing fight had brought distance, not reconciliation . . . the one time Darame had considered leaving Nuala.

"But you talked me into visiting other points on Nuala, instead. And you were right . . . I finally saw why he tried to wrap me in batting, and he finally stopped trying to do it." The whisper echoed in the tile roof above the whirlpool. Lifting a hand, Darame peered at her fingers. Wrinkled, ugh—time to pull herself out. But the heat felt so good, the soothing murmur of the water a song in the back of her consciousness.

Ripples in counterpoint, changing the tune. . . . A strong, slender arm of tactile muscle curved around the small of her back. "You would think that nothing could be discussed unless Atare was present," came a grumble.

Smiling faintly, Darame replied: "Nothing has been happening here without Atare."

Response came quickly, she found herself simultaneously raised a good ten centimeters off the ledge and defending her breast from a sleek, persistent damp head.

"You are not supposed to swim in this thing—Sheel, that tickles!" Darame shrieked, knowing her laughter weakened her argument. In truth, his attentions were quickly waking up every nerve in her body. *Do not protest too much, woman, he may discover he is tired—*

Suddenly the room moved—there was no other way to describe it. Vibration continued, twisting Darame's stomach and toying with her sense of balance. Colored glass crystals hung against the picture windows chimed sweetly. Somewhere nearby she heard the sound of breaking glass.

Silence.

"Quake?" Sheel murmured. It was definitely a question.

"No," Darame heard herself say. Seeing the glint in her

husband's eyes as he glanced upward, she added: "No pre-shocks." Only then did she realize how tightly they were clinging to each other.

Gently releasing her, Sheel moved to climb out of the whirl-pool. He did not question her certainty; Darame had never become accustomed to the coast's tendency to shake, and always felt the minor tremors that warned that a large quake was on the way. Fortunately the Nualans built with fault movement in mind, and damage was usually minimal.

Still. . . . "Daniel?" she said aloud.

"I have just established contact with the nursery, Serae," the *guaard* responded from the darkness beyond. "All three of your children are fine."

"Thank you." *Now they are mind readers.* Reaching for her towel, Darame stepped lightly up the stone stairs and wrapped herself in thick, woven, looped cotton. Glancing over to the wall, she saw that Sheel had already used a remote to activate the omni. The screen flickered once as Sheel changed channels . . . and again. A third station was broadcasting a news bulletin.

"—and the cause of the explosion is unknown at this time. The area effected by the blast includes the warehouses for Coastal Grains, Incorporated, Fleetwood Enterprises, and Odyssey Unlimited."

"Daniel, will you contact Mailan and the seneschal?" Sheel requested mildly. Without haste, The Atare glided over to a robe tossed carelessly over the low back of a chair. Slipping on the garment, Sheel took his time tying the sash, his gaze becoming slightly unfocused as the station returned to its regular programming.

Reaching her velour, Darame dropped her towel and pulled its warmth around her. *Sweet Virgin, the warehouse district. A silo flare or a fuel blast?* "Are we still patrolling the warehouse district?" she asked quietly.

"Just Odyssey Unlimited and its competitors," Sheel responded.

"Would not . . . if Odyssey or New Age . . . lost control of their stock, the result—" She stopped, not sure how to ask the question.

"Actually, many things cause more energy release than antimatter," was the dry answer. "The question is, in case of a silo explosion or a gas line rupture, would the antimatter traps hold. I do not know."

Nodding slightly, Darame said aloud: "I think I will check on the children." No point in waiting around . . . until Mailan arrived, nothing was going to happen.

"I imagine they will be full of questions," was all Sheel replied.

"Theories, in Ardal's case."

Sheel smiled.

CUCKOO'S EGG   LAUDS

Pale omni light illuminated the tiny room, casting sharp, hulking shadows and bleaching familiar objects of definition. An announcer was speaking; he was saying nothing new, so Garth ignored him. Furious thought whirled through Garth's brain, but single images eluded him. What possibly could have gone wrong? The plan had been flawless—flawless! Most importantly, had anyone been hurt in the explosion?

By Sebastian's Arrows, at least I had the mother wit to change hostels, was his first coherent thought. Not that he feared being traced. Although he had compiled the instructions in Caesarean, he had made the four copies immediately, then erased the screen. Nothing had ever entered memory. Each of his three copies was stashed with a different persona, and each persona was in a very separate place. Two of them existed only as transaction accounts and rental boxes, but he could reach them if he needed to . . . all of his names responded to his own thumb print. It was a thin veil of protection, but so long as neither of those "people" did anything out of the ordinary, no one would notice the triple identity.

What if there *hadn't* been any portable traps at the storage facility? But merchants always used their own traps—it was the control unit that was special. Privately coded, the power boxes were brought from each ship when antimatter retrieval was necessary. Rex had insisted he could find a ship willing to part with a box. A defective box? Or was the explosion unrelated to their "little project," as Silas had taken to calling it? A grain silo blast, maybe?

He wanted to call Lucy . . . desperately wanted to call her.

Clenching his fingers, Garth controlled the impulse. Part of the reason he had moved was so that no one would know where he was staying. If he was going to call Lucy, he had to leave this place to do it.

I can't stand it. Climbing out of the soft bed, Garth quickly pulled on his clothes. Food was needed, as were answers. He'd return to the restaurant he and Lucy considered their own, then call her from there.

A pause to booby trap his room, then Garth was on his way. His system was simple—a temporary shelf was angled near the door, various rings and items of clothing piled upon it. If the door was opened by someone ignorant of the trap, the shelf moved, scattering his already-strewn possessions about the floor. It was the easiest way Garth had found to determine if someone had entered his room . . . and after moving to Cuckoo's Egg, its construction had seemed prudent.

His usual route, past the recycling plant, was barricaded. Standing on a shuttle bench, Garth could see down the cobbled street, beyond working street lamps into predawn light. In the drizzle that was falling, he could see nothing but dampened dust and fractured shadows. *How big an area?* Garth considered entering into the whispered speculation surrounding him—decided against it—and stepped down into the pulsing mass of third shift workers dawdling on their way home.

Limpin' Lobster already had a few regulars at their tables. They were methodically putting away vast amounts of breakfast, their attention mostly given to a screen switched to omni and showing a special report on the explosion. Garth sat at his regular table, angled slightly toward the omni but not looking directly at it. Interested, but not overly so. . . . He spent a long time looking at the menu.

"Where have you been?" The question was both indignant and tremulous.

Garth controlled his body admirably, he thought: no flinching, no facial expression. "Have a seat," he told the quivering redhead bundled before him in her reddish fur and a rain slicker.

Dropping onto the bench across from him, Lucy gave him a black look. "I could not find you, where did you move?"

"A different place, obviously. I'd been in one hostel too long," he added, trying to forestall more questions on that tack.

"We need to talk, but not here. Are you hungry?" *That came out rather well, actually.* . . .

Glowering at him, she ordered a basket of breads and a local tea from the native menu. Pointedly she tapped in her own code. Garth was not sure if it was habit, or if she was snubbing him. He did not ask.

Savoring a tall, frosted glass of juice, Garth kept his eyes on the omni. A preliminary sweep had been made for those people known to be working in those blocks. All but one had been accounted for; so far most of the injuries had come from flying glass some distance from the center of the blast.

"Interesting, isn't it?" Garth said softly, catching Lucy's reflection in the tabletop. "There are grain silos in that area. Dust is always a problem with silos."

Her jaw grew hard, jutting, but Lucy did not answer. They finished their meal in silence.

Filling disposable cups with hot tea, they made their way outside to the boardwalk benches. Prime was ringing even as Garth noted dull light growing in the east. Another day, and who knew what it would bring. One person still missing . . . what if that person was dead. . . .

"You should have told us you were moving," Lucy started huskily. "We were worried."

Garth was surprised. She *did* sound worried . . . why? "I have been taking care of myself for a long time," he replied, studying her face carefully.

"I know that, fool," she snapped, turning her head away. "But there are many things about this place that you do not understand."

"Such as?"

"What if you accidentally ate something native?" At his silence she continued: "If you had moved, then fallen ill, you might have died before anyone found you. And you make Rex nervous when you do that—he thinks you do not trust him."

I don't. "In a free-trader scam, everyone handles an assigned part, and doesn't worry about what people do in their spare time," Garth told her.

Lucy gave him a long look. "Do not play games with Rex Dielaan, Garth Kristinsson," she murmured. "He has been waiting for this for a long time. Rex has little patience and even less compassion. Do not give him reason to regret inviting you into his circle.''

"You're afraid of him, aren't you?" Garth said impulsively.

"I am wary in his presence. It is not quite the same thing. I, too, have little patience.'' Stretching suddenly, Lucy set her cup down between them. "If the price becomes too high, there is always The Brethren."

Garth worked his way through her maze of words. "Emigrate?"

Her glance was amused. "It happens, you know."

"But—"

"Oh, I would need to hide my planet of origin, but I have wealth Rex cannot touch. I could live very comfortably on Caesarea. However, one does not lightly contemplate exile . . . I love my family and my tribe."

Before she could continue, Garth said abruptly: "What happened last night?"

"It was as you said. The distractions went well; the watchman moved well beyond our target—and was locked in the last building—and the security monitors were shorted out before they could register the unexpected guests. Stennis punched in that request you created, and cycled it. It should implicate the *guaard* in this, by his neglecting to allow entry to a technician during a code yellow situation."

"So the data banks accepted the phony code yellow?" That had been the excuse for their entry, that something had gone wrong with an antimatter trap that required immediate attention.

"Yes, but they could not pipe it to the console, so the *guaard* did not know about it." Her nebulous words bothered Garth— "they" was too indefinite for him—but he did not interrupt. "Once in, they found a portable trap, just as you said. The control box worked fine, once they found a few wires long enough to stretch."

"The blast was not related?" Garth kept a sharp eye on the curve of Lucy's cheek. Her features did not change, but he felt tension in the air.

"It . . . was related," she whispered.

"Damn it, Lucy, what happened?"

"I . . . do not exactly understand it, Garth, but I know they did it on purpose. New Age Wares was down to medical levels on their antimatter, so that is mostly why they went to Odyssey. They took what was in the main trap, but . . . there was an active auxiliary trap on the upper level.''

Garth's eyes widened. ''An electrical field trap? Hell's Bells, I thought those things went out of use years ago. Active levitation traps can be dangerous.''

''Stennis says they are quite safe,'' Lucy replied stiffly, ''as long as the mechanism controlling the ice ball of antihydrogen is working well. This one had a back-up unit, in case of power failures. At any rate, it was holding little antimatter. Their medical stock for the lasers, I think. But it was above ground, like their main storage unit. Apparently. . . .'' She rearranged herself, her gaze drifting out toward the sea. ''Apparently Rex did not think that having the antimatter disappear into thin air was incriminating enough.''

''They purposely cut the power to an electrical field trap?'' Garth whispered. ''Do you know what happens when you do that?''

''Boom?'' she suggested weakly.

''Not exactly. First the antihydrogen ice ball hits one of the two electrically charged plates like a balled fist. Then 'poof,' not 'boom'. 'Boom' is as in disintegration, while 'poof' is as in annihilation. I can't believe they did it on purpose! Do they know anything about explosions at all? What are they trying to do, make us look erratic?''

''What do you mean?'' She was genuinely puzzled.

Silently asking unknown deities for patience, Garth said: ''The plan was flawless, Lucy. We could have gotten away with almost all the antimatter. No ships were going anywhere until we gave them permission to—and we left enough for medical emergencies! Strictly a power play, a sneer at the people guarding the thing, a . . . a 'we can run rings around you, and you have no idea who we are or why we're doing this' sort of thing. Now, we have marred a perfect theft by a clumsy detonation. We have destroyed what little antimatter was left for pending surgeries, and—'' His voice dropped to a hiss. ''We may have killed someone!''

''If things went 'poof' I fail to see what was clumsy about the maneuver,'' Lucy responded stiffly.

''Girl, have you never heard of explosives experts? They can tell what kind of explosion took place, they can usually pinpoint the detonators used—they can even tell you how much of the explosive material was used!''

That shocked her. ''But if antimatter annihilates everything—''

''Yes. But they know how much antimatter was stored in those two facilities. So they know how large an area would have been destroyed. It would have been so fast nothing else could have competed with it—gas lines, silo dust, nothing. So when they realize it was an antimatter explosion, they'll calculate it out . . . and discover that the entire warehouse is not accounted for. We've lost our edge of mystery.'' Garth fell silent a moment, then added: ''*And* a man has probably died.''

''No one was meant to die,'' she whispered petulantly.

''Does that matter, within Dielaan law? Within Atare law? Who governs Amura-By-The-Sea?''

''Ancient ship law of the original transports,'' Lucy finally answered. ''There is a difference between intentional and unintentional killings. But . . . can we prove it was not meant?'' This last was whispered.

Garth did not like that question at all. ''They locked the watchman out, at the far end of the warehouses. He was outside the blast radius.''

''Yes. But . . . a *guaard*. That is Atare business. Garth, I do not know if Silas would have bothered to make sure an Atare was clear of the site!'' She sounded genuinely upset.

Silence stretched between them. Finally: ''I don't understand. Either life has value, or it doesn't. Who cares what tribe someone belongs to?''

''It is not like that!'' Lucy responded quickly. ''But . . . if they were in a hurry, they may have forgotten about the *guaard*. I . . . do not think they would stop the time switch, not after setting up the explosion. *Guaard* are like soldiers, not like the regular populace.''

''*Guaard* are sentient life forms. The law is that anyone who willfully terminates a sentient life will be terminated in turn, after required genetic samples are taken.'' Garth's voice was harsh.

''Yes . . . they always want to figure out what went wrong,'' Lucy murmured in reply. She was still studying the turbulent horizon.

"Lucy, you lovely little scatterbrain, as far as I can make out from the net, Atare and Dielaan aren't at war. However—the premeditated death of a citizen is more than enough to start hostilities." Reaching suddenly, Garth grabbed her arm and pulled her to face him. "Rex didn't plan on killing that *guaard*, did he? It *was* an accident?"

Flushing, Lucy said evenly: "My cousin is not a murderer. Neither be my brother!" The last was almost spat in his face, the structure of the sentence a bit odd.

"Lucy, don't you understand? You and your family can run to Dielaan, can be protected there. If a *guaard* is dead, I could be terminated for it!"

"You were not present." This was adamant.

"But I planned the theft."

"They changed the plan."

"If The Synod needs someone to blame, will that stop them? If they can't reach any of the other people responsible?" Garth shook her slightly, forcing her gaze to meet his own.

"If Rex Dielaan controlled The Synod, perhaps," she whispered. "But Atare has the strongest voice, and Atare does not place himself higher than his own laws. It is that simple." Taking a deep breath, Lucy added: "If necessary, *I* will protect you."

"You?" From her thin smile, Garth guessed that his tone was tactless.

"I am not the future ragäree, but I am not without influence."

This was said with more dignity than Garth would have thought possible, under the circumstances. Realizing his grip might be a bit tight, he released her arm. "You made your conditions plain when you joined us, Garth. I will remember that." The expression in her dark eyes was odd as she added: "At the end of all things, we desire peace."

"And Rex's vendetta with Atare?"

Lucy shrugged. "Say preoccupation—it could change tomorrow. We are still human, Garth. We desire security, wealth, power—our own place in the sun. Yet if you stop any Nualan on a street corner, I think you would find that he would put peace and harmony before almost anything."

"Before freedom?"

Lucy tilted her head slightly as she studied him. "How can one be at peace if one is not free?"

It needed a month's answer, or none. Turning his eyes toward the sea, Garth leaned back into the bench once again. Gray mist was beginning to obscure the horizon . . . a storm was coming in. *Foul weather ahead.* . . . His grandfather's words, carried by Kristin Arnason to another world. Only Garth's father had never used them to comment on an incoming squall. Funny how long it had been since he'd thought of that phrase. . . . *Mother, Father . . . You left me too soon. No one can jump into this business without training. Have I done the right thing? If not . . . can I ride out the tempest?*

ATARE WINTER PALACE   TIERCE

Color blurred before his eyes; Sheel blinked suddenly, and the bright splashes solidified into the majority of his clerical entourage. Sweet Mendülay, he hated things like this; crisis always pointed up that there were all too few Atares left to act as intermediaries between the public and the throne. Even now, his shy brother-in-law, Richard, was verbally fencing with the press, giving them the statement agreed upon by Avis, seneschal Zaide, and himself. Avis's husband Stephen was where he could be most useful—slapping the embassies into line and pumping them for information.

Unfortunately, the off-world representatives seemed as shocked as everyone else. Stephen had just called in, and the verdict was not good; his contacts knew nothing, and were full of questions. That meant that the next step was closer to home . . . the clan embassies. Either Darame or one of the throneline would need to attend to them.

Sheel flicked a glance past faithful Elek, who was busy serving tea and saffra to all who had requested it (and a few who had not). Near the window was another communications station, a screen equipped with everything from omni and vid to RAM/ROM features. Oblivious to the crowd, Zaide was simultaneously tapping something into a side console even as he read the reports appearing on the main screen. Since his lips were moving, Sheel guessed that he was on a call box, speaking to someone without benefit of a vid picture. Praise Mendülay for Zaide's calm efficiency.

Across the room, a door slid open. Darame had finally dressed; she was a slash of negative space in a simple, close-fitting costume of black syluan pants and shirt. Gliding into the room, the *guaard* who was her shadow three steps behind her, Darame went immediately to where Avis was seated.

A few private words, a muffin on a tray seized in passing— Darame moved in his direction. Sitting down next to him, Darame pulled one leg up onto the couch, rearranging herself so that she was facing him.

"Leah is fretting. I think she could use distraction. Do you have anyone she could make a statement to, or fence words with?"

The look Sheel returned to her was hooded. Of all the things he did not need right now. . . . "Does she need me as a sedative?" he asked obliquely, knowing that Leah refused to take any medication during pregnancy. Hot healers, fortunately, could soothe nerves and muscles as well as any drug.

"No, I do not think so. It is not that kind of thing." This was studied; what did Darame know?

"She is on vacation." His words prompted a steady gaze. "I know it is hard to sit during a crisis . . . Avis and I are doing little more than that." He was about to mention the embassies, then paused. Although a clan leader could summon an off-worlder to his presence, relations among the tribes themselves were more nebulous. If Darame was going to deal with high officials without every spy in the city knowing it, she would have to go to them personally. Which let out Leah serving in the same capacity—Sheel did not want her that far from the family compound, not so close to her delivery date.

"She is in the morning room," Darame said easily, turning her body so she could view a nearby omni broadcast. "I believe she wants to talk to you about Tamara." There was emphasis in the name.

Surely her children could wait until— Sheel felt hot, then chilled. Finally we will talk about Tamara . . . about Tamara's father.

Standing, Sheel touched his wife's shoulder lightly in passing and moved over to Zaide. "I suspect an emergency meeting of The Synod will be necessary. Could you see to it, please? I will be in the morning room for a time." Turning back to Darame, he added: "Perhaps you and Avis can decide how we will brief the clan ambassadors?"

"Without reminding them that the Amuran police will inform you first, as a matter of tradition?" Darame added with a smile. "Consider it done."

Nodding once, the dimple he reserved for her pulling at his face, Sheel left the room quickly, *guaard* Zara and Leo at his heels.

The doors to the salon were totally silent; Leah did not hear Sheel enter. She had her back to the entrance, her thick, dark hair, a sleek blanket tracing her spine, obscuring her swollen state. Pale, icy green, her favorite color, peeped out through the long strands reaching nearly to her knees. Reflection from the windows gave her face a ghostly expression.

How many years have I waited for this conversation? Sheel thought. Following the upheaval of more than a decade ago, Leah had retired into extensive counseling. At the same time, Sheel had tinkered with her reproductive system. Hot healing was far from a miracle cure, but it was very successful with certain types of illness and injury—radiation-induced problems, especially. Thanks to his own efforts, Leah had bore four children in the last nine years; a fifth child was expected momentarily. *Ironically fertile, since she has taken herself out of the succession.* How grateful he had been, when she had announced it, not long after she conceived the twins. Sparing him removing her . . . having to somehow explain his actions without admitting that his sister had once tripped over the edge of sanity and plotted the deaths of her siblings.

Now, we get to Tamara. Ailat was visibly her father's daughter, but Tamara favored Leah . . . and Sheel knew that Leah had gone to the labs after her release from the convalescence hospice. *You wanted Dirk's daughter. Did you want her badly enough to create her after watching him murder half your family?* Sheel moved to touch her shoulder.

Startled, Leah whipped her head around, a smile touching her lips. "I did not hear you." Glancing past him, she reassured herself that he was alone, but for his *guaard*. "It is starting up again," she said simply.

Sheel studied her face. "You are suggesting. . . ." he began.

"Someone who hates us has targeted our house," she replied, folding her arms across the top of her stomach. "It was mostly hate which spurred on Brant—hatred of anyone who had more possessions, more power than he did.'' Her words were relaxed, easy, as if the memories of a faithless lover were no more than echoes in her mind. ''At least Dirk did what he did mostly for love . . . or what he called love.'' Leah's face lost its sharp focus for a moment, as if she saw something Sheel could not.

Not quite sure how to proceed, Sheel said: ''You have loved three times in your life, and only once was it a mistake. Be comforted in that . . . I found my judgment faulty twice.'' Rarely did he refer to the two women he had courted on Emerson, but Leah seemed to need some support. At times like this, it was not hard to remember that the neurotic woman caught up in treason had long ago integrated into health.

''Yes, the first two times I was fortunate,'' she admitted, her expression returning to the moment. ''More than I knew, that Richard could be so generous after it was all over.'' Sighing lightly, she glanced at Sheel. ''You must let me help, brother.''

How to answer this? As a family court judge, Leah had proved highly successful. Sheel no longer feared her conspiring against the throne, but still. . . . ''I am not sure there is anything you can do, Leah,'' he began slowly. ''Stephen is dealing with the off-world embassies, and Stephanie and Ting are representing us at the accident site.''

''Surely you do not think it was an accident?'' This was almost amused.

Privately, Sheel doubted it was an accident, but appearances had to be kept up. ''We do not know yet what caused the blast,'' was all he said. ''Richard is dealing with the press—''

''Poor darling,'' she murmured, smiling. ''But he is the best of us to do it, when so little is known. What of The Synod and the clans?''

Ouch. ''I was thinking of sending Darame to the clans,'' he admitted. ''I do not want either you or Avis away from the compound right now, and the clans require a personal touch.''

''Unless we want the entire planet to know what is going on,'' Leah agreed. ''You would let Avis face The Synod?''

''Of course not. Someone must remain poised to respond to any new information. I suspect Avis would prefer to be well away from the hysterics The Synod promises to share with us.''

''The presence of a pregnant woman might help things,'' Leah suggested.

Two voices immediately answered in Sheel's mind—one screamed "No!" even as the other murmured: "Possibly." Suddenly torn, Sheel did not immediately speak.

Leah was not facing him as she continued. "Let me help with this, Sheel. If you only understood how much I need to help."

The whisper suggested genuine emotion. How could he decide? "Leah . . . Darame said you wanted to talk about Tamara."

"Yes." She did not look toward him. "I found out from Dr. Bartholomew that you had Dirk's deposit altered. 'To reduce aggression and introspection,' I believe were her words. I found out eightday ago, actually." Just as Sheel thought he would have to speak, Leah added: "It was unnecessary. You see, Dr. Bartholomew told me about something else, when I went to her after my release. Tamara is Donal's daughter."

Donal? Who was—Sheel realized he was staring at his sister, and looked back out the window. Now he remembered the name . . . he had never known the man. Donal had been Leah's first husband, who had died in an accident scant years after they had returned to Nuala. Sheel had left on his own trip off-world before Donal's arrival in Atare—Leah had traveled the Caesarea route almost twice before the Emerson group had returned. *Mother said Richard and Donal were as different as night and day. Yet Leah found something she needed in each of them. Forgive me, Richard, for thinking she wanted you only because she could manipulate you.*

"How?" Sheel asked aloud.

Leah smiled faintly. "Because Donal was such a gentleman, and so protective of me. Of course women started chasing him the moment he arrived on-planet. And he ignored them. But our own attitudes finally affected him . . . he felt guilty denying potentially healthy children to Nualans. So he made several 'deposits' in the gene banks, and cleared his conscience." Now she turned her head toward her brother. "Ironic, is it not? I might never have left to find Richard . . . might never have damaged myself with my sexual wanderings . . . if only I had known about that sperm." Her smile was softer now. "She is the image of Donal . . . of the daughter we lost. I understand there is enough left for another attempt. If I can conceive after this one, I would like to try once more. In his memory."

Sheel remained silent, feeling very foolish. *Ah, Leah, it took*

you so many years to mature, but finally, you are my older sister.
Here he had been worrying that she was building some new
empire, when in fact she had been building a family—which
was what she had wanted all along.

Her brown eye studied him. "Could I regain my balance and
not know my responsibilities to my people? And possibly bringing another Dirk into the world . . . Avis is a better ragäree than
I would have been." Leah looked tired momentarily. Then she
drew herself up, straightening her shoulders. "Now, brother—
shall we see when The Synod shall meet?"

Extending his arm to her, Sheel said gravely: "No doubt Zaide
has already made arrangements."

His words proved to be an understatement. They had scarcely
reached the corridor when Zaide came rushing toward them.

"Zaide?" Sheel said, the name sounding uncertain. It was as
close to alarmed as Sheel had ever seen his seneschal.

"My Atare, you are needed immediately in The Synod cham-
ber. It seems that synod representatives have been arriving for
the past hour." Now that he had found them, Zaide seemed more
controlled.

"Please inform the ragäree that Leah and I will attend to The
Synod. Has The Atarae left for the clan embassies?"

"I believe that was her intent," Zaide said vaguely, falling
into step with the couple. "We are waiting for Seri Ting's
report—" He broke off suddenly, his head lifting and turning
toward the east wall. Dimly they could hear the sound of a great
bell.

"Surely it is not sext already," Leah began, then paled
slightly.

"It is confirmed, then," Sheel whispered, as the three-minute
peal for a *guaard* killed in the line of duty began to ring.

"Serae, do you feel up to a synod meeting?" Zaide asked
after a few silent moments. "I can escort you—"

"I am well, Zaide, thank you," she replied, touching his
shoulder gently. "Perhaps you could order some mid-morning
refreshment for The Synod? Not . . . no hot fluids," she added,
giving Sheel a quick glance.

You are thinking faster than I am, Leah. It had been years
since a clansman had thrown hot tea in a rival's face, but why
chance it? "The meth car is waiting?"

"At the front."

THE SYNOD   TIERCE

Three *guaard* were waiting for them at the outer doors of The Synod. Sheel briefly considered protesting the visible increase in their number, but something in Crow's dark gaze held him silent. Atare had lost too much, that night Cort Atare and his heirs died. . . .

Although they were still half a dozen strides from the inner doors, Sheel could already hear the gathering. Sweet Mendülay, what was he going to say to calm this bunch? At the end of things, the antimatter was gone—how and why was another matter entirely. If his informants were correct, this meant that no ships would leave Nualan space until almost Midsummer's. And the price of the next shipment! It made him cringe to think about it.

Sound hit them in a wave, as shocking as seawater. At least three people were shouting at each other, and Nadine of Kilgore had actually backed Alasdair of Wallace into a corner. Feeling one eyebrow raise slightly, Sheel escorted Leah to the chair at the right of his own.

Their entrance had not gone unnoticed; stillness rippled out into the current of noise, pushing aside threats and questions alike. "Shall we come to order?" Sheel suggested easily, nodding slightly at the newest ambassador of Dielaan. The older man nodded back; his expression could only be called cold. Surprisingly, Rex Dielaan was also present.

"Welcome, Serae," Alasdair of Wallace said politely to Leah, his usual smile for her on his face. "To what do we owe this honor?"

Even through manners, Alasdair was no fool.

"I thought you might need a referee this morning," she told him simply, reaching to touch his arm in a reassuring manner. "I have requested a brunch for the group," she went right on, a slight smile acknowledging the few chuckles she received. "No doubt many of us were up very early."

"I am afraid that tea and muffins will not erase the events of last night," Rex Dielaan said acidly.

"But they will make the discussion of it more comfortable." She tilted her head toward Sheel as she spoke, waiting for his cue.

"I know I have had no breakfast," Sheel admitted. "I would

like to call to order this emergency meeting of The Synod. Please enter your codes now.'' He brought up the Amuran infonet as he spoke, quickly scanning the news for any change in the status of the warehouse district. Dare he use a net receiver today? Yes; something might come through on audio. ''Let us reiterate the information we already have on our current crisis, so that each member of The Synod has the same knowledge.''

''Nothing,'' Alasdair growled at him. ''We know nothing.''

''A bit more than nothing, Alasdair,'' Sheel suggested, tapping in a query to Avis. ''Even now the area taken out by the explosion is being measured, and all computer monitoring up to the blast evaluated. Once we know what was stored at Odyssey and New Age, we will be able to determine what we have lost.''

''Some things we have eliminated quickly,'' Leah went on, her eyes meeting the senior Dielaan ambassador's. ''For example, it was not a gas line explosion—the line to that district had been closed for repairs.''

Amused, Sheel kept his eyes lowered. Leah had just read that information off the infonet.

''So, was it silo? Sabotage? Carelessness?'' Rex's smooth voice slid across the table toward them. ''I understand that such a sensitive area is heavily monitored. What of the code banks?''

As The Dielaan spoke, the dark, polished doors slid open to reveal Quen reh Livia Dielaan. He was a bit pale, but dressed with his usual elegance. Without comment he walked to his seat, at his brother's left hand. Immediately he tapped something into his membrane—it caught the attention of his party. A visible smile briefly touched Rex Dielaan's lips . . . then it vanished.

''Tell me something else, Atare. Do you have anything on the last report your *guaard* filed? Does he explain why he refused entrance to several technicians who responded to a code yellow?'' Rex somehow kept the triumph from his tone.

''Your source, Quen?'' Sheel asked quietly.

Rex flushed at being cut from the conversation, but Quen answered readily enough. ''I checked in with the Odyssey group this morning. They are in the process of breaking into their drums, but the narrative messages from the monitors indicate that a trap began to deviate from norm sometime during matins. Shortly afterward a technician request was denied. That was almost the last reading before the monitors shorted out.''

''And all information stopped?''

"All audio and visual information. The climate control monitors were still working."

Sheel was entering it all. "So the monitors stopped before the explosion. Does Odyssey have any reason to believe that one of their technicians overran the request system and entered the building?"

That apparently had not occurred to Quen. "No, they did not mention it. As I said, they have yet to breach the drums."

"I trust they have called in the Amuran police, and are providing copies of internal and external code," Sheel stated for the record.

"Right now I have no care as to how careless the watchdogs were," the representative from Boone interrupted testily. "What I wish to know is how long will our joint venture be delayed by this mess?"

"Unless the captain had already retrieved his antimatter, our venture will be delayed until the next shipment arrives," Nadine said succinctly.

"This was the reason the *guaard* was reinforcing the watch system!" It was Valdez who had erupted. "I thought your people were competent!"

"Only so much can be done against either accident or sabotage, Valdez," Sheel said mildly, hoping the caterer would interrupt.

"Denying a technician's request for entry in the face of a code yellow strikes me as poor protection!"

"Would the *guaard* have known about the code?" Alasdair mused aloud.

"It should have gone to his console," Sheel said slowly, reviewing a passage on the watch procedure at Odyssey. "But the fact that part of the monitoring system shut down without explanation may mean he never received the message." The thought faded off as a new message came over the line. Someone at either Odyssey or the police had leaked information—the infonet now knew about the code yellow.

The murmur had increased—no doubt others were reading or hearing the same words. Wonderful.

"Tell us, Atare—the *guaard* is not 'protecting' anything else of value to The Synod, is it?" the senior representative from Andersen asked gently.

Yang sniffed contemptuously, even as Valdez leaped to his feet.

It promised to be a long meeting.

BOARDWALK   SEXT

Light rains had come and gone, leeching the stone dust from the air. Garth did not know how many hours he had sat beneath the Lobster's awning . . . it was too much trouble to glance at his roman for the time. Most of the morning had simply slipped away; Lucy had left soon after their talk. Her final words were meant to be consoling, but they had begun to echo ominously in Garth's ears.

We are immune from prosecution. It is an old privilege of the aristocracy; we may be questioned to our faces, but only the old way . . . no drugs, no wires. Lucy had spoken to reassure, her words careless and without conceit, but Garth's thoughts had woven into a double meaning.

I have my ring—proof of the original plan No one was to die! "You'd think I was Nualan, the way I carry on," he murmured aloud. But a *guaard* was dead, and the stillness of the city indicated all too well how seriously the Amurans took the death. A hundred years looking for one woman. . . . *I have scarcely begun to live. You may have deprived my parents of their lives, but you won't get mine. Caution, caution . . .*

No way to prove I was involved, but no way to prove who *was* involved. No names except Rex, Lucy, Silas, and Malini . . . all immune from prosecution. The technicians, the data bank operators? Unknown, every one.

They can wire me to tell I speak the truth. At the last, he had that. It might be his word against Dielaan, but he'd go down fighting, if need be. Still, he did not think Lucy would betray him in such a way—

"You are still here." She had crept up quietly.

"Where is there to go?" Garth asked in turn.

"You should come with me," Lucy told him, extending her hand.

"Where were you?"

"I went to see *it*, and to talk to Rex. He is in Synod now. I think he is pleased; the code yellow was clearly marked."

Taking her hand, Garth pulled her down to the bench. "It won't help, Lucy—not now. When they figure out that some antimatter was stolen, they'll dig into the code. I couldn't manufacture the code in its entirety; they'll realize it's fake. Then they'll start looking for people with access codes to that building. There's a death, several injuries, and a warehouse of antimatter to explain."

"You worry too much. Why should they question you?" Her head was tilted in a most appealing manner.

"I'm an outsider. Off-worlders are usually among the first to be questioned. As soon as they decide it wasn't an accident, they'll start hauling us in and asking where we were—" *You idiot. You total fool. You have no witnesses to where you actually were last night.*

"You were not there. The tests will show that. They will probe no deeper." Her eyes were shadowed, as if she had not slept well. Had any of them? "Do not waste energy worrying; Rex protects his own."

"But I'm not really one of his, Lucy."

"Nonsense! Rex has taken you under his wing. It was not oath, true, but it was similar. Trust him and be loyal, and you will receive the like in kind." Suddenly blazing, Lucy pinched his hand for emphasis.

"You cannot see it, can you?" At her stare, Garth went on: "You said it yourself, Lucy—Silas wouldn't bother to see if an Atare was clear of the site. Rex wouldn't think of a *guaard* as anything except an enemy soldier. *I* am not Dielaan, Lucy. I'm not saying Rex is planning on tossing me off. I'm just being practical. If he has to choose between giving me to the authorities, or giving up an old family retainer, who do you think will be the offering? Don't even consider that it might be family."

"You might be surprised," she replied softly.

Time to change the subject—this quibbling was solving nothing. "Let's run away somewhere. How about buying lake property on Caesarea?" Garth wanted to tease her, but to his surprise she looked disconcerted. "Okay, so we fight it out. Surely we can knock Rex into line. Too bad the last Dielaan died so young; he seemed like an intelligent man."

"He was a good man," she whispered almost inaudibly.

The mood had changed . . . Lucy seemed to echo the dark sky above. "Something to eat?" Garth finally suggested. "We need to keep up our strength. Who knows when we might end up as fugitives?''

It was a tentative smile that answered his, but Lucy indicated with a nod that she was willing to eat. ''Here?''

''Unless you want something else.''

Shaking her head, Lucy wrapped her long, manicured fingers around his wrist and drew him to his feet.

It was a lazy meal, encompassing several hours. The omni was still on; one station continued to monitor the investigation at the warehouse district. Lucy pointedly kept her back to the set, but Garth occasionally gave it his attention. Somehow it didn't seem wise to appear blasé about the incident.

''Will you come back with me?'' Lucy asked just before they left.

''Not right now,'' he replied, his glance taking in all the exits. ''I think that vanishing for a bit might be a good thing.''

''Do you want me to come with you?''

From her earnest tone, Garth knew she had misunderstood. He was going to change hostels again—that required privacy. ''How about meeting me for a late dinner . . . at Olive Grove?''

His request seemed to relieve her fears. Nodding her agreement, Lucy leaned over and added: ''Remember—do not push at Rex. Compline?''

''Compline,'' he agreed, tapping in his code. Impulsively he seized her hand and kissed its palm. ''Don't worry. It will come out right.''

Her smile was tight, but Lucy's expression grew soft. ''Take care.''

It was only a short walk to Cuckoo's Egg, and Garth was climbing the stairs to his room before he knew it. Punching his codekey, he opened the door and cautiously reached around to keep his booby trap from falling. His hand closed on air.

Slowly, Garth pushed the door away from himself with one finger; his make-shift shelf had collapsed when someone entered in his absence. Cleaning? No—he had left his room marked Do Not Disturb.

Then who?

Eyeing the friendly jumble of the compartment, Garth carefully shut the door behind himself. There was a method to his disarray, and at first glance nothing looked disturbed. Or had it been? Methodically he began searching for any type of monitoring device. That theory exhausted, Garth switched to counting his valuables. Again, everything was in its place.

It was almost chance that he found it. Activating the overhead light in the sanitation, he saw a quick flash of amethyst out of the corner of his right eye. Over by the commode . . . a sheer packet, fastened behind the porcelain. Taking one of the clean, woven, hand towels, Garth folded it around the item and detached it from the wall.

A plastic tab box, translucent and divided into sections. Opening it with a thick cloth barrier was difficult, but Garth finally found the pressure point. The contents made him slowly settle upon the tile floor.

Fride. It had to be fride—nothing else had that brilliant amethyst tinge to it. Holding up one vial, he tried to gauge aroma. Too good a seal. . . . Carefully replacing the vial in the box, he considered the implications of its placement.

Think fast, fool, if someone's called the police, you'll be leaving the planet in a hurry. Fride was illegal everywhere— even Kiel and Norwood. It was considered one of the deadliest of artificial drugs. Not for its addictive properties, which were considerable, but because it scrambled the circuits of the brain. A fride user was a chronic liar not through choice but through usage—information that entered the brain in one form rarely reappeared. If it did, it bore no resemblance to its original version.

No one would believe a fride user's testimony . . . not even under the wire. So . . . was this a warning, a threat, or a set-up? Garth used part of his towel for the lid of a vial and part for the glass tube. The smell of rotten nuts . . . fride. He poured it into the tiny amount of water suspended in the porcelain bowl. A small fortune in fride followed the first container.

There was a recycling plant near the waterfront, beneath a row of shops—just before the Limpin' Lobster. *No observation is ever worthless.*

They went to the trouble to use real fride. Yet the police were not hammering at the door. Full circle, then—*As soon as I identify the danger, I find I have been anticipated.* How did they *find* the place? Had Lucy been instructed to keep him away from here for a time?

First things first—a walk past the recycling center. Then reassessment of his options. If someone in Rex's entourage thought that threats were needed to keep him in line, he was already in trouble. Time to get out of the line of fire. *Rex and I can explain it to each other over a vid, at a distance of several cities*. If he could get out of Amura.

What if this was a back-up measure for *them*? Not meant as a warning? Meant to be used if he became unmanageable?

Packing could wait; if the authorities came by, he did not want to look as if he was in a hurry to leave. Wrapping the box and vials in the cloth towel, Garth hurried out of the room.

He thought to check for watching eyes in the lobby and entranceway, but he did not pay a great deal of attention to the various people in multicolored rain slickers walking down the boardwalk. It was not until much later that he noticed he had attracted the attention of the *guaard*.

(to) flee: [v.i.] 1) To run away, as from danger, pursuers, etc. 2) To move swiftly: SYN *vanish* 3) To hurry toward a source of sanctuary. [v.t.] 1) To run away from; to attempt to elude (a sentient enemy) or to escape from (a natural threat): SYN *avoid* and *evade* 2) To leave abruptly or unexpectedly; Compare *ABANDON*

CHAPTER EIGHT

AMURA-BY-THE-SEA
    ONEHUNDRED NINETYONEDAY   VESPERS
ATARE WINTER PALACE

"He went to the Caesarean embassy afterward?" Darame asked softly, leaning back in her seat and absently toying with a long, silver curl.

"Yes, Serae," Jude replied. "I took the liberty of contacting our plant there. The Caesarean went to request a travel visa. He was told it would take a minimum of ten days."

"Any idea how he took the news?" Darame kept her eyes on the empty vial laying before her on the table. It was a fluke that Jude happened to see Garth Kristinsson leaving his hostel. Only trained observation could have brought Darame the next piece of news—that the youth had been corpse-white in color and wholly preoccupied with an errand. On impulse, Jude had followed Kristinsson, and had been led to several selected bins at the recycling center. Once she had confirmed that Garth was entering the embassy, Jude had returned to the center. The plastics belt had already destroyed whatever had been dropped upon it, and the incinerator ran constantly, but the glass bins were full to overflowing—an incriminating item perched precariously at the bottom of the chute.

Even more fortunate was the tiny half-moon lightly brushed on the container's surface—it matched Kristinsson's right third finger.

So. . . . Pick him up as a fride user? No. Kristinsson was not a user. Fride lingered a long time; his planetfall blood work would have shown traces of the drug. A new vice, picked up from the hordes who attended Dielaan's parties? Probably not . . . even Rex Dielaan preferred not to associate with fride users. He certainly would not let a known user sleep with his cousin —fride damaged chromosomes as well as nerves.

"Why would someone want to incriminate Kristinsson?" she murmured.

"I left Marc on watch, Serae," Jude said pleasantly, her square, dark face set in the expressionless on-duty *guaard* mode. "If we have some luck, we will discover that answer."

"Yes, watch him," Darame agreed, indicating that Jude could remove the vial. "And put that in a safe place. It may be all the evidence we ever have against Kristinsson . . . and sometime we may need something against him."

Nodding her understanding, Jude lifted the vial with a pair of tongs and sealed it in a sheer bag. By the time Darame thought to look up again, the big woman had disappeared.

Kristinsson . . . what was that young man up to? *And I was vain enough to think it concerned me,* she thought ruefully. *Obviously he has foes enough without pursuing ancient business.*

Still, he had searched for her a hundred years. *Waiting until the time is ripe to ask me something?* Or was his plan more devious than that . . . and already implemented?

Idly reaching to one side, Darame tapped the membrane before her screen and brought up the infonet. Touching the remote again brought her the news channel. Carefully she began scrolling through recent articles. Give it two, three days . . . even the best free-traders needed some time to work—

Darame straightened in her chair. Garth Kristinsson was not a free-trader, not as Darame used the word. The son of free-traders, he was at least an apprentice . . . but not a free-trader. *I have been thinking of him as trained. Therefore, I have over-estimated his potential for mayhem . . . and underestimated his potential for mischief.* She continued scanning the net, looking for anything that might be pointed at her.

Nothing interesting, not at all. The explosion had driven every-thing else off the infonet. No intriguing thefts, no innuendos, no. . . . Her eye stopped at a small notice. Earlier that day, a student at the university had been interviewed about the blast by the press corps. Peter's Keys, wasn't there enough information floating around? They had to manuf—Darame began reading in earnest. The student was studying explosives, researching better compounds for the mining industry . . . he claimed that the blast wasn't large enough to account for the amount of antimatter usually kept on-planet.

Should have found a prizewinner to say it, she thought idly, as she reached to increase the speed of the scan. *No headlines for students.* . . .

Something crystallized in her mind, and Darame tilted her chair away from the screen. Any antimatter in the vicinity would have blown. . . .

You were looking for theft that might effect you. A slow smile crept across her lips. Even as the thought was occurring to her, Darame was switching to vid and entering the code for Halsey's retreat.

"The Atarae for Halsey, if he is available," she said to the still picture which accompanied an audio recording.

Abruptly the picture of the mountains disappeared, and Halsey's cheerful countenance filled the screen. "Darame! How lovely! Is this business or pleasure?"

"It be always a pleasure, dear," she said gently in Gavriel-

ian. "Tell all—be there a plan to seize the antimatter before?"

Halsey's thin eyebrows lifted visibly, but he responded, and
in the same tongue. "Be not clear with me before. Why?"

"Connections, connections," she murmured, indicating by
the repeated word a drop into free-trader cant. "Connections"
meant free-associating.

"You be looking for work?" This was very amused—he was
asking: *Do you want in on such a plan?*

Burbling with laughter, Darame shook her head. "No. Suspect
it be before . . . and I be not welcome."

The eyebrows drew together thoughtfully, then relaxed. "Post
me." Winking once, Halsey cut the signal.

*Of course I'll keep you posted, my friend . . . just as soon as
I find anything worth sharing.* Tapping her fingernails against
the frame of the screen membrane, Darame considered her next
move. *Either Mailan or Sheel—*

Before she could reach to re-activate the vid, a sweet chime
announced an incoming call. "Yes?" Realizing she had spoken
in Gavrielian, Darame repeated the word in Nualan.

Mailan's triangular face and huge, gray eyes leapt out at her
from the screen. "The subject is moving," she said without
preamble.

"Where?"

"Methplane terminal."

Darame felt her own eyebrows arch at the words. So, neither
tourist nor conspirator—Garth Kristinsson needed to leave
Amura in a hurry. A visa would have smoothed the way, but
his spacer skills would get him out of town. To where? "Do not
lose him. I will be there as soon as possible." Before Mailan
could reply Darame terminated the call.

Moving to her cedar wardrobe, Darame pulled out a small
waterproof bakit and immediately began throwing clothing into
it. Both water and desert gear, cold and hot extremes—the bottom drawer of the dresser produced the small bag she always
kept packed for trips. It contained items no woman enjoyed being
without, as well as numerous energy bars and vitamin supple-
ments. But would it fit into her bakit? Yes.

Wear boots, take sandals, something for nausea (she had felt
queasy since the meal at sext) . . . on impulse she threw in a

delicate, black syluan dress. Who knew what company she was going to be keeping?

Was there time to call Sheel and tell him—what? That she was going to shadow a suspected thief, and that she had no idea if it meant a trip to the airfield or a trip to the ends of the continent? No time even to coin a message. Returning to the dresser, she opened the top drawer and reached beneath it. A familiar twitching sensation as the pressure-sensitive latch read her print, then the quartz pentimento dropped into her hand. Releasing the drawer, she let it slide shut as she coiled the silver chain.

Artistically she arranged the pendant on the table by Sheel's favorite chair. Once he had commented on her simple, teardrop necklace—only once . . . he had never asked again. Perhaps her response had surprised him. *"It is the most precious material thing I possess,"* she had told him.

Moving back into her sitting room, her fingers trailed near the floating images of several holos. Candids, chronicling the people most important to her; Sheel had been caught glancing over his shoulder, that startling dimple beginning to pull at one corner of his wide mouth; Ardal concentrating, his thin face as carved as his father's; the twins piled in a heap on top of herself, Caolan the picture of Darame's father with his black hair and wicked grin—only the one amber iris contrasted with his dreamy Irish face—while Sabrann hinted at her mother's checkered past. Who would have expected her black hair to have silver trickling through it? A change on the genetic level . . . yet they had a Nualan's natural immunity to Nualan radiation, and wasn't that just as uncanny? Sabrann, too, had one black iris; the other was azure blue, a legacy from her mother's mother's people. Avis and Stephanie, one of Sheel's mother Riva—tiny figures frozen in time, littering her desk.

Whirling, Darame hurried to fetch the last of her equipment. Twisting her hair into a knot at the nape of her neck, she slid her sheathed stiletto through it. Secure hair, decorative clasp . . . and deadly weapon. Flexing her fingers, she checked to be sure the blade would slide free with its usual speed. Then she lifted a woolen sweater and removed her other weapon, carefully drawing it to examine its edges.

As if she needed to check—this blade was one thing she never neglected. The Nualans universally called this design a cat knife, but in truth it was a dagger, its sides symmetrical and equally sharp. *You represent Nuala*, she told it silently for the thousandth time. Darame held in her hand a *guaard* regulation issue "cat," complete with a solid wadeyo wood handle carved to her personal grip. The Trinity alone knew what made up the alloy of the blade. Platinum and even trinium were involved, and of course the metal was doped to protect it from the hungry irradiated microbes which flitted through Nuala's atmosphere. An extremely valuable weapon, and beyond price—only *guaard* possessed them. They could not be bought, or traded for, although visual replicas existed. When a *guaard* died of age or illness, the blade went on the wall of the family homestead, honored for generations. If a *guaard* died in the line of duty, the blade was kept by the *guaard*. And if a *guaard* died to save an individual life, that individual kept the blade.

Sheel had Fion's blade, in an unbreakable case. He never spoke of it.

Only *guaard*. And one tiny off-worlder. Through channels, Darame had learned that every active and retired *guaard* had agreed to her receiving the blade. No other Atare, by blood or marriage, had ever been given one. Darame still wasn't sure why she had been so honored. Perhaps it was the hours and hours of practice she had put in, patiently strengthening her wrists, working up to the weight of the seventeen-centimeter blade. Perhaps it was because she so obviously respected and loved the sleek things.

Perhaps it was because, when in the presence of former Captain Dirk's cat knife, shortly after the events which had sealed her future on Nuala, Darame had tried (futilely) to snap the blade.

Only a moment of consideration, her fingers caressing the sleek, reddish wood. Then she carefully strapped the blade to her right calf, making sure a slight flex at the knee parted material and gave her access to the weapon.

Hoisting the bakit over her left shoulder, Darame left without a backward glance at the *guaard* who shadowed her.

ELLIE'S FOLLY
ONEHUNDRED NINETYONEDAY   COMPLINE

All those trips spent loading cargo finally counted for something.
Finding the posting of berths and manifests had not taken long;
getting access to the loading docks had taken longer. But the
Nualan spaceport security was no better or worse than that of
any other ground base, and as the bells announced compline,
Garth found the transport he was seeking.

A stroll past the area, as if taking a final stretch . . . no one
visible. Cargo cubes were rolling up a conveyor and feeding into
the hold of *Ellie's Folly*. Listening intently, Garth heard a familiar scuffling and click. He smiled; automatic stacking near
the doors. Reversing direction, Garth tossed his bakit casually
over a shoulder and paced the conveyor. If he could cross the
watching eye simultaneously with a cube, his presence would
be canceled out by the code emblazoned across the packing
container.

Flickering began, then ceased. Leaping past the open hatch,
Garth ducked behind a row of secured cubes, settling to one side
of a running light. Now the wait began. The last hurdle remained:
would they notice a weight discrepancy? Unlikely. This methplane was a local version of an older design; unless they had
brand-new internal monitors, they would not be able to sense
the change his presence created.

*Andersen. As far away as I can get from here, except maybe
Wallace, and nothing's leaving for Wallace tonight.* If only he
knew a bit more about Andersen . . . ah, well, it couldn't be
that different from Amura-By-The-Sea. He had some concen-
trates, at least—they would tide him over until he reached another source. *If you had nothing to do with that fride, Lucy, I'm
sorry I stood you up. I'll make it up to you as soon as I can.*

Now why should he feel bad about standing her up? *Just
another one flitting through.* . . . A pair of narrowed black irises
suddenly glinted at him, and he smiled in spite of himself. What
would it be like, staying with someone? Finding someone like
his parents had . . . like Lise had?

The possibility that there might *not* be any off-world food in
Andersen did not occur to Garth until long after they were in
the air.

ARGOS   COMPLINE

It was not until Darame was strapping herself into a seat that
her thoughts stopped running on before her. Motionless, the
woman took a deep breath and tried to consciously retrace her
steps. Reaching the spaceport, she had hurried to the air terminal;
Kristinsson had no chance to get off-world, not without the
proper passes. Several *guaard* had been waiting at the scheduling
screen—had they run off in an attempt to find Kristinsson, even
as she approached?

I told them not to let him take off, Darame remembered. And
they had scattered, even as she had scanned the possible transports. No, not Dielaan, else why run? If he was leery of Atare,
he would not head to their capital city . . . the Kilgore flight
was hours away. Seedar felt too close, but still, he could slip
back up the coast on a ship—

Seedar or Andersen. Turning to her *guaard*, she had sent the
man to the Seedar-bound ship, even as she started off toward
Argos. Raising her trinium signet ring to the steward had gained
her automatic entrance; there was no question that the family's
credit was good—

Vibration momentarily traced her bones, and suddenly Darame
was drawn back to the *now*. Airborne and heading for Andersen
. . . how soon could she finish checking the passengers? A list
was no good; identification was not required for actual gold ticket
sales.

She walked the length and breadth of the compartment, and
no one remotely looked like Kristinsson—not even the exact
height and build. He could have changed many things about
himself in the past few hours, but changing height in a sitting
man—or woman—took time. In with the cargo?

A touch of nausea fluttered in her stomach, momentarily dis-
concerting her. What a time to get a virus. Strolling back to her
seat, Darame dismissed her abdomen and started reevaluating
her decision to board the *Argos*. The reasoning was valid. All
the instincts which made her what she was said *Andersen* in a
loud voice. Andersen was even close enough to Dielaan that
Garth could keep tabs on and or contact with Dielaan . . . if he
chose. Was he running from them, or being sent away? Still,
the fride. . . .

Running away.

You cannot run far enough, Kristinsson. I was not a hunter by trade . . . but I was a predator.

ATARE WINTER PALACE
ONEHUNDRED NINETYTWODAY   MATINS

If only his head would stop throbbing. No one could be expected to think through such a haze. Sheel settled back on the low couch in Darame's sitting room, closing his eyes. Carefully focusing awareness on the muscles of his skull and neck, he gently pushed blood into the strictured tissues. It took a few moments, but it usually worked. Not as pleasant as one of Darame's neck rubs, but effective.

Where was the woman? Surely not still at the clan embassies. *Probably Alasdair of Wallace went over the edge and is holding her hostage,* came an idle thought, and Sheel smiled in spite of the subject.

His eyes focused, and he saw the pendant. Nothing they owned reflected quite like that polished piece of quartz. What was it doing on his desk? Standing slowly, Sheel moved through the arched portal into his own office. Yes, it was her pendant . . . her pentimento. He had looked up the word, after she had used it. A form of memory chip . . . Why was it in plain sight?

Because she is not. So simple, the answer. *Missing, one wife. Pentimento left in trade.* No . . . in promise. Whatever she was up to, she hadn't abruptly tossed over the last ten years. *Well, it is comfort of a sort . . . but I would have preferred something along the lines of "I am going to do so and so, I will return in three days."*

Whom to ask? Avis? Before he finished the thought Sheel was seated before the room's RAM screen and calling up the relay record. No calls in the city, one call received—from the methplane terminal. No calls outside . . . except to greater Amura, a call to Halsey.

Switching to vid, Sheel punched in Halsey's code. His latest picture was of the Sonoma Mountains at starset. "Very elegant," he commented aloud. "Ask Halsey to contact The Atare as soon as possible." Even as he reached to disconnect, Halsey's arm flashed across the screen.

The focus shifted, the other monitor panning around to show

Halsey seated at his work unit, a half-dozen screens at his disposal. He was still dressed, his ever-present cup of kona at his side. "Atare! So many callers this evening. When will you come visit?"

"As soon as I can escape," Sheel said dryly. "Have you talked to my wife recently?"

"Indeed I have," was the smiling reply.

"May I ask about the conversation?"

Halsey tilted his head thoughtfully. "Yes and no. I would be happy to relay the discussion to you . . . but we spoke in another language. This leads me to suspect she does not want the subject to become common knowledge. Shall I come to you?"

"Can you receive a full band of signals?" Sheel asked in turn.

"Indeed."

Reaching to one side, out of sight of the vid, Sheel touched a blue button. The color was actually reflected in the screen.

"My, Atare, we are a bit blue this early morning. Some sort of scrambler?" Halsey had his professional gleam in his eyes.

"Indeed," Sheel said with a grin. "A new toy. Mailan can arrange one for you, if you will keep it close to your heart."

"Oh, I will, I will! Now—she called during vespers. I suspect she was working on your little problem, because she immediately dropped into Reykjavik Gavrielian and started asking questions. It will take any eavesdroppers time to find anyone who speaks that, except in the Gavrielian embassy . . . and I doubt they will share their tapes."

"Remind me to tell Darame about the new toy. I did not realize she was absent when they installed it," was Sheel's rueful confession.

"She wanted to know if I had heard anything about a plan to steal antimatter."

Sheel felt his left hand freeze against his cheek. "Planning to steal antimatter?"

"Past tense—whether someone had planned it." Halsey frowned. "I heard nothing at all about such a scam, and it would have been big enough that I would know something—even if only a contact in the group. She was free-associating with information, Atare, but she did not volunteer anything other than the possibility of such a plan being implemented."

"By—" Sheel stopped himself, and tried to think like a free-trader. Darame had some reason to suspect an antimatter theft,

or she would not have called Halsey to see if a free-trader group
had arranged it.

"Have you since found her source?" Sheel asked finally.

"I think so. A small article early yesterday on the net; an
explosives student was quoted as saying that the blast was not
large enough to account for the amount of antimatter stored at
Odyssey and New Age."

"Sweet Mendülay," Sheel muttered, and there was no irrev-
erence in his tone. An unspecified amount of antimatter at
large. . . .

"Can I be of assistance, Atare?" Halsey said seriously.

"Keep looking for information on this, Halsey. Darame has
vanished, or so I suspect, and I will need all the help with this
I can find." Sighing, Sheel considered his next tack.

"I will call if anything interesting turns up, Atare," Halsey
replied. "Do not fret for Darame—she has taken care of herself
for a long time."

"Not in the last ten years," Sheel replied, tension creeping
into his voice. "Thank you, Halsey. I will be in touch." Nodding
farewell, he let the vid go dark. More headache exercises . . .
he punched up his messages as he let his concentration seep into
his muscles. A "thud" in his lap announced the arrival of a cat,
but Sheel did not need to open his eyes to see which one. "Audio,
please," he told the RAM.

Rugged purring arose . . . it was Faust, the huge coon cat.
Letting his hand shape the animal's back, Sheel listened first to
a note from Avis, then the seneschal's report. The third message
made him open his eyes. It was scrambled.

"Captain Mailan reporting. I am at The Atarae's back. We
are following one Garth Kristinsson, believed heading for Andersen. I will call by scrambler when we reach our destination.
In my absence, Trainers Crow and Henderson will deal with all
guaard business. Take care, my Atare."

Crow and Henderson . . . good choices, aside from Crow
being Mailan's husband. He had matured quite nicely the past
few years, and was an exemplary trainer. But to leave like
that—*There must have been no time to call for backup. I wonder
where Darame lost her assigned* guaard. *Maybe she needs two
people on her at all times*. . . . Mailan hated being far from
Sheel, yet she understood what Darame meant to him. . . .

"My Atare?" Gentle Elek had appeared at his shoulder. "You

have a visitor." Sheel could not help but raise an eyebrow at
the news. "Since you are still awake . . . the young woman is
from one of the fuel merchants."

"Name?" Sheel straightened in his seat.

"She gave the name Rebekah Finnsdottir, Atare," Elek said
simply. "It seems that Zaide arranged for her to come. The news
cannot wait."

"And the seneschal?"

"I am not sure . . . his assistant, Dalis, is escorting her."
Elek stood his ground, his expression faintly disapproving.

"Saffra, cheese, and bread would be nice, Elek," Sheel finally
said. The man's face smoothed slightly, and Sheel knew he had
made the proper response. What had he had for dinner? *Had* he
had dinner?

"Has she taken the series?" Elek asked.

"I believe so; undoubtedly she is in the record banks, she is
currently involved with a member of the Dielaan throneline."
Lowering his head in his quaint bow, Elek withdrew into the
shadows. Only after the door had slid shut behind him did Sheel
stand and move back into Darame's spacious sitting room. Settling in a chair by the huge arched windows, he let his gaze rest
upon the dark water. Something that could not wait. . . .

Sheel chose not to turn when the door slid open; Ayers was
one of the *guaard* on duty, there was no danger here. Only after
the reflections in the windows stopped moving did he face his
visitors. "You requested an audience?" He looked at dark Dalis
as he spoke in Caesarean. .

Zaide's quiet assistant gave him one of her fathomless stares.
"The seneschal is preparing a statement," she said meaningfully,
and nodded her obedience as she backed from the room.

As the door slid shut, Sheel gestured to the chair across from
his own. "Please, be seated."

"Thank you, Atare." Her voice was strong and without accent, marking Caesarean as her second language. "I have come
to offer you an apology, and to assure you that Odyssey Unlimited did *not* leak the code yellow information to the net."

"If you did not leak the information, then I do not see the
need for an apology," Sheel responded in turn.

The woman's lips tightened momentarily. "I am the one offering the apology, Atare—not Odyssey. While we were breaking into the drums yesterday, we carefully kept the net out of

the building. Only one of the local police force witnessed the information-gathering. But . . . a friend of mine was concerned about me, and came to the offices. He was present when we discovered the code yellow, and mentioned it in The Synod meeting which followed. I think that caused some problems for you.''

Two delegations walked out, and two others had to be physically separated. Problems? But he did not volunteer his thoughts. "Quen leaked the information to the net?"

"No! But . . . one of the attendants with him. . . ."

"Is now unemployed?" Sheel suggested.

There was a swift expulsion of air through the delicately-chiseled nose. "He is Rex Diclaan's servant; I suspect his is a life position."

Zaide would not be drafting a statement over mischief. . . . "It would be unfair to blame you for actions beyond your control. You had no way of knowing that Rex Dielaan would choose to reveal that information."

"Quen is very angry about it. I think he plans on apologizing to The Synod tomorrow." Her expression was both contrite and hopeful.

Not if Rex finds out his plans. Instead he will be on his way to Dieluun. "I take it you have further news to share?"

This brought on a sigh—the kind that was more a drawing of fortitude. "The code yellow was false."

Sheel stared at her. "Explain," he said finally.

"I mean that it was unnecessary—no code yellow situation existed at that time. It was well-done, and we never would have discovered it if we had not delved into the drums, but it was counterfeit. Also . . . one of our technicians is missing." The last was reluctant.

"Someone else *was* in the building?" Without looking, he reached to where he knew Elek had placed his mug of saffra.

Slightly distracted by the realization that she was about to share a private snack with The Atare of Nuala, Rebekah stumbled slightly over her reply. "No, Atare . . . he is simply missing. We . . . we fear he may have been part of the sabotage."

Leaning forward, Sheel asked: "You have proof of sabotage?"

"We have a counterfeit code yellow. The penalties in such cases are severe." Rebekah graciously took the cup Elek was offering. "Someone wanted entry into the building at a certain time. You see, the code keys we issue our employees only work on certain shifts—and their jobs depend on guarding those keys. This man could not arrange third shift access without arousing comment."

"Did he have the skill to create a faulty code report?"

"If he did, we never knew of it. The pay scale is higher for bank programmers; he could have made a great deal more money if he had mentioned that training." Rebekah paused to sip her saffra. "My uncle suspects that someone bribed him, then gave him a new codekey. Possibly one which somehow loaded a program through the lock."

"Is that possible?" At her blank look, he glanced over his shoulder to Ayers. "Have you heard of such a thing?"

"Programming is involved, Atare. It is possible, but it is so rare, few locks have defenses against it," Ayers responded.

"Not so rare anymore, it appears. Why did they want access? Why not simply plant a bomb of some type outside the building?"

"Ingredients for bombs are restricted, Atare. It would take a long time to access the smaller types of explosive devices. Easily located weapons are bulky, and someone walking the rounds might find them. Then there is the problem of timing devices and detonators. Detonators, especially, are not as easy to acquire," Ayers explained.

"While antimatter needs no detonator . . . not even a timer. All it needs is to combine," Rebekah finished for him. "Most of our traps were magnetic. We had only one active trap, Atare, and it had a *very* good backup generator. The odds on both sources failing simultaneously are more than coincidence can explain."

"Sabotage," Sheel agreed.

"There is more." Taking one of the tiny, round rolls, Rebekah ripped it apart with considerable strength. "My uncle believes that the purpose of this exercise was to steal antimatter, not destroy it. If that turns out to be the case, then an unspecified amount of antimatter is at large."

"Unspecified." Sheel picked up another cube of jack cheese. "Can we determine how much antimatter was taken?"

"If we can get New Age to cooperate with us. Normally we are vague about the amount of antimatter on hand at any given time. It is traditional, more than anything else, although of course it keeps people from studying our trade secrets." She lowered her eyes modestly at these words.

"There is no cause for condemnation in a fair profit," Sheel said, amused at her expression.

"Exactly! But we have leverage with the owners of New Age, and we can convince them to pool figures. The difference between the blast radius and the amount of antimatter in storage can then be determined." A veil of relief seemed to cross her features.

There was several moments of silence, as Sheel considered the problem. How much should they reveal to the public? Would the knowledge that antimatter was in an unsecured area panic the Amurans?

"How safe is the antimatter?" As much as he hated even to mention it, safety was first in his mind. Ransom—or other motives—could come later.

"If it *was* packed by Stennis, it should be fairly safe," she replied quickly. "He is quite competent. We had portable traps on hand with exemplary superconducting rings. The danger lies in the control box and the refrigeration unit. As long as they used compatible systems, there is no danger. The power cells must be recharged, of course, but each trap comes with an extra power strip. If they knew about the duplicate and took it, exchanging the strip is simple—I've done it myself."

"I thought that control boxes were tightly regulated, and individual to a ship," Sheel stated, probing.

"They are. Only the largest ships have two of them. Therefore, either a ship up at the wheel is missing its control box, or someone bought one on the black market, from a derelict or scrapped vehicle."

"Older, in other words," Sheel amplified, beginning to tear up a roll.

Rebekah nodded hesitantly, sensitive to his tone of voice.

"So . . . we can call in a search for control boxes, and we can check to see if anyone is drawing a sudden excess of power."

The young woman's face brightened. "Yes! Recharging a power strip or attaching the trap to a main source would produce a draw visible to a sensitive gauge. Only I hope they don't . . . a straight drain from a line. . . ."

"Why would there be a difference?"

"Surges," she said promptly. "Surges and outages. The

power in Amura is intermittent during storm season." Rebekah gestured out the window at the blackness beyond. "That is why we have backups on *every* trap, not just the active one. The power strip would continue to drain if left on . . . and could not pick up quickly enough in an outage. It is for main power, not emergency backup. The systems are wired differently."

Both of them turned at the whisper of the door sliding open. It was Zaide, his dark countenance gleaming through the intensity of his eyes.

"Just the person I needed," Sheel said briskly. "Saffra?"

"Please," was the response—a dry and windy response.

Gesturing toward a chair, Sheel asked: "The statement is complete?"

"The first draft. I wanted to check a few points with the serae before she retired for the night." Ignoring Rebekah's blush at the word "serae," Zaide continued: "At this point I do not know if it is wise to mention possible 'theft.' Can we reach your uncle at Odyssey headquarters?"

"Or at New Age, if he's left our offices," she suggested.

"Excellent. Thank you, Elek," Zaide added. Reaching with one hand, he pointed Sheel's pocket controller at a wall screen hidden behind draperies and activated it. The gauze began to draw back. "Now, what code reaches the private office of your uncle?"

ELLIE'S FOLLY
ONEHUNDRED NINETYTWODAY   MATINS

Garth was awakened from a fitful doze by the sensation of falling. He had just enough time to remember where he was, and to wonder why it felt like they were falling—*The engines are dead. Dead?* Before he could follow up the thought, pain and darkness overwhelmed him.

LAUDS

When he awoke the second time, all was quiet . . . too quiet. Even the gentle drone of the engines was missing. Electrical failure? Reaching slowly, he touched a lump on his head. Magdalen's Hair, that hurt!

Then he realized that the running lights had been extinguished. Over the exterior hatch door, the green emergency EXIT light glowed softly. Where had they gone down? Andersen was half a continent away . . . most of it desert. Swallowing in a throat suddenly gone dry, Garth moved shakily toward the beckoning EXIT light.

It took time and strength to trigger the emergency release on the hatch. First Garth had to pick the lock on the control panel, and lockpicking had never been his strongest skill. Finally he gained entry to the wires. He recognized the connections to the locks, and was able to override them—but the schematic was in Nualan, and the door itself was a mystery. Rather than risk fusing the panel shut, he rigged a pulley around a conveyor bar and slowly hauled the hatch aside.

Although he had suspected what he would find, from the continuing silence, Garth was not fully prepared for the scene outside the cargo door. Sand . . . shifting, undulating, white sand, as far as the eye could see. At the horizon was a pale promise of starrise, but it was no comfort, except to point out the east. *Now this*, he thought grimly, this *is a desert*. Pushing out a ladder, Garth carefully made his way to the sand below.

Circling the methplane told him one thing—there had been an electrical short in one of the engines. All things considered, the pilot had made a decent landing . . . if he had only been wearing a harness, Garth might not have hit his head.

A dark cockpit . . . injured? Sleeping? Or had he actually left the crash site? *Why would anyone risk leaving?* Unless he knew the area well enough to reach help quickly. . . . Garth climbed to the hatch leading into the narrow crew quarters, and found it unlocked. Someone had left, then. . . .

Punching the lights brought up the emergency floods. Wincing at the brightness, Garth settled into the navigator's chair and looked for the comp. The panel was dark, locked and silent. Damn! How about simple charts? No manual charts, but the rest of the readouts could be operated . . . ah. Power filled the screen, lighting up several dials and scopes. General planetary information wasn't restricted, then. . . .

There was a beacon broadcasting. It was in Nualan, unfortunately. Recognizing the Nualan words for Amura-By-The-Sea, Garth brought up the chart for the coast. Numbering was se-

quential from left to right, so he started looking for a time log.
Was it tied into the comp?

It was . . . but there was a separate log-in for the pilot. He
had logged out at 0303 A.M. Ciedär. It was now 0546 A.M.
Ciedär. That meant. . . . *I was unconscious nearly three hours*.
Checking the pilot's log-in, Garth tried to remember the time
zones. Coastal, Dragoche, Ciedär, Andersen . . . they had made
it as far as the Ciedär zone, which meant the mountains to the
west of the downed ship were the Dragoche Range. Effectively
the middle of nowhere. Had the pilot been flying slower than
usual, because his readings indicated engine trouble?

Had he been a smuggler? *So who is coming back for the cargo?*

ANDERSEN
ONEHUNDRED NINETYTWODAY   LAUDS

"He *has* to be here!" Darame gave the young man at the information desk her blackest stare.

It was as effective as usual—he squirmed and became paler
—but no more information was forthcoming. "I am sorry,
Atarae, but he was not on the passenger list of *Argos*. He was
not on the cargo ship *Sweet Dreams*, either. The captain has had
the hold searched from top to bottom."

"I thought there were three ships due in from Amura?"

This pointed question seemed to distress the clerk further.
"There were—are—three ships due in nightside, but *Ellie's
Folly* is overdue."

"Why?"

"There is a hold on information—"

"Circumvent it."

Sighing, the terminal employee delved back into his RAM.
Although Darame had no legal authority in Andersen, the House
of Atare was highly respected, and the youth would bend over
backward to fulfill her request.

"Atarae, satellite picked up a report of engine trouble at the
end of matins. The plane lost contact with all stations shortly
afterward. That . . . usually means a crash. The winds are so
treacherous—"

"It is not storm season. What else produces that type of blank?
A power failure?" She gave him a hard look.

Wincing again, the clerk said: "Yes, possibly—Wait. The pilot has checked in with the Cied who do retrieval in that area. Electrical failure in a port engine, resulting in an emergency landing in the ciedär."

"Was he alone?" she demanded.

"Yes, Atarae."

"Hell's Bells!" This outburst silenced the clerk—his round face became paler still, and his Adam's apple bobbed in protest. Flinging her hands into the air, Darame yelled: "Then where is he?"

"Undoubtedly still aboard *Ellie's Folly*." The low, alto voice startled Darame, but she did not let the clerk know. "I have already contacted center command. The terminal and all other outgoing flights were searched. The flight to Seedar was searched before disembarking was allowed. Garth Kristinsson—or what is left of him—is on *Ellie's Folly*."

Her years of experience rising to the fore, Darame turned to Mailan as if the *guaard* had been seated next to her the entire trip. "Suggestions?"

"The Cied will find the ship and strip its cargo, bringing it back to their outstation—that is how they earn their 'fee.' Let us charter a small plane, and go to the outstation. We will arrive before the representatives of *Ellie's Folly*, and can negotiate, if necessary, for Kristinsson."

Negotiate? Ah, yes—a stray off-worlder, adrift without a visa . . . the Cied had been known to keep them to improve their genetic outreach.

Whether they wanted to be kept or not. . . .

Twisting back toward the clerk, Darame raised her voice and asked: "Can you charter me a methplane from that screen?"

ELLIE'S FOLLY   PRIME

Far, far to the east, a small, pale star was rising. Garth had known the planet was huge, but he had not expected the horizon to seem so . . . dreamy. It floated, as if nothing about it was quite definite. A small thing, admiring the Nualan star before it rose into its fiery glory, but it kept him from thinking too much about his predicament.

Leaving the plane would be foolish. He had no idea where he was, aside from somewhere east of the Dragoche Mountains.

He had no water—he didn't want to think about that. Attempting a trek by day would be suicidal; the monsoons had not yet reached this desert. Maybe never reached this side of the desert. . . . Certainly the desert dwellers had wells, but they were both hidden and guarded.

They must have boundaries . . . someone must consider this hill of sand their territory. Eventually they will investigate. Soon? No sense worrying about it. Better to close the hatches again, and try to keep cool without a breeze. Delayed stress, a headache, and rising temperature made Garth both sleepy and irritable. Maybe if he just sat quietly. . . .

The sound of the cargo hatch door rolling open awakened him. Reflexively Garth rolled into a sitting position on top of the cube nearest the conveyor. To his surprise, the individual standing at the top of the ladder was wrapped in some type of gauzy robe, several scarves of the same delicate beige completely obscuring a face.

A mummy, Garth thought vaguely, memories of musty museums fogging his thoughts. *No . . . a Ciedärlien.* A tribal desert dweller. . . .

The faceless creature "stared" at him for a moment, then turned slightly, speaking in swift Nualan to someone out of sight. It was a stronger language than that of the western coast; more rolling, with harder emphasis at what appeared to be the beginning of sentences . . . or the end of sentences? It scarcely seemed to be the same tongue.

Maybe it isn't. "Does anyone speak Caesarean?" he asked softly.

Another gauzed head popped over the lower edge of the hatchway. A third head appeared . . . hanging down from the top of the hatch. *Sweet Peter, how does he* do *that?* This individual had real eyes—the scarf covered only the lower face. Dark orbs studied him for a long moment.

"#**((?)) + ?!" said the hanging apparition imperiously.

"I know I'm not supposed to be here, but I would like to explain to whoever is in charge . . ." Garth began carefully, finding the tone they were using alarming. He was careful not to move his hands abruptly.

A blur of movement at the corner of his eye—had they somehow opened the inner hatch to the control room? Strong fingers seized flesh, and a searing prick followed. Pain spread up his arm, sweeping like a wave to the spine, then throughout his body. It was much like bumping an elbow abruptly, only worse, much worse—his entire body was going numb.

Ah, well, they couldn't take your word for it that you're harmless, now, could they? It was the only coherent thought he had before the pain reached his head and exploding bursts of color swept consciousness away.

> sanctuary: 1) A place providing refuge and
> protection; a place guaranteeing immunity from law
> once its boundaries have been passed. 2) A haven
> from strife. 3) A consecrated place, dedicated for
> worship.

CHAPTER NINE

AMURA-BY-THE-SEA
         ONEHUNDRED NINETYTWODAY   PRIME
ATARE WINTER PALACE

"Atare?"

Pausing in the act of adjusting his collar, Sheel glanced over to the door. It was Zaide; the seneschal did not look as if he had slept, either.

"Something cannot wait until court?" Sheel asked, glancing over to see if the star had crested the temple.

"I think the ragäree and I should call the court into session, Atare," Zaide replied, his deep voice rumbling like gravel down a rocky slope. "You have a visitor. Nadine reb^Ursel Kilgore."

The words caused Sheel's muscles to feel momentarily nerveless, as if he had no control over his body. Wishing there was time to examine that physiological reaction, Sheel slowly walked over to Zaide.

"She wishes to speak to you alone," the seneschal added blandly.

"Anything else?" Sheel said, his fingers rearranging the chain of office.

Zaide knew what he was asking. "She looks rather grim."

Ah. . . . The announcement had been made; better to beat the infonet to the discovery of false code yellows and breaking and entering, than let them report at will. Of the missing antimatter they had kept silent.

Although not the equal of the *guaard*, the informants of Kilgore were skilled. What had Nadine found out to bring her to Dragonhold so early?

Raising his voice, Sheel said: "Elek, will you call down for saffra and tea? In the Green Room; Serae Nadine of Kilgore has come to call." Giving Zaide a lifted eyebrow and a slight nod of farewell, Sheel moved toward the doors.

Tierce was ringing through the cloudless sky as Sheel entered the Green Room on the north side of the dwelling. It was a pleasant place of subdued greens, blues and lavenders, echoing the water which could be seen out the window furthest to the west. Elek had been swift and efficient, as always; the mid-morning repast was already steaming on a center table. Nadine of Kilgore, dressed in contradictions, all severe edges and flowing material, was standing over by the western window. She was alone.

Pausing as the door slid shut, Sheel studied her hard profile against the clear morning starlight. This woman actually looked as strong-willed as she was, the long, softly curling, ash-blond hair a complete smoke screen. Alone . . . Kilgore never approached other clans without at least a trio of family in tow. When one is always ready for a fight, one brings along reinforcements . . . unless one holds all the cards.

"Good morning, Serae," Sheel began, moving toward the center grouping of chairs. "It is early yet. Will you join me in a cup of saffra?"

"I know about the antimatter." Very low, her voice, yet still pleasant. Nadine did not turn as she spoke—her arms crossed before her, she continued staring out the window at what could be seen of the horizon.

Sheel watched her for a few moments, waiting . . . she did not speak again. Deciding that she was looking *at* something, he moved over near her and glanced out the windowpane. Beyond the cloudless blue of sky and sea, empty of even a sail skimmer, there was a dark horizon. More rain. It was needed; the precipitation was low, so far this season.

"We need rain," Nadine said without preamble. "Our farmers do not irrigate in spring . . . the cost mounts daily. Where are the monsoons?"

Since the farmers in Atare region had more than enough for their grape crop, Sheel had no answer for her. With a double harvest growing season in Seedar and Kilgore, the timing of the weather was precise. If the rains came too soon, delicate wheat seed could be washed away and ripening ears dashed to the ground. If they came too late, one crop would be stunted and the other rot on the vines.

If the rains failed to come, there would be famine.

"Things have been slow this year," Sheel finally started.

"We are behind," she murmured. "Far, far behind . . . less than a third of the usual rainfall has reached Seedar and Kilgore."

Somehow, this is related, was all Sheel could think. Finally, Nadine turned her head slightly and looked at him. They were of a height; her brilliant amethyst eyes did not flinch from his mismatched pair.

"I have a present for you," she said simply. "Stennis."

Sheel did not pretend to misunderstand. The technician who had disappeared from Odyssey Unlimited. Coincidence or not?

"Where did you find him?" he asked, settling against the windowsill.

"On a boat to Kilgore. It happened that he chose a ship that maintains close contact with the shore. His identification was not satisfactory, so they prevented him from leaving at the first port of call. When word went out at lauds, the ship started back to Amura. What with the winds in their favor, they may make it by matins."

"Then we have our saboteur?" Sheel suggested, watching her closely.

Nadine actually smiled . . . a genuine smile, faint but with warmth. "We have the key to the lock. There is more beyond the door, Atare. Stennis has yet to be questioned—we thought to leave it to Amuran security. A courtesy. But he has said this: he claims Dielaan immunity.''

It only needed this. He studied the woman before him. Her eyes matched the chips of gemstone woven in her hair—glinting, yet holding all images as their own.

"We must assume that Dielaan has the antimatter." The tone was flat, deliberate . . . there was no flexibility within it.

Sheel felt something uneasy trace the lining of his stomach, working its way up to his breastbone. *Or Dielaan knows who has it.*

"You know all too well what happens when the longhaulers arrive," Nadine went on. "We buy from them, they buy from us. They try to choose what costs them least, yet will bring the most amongst The Brethren. We hedge our bets, sending both tried-and-true and new things to tempt. And we send our children, Atare . . . we send our children into the void, to bring back Nuala's future. We have paid for that antimatter . . . and we want it back."

"Many have undoubtedly paid for the antimatter," Sheel replied slowly. "The question is, how much is left?"

"Enough for the three ships that were taking passage this month," she told him. "The others can wait until the next shipment, if necessary."

"Will they agree?"

"Have they paid gold in full for their portions?" This was very cool.

Sheel felt as if he had been struck. Paid gold in advance? No wonder Kilgore had their pick of the longhauler trade! Normally that would give them a tremendous advantage. But this time—

"You are over-extended," Sheel said aloud. "How badly?"

A minute shrug. "My siblings do not brief me on everything," was the answer. "For your ears only, I suspect one third of the tribal assets."

One third! Nadine was always careful in her speech: she had said *assets*, not liquid assets. Everything that Kilgore had . . . in other words, easily seventy-five percent of their available assets. Which would come rolling back with the next ship's arrival, in two months or so. But until then. . . .

He had to offer. "Do you need a loan?"

Again, that faint smile. "Do you think my brother would ask, much less accept one?"

No . . . Klaas Kilgore would go down in a sinking ship before he would ask for a life jacket. Marlis Ragäree had a reputation for a fierce temper, which cooled slowly. If Nadine was ragäree . . . but she was not.

"I wish he had your vision," Sheel said simply.

"His eldest daughter and both their heirs are due to go on this ship," Nadine announced. Sheel blinked once; which members of a royal family were traveling was usually a dark secret. "Drought, a trading exchange crisis, and hysteria in the royal houses. Do you know what we are facing, Atare?"

"Impossible. Even Klaas would not do that." It was Sheel's turn to sound flat, hard-edged.

"We must get it back, Atare, or my brother will go after it . . . even if he has to sail into Dielaan harbor itself to recover the trap."

What response was there, really? What would he do if he were in the same position? "We need time, Serae," he told her. "We must determine whether the regent has any knowledge of this, or if it is merely another of a long string of diversions."

"He had best learn to curb his 'diversions,' " was the tart rejoinder, "or his family will be spared slipping a knife between his ribs."

"You see my point?" Sheel pressed the words lovingly.

Nadine's long, spidery lashes veiled her eyes momentarily. "Others may already know . . . about the stolen antimatter, certainly. About Stennis, possibly. All spies are spied upon."

"Then I suggest we plan just how we will approach Dielaan on this subject. Can I interest you in that saffra now, Serae?"

"Nadine," she said slowly. "Do you by chance have darjeeling tea?"

"Of course."

CIEDÄRLIEN CAMP
ONEHUNDRED NINETYTWODAY   TIERCE

Light was filtering through the walls when Garth awoke. Through the walls. . . . Carefully opening one lid slightly, he let his eye become adjusted to the brightness. Slight flexing of his limbs told him that he was not bound. Interesting. . . .

What peculiar dreams. There had been a dark-haired girl with honey-colored skin, skin scented like terran incense . . . why dark hair? Lucy had red hair. . . . *Sweet Peter, what did they hit me with?* Fascinating. He'd always thought Nualans used no hand weapons other than knives, but that little trick required investigation. True, he did not seem permanently damaged . . . a good weapon for a Nualan, then. Nasty at the receiving end, though. He was so thirsty.

Someone was lifting his head and offering him water. Gods, he felt so drained. What kind of weapon was that? Great dreams, though—

Dreams. . . . Garth let his other lid open fractionally. The figure hovering over him was wrapped loosely in an embroidered, gauzy, sand-colored robe, but without the intricate head and face covers. These hung down on either shoulder. Her skin was the color of honey, and her eyes very dark. . . .

I think I've been raped. He was too surprised to be angry. The smile the stranger favored him with was very warm, if uncertain. Did that weapon make the senses more acute? How would he *know* she felt uncertain?

The woman offered the oddly-shaped ceramic cup once again, and suddenly wisps of haze cleared from Garth's brain. *Water. Clean water . . . I must have treated water.* How would they know—He struggled to sit up.

Gentle hands held him down with strength. Cool detachment was in the eyes, but she seemed neither angry nor worried. *In control of the situation, are you?* "Do you understand Caesarean?" he croaked.

A slight tilt of the head . . . there was no recognition in her eyes.

"I need someone who speaks Caesarean . . . or Gavrielian! How about pidgin Norwood—" Garth broke off, trying to swallow in a dry throat. The Cied woman reached for the cup again, but Garth pushed it away. "My bag . . . I need . . ." *Peter's Keys, did I even bring those damn pills?*

Groping with one hand, he seized the pack and pulled it to his side. He still felt too dizzy to sit up, but he knew every item in the bag by touch. His other two ID cards were still there, hidden in the walls of the bakit, but the pills, and other small items of his travels. . . .

Forcing calm, Garth indicated the size of the packet with

cupped hands. Then he mimed turning the dial, and tipping out the tiny pills.

At first she merely stared at him. Then her eyes widened. Gently pushing him back down to the woven pallet, she reached to veil her lower face. Soundlessly rising, the young woman slipped out a slit in the wall.

Well, she understood something, Garth decided. *What* was another matter. Was she in search of his other belongings, or someone who spoke Caesarean? They had his identification card. What would Cied do with an ID card? Why was he so dizzy? Residual from the weapon, the water, or the blow on the head? Could the pills work *after* ingesting untreated materials?

There was a strange taste of salt and sour in his mouth, and Garth recognized it as his own personal brand of fear.

MAIDEN'S HOPE   SEXT

Too long, everything is taking too long. Darame tried to keep from looking out the window, but she could not halt the impulse. So long to charter a plane—who would have thought that flying to the Cied base camps was such a specialized art? But the camps moved constantly, and only certain pilots could guarantee that they would be answered when they sent their landing request out into the cloudless skies.

Beside her, Mailan was silent. The *guaard* was in that strange trance state used on long shifts. *She never scolds,* Darame thought. *She must have believed me.* As soon as they had left the Andersen clerk's hearing, Darame had immediately stated: "I did not lose him intentionally."

All Mailan had said was: "I know, Serae." She had then led the way toward the flight gates.

And who is guarding Sheel's back? she wondered. But Mailan undoubtedly had things under control. *Please forgive my haste, husband. I will bring you the answers if I can.* If her mind did not grow dull with exhaustion. *If I had been able to sleep more on the flight. . . .* But nausea clung to her, and even saffra did not keep it at bay.

From what little net information Darame had been able to acquire, Sheel was already gleaning answers from various sources. A false code yellow, and sabotage . . . was there more?

Why destroy something if there was no gain in the act? Not even to claim power by the act of destroying. . . . *What were you trying to destroy, Garth Kristinsson? Be alive, Garth Kristinsson. Your death would leave more questions than answers.*

Mailan's eyelids flickered; she straightened in her seat, a circular glance taking in the immediate area. In moments Darame realized what had awakened her—the tempo of the engines had changed. Looking out the small window, she saw dark, scrubby lumps dotting the foothills of the Dragoche Mountains. In reality the inundating sand and sage gray brush obscured the outline of an extended tent site. Cied were known to train the sparse plants to grow upon a thin layer of sand spread over their tough tents. Somewhere in that thorny undergrowth was a Cied trading center.

What can I trade you for Kristinsson? It could conceivably be a problem. After all, Garth was on the run; hiding out in a Cied village might be to his taste. If that was the way of it, she would need to impress upon him that the Cied kept what they claimed—forever. Trinium would be a possibility . . . or specific goods that they rarely acquired through their recovery operations. If necessary, she would even offer a favor, although she hesitated to do that. It would be her own favor, not that of the throne; Darame would never risk offering the word of Sheel and Avis. Still, it was worth something. *I speak your language . . . I suspect I think as you do. That is power.*

Her charter was constructed for landings on water, sand, or snow, and it performed its job with precision. Even before the small methplane had come to a stop, Mailan was shrugging her shoulders into her Cied outer robe. Adjusting her double veil like a professional, she courteously offered Darame help with the arms of her Atare garment.

Embroidered robe wrapped correctly, veils attached . . . Mailan gave Darame a long look out of indomitable gray eyes before fastening her veil. Darame straightened in response.

Together we will have them at our feet.

Although the star was high in the sky, the city of tents seemed almost deserted. Only three robed figures could be seen. So, who was in authority? The "organizer" of a Cied trading camp changed with the moons, each clan taking its turn. It all had Darame slightly nervous; she had counted on many things, but not bargaining with Cied. Their protocol was precise. *Mendülay, say we have not already offended them.*

Pale robes mingled with tents and dunes beyond. Two of the visible Cied moved toward them, soundless over sand. One was wearing Dragoche tribe colors, the black and gold trim of a warrior, while the second was a scholar of . . . the Kalel tribe? Greens and yellows marked them, for they were out of Seedar, long ago.

"Welcome to our meeting place," the scholar said politely in Ciedärlien. Actually, a better translation would have been "place of trade," since the Cied never met with coastal dwellers for any other reason, if they could help it. "How may we serve you?" Translation: How may we serve our mutual interests? . . .

Now came the rub; normally Darame would have had someone to speak for her. Royalty did not press its own suit. A *guaard* increased her status, but if Mailan chose to handle negotiations, that could reduce the *guaard* to a simple warrior in their eyes. . . . So, how to begin.

"I have come to retrieve something," she said simply, holding up her signet ring to identify herself. "I believe he is in your custody."

Silence. Darame was quite certain of what she had said; by naming Garth as "something," she had termed him an outsider, and not worth taking under her protection. But by using the words "he" and "custody," she had implied that he was of interest to her house, and possibly dangerous. That would keep them from treating the negotiation as an immigration question.

The silence continued. Darame grew keenly aware of it; nothing stirred beyond the tents, nothing seemed to stir within them.

"We have found a stray," the scholar said finally. "Would you care to see him? We have sent for a hot healer."

Worse and worse. A hot healer? Why would they need—how badly was he injured? Or had they given him native food? This Cied was not sanguine about his chances, or surely he would not allow her to see him . . . not yet.

"That might be best," Darame replied coolly.

Without further comment the scholar turned and started down an intersecting corridor. Mailan indicated by a nod that Darame was to follow. She remained a half-step behind, the Dragoche warrior bringing up the rear.

Their destination was only three tents away. Gesturing, the Kalel scholar pushed aside the entrance for Darame. With a polite nod, he continued off down the row, the warrior still in his shadow.

"High-ranking," Darame murmured to Mailan. The *guaard* nodded, then preceded the woman through the opening. It was only moments before Mailan spoke.

"Come, Serae." Darame ducked under a rolled inner flap and entered.

Mailan had already circled the area, investigating every fold of canvas. Apparently satisfied with the security of the perimeter, she moved back out the slit, holding it closed with one hand. Darame knew she would keep one ear pressed to the crack, even as she watched the dusty street beyond. It would seem that Garth Kristinsson did not worry her.

It was easy to see why. He lay quiescent on a pallet, eyes closed, breathing slow and shallow. Darame knelt and lightly pressed fingertips to the youth's temple. His skin was very warm to the touch; he was visibly shivering. Occasionally a whispered word passed his lips, but for now he would tell her nothing: all he could say was "pills."

You waited too long, Garth Kristinsson. Unless they have a hot healer within a day's ride of here, your story has reached its end. No one could blame the Cied for what had come to pass. That an off-worlder had made it this far was amazing. That it should be one who had avoided the pill series? Even more incredible.

Methodically Darame loosened his collar, and reached for a rag laying in a shallow pan of lukewarm water. Wringing out the cloth, she gently pressed it to Kristinsson's forehead.

"Lucy? I would have come, I meant to come, but I had to leave." No more than a whisper . . . he did not even open his eyes.

Lucy . . . *Lulani reb´Carlotta Dielaan.* In Rex Dielaan's circle, yet not truly of it . . . one of those who knew it was expedient to pay homage to him, and yet. . . .

Darame startled herself; she had spoken aloud. The youth did not seem to hear her; his whispers continued, too softly for her to decipher them. Letting his words trickle over her like grains of sand, Darame continued to apply moist compresses. Eventually they would send someone to her—

The hand gripping the rag tightened spasmodically. That name . . . surely he had not said *that* name. But if he had said—

He spoke again. "Aesir considers the debt to be paid. Aesir. . . ." Dry and soft; needing water. . . .

Darame suddenly found her cat knife in her hand, although she did not remember reaching for it. Not life, but death—her hand tightened on the hilt until the knuckles turned white. *By all the varied saints of my childhood—Aesir!* What had she done to attract their attention? Would they send this child as their weapon? Or . . . a witness. Sometimes Aesir required a witness, when a killing was to take place. Those words were ceremonial for them, used when their part of something was about to end. . . .

No. She could not kill him—not now, at least. Fear was a pitiful reason for a free-trader to take a life. *I have been warned.* Slowly she lowered her cat knife, bending her knee to expose the sheath.

There was someone else in the room. Whirling, she found herself facing a shrouded Cied. Mailan must have let this one in, but why without comment—Then she noticed that the robes were brilliant white, not sand-colored. White . . . only The Dragoche, the spiritual leader of the Ciedärlien clans, wore white robes. Why was the old man here? Sheathing her knife and straightening, Darame waited to be addressed.

A slender hand reached for her left wrist. Even as Cied flesh touched her own, Darame realized that there had been a change in the ciedär. The old Dragoche had died, and his successor stood before her. Female . . . and very young—younger than Darame herself? There was something familiar about the silence that wove around them. . . .

Healer. Hot healer, to be precise. A Dragoche who was a hot healer! How the tribes must have rejoiced. Some healers automatically examined every person who came within arms' reach; others avoided healing, except when absolutely necessary. *What are you seeking?*

Finally, the Cied released Darame's wrist. Nodding slightly, politely, the woman moved past her guest and knelt at Kristinsson's side. Placing a hand at either temple, the newcomer paused. Then the veiled head slowly sank forward as healing actually began.

To be alone with The Dragoche of the ciedär . . . never could Darame remember seeing a Dragoche unattended. Idly she studied the embroidery on the woman's robe. She wore black and gold—Dragoche clan since birth, then—and the back of her white robes were unmarked, except for an ancient astronomical sign used to indicate a hot healer . . . the exploding comet. There was embroidery lining the cowl, which meant the priesthood. What had been on the front? Scholar's signs, and the makermother. . . .

Once again, there was someone behind her. Darame turned slightly, and saw two Cied warriors enter the tent, Mailan shadowing their footsteps. The two strangers settled themselves on either side of the slit, while Mailan blocked the opening with her body.

Very well guarded. How long would they remain here?

It was well into the afternoon, if the shadows in the tent aisle were any indication, before The Dragoche completed the healing. By then Darame was parched with thirst, and keenly aware of her disadvantage. But the healer would require sustenance, after such an effort. . . .

A warrior stepped forward to offer The Dragoche an arm, and gently led her from Kristinsson's tent. The other remained with the sleeping off-worlder even as Mailan indicated that it was time to leave.

Darame spared Garth one last look. Breathing normally, now, and sweating freely—the fever had broken. *Although he will be weak . . . that will slow us.* The thought occurred to her before she realized she had unconsciously decided to take him back to Amura. *Or even Atare? It might be safer for him. After all, I doubt you were running from us. . . .*

But now, to pry him from Cied arms. How to go about it. . . .

There was a huge tent at the end of the row; a bit whiter than the rest, but more star-bleached than dyed. The warrior and the healer disappeared beneath its eaves. Without shortening a step, Mailan moved up to the opening slit, then paused, her body angled to take in both the entrance and the woman following. Darame caught up to her, taking slow, deep breaths to control any flush to her pale skin. Just as they both locked glances, the canvas twitched aside and a khatta ushered them in.

Inhaling carefully, Darame moved past the khatta without a show of revulsion. How could she condemn them for fearing to leave everything they had ever known? But Toki would have been a khatta, if she had remained—a servant of the lowest caste, considered almost a beast of burden. No hunting skills, no fighting or scholarly skills, no conception before the twentieth birthday—*You never noticed that the finest embroidery came from her hands, did you? Do not bother wondering what happened to her* (though Darame doubted anyone ever had) *because we appreciate her in full measure.*

A cozy pile of pillows awaited her; The Dragoche was already seated, her hands hidden in her robe, her upper veil thrown back. Darame moved to settle gracefully in the place opposite the leader.

A khatta magically appeared to one side, bearing a tray of foodstuffs. To Darame's surprise, she was served chilled hazelle milk, spiced with a pinch of chocolate and vanilla and whipped to a froth. The tray was placed between the two women, so that each could reach the steaming, fresh rolls and pot of soft cheese. In the fragile, fired pot Darame could smell strong saffra. *Ugh —they drink it so sweet.* But then she spied a pot of honey. *Ho—they cater to the tastes of the coast!* Almost as if in response to that sign, she pulled back the film of her upper veil.

"Welcome, Darame Atarae," The Dragoche said suddenly. Her soft, husky voice sounded tired, but not strained. "It has been many years since one of the House has graced our tents. To what do we owe this pleasure?"

That they knew her first name could be good or bad—what had preceded her into the ciedär? Not that Atare were secretive about their names, as the Dielaan were, but still. . . . "I have come to retrieve something," she said simply. "Thanks to your presence, he should be able to travel soon."

"If you travel by night, yes," The Dragoche answered steadily. "But what of this off-worlder, traveling the wastes without the documents valued by the coast? Does he so desire to see our world?"

Vague, but it could have been worse—"He flees, Dragoche," Darame replied, flicking her eyes momentarily in the direction of a khatta who anticipated her desire for saffra. "Unusual things have been happening in Amura. I would know if these two events are connected."

"And if they are not?"

Darame felt the barest of smiles cross her lips, and was grateful for the lower veil. "Why, then I have no reason to retrieve him,

and you are free to ask him if he would care to visit among you
for a time.'' The words were chosen carefully; Garth could throw
away his freedom without realizing it.

"He might not care to visit,'' The Dragoche said tonelessly.
"He has not taken the pills. He will not love us for forcing that
choice.''

"You saved his life.''

The Dragoche's eyebrows flicked fractionally. "He has given
us life; it was a satisfactory trade.''

*Already throwing women at him? Did you give him time to
recover from your jabbers?*

"You could not have known he was limited to off-world
foods.'' Darame saw the slightest relaxation in The Dragoche's
posture, and knew the woman had been expecting Darame to
demand restitution.

There was a pause, as both women sipped at their beverages.

"Might we be permitted to ask if this young off-worlder has
anything to do with the troop ships off our coast?''

Dear Jesu, thank you for black irises and black nerves. Without the slightest tremor, Darame settled her cup back upon its
saucer. "Tell me of these ships. Are they known to you?''

"They fly no colors, but the construction is Dielaan. They
have been moving south, toward the Amber.'' The Dragoche
bent her head to her cup.

Darame knew where she stood . . . but she had to make sure
the Cied knew it in their own time. Despite their occasionally
vicious clan fights, the Cied hated war perhaps even more than
other Nualans—it was one of the reasons they had ritualized it
to such a degree. Sometimes they settled arguments which encompassed thousands of individuals with one knife fight between
two 80s. The blood of one symbolized the blood of many, and
there would be no further reference to the incident. . . .

*They think a war is brewing. And they do not like it, not one
bit.* Ships, dear Mendülay, ships—Livia, what are you thinking?
Granted, the Dielaan net would not report their presence, but
surely satellites would notice, if they had failed to up to now.
*Unless you are sailing them like trade boats, and with all these
rumors flying around about the antimatter, people will start
hoarding, then prices will rise, and*—

"Dragoche, you are aware there was an industrial accident in

Amura-By-The-Sea? That antimatter was destroyed . . . and stolen?''

At this The Dragoche leaned forward slightly and gestured for the khatta to leave. "Stolen?"

"It is the only explanation. I hope that this youth knows something of the incident, perhaps even knows the location of the antimatter. This is serious for our trading synod." The last was a chance—*I have bet that stopping a war is more important than exploiting this situation.*

"Will he give you the information?" This was blunt.

"I do not know."

"Will you take the information?" This was much gentler.

"Not yet. But it is possible." It might take time to arrange for the proper charges, but if it was necessary to drug Kristinsson to find that antimatter, Darame was perfectly willing to do so.

"Can you speak for your people, Atarae?" she was asked.

A slight shake of the head. "That is not my place, Dragoche."

"But you can speak for yourself."

Huh. Jumped to this one a bit fast, but with ships going down the Amber toward the Alameda Sea. . . . "What would you ask, Dragoche?"

"I offer the warriors of the Cied."

Darame stared blankly at her.

Evenly, The Dragoche continued: "Dielaan will not cross the sands."

Ah. *That* made sense. Whatever was going on, the coast would not have to worry about invasion from the east, over the mountains. Not even methplanes bringing trouble—the Cied would see they never left the ground. What could they want that was worth offering first?

"And Kristinsson?"

"Your claim is great. We will give him to you."

Will give him . . . no, the negotiations were not over. "What will you ask, Dragoche?"

"I would ask for seed, Atarae. Human seed."

Darame was literally too stunned to speak. Ciedärlien, asking for . . . genetic help? The origins of the Cied were shrouded in a thousand years of isolation, but one thing was well-known—the followers of Lien had left the coasts because they had believed that holy Mendülay was punishing the Nualans for using technology to attempt to control their planet. Given the proper time, Mendülay would heal both the Nualans and their home.

"You ask much, Dragoche," Darame finally said softly. "Is this asking for Ciedärlien, or for others?"

"*We* ask, Atarae." There was silence for a time, and finally The Dragoche began to speak, her gaze fixed upon an invisible mark on the tent wall. "For many generations, the borne healers of our people have known this truth—we are outkin all, we Cied, and eventually it will destroy us. The followers of Lien were strong of heart . . . and we believe in the choices of our ancestors . . . but we are too few. The ties that bind us begin to fray within, and the future is too terrible to contemplate. If it continues, live births will diminish, and our numbers wither like monsoon grass."

Inbreeding. Of course. The coasts had always traded among themselves . . . but when the Cied left for the sands, their only diversity was in believers from every tribe. When Nuala returned to the stars, seeking immigrants, the Ciedärlien remained apart . . . interwoven. Slowly, steadily, natural defects and Nualan mutation would begin to take their toll. *The genes begin to fray . . . never doubt that she is a true healer, even if her terms are strange*.

"You wish aid from our labs?"

"We wish to send volunteers to the coast, to bring back our future," The Dragoche clarified. "It should have begun years ago, but . . . there has been resistance." A tiny shrug. "Now that healer and Dragoche are one, I can say: 'Mendülay requires this of us' and it will be done. Why would a healer be chosen Dragoche, except to bring new life to our people?"

"Why, indeed?" There was nothing else to say—the labs never denied aid, ever. "I cannot speak for Atare, but I have the ear of The Atare and Avis Ragäree, and I believe I can sway this to your favor." Choosing her words carefully, she continued: "You know that we seek to return to the mold of our ancestors, but with the strength to withstand the planet's heat. You care only that the seed is as healthy as possible? The coloring of the Cied may begin to change—"

The Dragoche straightened. "My own daughter has blond hair. It will be a new generation in more ways than one." Her head snapped back toward Darame. "This can be kept among Atare?"

Ah. Friction remained with the other clans. . . . "If it can be done, it will be done." *Your reasons for remaining apart are subtle, but you do not need ridicule from those who do not understand.* That they could bring themselves to ask . . . no, the coast did not understand the Cied. A touch of awe threaded Darame's impression of the new Dragoche. Perhaps there was more to the selection of a Dragoche than politics and tribes taking turns. . . .

It was that simple. "I would recommend remaining with us a full turn of Kee, before escorting Kristinsson to the coast. Will you join me for a light supper, Atarac?"

"I would be honored, Dragoche," Darame said with complete sincerity.

> improvisation: The act or state of being improvised, as in 1) a] A course pursued with no previously conceived policy, plan, or consideration in mind, or b] The extemporaneous quality of such a course— spur of the moment; 2) a] extemporaneous creativity b] the extemporaneousness of said creativity; 3) Something improvised, or designed to appear improvised [IMPROVISE—to devise from whatever material is available.] Compare *IMPROMPTU*.

CHAPTER TEN

CIEDÄRLIEN TRADING CAMP
        ONEHUNDRED NINETYTHREEDAY   PRIME

Starrise was a singularly unpleasant experience for Darame. Before the star had fully cleared the horizon, she was prostrate with dry heaves.

Now I am for it . . . must be some form of influenza. Wryly, she congratulated herself on picking the location of a hot healer. Sweet Mendülay, she hated to be only a *little* sick. It would be embarrassing to ask for assistance. . . .

"Atarae?" Mailan's soft, low voice was close by in the gloom. "I have brought you some water."

"Thank you," she managed. Sitting up took time, but she accomplished it on her own. Reaching for a mug was temporarily beyond her; Mailan finally poured her a small amount and closed her fingers around the ceramic sides.

"The body is always the weak link," Darame said lightly, slowly sipping the water. Part of her wanted to rinse her mouth, but old habits died hard—this was the ciedär, and one did not waste moisture in the ciedär.

"Do you wish me to ask for The Dragoche?" Mailan asked.

After pausing for another sip, she said: "We must talk first."

"About Garth Kristinsson?" Mailan's rise to captain was threatening to make her garrulous; *guaard* did not ask questions often.

"Partly." A night of restless sleep had crystallized several things for Darame. First and foremost was the need to tell Mailan about Kristinsson's words. If Aesir was able to reach her, she was uncertain that even the *guaard* could prevent her death. But she could not leave Sheel to wonder why an assassin had struck in the night. "Kristinsson mentioned something in his murmurings that you should know about. He said 'Aesir considers the debt to be paid.' Are you familiar with that phrase?"

"I believe it has something to do with the Gavrielian underground," Mailan said calmly, startling her Atarae.

"Now how do you know that?"

"The security forces of different worlds occasionally are pushed into alliance. During one of those times, the *guaard* had access to the data banks of the Reykjavik Internal Police."

"Indeed." Perhaps the Reykjavik police had not known they had volunteered quite so much information? "That is essentially correct. They are . . . have you ever heard of the Mafia? The idea of one nationality having a group which protects its interests . . . at a price?"

"Born on Earth, was it not? Somewhere in the nineteenth or twentieth century *anno Domini* nation of Italy. They took the law into their own hands to satisfy blood feuds, and progressed into a strong criminal syndicate." Mailan sounded momentarily like a history teacher.

"Exactly. The progression on Gavriel was much the same, only Aesir still exists mainly to settle wergild. Aesir loans money and seeks information, all to protect the interests of people who come to them—Gavriclians, mostly. Aesir gets a cut of the wergild, of course. If the person who borrowed metal or asked for information doesn't pay up, his family may suddenly have even more reason to seek wergild."

"And what has this to do with you, Atarae?" Mailan asked neutrally.

"I am not sure." Frowning, Darame dug into memory. "Those words are traditional—Aesir uses them when they consider their part of a job to be complete. The question is, why was Garth Kristinsson using those words?"

"I would imagine he will be unlikely to volunteer a reason."

"I imagine you are correct," Darame said wryly. "Aesir said those words to Kristinsson, I would guess. Again—why? To signal that he, or someone close to him, had paid a debt? To offer ceremonially to someone else, once he had made sure that they had satisfied a debt? If he *is* Aesir, he is one of two things—an assassin, or a witness. If he is not. . . ."

"You are in danger, Atarae," Mailan stated.

"Possibly. Words spoken in a delirium may be long past—or not connected to me at all. So—" Darame carefully settled her robes around her knees. "If there is a threat, it is off-world—Aesir does not hire native mercenaries to make their lessons plain. But I am not sure the *guaard* can anticipate Aesir, even with prior knowledge. Should something happen, at least you will know why." This last was brisk.

"Atarae." This one-word sentence caused Darame to glance up from the hem she was smoothing. Mailan's face was peaceful. "Did you in the past ask Aesir for either wealth or information? For any reason?"

"Lucy's Light, no! I stayed as far away from them as possible." Darame shuddered, wrapped in distant memory. "It was not wise to draw their attention to yourself . . . Aesir never forgot someone who was useful. I always thought myself fortunate that they never seemed to notice me. Perhaps I was hasty, thinking myself secure from their eyes."

"Then they have another reason for seeking you, if they do. Are you not allowed to speak in your defense?"

Darame smiled mirthlessly. "Another reason to treat Aesir with respect; if they are satisfied with a claim, they do not bother with counter-claims while attempting to satisfy ancient law." Sighing, Darame gave her shoulders a twist, then pulled her first veil across her face. "It is time to approach Garth Kristinsson. Where to start. . . ."

"From his advantage, of course—as you always do. But not quite yet," Mailan replied, securing her own veil and rising to stand to one side of the tent slit. Fabric slapped as someone requested entrance.

"Come," Darame said in Ciedärlien. *Ah, to have Mailan's hearing.*

The warrior who entered was not familiar, but the individual behind him was The Dragoche. The woman did not wait for an invitation to sit but immediately lowered herself onto the cushions next to Darame. Reaching for her guest's wrist, The Dragoche was attentive to every twitch and pulse.

"You are well, Atarae?" she asked gently.

"Well enough, Dragoche," Darame said carefully. "Well enough to travel, and to take Kristinsson to the coast."

"Yes," The Dragoche agreed, releasing Darame's arm. "Does your husband not know, Atarae, or did he choose to wait to tell you? You must be careful—the early time is the most delicate."

Darame studied the woman's dark eyes intently, weighing her words. Surely not . . . nothing like the other two times . . . but later ones were often different, either easier or harder—

"How long?" she asked steadily.

"Say rather how far," The Dragoche answered, meaning it was still prudent to count from the beginning, rather than toward the end.

So new, this life . . . Darame had begun to wonder if three children was her allotment. *How odd—before I came here, I would have thought that three was two too many.* Yet fertility came and went, and sometimes the heat of the planet dulled its edge. Sheel, too, was still Nualan, for all his heritage of off-world men who had given their ragäree wives children. His fertility was cyclical, not constant, as was the case off-world.

"I will be careful," Darame said aloud. Another child. . . .

She felt a smile creep across her lips, and was glad no one could see it. Some things could not be shared with strangers, no matter how sympathetic.

Nodding once, almost as if giving Darame permission to use her own judgment, The Dragoche straightened her already upright stance. "Before we part, I would give you a gift, Atarae."

Oops. Darame had nothing to match such an offering. "It is enough that I have spoken to The Dragoche, and heard her words," Darame responded.

"Your promise means much to us," The Dragoche continued, as if she had not heard Darame speak. "If it can be fulfilled, it will be fulfilled—though it take generations, it shall be fulfilled."

"Yes," was the simple affirmation.

"Your will is strong, ice woman," The Dragoche said firmly. Startled, Darame did not reply. That was a nickname a sini of Lebanon had given her . . . had it traveled this far? "Not mere will, but sense of honor—I would pay homage to the morality of Atare." Her hands disappeared momentarily into her voluminous robes; they reappeared holding a sheathed blade.

The leather was old and worn, but well-tended, the repeating gold design circling the hilt known as soft diamond. *Ebony . . . the black must be ebony.* It had traveled more light years than she could imagine. . . .

Gracefully The Dragoche extended both hands, offering the knife. "It has waited for one who cannot dishonor it," she said gravely.

Hesitantly, Darame reached for the blade.

The grip was warm, that smooth heat only wood conveyed. So delicate, the worn gold tracings overlaying the woods . . . was there cherry in this blade? The only species she recognized for certain was osage-orange; its wood was blood red. At least three woods, with a grace that spoke of great age. This blade was so old it was almost sentient. Courtesy demanded she draw and examine it; the action almost lost her any claim to composure.

Just below the hilt, delicately engraved upon the alloy itself, was the fragile symbol of a crane. . . .

Dear, sweet Mendülay, it is a Crain. It was a very old name in metal lore, a family whose work spanned generations. Crain blades had been cherished by more than one member of the original Nualan landing party. She had thought all of them were in private collections, but one, at least, had escaped being buried forever beyond the sight of commoners.

Finally Darame lifted her head to meet the woman's gaze. "I saw the look in your eyes when we first met," The Dragoche said simply. "It was a look of blind terror . . . I must assume it was the young man's words which inspired your fear. But you did not kill him; to place justice and moral responsibility before self-preservation is an act of which few are capable. We are no longer worthy of this blade, and have not carried it in generations. I trust you will prove a wise guardian."

So that is how you knew . . . that I would keep my word to you. "I will do my best, Dragoche."

One nod, as in satisfaction or dismissal. "Join me now in a cup of special tea, Atarae. It will help soothe your stomach. By the time the star has crested the sky, you will be ready to speak to Garth Kristinsson."

CIEDÄRLIEN TRADING CAMP   SEXT

They were slightly bitter, the pills; the slick coating on them was not nearly thick enough. There was no longer any choice, however—Garth knew when it was time to capitulate. *So I take the pill series,* he told himself grimly, downing the rest of a precious glass of water.

No one had to tell him the value of fluids. Shrouded figures appeared at regular intervals, offering coldseal containers filled with cool water. No one who came spoke Caesarean, but Garth figured he was meant to drink all of it—he had been there a long time, and had had no need to pass water.

My skin is doing the work, Garth told himself, trying not to move. So tired . . . he had done too much the night before. He found himself wishing he had one of the gauzy Cied robes. They were in three layers; an outer robe, a long-sleeved caftan over drawstring pants, and beneath that a skinsuit, which was light-colored and made of something highly absorbent. *Actually, it's rather stimulating, watching them peel off those layers.*

A smile touched his lips. Who would have thought he'd have energy for sex? But he had surprised himself last night. The shadowed figure who had been present when he awoke had been female, but her amber-colored eyes indicated still another stranger. Without comment she had brought him an herbal tea and a moist, soft cheese, which he had finally let slide down his throat. What point in protesting, after she had pressed the pill packet into his hand—and two were already missing?

If the woman had been disappointed that he seemed languid, she had given no sign of it. Rather, she actually had a sense of humor about her presence—while removing her robes, she had winked at him. Garth had been surprised that she had stripped nude (hadn't he read somewhere that the people conserved body moisture by always wearing clothes?) but after peeling off her skinsuit, the woman had pulled her caftan back on. Swiftly braiding her long, dark hair, she had curled up next to him and closed her eyes.

At first the added heat had been unbearable, but Garth had feared to offend her, and had not moved. Later on, sweat and desert shadow had cooled into comfort, and when the young woman's fingers had trailed across the back of his right hand, Garth found that he had made a decision. Whether this was tribal courtesy, that a "guest" should not sleep alone, or private initiative, or even stud service in return for his rescue, was no reason to turn down an interested female with beautiful eyes and a friendly smile.

Morning bore a definite air of fantasy. Not only his companion of the previous night, but the first woman as well had been in attendance, accompanying the servant who brought them a light breakfast. The women had dismissed the servant, then removed their veils, revealing dark and golden beauty, both black hair and dark chestnut, and that same, slow smile. . . .

The pattern of starlight through the tent slit drew him back to the moment. Another coldseal of water had arrived; how long had he been awake? He had napped again, after breakfast, once the pair had left—

"Enjoying your prison?" came a low-voiced question.

A sharp turn of the head, and Garth saw that others had entered his tent. Two more Cied, with different color patterns on their robes— The eyes of the smaller one were familiar. He knew that voice. . . .

Garth struggled to sit up. Holy Jesu, where did *she* come from? And how did she find him, for pity's sake? *He* didn't know where he was. . . .

"They . . . have been kind, as far as they could," Garth began slowly.

"You were lucky—their hot healer was nearby. Otherwise, you would have been dead yesterday."

"I am a prisoner, then?" he said steadily.

"I have arranged to take charge of you, in exchange for some things the Cied want. They are great traders, and famous for getting the best part of a bargain. It all depends on whether you wish to leave here with me." She stood with folded arms, a still, shapeless pillar of sand—

"You're welcome to sit," Garth blurted out.

He was correct; she had been waiting for an invitation. Irritation at his own lack of courtesy momentarily obscured the meaning of her last words. *Whether you wish to leave with me? What is going on?* Silently Garth watched the woman settle herself onto the floor of pillows. By the time she was facing him, eye to eye, her veils to one side, he was ready.

"Why are you here?" Garth asked simply.

"Looking for you, of course," was the reply. "You left in a hurry, and without the proper paperwork. That smacks of fear. I suspected that you . . . overheard . . . some information that might be dangerous, and accordingly ran from those who might have silenced your knowledge."

Had he imagined the pause, before the word "overheard?" "It seems a small thing for The Atarae of Nuala," he suggested, probing.

"You are Lisbet's son," she stated, the spread of her hands indicating that there could be no question of her involvement. "Also, there is a very serious situation brewing on the coast. Some antimatter has been stolen. I was hoping that what you heard might be connected to the theft. I do not have to tell you the dangers of an antimatter trap in unskilled hands."

"We will return to Amura-By-The-Sea?" Garth continued.

"Eventually. We will go to Andersen first."

First. Ah—and if you needed to run again, there would be room. "How would I get out of the desert, if I did not leave with you?"

Darame smiled slightly. "I am not sure you would. Cied have a way of keeping stray off-worlders as long as they can. If they thought they could convince you to stay permanently, they'd put their hearts into it. Clean genetic material, you see. They might let you go, when the owners of the freighter came for their property. Then again . . . they might not."

"What makes them so sure I am clean?" Garth responded evenly.

The woman's smile widened. "I doubt they trusted to luck; I imagine that they ran a few tests of their own. Any young woman close to cycling would have been in the lottery for the first night with you . . . last night, I imagine The Dragoche sent the woman most likely to conceive. But it never occurred to them that someone who had failed to take the series would get this far into the ciedär. They have tried to make your stay as pleasant as possible, all things considered—and they sent for The Dragoche herself to heal you. As we have already discussed, you have given them return for their hospitality—a tenfold return, if either of those women conceived. You may leave them without a feeling of debt."

"I do not know where the antimatter is," Garth said slowly. "But I had a feeling . . . someone thought I knew too much."

The look he received was intent; he was not certain she believed him. "That does not mean you cannot help me. At any rate, I can protect you."

"There are some things Nualans do not wave," Garth replied.

"I choose to be Nualan—and if you help my people, I can arrange many things. For the time being, I can get you away from here, and keep you safe from any who might threaten you. Few would have the nerve to cross the wife of The Atare." Standing slowly, the woman pulled the lower veil across her mouth. "Think about it; my charter will not leave until the star is low."

"I will go with you." What was there to think about? And if she knew nothing, he was safe enough with her.

If she suspected his involvement? So far she was not pushing . . . so he was still safe enough with her.

For now.

AMURA-BY-THE-SEA
ONEHUNDRED NINETYTHREEDAY   NONE

Kee's rays danced across the water; the reflection was as painful as light against metal. Clouds billowed across the horizon, promising rain. They had promised several days . . . it was as if the shore held its breath, waiting. . . .

It was irrational, the guilt Sheel felt. He could not make it rain—why did he feel he should be out in the heat, suffering with the drooping plants outside his back door? At least Atare had something to be happy about—Avis had delivered a healthy son in the early hours of morning. Curled in a sloping chair, she cradled the sleeping child close, talking earnestly with her other children about the new arrival.

"Yes, he is tiny, but you were smaller, Jul," she told her four-year-old daughter. Blond curls bobbing, her mismatched pastel-hued eyes wide with interest, Juliana compared the bundle in her mother's arms to her own long legs.

"What are we going to call him?" Drew asked.

"Well, your father and I have a few ideas, but there is time —we shall not name him for a good thirtyday yet. Your Aunt Darame and Aunt Leah will help." Avis winked at Sheel and her husband Stephen as she spoke. Traditionally the mother, the eldest female of the House, and a friend of the mother's choosing named a highborn child. Officially, the family representative would be Leah and Darame the friend. If Darame had returned by then. . . .

"Come along, troops," Stephen told the small gathering. "Your mother could use some rest. You can come back later." Bending to give Avis a quick kiss, Stephen scooped up Juliana to his shoulder and lead the way toward the door. *"Rest,"* he told Avis, his voice firm.

Chuckling, Avis nodded assent, her eyes already slipping back to the new life she held. She ignored tapping at the doorframe.

"Enter." Sheel turned back toward the window as he spoke. Behind him, Avis graciously responded to compliments rumbled her way; Sheel waited to hear what news Zaide brought. It would not be good—that was a certainty.

Finally Avis asked: "And what else brings you here, Zaide?"

"You know me too well, Ragäree."

"You always make purely social calls after vespers," was the amused response. "Come now—what new horror have you dragged into the light of day?"

"Only a potential horror, Ragäree. Dielaan vessels are sailing down the Amber."

Silence. Sheel twisted his torso toward the seneschal. "Not trade, then?"

"The wrong shape for traders, Atare. They are neither swift moonrakers nor heavy haulers. They can only be transports. And they do not fly colors."

That was interesting. One side of the Amber River was controlled by Andersen, while the other paid nominal heed to Dielaan, much like Amura looked to Atare. Ships could sail without colors in their own waters, but not in open territory. . . .

"How do we come by this information?" Avis asked, her concentration on her son's face.

"Satellite, Ragäree."

"So others know of this development."

"Oh, yes—most of the omni stations have already mentioned the event." Zaide's voice hinted at unvented irritation.

"Have you taken any action yet?" Avis continued.

"I contacted a friend at an Amuran net link. More than one group has asked Dielaan for a statement concerning the ships. It is interesting to note that none of the embassies, either clan or off world, have inquired about the vessels." A familiar, deadly blandness had slipped into Zaide's voice.

Sheel turned completely, leaning against the heavy thermal glass and meeting his sister's glance. Her face was suddenly devoid of expression—Zaide's last words had disturbed her. With good reason; when the clans were screaming and throwing insults at one another, the actual situation was sound. But when silence grew among them. . . .

"Have we been contacted? Has anyone requested a synod meeting today?"

"No to both questions, Atare."

"They wait," Avis murmured. "I wonder how Dielaan will explain the ships."

Vespers brought an announcement by the House of Dielaan. Sheel, Avis, Leah, and his sisters' spouses watched the conference from the comfort of the Green Room, then retreated to the starset level for an early meal.

Kee was low in the sky, slipping between the dark clouds like a wary ghost. "At least the cloud cover keeps the temperature lower," Sheel said aloud as he moved to the wall-sized window.

"There is that," Richard grunted, reaching for a hot roll and juggling it experimentally. "All we need right now is for the heat to touch off tempers. 'Maneuvers,' indeed! Do they expect anyone to believe that? A perfectly good body of water off their own coast, and they need to practice maneuvers in the Alameda Sea?''

"There has been a flurry of messengers wheppin' in an' ert of Kilgor' Herse,'' Stephen added, seating himself and passing a covered dish to Avis.

Sheel gave his brother-by-law a hard look. Stephen's Garrison accent rarely surfaced—especially when he spoke Nualan. Then he moved away from the windows and toward the small group. "Zaide, please join us.'' Sheel gestured to a seat as the man entered the room. "Stephen tells us that Kilgore has had a great deal of activity today. Anything on the grapevine?''

"Their coastal watch is on alert,'' Zaide said simply, nodding his thanks as Leah passed him the fruit. "Shall I arrange table service, Atare?''

"No. We can do without this evening.'' Sitting down, Sheel let his long fingers toy with a utensil. "No more than could be expected, since they are at the curve of the coast. Anything else of interest?''

Zaide smiled. "I am not sure. Would you find it interesting to know that Lulani reb^Carlotta Dielaan left Amura today—for Andersen? And that Rebekah Finnsdottir was turned away at Dielaan House with the news that Quen reb^Livia Dielaan is ill, and cannot have visitors?''

The utensil paused in mid-flip. "And?'' Zaide's smile was satisfied.

"It is time to pass along the other news; I have been saving it for a time when we needed cheering, but the deadline draws near. In less than thirty minutes, Darol University will be making an announcement on the infonet. The intelligence branch of the *guaard* reports that the Physics Department has made an incredible discovery. They have been experimenting with the platinum group metals in antiproton targeting and lens work. Using trinium as the metallic target for a proton beam in a particle accelerator, the energy efficiency of antiproton production can be raised from a part in ten thousands to—'' Zaide paused to take a sip of wine.

"Well?'' Avis said, her expression curious.

"A part in hundreds.'' Zaide's amusement was clear.

Silence. Sheel kept his eyes upon Zaide, so he could not see

Richard's face as he spoke—but his brother-by-law's voice reflected astonishment as clearly as a mirror. "Hundreds?"

"Hundreds," Zaide repeated, reaching casually for a roll.

"We r' rich," Stephen exclaimed, amazement threading his words.

Avis started to giggle. "We were already rich, love. I do not think the tribe need consider the subject of wealth anymore— . . . with this boost, we are considerably beyond the concept of 'wealthy.' " Her eyes strayed to Sheel as she spoke. "Is it safe to celebrate?"

Stephen looked puzzled, but Leah's and Richard's demeanor was subdued. Leah said simply: "Consider how the other clans will react to this news."

After a moment, Stephen said precisely: "Half the planet will be applying for entry to the tribe—pickaxe in hand."

"The least of it," Sheel agreed. "Scedar and Kilgore will not care for it . . . and I think I can guarantee that Rex Dielaan will go up in flames."

"But it will mean both power and freedom," Zaide pointed out, abandoning his offhand manner. "There are things Nuala requires; things our desire for trade forced us to set aside. Now we need have no fears, for they will line up at our door, attentive to our every word."

"Hungry for our lifeblood," Sheel murmured. Standing, he moved back to the huge window. The star was disappearing into a swirl of red, black, and yellow, the horizon seemingly burning. "Is Quen of Dielaan really ill, and why did Lulani leave Amura?"

"How can we find out?" Avis asked.

Sheel reached for the membrane of a RAM, set inconspicuously to one side of a planter. Tapping in a code, he waited for the selection to appear. "I am both doctor and healer, and I have access to medical information. If his illness is serious enough that he has no visitors, tests were run; the results will be at the hospice."

"Can you do that for anyone?" Leah asked.

Smiling, Sheel placed a finger to his lips in warning. "And the answer is . . . Quen's record has not changed since his arrival. . . . Lulani has been in her cousin's shadow for months. Why Andersen and not home?" His wandering fingertips tapped lightly on the edge of the RAM.

"Kristinsson?" Zaide asked.

"Crow tells me it was the only probable direction for him."
His gaze shifted to Avis. "It is about time for you, is it not?"
She looked startled, then nodded.

"As soon as you finish nursing, I think we should call Nadine
. . . before Andersen's announcement, if possible. I want her
disposed to listen to us."

"What will we discuss with her?" Avis asked, her eyes twinkling.

"Do you remember what I said about Stennis? Nadine was
going to choose her time, and bring it up to the Dielaan ambassador . . . privately. And Kilgore has its ear to the waves,
even as we guard the northern mountains."

"I will send for the baby," Avis said suddenly. "With some
strategic draping, I can nurse him without anyone knowing—
though I doubt Nadine would care. We should catch her before
Andersen makes that announcement."

"Of course she may already know," Zaide pointed out.

"Everything is a risk," Avis replied, rising and moving to a
wall vid.

It took three different transfers to reach Nadine of Kilgore;
fortunately, by Amuran standards, Kilgore house had meals at
odd hours. Nadine appeared with a glass of white wine in hand,
her mood clearly mellow.

"Redfish is always best with Sonoma River whites. I fear I
envy you the vineyards, Atare. Would you care to work out a
trade of some type?"

"A warm-water shellfish bed for a vineyard?" Sheel suggested.

Nadine's expression was momentarily remote. "Two vineyards," she countered.

Smiling faintly, Sheel said: "Two beaujolais vineyards."

"Chardonnay."

Sheel shook his head slightly.

"A dozen bottles of this year's crop?"

"For . . ."

"A preview of tomorrow's Synod meeting."

Silence. "Am I going to like the preview?" Sheel asked softly.

"Why do you think I am drinking before compline?" This
was precise, the enunciation artificially clear.

Avis allowed her chair to turn slightly, angling her body toward the screen. "Burdens shared are halved."

"For that, ragäree, I shall arrange a basket of fresh shrimp for you." She sighed. "I do not have the temperament for this, Atares. I fear I may have provoked something . . . but I am not sure what I triggered."

"Let us reconstruct the scene," Sheel suggested.

"Are we alone?"

Sheel glanced around the room. Leah, Richard and Stephen had left before the call was made. Zaide remained just beyond the screen.

"The seneschal listens."

Nodding, Nadine said: "As we discussed, I intended to present the case of Stennis to the Dielaan 'advisor' earlier this afternoon. Our embassy representative had business with their ambassador, and I went along as backup. Upon arrival, I was informed that the man was not going to be available—that he was no longer attending to Synod business. Rex Dielaan would see me instead." Smiling faintly, Nadine continued: "It is well-known the 'advisor' was sent to knock some sense into Rex. He is a partisan of Livia Ragäree." Nadine leaned forward. "And at odds with his sister's children, who are currently out of Livia's favor."

"Tsuga and his brothers," Sheel supplied smoothly.

"Tsuga is heading up those ships, Sheel Atare. Now why would Tsuga leave behind all his responsibilities to conduct maneuvers in the Alameda Sea?"

Avis drew in a deep breath, but Sheel did not turn to catch her eye. Sweet Mendülay, Tsuga. The last three years he had quietly undermined Livia's position . . . was he ready to openly back her son against her? Traditionalists would say Rex should go off-world, should find his wife and "serve his time" in the outer lands, as many put it. But others . . . outkin, outclan . . . what could they gain, if he tried to force Livia's hand?

"Do you know anything for certain?" Sheel finally asked.

"We were able to tap a final message before their code changed . . . we have yet to break the new one. 'Do not concern yourself with the regency problem, I have attended to it as per your instructions.' " Nadine was silent for a time, idly twirling her wineglass. "I told Dielaan that a man named Stennis had been picked up by the Amuran security force . . . and that he was claiming Dielaan immunity. I asked him if he was prepared for the questions Stennis's claim was bound to raise in The Synod.'' Her pause was fractional, but crisp. ''Dielaan told me that if The Synod was so paranoid it saw enemies at every turn, it had failed as a body for mediation. It had failed,'' Nadine repeated, ''and so far as Dielaan was concerned, it had outlived its usefulness.''

''Finally he is pulling out?'' Sheel said quietly.

''So I gather from his words.'' She suddenly looked worn. ''I was so careful, Atare . . . delivering a friendly warning. Dielaan was looking for insult. He told me through a sheet of ice, centimeters thick, that I should be careful of accusing anyone of having that antimatter—that I might be laying the groundwork for a 'prolonged disagreement,' as he put it.''

''Who was threatening whom?'' Avis said dryly.

Nadine nodded, and downed the last of her wine.

''Let us speak before the meeting tomorrow, Nadine,'' Sheel said.

''Call me,'' she said simply.

''After sext, unless something comes up,'' Avis promised.

''Good E'ven.''

The seneschal moved to disconnect the huge RAM vid. He stood by it, not speaking, his hand resting on the membrane.

''Zaide . . . have you heard anything from The Atarae?'' Sheel asked quietly.

''No, Atare. Nor the captain.''

''If anything was wrong,'' Avis said firmly, ''we would have heard. Go put your children to bed.''

One last night . . . tomorrow will change everything.

MAIDEN'S HOPE   COMPLINE
VILLAGE OF KRISTINE

It was only a refueling stop, but Garth wanted to leave the ship. ''The inland sea is very different, isn't it?'' he asked The Atarae.

Shrugging, she responded: ''The colors seem more intense here. Something about the combination of salt and starlight and particle density, I suppose. It is a beautiful body of water, but you will be able to see little right now; the star still sets early this time of year.''

"Do you care if I try to see from the tower?" he asked, keeping his voice relaxed. It was as good a time as any to examine their precautions.

"Not at all. We'll all go." Standing, the silver-haired woman led the way, her tall shadow only two paces behind her.

Why do I feel like you follow her but watch me? Garth knew better than to ask the *guaard* anything at all—his question was doubly unsuitable.

The Nualans knew their planet—it was already too dark to see the water, although several boats at anchor were outlined by tiny lights along their rigging. A different smell, this sea . . . saltier, harsher.

"Tomorrow morning in Andersen," Darame promised him, nodding at the darkness beyond. "Directly across the water, oh, several hours by meth. The place I usually stay has a beautiful view of the sea."

"You will like it even better from a ship," came a familiar voice.

Garth whirled around, even as the *guaard* blurred past him into a solid wall between the voice and The Atarae. No, his ears had not deceived him—it was Lucy, with at least a dozen uniformed Dielaan warriors in tow. *How in Seven Hells*—Looking quickly at Darame, he saw the woman was watching his face.

Whatever she saw there seemed to satisfy her.

gauntlet: 1) Two rows of armed people facing each other and striking at an individual who is forced to run between them. Activity attributed to a small group of Terran northwest hemisphere *Homo sapiens*. 2) A cross fire of some type. 3) An ordeal or, more rarely, a punishment.

CHAPTER ELEVEN

DIELAAN HARBOR
     ONEHUNDRED NINETYSEVENDAY   NONE

Waking was hard. Not that there was any reason to wake—what could be done on a ship at sea? *A ship approaching harbor*, Darame suddenly remembered, and fought her way toward consciousness. *Your own fault. If your reputation was not so pervasive, they would have left you in Kristine.*

But for some reason Lulani could not do that. There was a timetable involved . . . that worried Darame. Rex Dielaan's cousin needed Garth, but wanted neither an alarm sounded nor a tracker at her heels. So Darame and Mailan had been "invited" to accompany them to Dielaan. *Protective custody, my father's black eyes.*

Someone was placing a cracker in her hand. Convenient of the cook to have some on board—

"Atarae, can you hear me?" came Mailan's patient voice.

"Of course I can hear you, you are shouting in my ear," Darame mumbled.

"Can you open your eyes?"

That question was not quite right. Darame experimentally lifted an eyelid. The room was dancing without her permission. Slowly propping herself up on one elbow, she gave Mailan a blurred look.

The *guaard* was unruffled. "Drugged," she said simply. "In the tea served last night. I did not drink of it, but they knew I would not leave you. We have had a seventy-five-hour lock placed on our codes—we cannot call out of the city. Apparently there is no such thing as a cash call here—you must identify yourself to get net access. Other than that, we are alone. The remaining sailors will not prevent our leaving—"

"Since we would have to travel quite a distance to get to an outside line. A complete code block? How do they expect us to eat?"

"Food was left. The sailors plan to host us several days yet."

"Other avenues open to us?" Darame found that her head was no longer spinning and forced herself to stare at the *guaard*.

Mailan knew what she meant, even as both women glanced down to see the faint, gray sheen tinting Darame's roman. Their conversation was being monitored. "I sent a little bird two hours ago."

More than ten hours before the satellite went over again. But Mailan *had* been able to tap directly into it. "How long was I unconscious?"

"From compline last night. None rang not long ago." Mailan's gaze was steady, her gray eyes questioning.

Of course—Mailan *was* asking a question. Did they have any options? Were they forced to remain on shipboard for three days? If the warriors were gone, no one would stop them from seeking Garth and Lulani, but trying to track a cold trail through the maze of Dielaan would be a hopeless task. . . .

"Is there still a regent?" she said abruptly.

Her eyebrows lifted slightly at the phrasing, but Mailan nodded.

"In the city?"

"There has been no mention of her leaving Dielaan."

Slowly Darame swung her legs over the side of the berth. With exquisite caution, she raised herself to a sitting position.

"I am not sure it would be possible to approach the regent," Mailan offered. "Dielaan news being what it is, I have not discovered the problem, but there is tension and hostility toward Atare right now. All Atare traders have been warned to remain in their hostels."

"Wonderful." Thinking furiously, Darame flexed her fingers and toes, wondering if the life-to-be had taken the drug in stride. Mendülay, if a miscarriage was triggered, what would she tell Sheel? What it would do to Atare-Dielaan relations—"The robes! We still have Cied robes!"

"Marked with the emblems of the royal line," Mailan pointed out.

"Mailan," Darame began patiently. "Does the average Ataran know *any* Cied patterns? The ruse only has to get us to the firerose garden before the Hall of Judgment."

"Atarae?" Mailan actually looked skeptical.

"The trellis at the entrance to the gardens," she specified. "There is a procession back to the palace every day at vespers. I know for a fact that Livia always glances at those fireroses. If we place ourselves carefully, we will be invisible to the crowd and in plain sight to Livia. And if it fails to work," she added quickly, "we will return here for dinner and think of other ways to occupy ourselves. But Livia *did* ask me to visit before the turn of the year." *That* for anyone who was listening.

"Very well, Atarae," Mailan said quietly. "Would you care for another cracker while I locate the robes? That is one," she added.

Darame struggled not to laugh, and lost the battle. Sweet Magdalen, were they back to owing favors? Whenever the young *guaard* had done something normally beyond her duties for her then-liege Serae Sheel, seventh son of Ragäree Riva, he had owed her an unspecified courtesy—whenever Sheel had done something normally not asked of the Line, she had owed him. Mailan had apparently decided that it had amused Sheel and drawn him out of his solitude. *Do I seem to need a laugh?*

"More than one, I fear," Darame finally got out, wiping away a tear. "Yes, Mailan, I will have another cracker. But I will get it myself."

VESPERS

They reached the trellis of the firerose garden at the stroke of the vespers bells. Quickly taking in the area, Darame decided that the simplest arrangement would be to lean against the heavy trellis in full view. Leave her head uncovered? Perhaps that was too exposed . . . a curl or two trickling down her shoulder would be enough. Livia would recognize the ciedär patterns of Atare —Livia never forgot anything.

Fireroses were a late summer-early fall plant, but a few subspecies bloomed the entire growing season. A magnificent pink variety swarmed thickly up the trellis and across the arch like a bolt of velvet. *Just the thing for Atare colors,* Darame thought, choosing her corner with care.

"The unease in the city does not concern you, Atarae?" Mailan said quietly from the shadows behind her.

Then a horn blew, and there was no more time for conversation. Just down the street and across from them, the gates of the Hall of Judgment swung outward. Four pairs of warriors mounted upon black hazelles indicated that the regent of Dielaan was returning to the palace. Darame was intrigued to see that Livia was riding in a drawn carriage. *I know we rode in a meth when I was here last.* "Why a carriage?" she murmured aloud.

Correctly deducing that she was being addressed, Mailan said: "A meth can be tampered with; hazelles and carriages are harder to sabotage."

Sabotage. Huh. . . . "Remind me to tell you about my little talk with Tho Dragoche," Darame told her. "Someone else besides myself should know what was promised in return for cooperation."

The carriage slowed and a young warrior stepped out onto the running board. With a spring to his step, he leaped from the vehicle and moved off into the crowded street. Darame watched as he momentarily disappeared into a shifting blanket of bodies, then tucked her hair back into her robe. He came up to her and, offering her a delicate filigree ring set with a marquis-cut emerald, spoke without preamble.

"I am to escort you to the palace. A carriage will be sent." Remaining silent, Darame accepted the ring. Spreading his legs, the young man folded into a resting stance and proceeded to ignore Darame.

A ring of passage . . . interesting. Announcing that she was under Livia's protection; Darame recognized it as a gift from Livia's mother, one that never, to her knowledge, left Livia's hand. Necessary? Mailan had said there was a problem . . . she slid the band onto her right ring finger.

Reaching up above her head, Darame selected a firerose that had been creased by someone's carelessness and gently broke the stem. Tucking the fresh blossom behind one ear, she gave Mailan her most confident smile and turned back to watch for transportation.

COMPLINE

Dinner was full of exotic foods—an impressive spread on short notice—and the wine was a full-bodied Amuran cabernet. Cheese, chocolate, and madeira made up dessert, but Darame chose lemon-flavored water from the offered serving tray as she let her eyes flit toward the horizon. *Good night, husband. Sleep well.* Hours yet until Mailan could contact the satellite.

And tell them what? That they were free of the ship, but had definitely lost Garth? She would mention that they were guests of Livia—and host-guest law was practically engraved in granite. Safe for now.

A rustle of cotton skirts, and Livia reappeared from the inner dining area, moving languidly past the departing servant. Behind them, Mailan and a Dielaan warrior stood like signposts on either side of the entry door. Below, in the courtyard, several warriors stood within the shadows. Did Dielaan always have so many present, beyond the usual door wardens?

Otherwise they were alone; Livia's husband had joined them for dinner, but had excused himself after the meal. Darame had not missed the intent gaze he had given his wife before his departure.

"I have not seen us so quiet since right before Pamela and the twins were born," Darame finally offered.

A faint smile touched Livia's lips. "We were both carrying during the heat, as I recall. It was not a pleasant time to be dropping a child. And you," she added, "looked like you were carrying every promise in Atare."

"I *was* big," Darame admitted. "But they were big babies."

"How long were you on shipboard, my friend?" Livia asked quietly.

"Almost four days," Darame decided to say.

"Did you have access to the infonet?"

"Not exactly." This was dry, and amused. Livia must not think she was claiming insult. . . .

"What part does Lulani have in this?" Livia whispered, sipping her wine. She still drank red grapes, the heavy, heady taste suiting her mood. "Were you aware of the announcement from Andersen?"

"Enlighten me."

"Some physicist at their major university has been playing with antiproton production. He has discovered that platinum group metals raise the energy efficiency of production." Livia took another sip of wine. "Trinium, especially."

"It will be good for Nuala," Darame chose to say. Would this help the trade balance? They just barely broke even some trips—

"It will raise the efficiency level from a part in ten thousands to a part in hundreds." This was remote, as if Livia's mind was elsewhere.

Darame was grateful that she was resting her water glass on the edge of her seat. A part in *hundreds*? For a moment the sheer value of it numbed her—the free-trader might be buried, but she was not lost within. Then ten years of casual wealth snapped her attention back to the moment at hand.

"Could Tensar have done anything?" Livia murmured. "Would his life had made a difference?"

She spoke of her eldest brother, the previous Dielaan, dead ten years and more at the hand of Darame and Halsey's unmourned partner Brant. Sensing that Livia was struggling with something, Darame kept silent.

"It is over, for better or worse . . . the world I have known. I have tried to be a good regent, Darame," the regäree said steadily. "I have raised the standard of living among my people to new heights. I have opened lines of communication with ancient enemies, building for the future. I have borne six children . . . children I have been proud of." Her porcelain features turned slightly, and Darame realized that she was crying. "Five days ago, my second cousin tried to poison me. He then took off with a substantial part of our navy. The order for the ships was issued in the name of Rex Dielaan."

What was there to say? If Rex had ordered the ships, he had also ordered . . . what? Tsuga to take care of the problem of the regent? Dielaan was probably the craftiest and most violent of the tribes, but even *they* usually sent warning to a ruler that someone wanted them ousted.

"Obviously Rex does not know about the corner of hell the Cied claim is reserved for matricides," she suggested.

Livia started laughing. It went on too long; finally Darame reached over and firmly gripped the woman's shoulder, shaking her. Dropping her wine, Livia covered her face with her hands. The sound of shattered glass chimed discordantly; Livia's emerald, returned to her hand, seemed to flash in reply. "What is he doing with those ships?" she whispered. "Have I built a new house only to have it pulled down—and for what?"

"Do you know where the ships are?" Darame asked after a long silence.

"Two days out from the Amber Delta," was Livia's listless response.

"Heading . . ."

"West."

Ah. Toward the west coast . . . Kilgore, Seedar, Amura, the sini alliance . . . Atare. Was it a simple threat, or a promise?

"You are a very good regent, Livia," Darame whispered, her eyes shifting to the sky, where the stars began to come out. "All that has happened in the past few days, and your first thought is for your land and its people. That is as it should be."

"But I am also a mother, Darame. What do I owe my children?"

"You are the ragäree of Dielaan. You are the mother of your people, as much as the mother of the heirs." Darame spoke flatly, grinding the words.

"Those ships are full of outkin, Darame, most of them trained warriors. And I have no idea what Tsuga and Rex are going to do with them. They could be planning on starting a war—and I have no idea whom they plan to fight!" This last was almost bitter.

"I can assume you frown on this decision?"

"How can I know what I think if they tell me nothing? Even my—contact—in Amura has not sent word. And if he knows nothing—"

"Or is unable to send you word." Darame continued into the silence. "If someone tried to poison you, Livia, you must assume that they have set aside anyone they suspect of being your partisan. What is the provision when an heir reaches for the throne before he is confirmed? Livia . . .'' Darame decided they were good enough friends that she could speak bluntly. "If you think Rex is taking a fatal course of action—stop him."

"He has the right." This was both tired and bitter.

"No, he does not!" Darame leapt to her feet and strolled angrily toward the brick wall. "All this talk about his *rights*. Damn it, is there no talk of his responsibilities? Does he have the right to throw his people into a war that would drag them back down into grinding poverty? That might even *annihilate* them as a tribe?" Turning back to Livia, Darame added: "We have spent so much time building our synod for trade we forget that others watch what we do. What do you think will happen to the prices offered to each clan, if we return to bargaining alone? We *need* each other! Do you think the other tribes will *allow* Rex to kill the goose laying golden eggs?

"I do not know what will happen, either, Livia. Rex may make some brilliant strike and have you all applauding. Or he may ruin all of us."

Livia did not respond. A dark outline in her cushioned chair, she methodically twirled the wineglass stem she had retrieved; she would not look at Darame.

I cannot stand it. "Livia . . . there is a very good possibility that Rex and Lulani know something about the missing antimatter."

That got a reaction. Straightening, the woman turned imperially toward her guest. "Ah. And that strange-eyed, young offworlder is also part of it? Of course—I was obtuse not to see it. But Luzige pays little attention to the cousins; I warned him not to leave them out of his thoughts." That easily, Darame discovered the name of the diplomat recently sent to Amura. "This makes sense." Her deep green gaze flicked out toward the horizon. "Now I can explain. Rex absorbed much at Tsuga's knee . . . mostly poison against the other clans, I fear. Tsuga felt The Synod diminished the authority of The Dielaan, and so opposed it. I felt The Synod relieved The Dielaan of playing merchant, as well as gaining top prices for our goods. We stopped talking to each other for a time over it—you knew that?" Her sharp glance made it clear she asked a rhetorical question.

"So as soon as he was old enough to deal with The Synod,

Rex started trying to dismantle it?'' At Livia's nod, Darame grew bolder. ''You evade the question—what can you do? If Rex has the right, can you do nothing?''

''Not exactly.'' Now Livia looked tired. ''But there is only one thing to do, and it might . . . get out of hand.'' A smile touched her lips as she studied Darame's face. ''Do not eat me. Officially I am regent. Although Rex is heir—is Dielaan, since he is of age—he is expected to take care of certain matters before coming to the throne. Of course, sometimes the requirements cannot be met . . . a time of war, for example, where the Dielaan dies and his heir must take over.'' Livia's smile grew brittle.

''To whom does he answer to, if he fails in any of those matters . . . without a reason?'' Darame asked.

''To the family,'' Livia said steadily. ''Not only outkin, but outclan. There are many septs of Dielaan; their power is the pyramid upon which our throne rests. If he is a failure as a Dielaan, others will move in to 'advise' him. To keep the septs at bay, the family must move first.''

''But the family is divided. Some of the outkin are backing Rex.''

Livia's eyes flashed. ''Backing him in idiocy! If it was not so ludicrous, I would suspect them of trying to pull Rex down and push another branch into his place!''

''Why is that ludicrous?''

Silence. Livia slowly stood and walked over to the silver-haired woman. They were of a height; Livia's gaze was now steady. ''Because I have three sons, not one.'' A dare threaded her words.

''Rex already watches Quen like the proverbial hawk. What if Quen conveniently dies during a nice little war someplace? Either Rex or someone with darker plans could arrange it. You are supposed to be dead; if you were, who would be Coll's regent?''

''Lulani, oldest of the outkin . . . Lucy was named for her. But she . . . .'' Livia's face grew remote.

''You do not know!'' Darame said hurriedly. ''You cannot begin purging your family because you see phantoms threatening you! Lulani the elder may know nothing about this mess.''

''Then what do you advise?''

Dielaan historians would blame her sons, but the true surrender to Atare supremacy took place on a dark terrace in a coastal desert city when Livia Ragäree of Dielaan asked the wife of Sheel Atare for a course of action. What the free-trader Brant of Caesarea had begun, Rex Dielaan was about to finish—the autonomy of the clans.

"Stop Rex. If you show—right now, *before* he can start a war with somebody—that Rex has done nothing to prepare for his role, and now throws his people into battle like toys, I imagine the tribe will back you. Give your net some rein, and they will slice him up like a stew. I know your people follow you blindly, but are they suicidal?"

"If I do this, there is no turning back. I may not be able to save his reign." Livia's voice was finally calm.

"You have three sons, lady. Quen and Coll were born for this day." *Sweet Jesu, Livia! Twohundredyear ago your many times grandmother would have had Rex die in an "accident" long before now!* Darame realized with a shock how protective of Atare she had become, and felt momentarily ill. *Is this best for Dielaan—or merely best for Atare?*

"Can I save my house?"

The only way to make sure of her own motives was—"I have no authority to make promises, but if necessary I will browbeat Sheel into supporting Quen or Coll. Somehow, we will salvage from this wreckage."

Livia laughed— a real laugh, shorn of bitterness. "Ah, if only you had come sooner or later. Someone of Dielaan would have given Sheel Mindbender a run for the race!"

Darame impulsively stretched out her hand. "Kin cannot choose. Friends can."

The ragäree of Dielaan returned the clasp.

DIELAAN   COMPLINE

It was frustrating, knowing that there was an argument going on in the next room and being unable to understand any of it. Garth nibbled at a baked corn chip and considered his position. *Still alive . . . that counts for something.* But Lucy was arguing with Rex, via satellite, and Garth wanted to know what had made Lucy snap. Wandering over toward the window, Garth paused just beyond the opening that beckoned to him.

"Lebanon? #()! sinis? #()*!! * ?:<<—" Lucy stopped abruptly.

"That I have lost my mind?" Rex's sudden Caesarean words were very smooth. "Must I start explaining things to you, dear cousin, like a small child? The mines give Atare too much of an advantage."

"Where is the antimatter?" This was barely a whisper.

"Safe. Do not fail me, Lucy. I will be very disappointed if you do."

It was a moment before Garth realized that the harsh "click" he had heard was Lucy abruptly signing off. *Eat; the pills must have something to work on.* Biting into his chip, Garth continued past the windows, settling onto a pile of cushions decoratively placed in the corner.

Lucy whirled into the room, her color high. Without comment she marched to the table and slammed her fist down upon the plate he had been eating from, shattering both the tortillas and the pottery beneath them.

Gods, what does Rex want of us now? Rising to his height, Garth walked over next to her. "Did you cut yourself?"

Rubbing her fist, Lucy muttered: "No." She seized a glass of sangria and moved toward the terrace.

"Are you ready to talk about it?" Garth suggested. *Lucy, I've got to know what's going on, and your net doesn't ever say anything!*

Lucy froze, the glass millimeters from her lips; intent black eyes devoured him. "Whatever makes you think that talking would help?"

"Help *you*, I mean . . . not the situation." *So, we've been given our orders.* Queasiness touched his stomach.

"We are going to the Lebanon airfield. Lebanon is a sini village. Fortunately, we are merely going to 'borrow' their runways." This was very tart. Lucy tipped her glass, taking a swig of the sangria.

Well, if she intended to drink herself into the ground, he would have to ask questions fast. "In the north, then. Why?"

"Rex seems to think that the trinium mines give Atare too much power. So he is going to relieve them of it."

"The power or the trinium?"

Lucy snorted. "Both, I imagine. I have no idea. He may try to force Atare to divide the mines among the other clans; he may simply extort trinium from them; he may blow Atare to The Last Path for all I know."

Garth stared at her. "With what? Our antimatter?"

A faint smile touched her lips. "Now it becomes 'our' again. A few days ago you were denying you knew anything."

"I might as well be executed for a crime as for suspicion of one," was the even reply. "Lucy, I'm serious. What is Rex up to?"

Irritably she waved him off. "Something that Andersen announced, about antimatter production. He seems to think it will give Atare control of The Synod—or of all trading, if our actions collapse The Synod."

"I thought antimatter couldn't be produced here commercially." He poured himself some of the sangria and dug in his pocket for his pills.

"It cannot; the cost of protecting the facility is prohibitive . . . or always has been. I wonder if that will change?" For a moment she was distracted; then she announced: "No matter—we are all going to die."

Fighting the nausea the rav pills always triggered, Garth moved to her side and took her arm. "Take a deep breath. Rex scared you—he likes to scare people. What did he say?"

Oddly enough, Lucy did take a deep breath; it seemed to help. "Metals are used in antimatter production. Yes?"

"Yes. For targeting and—"

"Targeting! That was the word. Physicists can use trinium in targeting! It will make production *much* cheaper. Rex was livid; he is probably still yelling about divine guidance."

"In targeting? A better target?" *From a metal found hardly anywhere else?* "Gods, Atare is rich."

"Yes, they are," she agreed, starting to drink again.

Garth seized her wrist gently, stopping her movement. "No, I mean this will make them rich beyond anyone's wildest dreams! If they can produce more antiprotons faster. . . ." He considered it. "No wonder Rex is furious. Has anyone seen the process work?"

"Garth." She gave him a long look. "We are going to die. What difference does it make?"

Irritated, he moved back to the table and retrieved his sangria. "Stop saying that. You said Rex wasn't going to kill me—he just wanted to know where I was. Has it occurred to you that others might want to overthrow The Synod? That *our* movement signaled *their* movement?"

"He is not planning on killing you," she agreed carefully. "Whatever he did to warn you to be silent, he underestimated its effect on you. He was astonished and angry when you vanished." Crossing one arm over her torso, Lucy shivered. "He is not the one who will kill us."

Maybe I should have told you what he planted on me. Suddenly uneasy, Garth asked: "Who is going to kill us?"

"Atare."

"Lucy. . . ." He only had to take one step; quickly she continued.

"Rex does not believe that you told The Atarae nothing about our plans. He wants me to bring her with us to Lebanon."

"Kidnap The Atarae?" Garth stared blankly at her . . . and was surprised at the sudden rage that rose in his throat. "No. She's my business, not Rex's." *Whatever I finally decide is my business!*

"Do not be foolish. He wants me to take her out of the palace from under his mother's nose! Darame Atarae is a *guest* of the ragäree, Garth." Seeing that he was lost, Lucy said: "Even an enemy is safe once he has been accepted as a guest. I would be tarnishing Livia's—the tribe's—honor!"

"Where is the antimatter?"

"He would not tell me." Lucy was actually pale. "What am I to do?"

"Don't take her."

Wearily Lucy moved away from him, setting her glass down on the table. "You do not understand. Surely Rex switched his transmission to the leader of the group I brought with me. He has told them what he wants. I am sure the sergeant has already sent people to take care of it—"

"Then we won't go." Garth said it softly.

"They will make sure you go . . . just as they will make sure of Darame Atarae and me."

Garth stared at her. It was not her words that shook him . . . he had suspected it would be difficult to elude the warriors of Dielaan. No, it was the tone behind her words that surprised him. Lucy was afraid.

"Lucy," he said quietly. "Why are you helping Rex?"

"He . . . he is my cousin," she replied, bewildered.

Steering her toward the door, Garth maneuvered them both onto the terrace. "No, Lucy. That isn't good enough. Quen,

maybe, I could see you storming the gates of Heaven for . . .
or your brother. But Rex?''

"He has the right." This was stubborn.

"So? Let him go find his wife and learn something about the
rest of the Seven Sisters. Why help him get to the throne any
faster than usual?''

Now her concentration was on her wineglass. Garth leaned
against the brick wall and hazarded a glance at her.

"I think you owe me an answer.''

"You have what you wanted, do you not? Surely Atare has
been embarrassed by this, their trade damaged——''

"Not the conspiracy. I think *you* owe me one.''

"Will you tell me why you came here?" She did not look up;
her words were very soft.

He considered the idea. Was Lucy a good confidant? He realized that he had no idea. "I might," he said slowly. "If I
thought I could trust you with the story. Probably not now . . .
but someday.''

"Might is not a promise.''

"I said probably. Do you think I'd lie to you?''

"You might." She straightened, her frail form frozen, ram-
rod. "Words have power here . . . where you come from, words
are so much noise.''

"I don't think we're quite that bad," Garth managed to answer. "But you're avoiding the question.''

"I know." Another deep breath. "You will not understand.''

"Maybe not. But I'll try to understand.''

"I was afraid," she said simply. "I was suffocating . . .
watching my brother Silas, who is a born mythmaker, deteriorate
into a drunken fop. Watching my brother Madras drive himself
to the brink of suicide trying to manage the family estates, and
his judgeship, and a position at court—only his need to go to
Caesarea saved his life. Have you ever spent time in a . . . a
totalitarian regime? There is only one voice allowed. Otherwise,
those in power risk losing control. They control *everything*,
Garth. What you do, who you see, the art you view and hear
. . . even what you think, if they can. I was becoming stupid
and lazy and vicious, concerned only with the immediate future
. . . thinking about going to Caesarea and not coming back.''

"And you thought Rex could improve things?" This was hard
to believe.

"No, no—" Lucy was vigorously shaking her head. *"Change*, Garth. I wanted to force change. I wanted to bring down the house of cards we call Dielaan, and build something better. But I wanted to figure out a way to do it so no one was hurt, or disgraced . . . at least no Dielaan. If I had thought I could do anything under Livia's regency, I would have. But she was so careful of her trust—nothing changed that could help me or my class. We're nothing but pampered breeders, leading useless lives. . . . Even if Rex is no better, there is always a period of unrest after a new Dielaan takes over—things change."

"You're an odd sort of reformer," Garth said finally.

Lucy chuckled. "Hardly. I scarcely notice the lower classes; why should I? It was not until . . until I found out about the ships that I grew worried." Her voice grew suddenly husky.

"Ships?" Garth realized he was whispering.

"Ships have set out from Dielaan, Garth. Down the Amber River to the Alameda Sea." Finally she looked over at him, her delicate features backlit by the salon lights within. "I think Rex wants a war. My brother will lead soldiers from our lands into war, and they will all die." This was ragged, intense. "Do you think the clans will tolerate this? What if this time our people say 'No, we have too few sons left. Eighties they may be, but they are our life.' Or Atare decides to wipe us from the planet?"

Garth knew he was staring at her, but he couldn't help himself. *First murder, then war. Lucy is right; we are going to die.*

Was this what he had sensed, the fear that had gripped him the moment he had heard Lucy's voice in the terminal? Yet The Atarae had not been visibly afraid. . . . *Lucy couldn't have gotten me out of the Ciedärlien camp—she as much as admitted that. Did she guess that Darame would go after me? Was it all chance? But Rex sent her . . . or did Lucy tell him she would find me?*

"Lucy . . . do you realize what you're saying?" It sounded stupid to his ears, but he desperately needed time to think.

"We have been used," she said steadily. "My honor is stained. If I can make this right for you, I will."

"Screw honor! We're talking our lives, woman!" Garth thought furiously. "If I can get us off this planet—do you want to go?"

The silence stretched. "If we can stop Rex, I will go anywhere with you," she said with simple dignity.

It startled him, her choice of phrasing . . . as if she knew the words meant more to her than to him. Stop Rex? "How do you plan on stopping The Dielaan from doing anything he damn well pleases?"

"We must find new allies."

"Lucy, wars have a way of accelerating once troops have been mobilized. You've got to do better than 'We must find new allies,' " Garth hissed. "If you're going to find a conscience, find one with a few ideas!"

"You forget one thing. Because the warriors have gone to seize The Atarae, we will take her to Rex. Therefore, Rex has no reason to doubt *me*." Lucy studied him with her dark eyes, as if weighing him against an unknown scale. "Will you help me make sure there is no war?"

"There won't be a war. Your people hate war—that's why they fight so rarely." Garth stressed his words, trying to make them true.

"We only fight when there is something to gain . . . something we cannot acquire any other way. My father would never have started the last war if Sheel Atare had ruled. Trade routes and contacts caused it." Lucy smiled wryly. "I think that is why I have a secret fondness for The Synod. If it had existed back then, there might have been no war . . . no wedge for off-worlders to wield among us. I resent it that an Atare thought of it first."

As clearly as if she stood before him, Garth heard Silver's voice. *For prestige and power. To erode the power and prestige of the other. Sometimes you can win and still lose—or lose and yet ultimately win.*

"Then we have big trouble, because I think Rex is more interested in humbling Atare than anything else."

Lucy nodded, her face drawn. "He means to make sure none of the clans will trust Atare. This announcement by Andersen will help him, will it not?"

"Oh, yes, my love . . . no one trusts an individual who counsels gathering collective wealth, then suddenly ends up with the winning game piece." Garth stared at her, his thoughts furious. Was it enough? To destroy their synod and drag them to the

brink of war? He didn't want anyone slapping a charge of localized treason—or murder—on him. And that was what he was
facing. But he didn't want to leave this kind of mess behind
him, either.

Of course, if Rex held Silver in protective custody, that might
be the final move necessary to make people suspect she was a
part of the theft. . . .

"You are sure Rex won't hurt The Atarae?"

"Of course not. He wants a hostage to keep them at a distance." Lucy spoke with scorn, but her eyes betrayed her.

You are no longer sure what he will do. That chilled him.
Nothing happens to her without my permission. Sometimes you
can win and still lose—or lose and yet ultimately win. . . . So
it hasn't worked out quite like you planned—Lucy's right. You
got most of what you came for, didn't you?

"We stay," Garth said briefly. "And every warrior in Dielaan
won't be enough to help Rex once we get inside his defenses."

It was ridiculous how good he felt when Lucy threw her arms
around him.

AMURA-BY-THE-SEA   COMPLINE
ATARE WINTER PALACE

This section of the winter home had wooden floors; there was a
board under the third hall window which creaked whenever a
neighboring strip moved. Sheel found himself listening for the
sound as he walked toward the family room. Two moons had
already risen; just past the full, they illuminated the corridor with
their silvery light.

"I would guess that Rex Dielaan is playing games, Atare—
and with living pieces," Crow suggested. "Mailan had to be
brief—otherwise Dielaan might have monitored a surface-to-
satellite communication. But worry is premature. Mailan is competent, and The Atarae has guarded her own back for many
years."

"And the middle name of the House of Dielaan is treachery,"
Sheel murmured, moving past the dark *guaard* and into the
family salon.

"Even Dielaan has its own honor," Crow stated as he followed.

"Atare merchants being attacked on the streets of Dielaan, and you are concerned with honor," was the terse reply. Sheel cut off his words abruptly as he realized Ardal was in the room. The boy had just switched off a vid. Now he turned to his father, his face alight with excitement.

"There was a *riot* on embassy row today!"

Sheel stared at the boy. "What?" he said gently.

"A riot!" Ardal insisted. "I just talked to Denis—he could see it from his window! Amuran security arrested everyone," he added, sounding just the slightest bit remorseful. "I missed *everything*."

There will be more than enough action in the next few days, Sheel wanted to say. "Was anyone hurt?" he asked instead.

"Some people had batons, but Denis did not see any hospice staff."

"Do you know your lessons for class tomorrow?"

"Yes." This was prompt, but not overly so—Ardal knew better than to appear in the family room without his assignments completed.

"I would try the infonet, if you want more news," Sheel suggested. "But you should be in bed, oh, in an hour or so. Use the one in your room."

"Yes, sir!" Ardal started running toward the far door, his *guaard* in close pursuit. Slowing and drawing himself up, Ardal hazarded a look over one shoulder. "Has mother called?"

Such simple words. . . . "Captain Mailan called. They will be gone a few more days," Sheel said easily. Ardal continued out, but not without words.

"I wish she would take me sometime."

Do you know what you ask? Oddly enough, Ardal might indeed know what he asked. Turning to Crow, Sheel said: "A riot? Who started it?"

"It was between some young Wallace clansmen and Addams, a sept of Dielaan. The culprits have yet to be released—" The wall vid chimed, drawing their attention.

Sheel touched the membrane; the face of Leo, one of his personal *guaard*, appeared. "A Dielaan ambassador is here to see you and the ragäree, Atare. The latest arrival. Avis Ragäree has said she will see him; he waits in the Green Room."

"Why announce this afternoon that they were withdrawing

from The Synod, then demand an audience tonight?'' Crow was clearly off-duty.

"Rex Dielaan withdrew his clan from The Synod; this man was not present."

Alameda was a sheet of ghostly flames, as if radiating from within. It was impressive, the view out the windows of the Green Room. Dressed formally in a long gown of powder blue, Avis had waited for him at the double doors. There was nothing to say in private; offering her his arm, Sheel had indicated that the doors should be opened. *Guaard* had mysteriously appeared at their backs, doubling the ranks.

Tall for a Dielaaner, this man, and naturally grave of expression. He turned at the sound of the doors and nodded formally at their entrance. Ringed in ice, this one. Still dressed in silk mourning—for his wife, dead three years, Darame had discovered. But he had yet to offer his name.

"Greetings, ambassador," Avis said warmly.

The atmosphere thawed noticeably; Avis always sounded sincere, and it was hard to resist her. Bowing over her hand, the man said: "May I congratulate you on the birth of another heir? Mendülay has been kinder to you than to your mother—she had a great deal of suspense, did she not?"

"If you mean there were a lot of boys and not nearly enough girls to suit her, you are correct," Avis replied with a smile. "We have been fortunate. We do not hold formal court at this hour. Please, be seated."

Lowering himself onto a divan, the Dielaaner allowed a frown to steal across his face. "Since we shall wave a formal court, shall we wave other pleasantries? I hope you will forgive my haste, but there are important things with which we must deal. To begin with, you are aware that there was an altercation this afternoon before the gates of Dielaan House?"

Downgraded already, Sheel thought grimly.

"We had heard that some young men of Wallace and Addams decided to play," Avis said archly.

Smiling politely, the ambassador continued: "What has been kept darkly secret is that the Wallace youngsters were liberating me from a protective guard of Addams." Silence; Sheel could hear Avis's kid slipper slide across the loomed rug beneath her feet. "I say 'liberating' because I was truly in need of rescue. I have been virtually a prisoner within Dielaan House for several days now. In desperation I called out to the crowd as I was being taken from the embassy. I could not have hoped that a foreign clan would come to my rescue. Undoubtedly they welcomed the chance to pound a few Addams' heads,'' he added with grim humor.

"Have you come to ask for sanctuary?'' Avis said carefully.

"I have come to ask for your help. The young Dielaan left Amura-By-The-Sea early this morning. He has gone off on some scheme of his own, without consulting the Dielaan Council or the regent, much less discussing his plans with the embassy staff. It is irregular at best.''

"What kind of help do you ask?'' Sheel said formally.

"Stop him.''

"Stop him?'' Sheel could not keep the surprise from his voice. "By what authority? Amura is neutral, and has control only to the end of its own boundaries. We are not the law here.''

His face harsh, the ambassador said: "He has taken a large meth, with the bulk of the embassy warriors. The import of Andersen's announcement was not lost on him, Atare. Look to your own.''

Sheel was conscious of the *waiting* in Avis's posture . . . she would let him address the topic. Where was the family? Mostly within Amura or Atare, except for some outkin. Behind them he could hear a *guaard* leaving the room; before this conversation was through, every Atare on the planet would have had their ration of *guaard* doubled. "Is this a threat, ambassador?''

The man's face grew dark with blood. "No! It is a warning!''

"Has he begun moving troops?''

"I believe so. There are troop ships in the Alameda, of course. And I am suspicious of several traders just south of here—their manifests are odd. But what I fear is that he will strike somehow at the trinium mines. He sees them as the greatest threat in existence to clan autonomy.'' Something quiet, even sad slipped into the man's posture. "Cort Atare Ironhand did not come down heavily enough upon Dielaan, after the hostilities ended. And now we have the fruits of his kindness.''

"Ironic, that mercy is seen as weakness.'' Sheel kept his voice mild.

"We have more in common with the Cied than we care to admit.''

"The Cied may fight, but they do not have war, ambassador.

Dielaan chooses otherwise,'' Avis said simply. She continued, her voice stripped of its chiming humor. ''If Rex Dielaan thinks to threaten our livelihood, he has made a mistake. We shall not err as did Cort Atare.''

Now *that* was a threat. It seemed to surprise the Dielaan ambassador; it did not surprise Sheel. His sister took her role as mother of her people seriously. If a snake threatened your children, you cut off its head. . . .

''Atare?'' It was Zaide's voice; he stood at the open door. ''Alasdair of Wallace and Nadine of Kilgore are here. They wish to speak with you.''

Sheel was beginning to get a headache. ''Please escort them in.'' He flicked a glance at Avis as he spoke; her half-lidded eyes meant assent.

Zaide had not installed them far away; in mere moments the group had returned. Alasdair had several of his staff in tow, while Nadine was alone. Sheel noted the last with pleasure—she trusted them enough to arrive without the usual Kilgore battery.

Ready to breathe fire, my Alasdair, while Nadine is cold and silent. Is this more fallout from this afternoon's meeting? His head still ached from that one. Short and sweet; Nadine had implied that Dielaan knew something about the missing antimatter, and the young ambassador (the only one left since Rex's purge) had abruptly announced that he had his orders. . . .

''Please forgive this intrusion,'' Alasdair started gruffly. ''But it seems that a few of our coastal students have been involved in a street prank. I was hoping you might have a bit more influence with the locals than I do.'' He definitely had his eye on the Dielaan ambassador as he spoke.

''I certainly have not pressed charges,'' the older man murmured. ''I owe those boys my thanks.''

This completely silenced Alasdair. Taking advantage of the lull, Zaide stepped forward and said: ''The Amurans are being very careful with information, but it seems they are keeping the antagonists locked up merely to insure the fighting does not break out anew. They will be released sometime tomorrow, after tempers cool.'' With a nod, Zaide slipped back out of the room.

Now, what is he up to that he cannot leave it? Sheel wondered.

''Well . . . thank-you both,'' Alasdair said, bowing slightly to Avis and Sheel. ''Your staff is as efficient as ever.''

"No tea?" Nadine asked. Although the faintest of smiles touched her lips, it did not reach her eyes.

"We did not know it was going to turn into a conference," Avis apologized.

"Your shrimp is on the way to the kitchens," Nadine said simply. "I am leaving on the tide. I have been recalled."

"Recalled?" Alasdair turned and gave her a daunting look.

"Dielaan ships are coming around the peninsula . . . and we have an arsonist loose. Someone has been torching the wheat fields." Her tone was frigid.

"*No!*" Sheel rose to his feet; the others actually stepped back a pace from him. "Can you not see what is happening? This is exactly what Dielaan wants! All of us, drawing into our enclaves, suspicious of each other—"

"How can we trust each other?" Alasdair growled. "Kilgore throws around accusations, but *they* are the ones who plucked this spy from the Alameda. No one else has confirmed any of this . . . although we caught Yang up to something, last night." Alasdair's face seemed to close.

"Do we really need confirmation of the essential fact?" Avis asked gently. "Rex Dielaan has gone off on a private vendetta. This ambassador tells us it was without the knowledge or approval of council or regent. Let us not be too hasty to blame Dielaan for all that hovers on our horizon."

"*If* this is not a ruse, to trick us into believing we but witness a rebellious heir kicking up his heels?" Nadine spat out.

"Has Rex Dielaan invited you to join his private little war?" Sheel looked directly at Nadine as he spoke. Shrugging slightly, she shook her head once.

"Of course not," Alasdair muttered. "Dielaan has no use for anyone but Dielaaners—and precious few of them!"

"Precisely. Dielaan dislikes us at best and even hates a few of us. A more subtle man would have sought alliances, even with intent to betray, before starting up disturbances." The Dielaan ambassador looked as if he was going to protest, but did not speak. "Would any of you trust Dielaan as far as you could throw him?" This time Sheel watched Alasdair. "Will we allow him to pick his time and place, striking when and where he pleases?"

"What are you suggesting?"

Sheel gestured to the Dielaan ambassador. "The ambassador

has suggested that Rex Dielaan has taken a methplane north, heading into the coastal mountains. His immediate goal is the Atare trinium mines. Andersen's announcement enraged him—which may be to our benefit."

"It enraged my brother," Nadine said dryly. "He is not starting a war over it."

"But if Dielaan was already planning a spot of war? His ships are three days, at the least, from Kilgore. They could not reach the trinium fields for eleven or twelve days, even with the monsoon winds. Surely his leaving Amura is premature."

The Dielaan ambassador seemed to be struggling with something. Avis gave him her lifted-eyebrows, entreating expression. "I think your guess is good, Atare," the man finally said. "Since I was 'safely' under his thumb, Rex did mention several things to me—some which made no sense earlier. Now I believe this was all part of a plan to discredit and destroy The Synod, gutting its bargaining power and returning trade responsibilities to each individual tribe."

"And return us to pre-synod prices," Alasdair mumbled under his breath.

"But he was truly enraged over the announcement by Darol University. He kept screaming about an Atare conspiracy, and that he would not allow Dielaan to slip beneath the sands of time. Whatever his original plans, I believe he revised them heavily last night." In the wake of his words, Livia's uncle actually looked his age . . . an exhausted old man who feared he had betrayed everything he had ever loved.

If I can do it, your sacrifice will not be in vain. Before Sheel could continue, Nadine spoke up. Her voice was soft . . . regretful.

"All I see is that Rex Dielaan has blown a synapse and gone haring off into the north. What are you asking, Atare?"

"Instead of each of us sitting back and allowing Dielaan to come at us when and where he may, I suggest we all send people north—and stop him before he truly starts," Sheel replied, studying Nadine for clues to her own feelings.

They might have been alone in the room. "Dielaan is right in one thing . . . he recognizes a threat when it presents itself."

"Which threat is greater?" Sheel responded.

Nadine was quiet. Then she shook her head slightly, the amethyst crystals in her hair tinkling like wind chimes. "He may be right in another thing. Nothing will ever be the same again."

"Do you think your arsonist is merely a random fool?" Alasdair asked carefully.

"My brother does." Nadine raised her chin aggressively. "I believe in coincidence . . . but not in a half-dozen fools spread over several kilometers starting simultaneous fires."

Avis's soft voice intruded, startling them. "A moment, and everything changes. Will you help Rex Dielaan drag us back toward the darkness, or will you try for something better?"

As Avis spoke, Sheel became aware of Zaide's presence. The seneschal had slipped back into the room sometime during their talk, and had activated the RAM which was inset behind a sliding panel.

"Zaide?" Sheel said, making a question of the name.

"The Amuran police have succeeded in convincing Stennis that he will still have his immunity even if he explains his involvement in the affair. Please note the highlighted portion of the interview." Touching the membrane, Zaide also activated the audio portion of the feed.

"The controller and the trap were not quite compatible?" came a smooth, even voice speaking Caesarean.

"No, but that often happens. I've jury-rigged many portable traps in my time. A Stanford trap can be hooked to almost anything. There were several wheels of wire laying around the control room. I chose the heaviest gauge available and wired it in. Worked like magic."

Zaide cut off the audio recording. Studying him from the back, Sheel noticed a slight tremor in the man's body, and settled himself on the edge of his seat. *Go ahead, Zaide. Now is not the time to be gentle.*

"The Stanford magnetic trap is off-world issue," the seneschal said as he turned to face them. "As was the pirated control box. *The electrical wire used to connect the two was Nualan, and doped.*"

"Well, man? What is the last word on it?" Alasdair demanded.

"I am not a metallurgist, but dissimilar metals are involved. Transference of molecules will take place slowly but steadily. Eventually the connecting wire between the trap and the refrigeration controller will fail. The superconducting rings will then overheat, and—'' Zaide's graceful hands gestured, turning palm-up and lifting slightly.

"Without warning?" Alasdair sounded incredulous.

"Without warning," Sheel whispered. "Once the transference blocks current. And that is unique to the conditions surrounding the trap."

A slight chiming noise . . . Nadine slowly sat on the couch near the door. "May I have access to a RAM vid? I need to make a satellite call."

DIELAAN
ONEHUNDRED NINETYEIGHTDAY   MATINS

He was surprised to see Lulani . . . afraid of Lulani? Unable to sleep, Darame kept going over the events of the past few days. *You did not imagine it; he was startled, even afraid . . . not necessarily of Lulani, but of what her presence meant. So, he ran from Dielaan . . . and Dielaan tracked him.*

Her knife chafed her leg, but something in her refused to take it off. She had been sleeping in her blacks for several days, now . . . tonight was the first time she had laid her stiletto on the side table. She was a guest of House Dielaan; others would touch her at their peril. . . .

"Why?" she whispered to the ceiling, her thoughts veering back to Kristinsson. "I think he spoke truth when he said he did not know where the antimatter was hidden. But there are other things he could know about it."

At first she missed the odor. It was no more than a cloying memory, like hothouse blooms left to wilt. Exhausted, to be manufacturing smell along with sight and sound . . . Why that scent? It was disturbingly like—

Instinctively she rolled off the mattress, digging her way under the bedstead. Someone—or several someones—seized the entire assembly and threw it head over foot toward the door. Still moving in a dream, Darame scrabbled at the nightstand, her hand closing on the stiletto she had been wearing in her hair. Even as someone seized her from behind, she twisted her body and stabbed backward past her hipbone.

The scream made her head ring. Free, she was free, and there were the balcony doors—

oathbreaker: 1) An individual who, after a solemn
calling upon a god to witness to the truth of words
or deeds, or to witness to the honest intent behind
words or deeds [See *oath*] violates, negates, or
otherwise invalidates said declaration. 2) One who
breaks trust with a formal affirmation which was
made solemn by its link with something revered or
viewed as sacred.

CHAPTER TWELVE

MARE IMBRIUM, LEBANON
ONEHUNDRED NINETYEIGHTDAY   COMPLINE

Peter's Keys, he was tired. Gaining two hours going west was
all to the good, but their destination required touching down at
many desolate airstrips. The control tower at Lebanon airport
had not interfered with them, other than requesting they park
their meth off the runway. After refueling, their group had swung
back east in the plane Lucy had chartered, the bulk of her warriors
following in a mid-sized carrier.

There would be fewer warriors than expected—even Garth
had figured out that much. There had been little time to talk
alone, since the warriors had returned with Darame Daviddottir,
but Lucy had managed to tell him that with the announcement
from Andersen's Darol University, Rex had drastically altered
his plans. Instead of a fleet at his back, Rex had but the group
stationed at the Amuran embassy—no token sampling, but apparently far from his original estimates. They also had another
hostage: Quen of Dielaan.

Just what we need, Garth thought, glancing over at Lucy. She was an interesting color, pallid yet with bright spots of color on her cheeks. Another fight had been imminent, over the Atarae, until the senior warrior had explained that they had used a knock-out dart on the woman. Only then did Lucy subside—she had been demanding a healer, terrified that the Atarae's continuing unconsciousness meant a fractured skull or worse.

Garth's eyes shifted fractionally—he did not wish to look upon the bonelessly limp bundle wrapped in a blanket and carried over one warrior's shoulder. This "cage," as the mining elevator was called, could hold one hundred miners at a time, but right now it seemed claustrophobic.

Trouble, trouble, trouble. How could they begin to sabotage Rex's plans? Time to bolt? Where? No, Garth needed to know where Rex was and what he was up to, before he could keep his promise to Lucy.

Oddly, the miners in the changing room had been calm in the face of their visitors. The one "boss" still present from the previous shift had been more upset at their intention to descend without hard hats, lanterns, and reinforced shoes than at their decision to go below. Lucy had ignored her warriors' restlessness, taking time to get tiny scraps of metal with arabic numbers stamped into them. She had handed one to Garth and kept two for herself, indicating with a vague gesture that the other was for the "bundle."

"Chits," Lucy whispered suddenly, recalling Garth to the present. "The pieces of brass are called 'chits.' Everyone who enters a mine must carry one—they use them in copper mines, too. To identify bodies in case of mining disasters, and to know how many people are below at any given time."

Comforting. . . .

"Mostly for detonation," the miner said suddenly. "We have to be sure everyone is out before we blast. We are the explosives crew—we get time between each shift to pop boulders and continue caving."

Garth considered asking what "caving" was, and decided against it. Mining surely had its private language, and one question would breed a dozen. His ears popped, and he wondered how deep they were going.

Finally the cage slowed to a stop. "2377 level," the miner announced briefly. "This is where we sent them."

"2377?" Lucy asked.

"Meters," the miner replied.

"Are we almost . . . 2377 meters beneath the surface?" she whispered, growing even more pale.

"Huh? No, honey, we are but 790 meters or so under. We name levels according to elevation. Did not your ears tell you?" He smiled faintly at this, then reached for the bar across the gate.

His motion triggered a seal, and the doors unfolded like a flower, panels sliding back and bolts clanking. Courteously gesturing, the miner allowed Lucy to step off the cage first. A warrior abruptly flicked a finger at him, indicating that he was to accompany them.

"Why?" Garth said aloud. The warrior turned and regarded him mildly. "Rex must have everyone he needs down here already. This man is a miner, not a supervisor—he has no authority, nor skills with the type of thing going on here. Do we even have enough food and water for ourselves, much less anyone else? Let him go back; you left a guard with the hoistman at the top of the cage, no one is coming down without his permission."

Neither the warrior nor the miner moved. Garth forced himself not to blink. He didn't know *why* it was important to get that miner back to the surface, but it felt important.

The warrior looked at Lucy; she turned to the miner.

"The way is simple?"

Lifting an arm, the man pointed. "Straight to the crossways, and turn right. Just follow the lights along the back of the drift."

As one, the group stared at him uncomprehendingly. A warrior started to move toward him. Lucy imperiously held up a hand of warning, once again a princess of Dielaan.

"Follow the light strip along the ceiling of the passageway," the miner said hastily, clearly after thought.

Translation, Garth did not say, but knew it to be truth. He had trained a few long-hauler dock loaders in his time, and vocabulary was always a stumbling block. Everyone waited to see Lucy's response.

Nodding slightly, gracefully, Lucy smiled her thanks and turned away, dismissing the miner with a flick of her fingers. A good move, that—the warriors were unlikely to pursue the issue.

It was white light that was used to illuminate the passageways

—dim to Garth's eyes, but more than sufficient for movement. Lips slightly puckered, Lucy looked impressed by the conditions.

"It is very clean," she said simply, stepping carefully over a pool of water dripping from pipe condensation. "Copper mines do not line their walls with reinforced cement."

"I doubt they line all of them," Garth murmured. "Probably only the ones closest to the eleva—cage." He looked up above their heads, where the lights ran in a single row down the center of the "back." "If they call the ceiling the back, what are the walls?" Lucy's shrug was eloquent.

Major lighting ran to the right, with spot lighting to the left. The cement floor had already petered out, replaced by native rock and dirt. Rough stone walls jutted toward them, reminding them they were within a mountain. It was eerie, seeing the next group of lamps just beyond a belt of darkness, watching a breath of air stir a wisp of Lucy's hair. . . . *Good ventilation fans,* he told himself. Surely nothing lived down here. . . . Turning away from the "drift" leading off into the heart of the ore body, Garth followed Lucy toward the control room.

"Have they dug the trinium out of this tunnel?" Lucy said aloud.

"Drift, not tunnel," he reminded her.

"There is a difference?"

"There must be—he didn't use 'tunnel' when he changed his wording, did he? As for the trinium, I imagine it's like many other metals—almost invisible to the eye. Processing has to take it out. They mine a lot of things up in these mountains—nickel, copper, gold, silver, other platinum group metals—chromite, too, I think." He looked intently at the sides of the drift. "This was probably cut for transportation, not mining. There's another name for finding pieces of pure metal . . . place . . . placer, that's it. Like placid. I did a bit of gold mining once," he added, offhandedly. "In a river on Gavriel." He was rewarded by her look of respect.

Reaching the control room door, Garth stepped aside to allow her to enter first. *Courtesy or prudence?* he taunted himself.

They walked into a model of efficiency. One entire wall was lined with screens, the diagrams animated upon them a marvel of complexity. It was all notated in Nualan, of course, but in Lucy he had an able translator.

"Ore pass," she read carefully, her finger tracing above a branching network of lines.

"Serae!" whispered an anxious voice. Turning slightly, Garth saw a lathe-thin, seamed old man, whipcord from years of weathering. "Those are active screens, with hidden controls. If you touch the wrong place, you could open a pass door, or stop an engine under a chute. Someone could be injured!" His Caesarean was stilted, but understandable.

"Of course, how careless of me," she said gently, and the man grew visibly calmer.

Rex has been baiting you. Garth could feel sympathy for the supervisor; this room was undoubtedly his usual domain, and in Garth's experience, plant managers took their duties seriously.

"The screens are a great deal of fun," came Rex's smooth voice. "The colors change on the temperature gauges, and when you cut the ventilation fans, everything turns red."

"Rex, for shame!" Lucy told him, trying to sound teasing. "There are people down here, are there not?"

"One hundred fifty, an entire shift," he agreed. "No need to stop work, if Atare is reasonable." Leaning back in a flexseat, The Dielaan looked to be in a very good mood. He nodded casually in the direction of the opposing corner, where Quen sat stoically. "Quen feels sure Atare will be uninterested in another war." Then he turned a hard eye on Garth.

"We need someplace warm and quiet for The Atarae," Lucy said quickly. "These clumsy idiots injured her."

"Not seriously, I hope?" He might have been inquiring about the weather above.

"I do not think so. Since they drugged her, I have yet to make sure of her condition." This was a trifle stiff. It seemed to amuse Rex.

"You may play doctor, if it amuses you. The lunch room is adjacent to here—through that panel," he added, flicking fingers in dismissal. "And Garth . . . how good to see you again."

"Dielaan," Garth chose to say, nodding a greeting.

"Do you know what that means?" was the purring response.

"That you are the hereditary ruler of twenty percent of this planet's population, among other things." Now that they had come to it, Garth found himself remarkably unafraid—at least of Rex. It seemed foolish to bring him here only to kill him.

And if that *was* Rex's plan, well, there was always dignity at the last.

"You will be pleased to know that each new plan takes us further from our initial problems. We should have everyone so confused, it will never occur to them to question you about the removal of the antimatter."

"Where *is* the antimatter?" Garth asked.

"Safe." He gave Garth a long look. "It never occurred to *me* you would run. Surely you knew that my position was as tenuous as yours? Your constant carping at Lucy irritated me—I merely wished to silence you."

"What is tenuous about being Dielaan?" Garth decided to answer.

Rex smiled thinly. "There is always someone else waiting in the wings, ready to take your place."

"The only people who wish to take your place will need to remove far more than one Dielaan," came Quen's voice.

"Since I will not be removed, it is a moot point," was Rex's casual response. The sound of footsteps caused him to turn his head.

"Do you know, I think we are alone on this level?" It was Lucy's brother Silas. "There is a maintenance shop of some kind, and equipment is humming, but no one is there. And there is no food, except for a few satchels in a cold box. Not good for a prolonged siege," he pointed out, taking a seat. "Good to see you, Garth. Did you enjoy Dielaan?"

"Not much time for seeing the sights," Garth admitted, and as the other laughed, he added: "The Cied women were beautiful, though." That seemed to disconcert Silas.

"What did you do with my sister?" he finally inquired.

"I think she's trying to revive The Atarae," Garth answered, craning his neck toward the panel at the back.

"Who?"

Garth turned his head back to the man and surveyed the other's frowning countenance. "The Atarae. The 'guest' Rex asked Lucy to bring along."

Rex started laughing.

"The . . . the . . . you mean Sheel Atare's *wife*?" He stared at his cousin, his expression a mixture of respect and chagrin. "Well, old cos, I *certainly* hope you have planned this down to the last iota, because Sheel Atare may dig a tunnel to this room to reach you. They say he is not a bit rational when it comes to that woman.''

Rex shrugged, flexing his fingers expansively. ''All the better. He will do nothing to endanger her. You—'' He pointed to the supervisor. ''Get a satellite line, I want vid and infonet access.''

The wiry man sucked his thin cheeks in, his pale eyes straying to the screens. ''I am sorry, Dielaan, but that is impossible.''

''Impossible?'' His velvet tone made Silas visibly wince.

''This is a completely enclosed line, to protect our secrets. We can communicate with any other control room within Mare Imbrium Mine, or the surface control. But that is it.'' Realizing this would not be a popular answer, the man spread his hands helplessly.

''Then how,'' Rex started softly, ''am I to know whether plan A is on schedule?'' He had not raised his voice, but several warriors looked very uncomfortable, and Silas had moved back into the shadows.

''Plan A?'' Garth asked, hoping to distract Rex with a solid question.

''A few fires among friends—my friends setting the fires, of course.'' Rex contemplated the screens, seemingly enthralled with the movement of ore. ''I decided to corner the grain market this year.''

''What?'' The volume turned the heads of everyone but Rex. Quen had actually turned and risen to his feet. ''You did *what*?''

''The wheat and oat fields of Kilgore and Seedar are burning by now,'' Rex explained patiently. ''They will extinguish the fires, of course, but not until a good portion of the new crop is cinders.''

''And what do you expect to eat, come the harvest?'' Quen said acidly.

''Dielaan can produce enough to make up for it,'' Rex replied, his dark brow slightly furrowed. It was plain he was not used to arguing with Quen . . . at least not past the first exchange.

''It has completely slipped your mind that we appear to be entering a drought? That we are down in rainfall inches by a good third, and no rain is in sight?'' Quen was furious, and fighting to keep control—his knuckles were flushed from clenching his fists.

''The monsoons—''

''Have not come! Spring rains, not monsoons! The weather

pattern has changed! And if the monsoons do not come in the west, then the overflow *does not pass the mountains.*'' Quen actually began to step toward the group.

Rex slowly stood, turning to face his younger, and taller, brother. Garth never knew what he was going to say—or do—for a beep interrupted the scene. Heads swiveled toward the supervisor. He glanced at the screen.

"Control Center," was his terse explanation.

"Answer them," Rex told him. "Remember my captain and his pallet."

Visibly trembling, the Ataran reached for the screen and touched one of the multicolored squares running along the bottom of it. A man with a face like a tarnished copper coin appeared on the vid mode. He was dressed in a tunic of heather gray, a yellow stripe wending its way around the hem.

Mock-sini, pricked Garth's memory.

"Your status, Campbell?" The man spoke accented Caesarean.

"All areas are working smoothly, sir," the supervisor replied. "The Dielaan would like a linkup to the infonet, I believe."

"One moment." The man turned to someone beyond their range of sight and conferred. Glancing back at the lens, he said: "It is possible, but will take a while. In the meantime, I have been asked to pass on to The Dielaan some information that may interest him."

"He can hear you," Campbell said after Rex nodded.

"The Amuran Forces have questioned the man Stennis, and have discovered the procedure he used to secure the Stanford antimatter trap. There is a problem with the jury-rigging of the trap and the control box. Dissimilar metals are involved. Transference is taking place—"

"How long is their estimate?" Garth asked, moving before the screen.

For the first time, the man looked uncertain. "I do not think they—"

"Well, find out, for Mary's sake! You don't expect The Dielaan to take your word for it, do you? We'll stand by." Turning to the supervisor, he said: "Cut the audio." Then Garth turned back to the others.

Lucy, at the open panel, was as white as new snow, while Silas looked like he might pass out. On the other hand, the warriors looked uncertain, and Quen thoughtful. Rex was openly amused.

"Surely they do not think we would fall for that?" Rex finally chortled.

"Transference is no joke," Garth said briefly, turning his back on them. "And any number of conditions can speed up or slow down the ion migration between the metals. We may have a big problem." He gestured for Campbell to reconnect the line.

In a few moments the man on top said: "Amura has suggested that, depending on humidity, power draw, and other variables, the minimum resistance point will change anywhere from 150 hours to twenty days from activation of the link."

One hundred fifty . . . six days. They had taken the antimatter eight days ago. "OFF!" he said to Campbell, then whirled to face Rex Dielaan. "We're already two days into the danger zone. We've got to get a new control box on that trap."

"Surely the system cannot already be corroded," Quen said uneasily.

"It doesn't work that way." Garth's growing fear made him snap. "We're not talking solid rust, here—all the metal has to do is corrode enough to block current. Then the refrigeration controller fails—that has to be what they're afraid will happen. If it does, the superconducting rings overheat and then—" He broke off at that, as he realized Rex was calmly extending his index finger to support his head above a carefully placed hand and arm. "You don't believe me."

"I do not know," Rex said candidly. "How long, on an average, does such corrosion need before resistance changes?"

"It depends on conditions! Where have you been storing it? Is the place hot, cold, damp, dry? I don't know how much current the wire Stennis used was meant to hold. But I'm not trained in that line." It was a helpless admission, but the look on Lucy's face demanded it.

"An average," Rex repeated.

No matter what I say, you are going to refuse them. "If the unit has been stored somewhere cool and dry, I'd say twelve days if we're lucky."

"And it has been . . . eight?" Rex considered the fact. "Then we have two days maximum before we must let them near the unit. Agreed?"

"That depends on the conditions where it's stored."

"It is with my captain at the bottom of the mining shaft we entered."

There was a gurgle of protest. Garth turned his head toward the supervisor. "You have something to say?" He hadn't meant to sound threatening, but Rex made him want to bully people.

"The . . . the mining levels are very damp and hot, and grow more so, the deeper you descend. That is the ore train level," he mumbled. "Not the best place for antimatter." Rex reached for the screen. "Not that one, that monitors the pumps!" It was a shout.

"Pumps?"

"We must continuously pump water out of the depths—over 4000 liters per minute. It is thirty degrees when we pump it up; we use the heat exchange to produce 25 million BTUs per hour." This last part sounded rehearsed, and Garth wondered if the man sometimes did tours for officials.

"Thirty degrees?" Silas whistled his appreciation. "A nice tub bath! Not quite enough for a whirlpool, though." The return to the subject of the mine seemed to reassure him slightly.

Lips thin, Campbell said: "Not so pleasant to stand hip deep in while reinforcing a drift."

"Is this a volcano?" Rex asked casually. Campbell stared at him, clearly afraid to answer. "Well?"

"No, Dielaan . . . it was certainly formed by volcanic activity, eons ago, but the active parts of the range are north and south of here. The heat comes from radioactive decay. Part of the reason our exhaust fans are so strong is radon gas." This was very carefully said; Garth could see the caution in Campbell's eyes, and wondered if Rex was paying attention.

"Pity," The Dielaan murmured. He flicked a glance in Garth's direction. "What would you say to half this year's haul of trinium as a ransom for one woman, one mine, and one trap of antimatter?"

ONEHUNDRED NINETYNINEDAY   MATINS

Such strange dreams . . . people meeting and saying the most bizarre things. *Always have options*, Halsey reminded her, even as Riva Ragärëe lovingly shook her ancient head at her favorite daughter-by-law. *A healer will always try to protect you, even when you shun safety*. And Sheel, his thin, worn features as familiar to her as the triple moons of Nuala, the expression crossing his face saying as clearly as words: *You enjoy this sort of thing. Danger is your lifeblood.*

Not danger; the game. . . . Through thick eyelashes she could make out a dim light. Coming from the next room . . . here, all was darkness. Night and pain—funny how things never hurt until they were noticed. There had been a fight . . . she remembered punching a hole in someone with her stiletto. Then a flash of light, and nothing. Sweet Mendülay, she was so nauseated. . . .

"Atarae?" Very soft, almost a whisper . . . not Mailan. *Gods, Mailan. If they got to me, then*—Who were *they*?

"Atarae? I have a bit of water. The mug is old, but it is clean."

Darame's suddenly acute senses could actually smell the water. A stoneware cup was thrust beneath her nose, and a hand reached to support her head. The shriek surprised them both; pain swept over her like a wave, momentarily extinguishing sight.

"Forgive me, I am not thinking—" This was cut off suddenly. "Perhaps . . . if you could roll over on your side? I could check the bleeding."

She did *not* sound steady, her accent from the interior . . . why was her voice familiar? *Since when do you know kidnappers?* Sweet Mendülay, what was she involved with, now . . . *I do not have time for this . . . would not another diplomat do?* How could one be sure of anything with such an ache—Blood? Instinctively she touched her thigh. "How much blood? From where?"

"The back of your head," was the brisk response. The "voice" carefully straightened her back and bent her legs. Steadying Darame's neck, she slowly tipped the woman to her side. "All right?"

"No worse than before," Darame responded, laying her fingers over her stomach. No hope, no hope of keeping this life. She would be lucky to get home alive herself. *If I had known, I could have sent Mailan alone*—Could Mailan have dealt with the Cied? Damn, the Cied, had she told Mailan about the bargain? A poor guardian of that knife she turned out to be. . . . Snips of conversations—Livia had been there, had she not—of course! Dielaan! "I was in Dielaan." Memory began to return.

"Yes." This was very strained. "There was little I could have done, except maybe sound the alarm, and I simply did not have the courage. I will be spending the rest of my life making it up to you and my aunt."

Aunt. Ah, the voice was familiar, after all. Lulani. Did that mean Garth Kristinsson was nearby? Darame could not help it; she started to giggle, ignoring the pain as her head vibrated. *One-track mind.*

"We are outside Lebanon, at one of the trinium mines, Mare Imbrium."

That snapped her out of her bleak humor. "Whatever for?"

Lulani sounded close to tears. "I am not sure Rex knows. He seems to be declaring war on several clans at once—at least Quen says they are acts of war. *I* certainly would look on them that way."

"Where is the antimatter?" Why did her voice have no strength?

"You *do* know—I was so sure you knew nothing." This was a whisper.

"I knew that the antimatter was stolen and I suspected that Kristinsson knew something about it. Your timely arrival kept me from pursuing the subject. Is this mine under siege?" Darame reached with fumbling fingers for the mug of water. So dry, why was her throat so dry? . . .

"Rex controls the elevator and the deep control bay," was the response. "There is still a shift in the mine, working. But it is only a day since you were taken—the ships have not even reached Kilgore."

"It is a cage, not an elevator. He has attacked other clans?" The water was actually chilled, who would have thought it.

"Not . . . there has been no challenge. But he sent people to Kilgore and Seedar to burn crops. We are having a drought, and he is burning crops!" This last was intense, and Darame opened her eyes in surprise.

Has he gone too far even for you, child? "Rich men rarely go hungry during a famine," Darame chose to say, closing her eyes again.

"I do not understand what he is thinking. It was that announcement Darol University made," Lulani muttered, her usually delicate voice flat and lacking resonance. "I am sorry, but he will not let me get water to fix your gash."

"There should be a first aid box close by, if we are near a RAM," Darame told her. "I would appreciate something for nausea, if you have it."

"In my catch-all, maybe—" Darame heard rustling sounds. "There *is* an emergency box, but Rex wants you looking green when he sticks you before the camera. Idiot." There were sounds of a seal breaking. "These can be chewed; they are mild, but they help me when things become too tense." Slender fingers pressed a flat lozenge into Darame's palm.

"Have the authorities arrived yet?"

"I think so—Rex told the supervisors not to call, but I think an alarm was sent before he thought to say anything."

The lozenge was effective, and worked faster than Darame had hoped. Already the nausea was retreating, although her head ached abominably. Slowly she raised herself to one elbow.

"Has Atare sent a force yet?" she managed to get out. Even the slight change in position made her dizzy.

"Careful, you may have a concussion. Oh, yes, they have the buildings surrounded," Lulani told her. In the dim light cast through the open panel, her usually golden skin was yellow, her copper-hued hair dull, lifeless.

Darame tried to keep her vision from doubling and fought for the right questions. "My *guaard*," she finally started.

"They swore she was alive when they left," Lulani said quickly. "But . . . she was not in the best of condition. Fortunately she was already unconscious when they grabbed you."

"Fortunately?"

Lulani smiled faintly. "You did a great deal of damage to the man who seized you from behind. They had to drop him off at a hospice. And of course they could not retaliate against you."

"Reflex." Darame dismissed the topic to return to her major concern. "Where is the antimatter? Did Rex hide it in Amura, or somewhere else?"

"It is here." Lulani actually began to tear up. "I do not know who is telling the truth anymore. Garth does not think they would lie about such a thing, and says it is possible. Rex thinks it is a trick."

"Lulani, make sense. What trick does Rex fear?"

"I am not sure I can explain it," the young woman started slowly. "Garth told me, after we stopped talking to the surface, but it is complicated. When metals are compatible—or is it when they are not compatible enough?—corrosion can take place. This can block the current. And if the current between the controller and the refrigeration unit fails, then the temperature rises, and. . . ." She swallowed visibly.

Gods, it was so hard to think . . . how could she deal with a crisis when it was so hard to think? What was this woman talking ab—"Transference. You are talking about transference."

"Yes! Transference. But Rex thinks it is all very convenient . . . and I think he suspects he is losing our support." This last was barely audible.

"Transference does not happen overnight, but the phenomenon is quite real. Where is the problem?" *Why am I so tired?*

"In the wire Stennis used to connect the controller to the trap. It was just laying around the warehouse," Lulani said promptly.

"Not that problem—the problem your cousin has with the story. Do they want him to send the antimatter to the surface?"

"Nooo, they want to send down some technicians to work on it."

Idiots. I have been abducted by idiots. "Has he no common sense? We want the antimatter back in one piece—no one is going to play games with him over it. He can have the technicians stripped if he wants; no one will smuggle down weapons. Does he value his skin so little?" Darame sagged against the rock wall behind her, grateful for its support. Glad, too, she had worn her blacks to bed. It was not uncomfortable in this section of the mine, but a nightgown would have been breezy.

Lulani shrugged helplessly, lifting her hands in entreaty. Before she could speak, Darame added: "If you say, 'He has the right,' I may hit you."

"No. I will not say it." Firm, her chin lifted. "I am no longer convinced there is any gain in this little game of his. Does he truly think he can blackmail three of the largest clans and get away with it? He cannot hide forever behind the walls of Dielaan . . . and if he does, he may have no people left beyond those walls once he comes back out." This last was sad, but it had the ring of long thought.

"If the fields of Kilgore and Seedar are burning, they will not burn Dielaan—I assure you." Now what? Was there any chance to reason with this crazy Dielaaner?

"Not that." Lulani shook her head. "I do not think our people will follow him to war. The outkin, yes . . . but not the masses."

Ah. So, if we can beat this brush-fire out. . . . Darame curled her knees up to her chest. "Help me sit up." Easier said than done, and Lulani clearly would have protested if she had dared. Moving told Darame something extra . . . they had not bothered to search her. *They left my cat knife!* How she would use it, she had no idea, but it made her feel a bit better.

"We do not have much in the way of food, but if you would like some? . . ." Lulani began hesitantly.

"Not unless you have tea and soda crackers," was the wry response.

Any Nualan woman would see through that statement. Lulani's face looked bewildered. "You . . . you are not. . . ."

"I wish."

Lulani actually looked as if she would spring to her feet, then stopped herself with an effort. "No; Rex must *not* know." Black eyes met black; Lulani's were filled with almost desperation.

"Well?"

"He *hates* your husband."

The intensity made Darame flinch. "He hates many people, your cousin."

"But you are here, and . . . I still do not think he will . . . kill you. I will *not* give him any more ammunition!" This was fierce.

Wearily, Darame said: "Lulani—Lucy . . . you must choose sides. All this vacillation is bad for your character. I do not know why you chose to back Rex in this ill-planned madness, but I do not think that remaining neutral will gain you anything."

"He said no one would die! That he would not dream of starting a war!" Somehow she kept her voice to a whisper.

"And you believed him . . . chose to believe him? Knowing his mistrust of the other clans, his hatred for Atare? Well, my dear, he has caused deaths, and he apparently has started a war. What are you going to do about it?"

"Me?"

She was so new to the game. "You. Who else *can* do anything?"

"What can I do? We have been trying to think of something—"

"We. Who else is here?"

"Garth and I. Also Silas, and Rex, of course. A supervisor from the mines . . . Campbell, I think he is called. Rex brought

Quen—a second hostage. Quen knew nothing of this, or never gave us reason to think he knew of it. And the guards from the embassy.'' She leaned closer. ''Do you have an idea? Garth said we needed to know where the antimatter was, before we could try to leave. But he does not want to leave you and Quen—he is afraid of what might happen.''

''Commendable of him,'' Darame murmured. ''Where *is* the antimatter?''

''Last I heard it was at the bottom of the ele—cage shaft,'' she said quickly. ''Rex's new captain of his guard is watching over it. They brought a communicator to use between them, but it does not work well in here.''

Darame considered the problem. ''Can you get to the surface?''

''I am not sure . . . there is a guard at the top, and if Rex did not call ahead on the vid, he might not let the . . . the hoistman bring up the cage.''

''So convince Rex to let you take out an important message personally—something he does not want to share with any others watching the vid. *One* of us must get to them and tell them where the antimatter is located,'' Darame stressed. ''And I am not moving very well yet.''

''You should not be moving at all,'' Lucy pointed out.

''Sometimes we must make sacrifices.''

''Do you think I can get out?'' This was blunt.

''Keep them busy; *I* may be able to get out the other exit.''

''There is another—'' A whisper of astonishment.

Darame raised a finger to her lips. ''A safety precaution . . . there is always another shaft in a trinium mine, although if you came through a 'dry'—a locker room, you came down the main one. I have never been in this particular mine, but they are all similar. How far along is the shift?''

Lulani shrugged again, although it was not quite as hopeless an expression. ''It had changed not long before we came down. It is well into matins, now, and we came down in compline. They mentioned hours for measurement.'' A frown puckered her delicate black eyebrows.

''Probably until prime, then. They cleared the mine, did you say?'' *Already I am forgetting what we have discussed. Wonderful.*

''No . . . the entire shift is still here, working. We have been monitoring the internal net; I do not think management has told them about the emergency." Very slow, this; Lucy was obviously still of two minds about it.

"Understandable, but that cannot go on, not if Rex refuses to allow the antimatter to be adjusted. Somehow you must get out of here! Lucy, I know not what you know about these mountains, but that containment trap must be working very hard to stay cool. The radiation level builds as descent is made, so the air and water are hot. Even the fans and pumps cannot pull out all of it."

"Garth tried to tell Rex that moisture and heat could speed up the transference," Lucy whispered. "But he has convinced himself that we have at least two days before we need to worry."

"Wonderful," Darame said softly, momentarily closing her eyes. Lids flicking open once again, she asked: "How do my pupils look?"

"What?"

"Are they the same size, or have they dilated oddly?"

Obediently Lucy leaned over and peered at her. "They look the same."

"Good. Now, we have two priorities—we must clear everyone out of this mine, and we must get the antimatter stabilized or out of here."

Smiling faintly at this blithe statement, Lucy said: "Rex is constantly monitoring the internal net and the cage hoist. How will you tell management to clear the mine? How will you get away from here?" she added, tilting her head curiously.

"Right out the opposite door, my dear. You will go tell them I am asleep again, and that you are still not happy with how I look. Make sure no one comes in here for . . . as much as an hour, if you can. I am not sure how fast I can walk. They do not expect anything of me, not after knocking me about as they did—and that is to my advantage, right now." It was tiring, conversation. How could she hope to stand, much less keep moving?

"I . . . I think you are right. Even if you get lost in this mine, it is better than waiting to see what Rex will do next. Before, he was predictable, if vicious. But now. . . ." She shook her head, bewildered.

"It is worse than you know." Darame considered a scrap of information; a trump, one might say in cards. "Your charming

cousin ordered your Uncle Tsuga to 'take care' of the problem
of the regent. He tried to poison her. Fortunately, your aunt is
a very suspicious and observant woman, or she would be no
longer with us.'' Darame slid the young Dielaaner a glance;
Lucy looked stunned. "Smooth your face, woman, and start
distracting. Remember—always keep a lie simple! Go!'' Almost, she forgot and tried to gesture with her head—pain warned
her to keep her movements contained. "Oh! Do you have a
pocket torch of some type?''

Lucy shook her head. "I am sorry, but we did not bring down
hats or lights. I *did* get you a chit—it is in your pants pocket.''

At least they can identify the body. "Next time pocket a
torch.''

"Next time?''

They both managed a faint smile.

MARE IMBRIUM, ENTRANCE GUARDHOUSE
LAUDS

"Then placement is everything?'' Sheel asked slowly, intently
studying the diagram on the wall before them.

"Absolutely, Atare,'' responded the woman to his right. "No
matter where the explosion took place, there would be structural
damage, but it could be dealt with later. Our major fear is prox-
imity to miners. Unless they have moved during matins, The
Dielaan's party is located . . . here.'' Extending a telescoping
pointer, the manager indicated an area near the junction of shaft
Number one and level 2377. "Half of our current shift is working
somewhere on 2377. Now, we can communicate with them both
individually and by crews, but not without Dielaan knowing
about it.''

"What can he do, other than decide to detonate the antimatter?'' Zaide asked from the shadows behind them.

"This is the main underground control room. He can arbi-
trarily shut down ore passes, play with the ventilation fans, delay
the cage—''

"Can you override him?'' Sheel looked up as he spoke.

The manager grimaced, tilting her head sideways in a nervous
gesture. "Theoretically, yes—but there are guards topside between us and the main board. Also, the crews who eat on 2377

now know the control room has been seized. Those who are deeper than 800 meters must come up to eat on the surface; this shift they were unable to leave the mine. Right now *my* greatest fear is that someone will think the major threat is Dielaan's access to the controls, and try to break in on them.''

"Access through a net tap?" Crow asked.

The manager shook her head. "We have so many safeguards to prevent that, it would take at least a day to break into the system.''

"I am not sure we have a day," Sheel murmured, his gaze returning to the diagram. "So Dielaan controls the main shaft. But there is a second shaft, to the north of the ore body?''

"The heavy equipment shaft, Number six. Miners mucking in that area often use it because otherwise it would take too long to get to their work areas.'' She turned back to the projection. "We could send people down the north shaft, and pass the word by mouth—clear the mine that way.''

"Could we reach everyone?"

"Impossible," said the second supervisor, who was standing next to Zaide. "We have literally hundreds of miles of drifts.''

"If we sent a few people in with porta-vids? And coordinates for working drawpoints?'' the other suggested in turn.

Her counterpart frowned in her direction, but Sheel could see that the stout man was considering the idea. "Maybe," he said finally.

"Every communication and alarm system runs through the internal RAM?'' Crow stated dubiously.

"Communications, yes—it is very hard to send messages through this rock. As for alarms, we have many kinds, but they all have different meanings. There is an accident siren, which clears the transpo drifts so that an injured miner can be removed. We also have a warning blast for 'fire in the hole'—a last call before blasting commences. Those signals will be worthless to us.''

Sheel stared at the diagram, letting the images blur into light. Sweet Mendülay, he was tired. Good thing these two had been late to their shift, or the advice being offered by the mines would be as scattered as his own thoughts.

No time had been wasted; over a thousand Atare warriors surrounded the Mare Imbrium buildings, and already Crow was trying to discover a way into the mine. This required all his

attention; he could not spare thought wondering how Leah was
doing, or why Mailan and Darame had not called in a third or
fourth time. His dreams had been uneasy, and his dreams were
often an uncomfortable window into the future. . . .

"If we could find out where the antimatter is, we could slip
in and seize it," Crow murmured, carefully scanning the diagram
of the mining levels.

"And if it is not with them? If they have sent it to another
part of the mine?" Zaide asked. "That seems likely."

"They could not move it far," Crow said, his voice indicating
his thoughts were elsewhere. "It must weigh a hundred kilo-
grams. If they have any common sense at all, they have it on a
puff packet." Now he turned back to the two mine supervisors.
"The ore train level—could we go in through that tunnel?"

"Not without alerting Dielaan. The bed through the mountain
is one track, with only enough room for the train itself. Possibly
you could ride a train back inside, but you would need to be *in*
the cars for about five kilometers, until you reached the chutes.
Then you would need to move quickly, before the train came to
a complete stop, for if we delayed the chute, it would register
on the screens in that control room."

"For how long would it register?" Clearly Crow had already
made up his mind; all that was left was to evaluate the risks.

"A yellow light would flash the entire time, indicating a
change in procedure. I would think that anything less than five
minutes would be dangerous. Light is dim down there, unless
we are working on equipment, and you have never seen what
you would be entering. A mine is like nothing you can imagine,
warrior, and even holos of what you would see would not prepare
you." The woman spoke soberly, her expression grave. Glancing
at the other manager, she suggested: "Volunteers to lead them
in?"

"Absolutely," the other agreed. "I know your people have
the best training possible, but even apprentice miners can get
lost in these drifts."

"Then you are in favor of the train tunnel?" she asked, surprised.

"I have no better alternative." Stepping up to the multicolored
diagram, his round face impassive, he pointed to three places
within the mine. "Assuming they know little about mining, I
would bet my next pay voucher that they have placed the anti-

matter in one of three places—between the ventilation shafts, as close to the center of the ore cave as possible, or at the foot of the main shaft. It depends on Dielaan's true goals. If he wishes merely to damage us, the shafts are best, although a greater threat to the air supply. If, however, he brought the ore cave down into the mucker level . . . well, we might have to abandon the level, and create a new east-west drift approximately twenty meters below it."

"Is there enough antimatter to destroy this mine?" Sheel said to Zaide.

"No. But according to the merchants' estimates, there is easily enough to seal any shaft . . . possibly both Number two and Number three shaft, since they are not that far apart. That would leave only Number five for ventilation."

"And the cage?"

"If they destroy the main transportation shaft, the only way out for those on 2377 would be the north shaft, Number six. It would require walking—or, if vehicles with enough fuel could be located, riding—approximately eight kilometers due north. All of this assumes that the concussion from the explosion does not cause cave-ins that far out. If the antimatter triggered under the ore cave, I have private reservations about whether any drifts in the area would withstand the vibration." He swallowed visibly. "I speak abstractly, of course. . . . if the shift is still below during an accident. . . ."

"So—we must get it out of the mine." Glancing at Crow, Sheel said: "I want entry from the train level and the north, simultaneously. You may need . . . additional weapons." This was almost toneless. Nualans had so few types of weapons; taking life was usually the last thing on their minds. . . .

"I requested Cied jabbers, Atare," Crow replied. "And a burn."

"Atare?" The unexpected voice caused both Sheel and Crow to tense. Simultaneously they turned toward the entry panels. No trick of the ears; it was Mailan, in day issue blacks, the left sleeve missing. Her arm was wrapped from bicep to wrist, and her forehead bore pale evidence of a cold torch sealing, but the gray eyes were as steady as always. "We have a guest, Atare." With that, she stepped aside.

Livia Ragáree, Regent to Dielaan, stepped into the room. Dressed in a skinsuit of vivid red, gold, and black, her house colors, she looked stripped for fighting, no older than her eldest daughter. Her porcelain features were now chiseled from rock rather than molded of fine bone.

"We must waste no more time, Atare," she said crisply. "I do not wish to owe you wergild, and I do not trust that dog I once called son. Your Cied allies did their work well; their sabotage prevented two squads of warriors from following the lead of my cousin Tsuga." She spit precisely to one side, then continued speaking. "What with repairs, a platoon of my own will be here within three hours. I understand that the heir to Dielaan is also being held hostage. What plans have you made to alleviate this situation?"

Sheel stood slowly, meeting emerald eyes that did not flinch from his gaze. It was all too obvious what her cryptic words meant; Mailan's condition had warned him. "Also" being held hostage . . . Quen of Dielaan, that was already known. Now Sheel knew why Rex Dielaan was so confident Atare would deal with him. *Blade and blood, stars and seed, Dielaan—until one of us is no more.* It was a very old oath, the war cry of Wallace; why did it come to mind?

Forcing himself to nod graciously, Sheel said gravely: "I should have proposed to you years ago, Livia."

Her smile was fierce, the lift of her eyebrows regretful. "Darame will not share." She stressed her tense, as if daring them to contradict her, and Sheel returned her smile.

LAUDS

Somewhere close by, water was dripping vigorously, splashing into fluid of unknown depth. The height and width of the darkened drift magnified the sound, causing an echo effect. Sweet Mendülay, how long had she been walking? Touching her roman, she veiled her lids, flinching as the light stabbed at her. Still lauds, just under two hours since she crawled out of the shift room. . . . A finger twitched, and the wall of black returned.

Darame would have killed for a "boss buggy," the little balloon-tired tractor transports often left conveniently at a widening of the route, but they were all in use or parked elsewhere. Still dizzy from the blow, she had set her course by the only two markers she knew she could follow half-blind and staggering . . . away from voices and away from lights. There was no way to tell how many warriors Dielaan had brought with him, and once free she could not risk falling into their hands again. At that point, she had not wanted to find a group of miners; there had been too much of a chance that they might have wanted to storm Dielaan's stronghold. Now, when she had some distance on the control room, *now* she wanted to find someone.

Lights had dwindled to merely intersections . . . then nothing. Once she had recovered enough to think clearly, every step into *nothing* required conscious effort. It was not the darkness, the sheer sensory deprivation that frightened her . . . it was the weight. The constant knowledge that a thousand meters of rock was between her and the sky. *This drift is at least six meters high and four meters wide. Relax, breathe deeply—*

Leaning back against the wall—the rib, it was called the rib —of the drift, Darame massaged her left shoulder and took slow, deep breaths. Damn the elevation! Breathing was hard enough right now, and when you started thinking about all that rock above your head. . . .

Do not think about it.

Finding a pole longer than she was tall had been incredible luck. She had used it to test for uneven ground, and to make large circles in the air in front and to her left. She had found the cords for two pneumatic doors that way—one she had missed, which required fifteen meters of backtracking and several minutes of slashing until the errant, dangling cord was discovered. While there was dim, distant light, she had shut the doors as well, but the last cord had eluded her. *Flagrant disregard of mining regulations,* she told herself severely, trying to work the pain from her shoulder. Who would think a little pole could be so heavy?

"Not used to it." The deep whisper seemed to carry, and Darame shrank into herself, waiting . . . listening. Only the water, and, further still, a distant vibration, scarcely felt through the soles of her boots, encouraging her on. Someone was working in this end of the drifts—maybe several someones. *You will find them.* A dull, snapping sound reached her ears, and the invisible band across her chest tightened correspondingly. Somewhere in this drift, the rock was "talking" . . . shifting minutely, moving toward either stabilization or collapse. *Miners who live listen to the rock.*

Water was Darame's primary guide. The suspension of rock

dust in the air of a mine would be fatal if not for constant wetting done by spraying trucks and piped-in water. Of course, these drifts were now for mucking, not drilling—here in a sense was the second stage of the operation. Some sixteen meters above her head, the explosives crew, through daily undercutting, drilling, and blasting, maintained the constant duty of making sure the ore body continued to "cave," by gravity, evenly into huge drawpoints—

Darame's flesh literally crawled, her hands gripping solid, comforting stone. *By all the varied saints of my childhood, the blasting crew!* Gods, what if blasting was about to commence? The mine was always cleared before detonation, but what if she was unconscious when the call went out—

Stop it. One hand reached and clutched the piece of brass in her pocket until a sharp corner drew blood. *This means miner below—they will not blast with a chit unaccounted for.*

What about the antimatter? Sitting at the bottom of that hot, damp, shaft almost like a bomb, ticking away. . . .

A miner. I must find someone who can help me. I must find a damn belt torch! On this level, most miners worked alone, operating unwieldy front-end loaders which would scoop up the ore from the drawpoint drifts and dump it into ore passes leading down to the train level. *I know there is someone out here—the belly of the drift is wet. Belly . . . is that the right word? When something goes wrong, you are on your belly fast enough.*

Enough rest. Darame had chosen this heading because it was so wet—surely someone was "mucking" here this shift. Now as long as they had not already moved on. . . . The pole extended cautiously.

Damp had become mud, and now a pool of water. Keeping a hand to the rib on her right, Darame probed continuously for shifting rock. A twisted ankle could be disastrous now . . . the water continued to rise. Past the ankles, to the calves . . . below the knee. A rock brought her left leg back up quite a bit, and then the pole slapped something. Another poke; almost a flap in response. . . .

A smile crept across her face. Yes, she had chosen well. Not a pneumatic door, but heavy plastic stretched over the opening, controlling ventilation and keeping dust at bay. Dear Mendulay, what she would give for a light, much less a breathing mask. How to gain their attention without being crushed by a many-

ton loader. . . . Working her way carefully to the center of the
plastic, slipping a few times, Darame finally found the overlapping
slit and yanked it apart. Instantly the sound of water changed
from dripping to hissing . . . they were spraying to control dust.

Pulling the plastic together, Darame worked her way back to
the right rib and started slowly into the heading. Already she
could sense the difference; dust and a whiff of methane fuel
stung her nostrils, and humidity brought home to her the increased temperature. Her body responded, breaking into a gentle
sweat. Only the hiss of sprayers and the vibration of wet rock
against her soles indicated a nearby miner. Darkness isolated
her, a vast, empty feeling which threatened kilometers until the
mucker was found. *Remember that sound is deceptive underground, and carries oddly*. The drifts had been exactly twenty-
four meters apart; drawpoints were only separated by half that,
as she recalled. Sure enough, her hand suddenly reached for
empty space. Poking with her stick gave the impression of rubble.
Reaching above her head, Darame traced the arch above the
drawpoint with the pole. Still intact—in use, but not today.
Twelve meters down the line, a second drawpoint contained a
huge boulder. Delicately her fingers crept over the face of the
rock; she found several holes which could only have been man-
made. Praise Mendülay—blasting holes, empty.

Her concentration had been on touch and sound . . . now she
noticed a change in her vision. No longer was there *nothing*
beyond her nose; the face of the drift was now dull black rather
than pitch black. *A light*. Gripping her pole tightly, Darame
continued walking.

A third drawpoint was operational—tiny jets of water shot
from the poured concrete insert at the back of the drift, coating
her hand and arm with a fine mist. Only a few steps farther, her
hand once again closed on empty air, even as her calf brushed
up against a rib. What—? Abruptly, she snatched back her hand,
her heartbeat racing. *Foolish*. Now she remembered. These
mines were designed so the mucker operators were able to dump
their dippers of ore directly down a chute to the train level, over
one hundred eighty meters below. To her immediate right was
an ore pass. Farther down the chute there were heavy directional
panels which could control the direction the ore fell, but if it
was open. . . . Shivering, she continued walking, and quickly
found solid rock once again.

Eyes stinging, Darame no longer merely felt the mucker—she could hear it. A low, growling rumble, increasing in volume, like an animal about to charge. . . . Accelerate, stop, creak, and groan—scraping and grating, as a dipper was filled at a draw-point. Faint light reached her, showing her that the drift was not truly straight—

Suddenly the light against the opposite rib was a thousand times brighter, a blinding reflection, illuminating thick, suspended dust which sparkled with the blaze of a crystal chandelier. A roar like a hound of hell overwhelmed her as monstrous inflated tires were momentarily within arms' reach. Dropping her pole, Darame threw herself against the rib of the drift, clinging for dear life, knowing the clearance on each side was only thirty centimeters, praying aloud as her senses were hammered flat by unimaginable sound and light and darkness. A fusillade of stone rained upon her left arm and shoulder even as the shattered pole shot across the mouth of an ore pass and fell into the depths of the mountain.

wergild: In ancient Germanic law, the value set upon a human life in accordance with a fixed scale, then paid as compensation to the family of the injured or slain person. Compare *BLOODWITE*.

CHAPTER THIRTEEN

MARE IMBRIUM, LEBANON
        ONEHUNDRED NINETYNINEDAY   LAUDS

Impressive invective. . . . As far as first thoughts went, it was not particularly illuminating, but it was accurate. Someone was

cursing vividly, with a variety in tone and word choice that part
of Darame found astonishing. Other parts of her were too busy
hurting to wonder why a voice was swearing at her.

Something about . . . why no light attached to my hard hat?
Gagging, trying to breathe through her nose, Darame reached,
gripping a projection of rock and hauling herself upward. Wincing from the glare of a spotlight, she saw bright spots of blood
on her arm, and remembered where she stood . . . sat.

"A mucker was going to eat me." Barely audible; certainly
not heard over the low mutter of an idling engine, but suddenly
the vituperative flow of words ceased.

Brilliant light slowly dimmed, becoming manageable. From
out of the darkness came a musical, husky voice, distinctly
female: "Serae, woul' you min' explaining what you are doing
creeping down my heading with no hard hat, no toeboots, and
no light?"

Darame tried to frame a coherent answer, then concentrated
on remaining upright.

A strong arm reached around her waist and slowly pulled her
to her feet. "If you ha' black hair like mine, you woul' be a
dea' cipher."

"Go to Norwood. The food does it—permanently." So
dizzy . . .

"Huh." It was not disbelieving, really—more considering,
withholding judgment. The arm guided her past the swinging
corner of the massive, empty dipper, settling her on the running
board edging the far side of the mucker. Cracking the passenger
door, the miner reached inside and pulled out a thermos. Pouring
something into the cupped lid, she thrust it at Darame.

It was an old-fashioned tisane, still warm from lunch, with
more herbs in it than Darame could readily recognize. Carefully
she sipped the fluid.

"Now, Serae, have you remembere' how you arrive' in my
mine? Tho I suppose it is as much yours as mine, eh?" the miner
added.

Sometimes silver hair is handy. "No. I was unconscious at
the time. But I can explain why I am in your heading. I was
looking for help. . . . Your drift was damp, so I knew someone
was working back here." Darame found speech coming slowly.
The tisane was staying down, praise Mendülay.

"Damp. Aye, it woul' be that." A throaty chuckle escaped the woman. "So, it has finally come, eh? We are under siege?"

"You know?"

"Know my shift boss came by an hour ago and tol' me to work through lunch. As if I usually stop!" A scoff, that.

"Your boss? Why did I miss him?"

"North en', Serae. My whole crew enters at north—we take a buggy over the surface instea' of through the drifts. But we all have ha' itchy palms lately, what with that antimatter missing an' all. Kooks bree' more kooks, eh? So, do they want infonet time, trinium, or concessions?"

Darame stared over the rim of the cup, then felt a rueful smile creeping up on her. That summed things up pretty well, actually.

"The last two, I suspect. They have other hostages, and are in what I think is the main underground control room . . . the one on 2377, just east of the cage. The bad part is, they are the same kooks—the antimatter is sitting on a platform at the bottom of the main shaft, and someone is sitting with it, in case Dielaan wants to set a timer and cut its power."

"By the Worn Ruts of The Last Path! They *are* crazy! So, they have the cage, eh? Not goo', not goo' at all. Nothing for it—out Number six. Another half a kilometer that way—" Her thumb jerked expressively over her shoulder. "Right at the intersection, go a kilometer straight on, then hang right again at the auxiliary east-west. Four kilometers to the junction, then left and out . . . after a long walk," she added.

"But how can we tell them to use shaft six?" The warmth was exploding in her stomach, making it easier to think through pain and grumbling machinery.

The woman sat down next to Darame. "Time is a problem, serae."

"The problem is the antimatter. It is unstable, and could blow up. Also, Dielaan is armed, but with what, I do not know."

"Huh." Much flatter this time; almost irritated. "That is the way of it, eh? I thought you use' that wor'. So—it begins again."

"Not if we can stop it," Darame said quickly. "One idiot is not going to topple ten years of good tribal relations."

The miner's light bobbed—jerked sharply to one side, as the woman detached it from her hard hat. Clicking it to a wide beam, she let the light diffuse around them. A dusky, oval face topped with ruffled dark ringlets was revealed. It was a strong face, not pretty by any definition except for a straight, elegant nose and brilliant blue eyes the true, deep, purplish sapphire. As for expression, the woman looked skeptical.

"Maybe, serae. But I was raise' in the mountains north of here, an' I remember when Dielaan came over the passes."

"That will not happen again." She could not remember why, but Darame knew that had been taken into account.

"Maybe. First we nee' to get you out of here."

"First we need to figure out a way to warn the miners that something is wrong. Diclaan is on the internal net, so anything we transmit will be at the least overheard, if not pre-empted." Darame's eyelids drooped as she leaned back against the side of the mucker. "Then we need to tell them up top where that antimatter is located."

Consulting a roman she had pulled out of a pocket, the miner said. "Two hours until shift change. We cannot wait?"

"To be honest, I am afraid to wait. The Dielaan is acting irrational."

A snort. "All Dielaaners are irrational. So—how to reach everyone without using the wall boxes or internal net." She thought for a minute or two. "Impossible."

"There has to be another way! Surely you do not depend on that system alone for things! What if there is a power failure?"

"Back-up generators," the woman answered calmly. "We use a few other systems— emergency alarms for injuries, bells for cage operation, a signal for when we are going to fire the hole. The wall boxes are separate, but they can be monitored by the internal net—do you see?"

Unfortunately, she did see. If they did not have to worry about Dielaan reacting violently, they could easily announce a problem and evacuate the mine. "We need something he cannot stop and cannot immediately assign blame to," Darame muttered, sipping at the tisane and absently offering the lid to the miner.

They sat in silence, sharing the cup of herbal tea and considering. Then the miner began to chuckle.

"You have an idea?" Darame asked, carefully turning her head toward the other. It was bleeding again, she could feel the trickle down her neck.

"A gag." The woman kept chuckling. "I wonder . . . if Doc is still in 2368 East, he coul' do it."

"Well?" Darame prompted gently. *All the time in the world, down here.*

A brilliant blue eye, momentarily flashing red, glanced her way. "A gag we pull on all the new han's. We tell them that we have a code we use for the siren—an' they have to memorize it. A huge list, really scares the whatever out of them, eh? They get a dozen or so down before they fin' out trinium mines stoppe' using the codes a thousan'year ago." She grinned; it was contagious, that grin. "We use the 'miner hurt' code and the 'fire in the hole' code, an' that is all that remains. But the thir' one on the list is 'evacuate mine, fire/explosion danger.' "

"Would anyone remember that?" Darame said, skeptical in her turn.

"*I* do," the miner pointed out. "Those who no longer remember will figure something is wrong. They will go to a wall box—an' will probably fin' another miner there, who knows what the signal means. By now folks down under know the main cage is blocked, so they woul' start for the other shaft, anyway." Straightening, the woman stood and reached for Darame's arm. "We nee' to fin' a first ai' box for you, an' then Doc for the wiring. My name is Kristori, by the way." Opening the cab, she helped Darame into the confines of the mucker. The compartment had its own lights in the roof and side panels; the soft glow was somehow comforting.

When Kristori had climbed in on the other side and shut both doors, silence descended upon them. The mutter of the engine seemed very far away.

"Good soundproofing," Darame whispered approvingly. Still dizzy, she leaned back into the padded seat and half-veiled her eyes.

"Hang on, eh?" With practiced ease, Kristori threw the mucker into reverse, engaged the engine, and started backing down the dark drift at full throttle.

Darame decided to close her eyes.

"Are you sure that will do it?"

The other hard hat light raised slightly as Doc continued separating wires, throwing his long, sharp nose into high relief. "Did I kibitz when you patched her head and arm?" The tall, bony man had a restful voice, almost as if he was trying to lull them to sleep.

"Nay."

"All right, then." He seemed to feel he had covered the topic; only the murmur of Kristori's engine filled the confines of the drift.

After a ride which had raised the hairs on Darame's arms, though it was apparent Kristori knew her business and had not so much as grazed a support beam in passing, the miner known as "Doc" had been ferreted out of a nearby drift. This had involved stopping the mucker at the mouth of the heading, and signaling with a pocket torch that had a red lens. The roar from the darkness had died to a mutter, and eventually a spider-shanked apparition had loomed into their spotlight.

Two minutes . . . five minutes. Kristori had returned to the cab and headed her mucker off down the drift. Tilting her head as far as she had dared, Darame had seen the light from the following machine.

"He is with us," Kristori had said succinctly. So it had proved.

Doc had turned out to be one of those people who could do anything with a pair of wire clippers, a clamp, and some industrial strength tape. Tenderly parking his mucker at a crossing and shutting it down completely, Doc had opened a nearby junction box and had had the face off before Darame had blinked. The hydra of wire within had fallen in coils to his feet, and he had immediately begun searching for the siren linen.

In the meantime, Kristori had hunted up peroxide and bandages, and had given Darame even greater appreciation for Sheel's healing touch. After thought, they had decided to pack the ore grazes with biosporin and wrap her entire arm with a support bandage. Small adhesives had worked for the two large lacerations on her shoulder blade, and a seal for the split skin over the lump on her head. Beyond that, Kristori had admonished her to sit quietly and keep out of the way. Meekly Darame had done as ordered.

"All right, now," Doc said suddenly. "We are ready for business. When I flip this—" his fingers hovered over a toggle switch— "the siren starts screaming 'emergency, injured miner.' Then the fun begins."

Looking over his shoulder, Darame saw that he had tampered with all the incoming wires from the emergency switches, and had attached small dials to them. "Are those . . . detonator timers?"

"Always like to see beauty and brains combined," Doc stated. "Yes, indeed, those are detonator timers. What will happen is the siren for clear the drifts will wail out. It is what we use to empty equipment from the transpo drifts, so an injured miner reaches the surface quickly. Normally it cycles three times, then shuts itself off. But I have bypassed the shut-off, *and* have rigged these timers. So it will blow until someone re-routes the thing, or someone cuts off the main line up top and outside, at the power station."

"Why the timers?"

"Those are for if someone tries to cut off the siren through the net. They will read the signal as coming from, say, 2380 East. So they cut it off. Well, then *this* one starts blaring. In another minute, *this* one starts signaling that someone is throwing the switch, and so on. Now, an electrician would know what had happened, but unless they have someone in there who has access to the wiring diagrams in the net, *and* can read them, they will give up before they figure out how to stop it."

Darame gave him one of her tremendous smiles. "Magnificent, Doc."

Straightening to an alarming height, Doc returned a toothy grin. "All right, then, serae."

"So, we flip it and hea' for shaft six," Kristori said briskly.

"*You* head for shaft six. *I* need to get to that antimatter." The two miners gave her a long look. Darame pushed irritably at the hard hat they had found for her, and smoothed her features. "If Dielaan becomes annoyed enough, he will slap his own timer on it; then where are we?"

"As isolated as the firstcomers," Doc agreed. "Might be good for us."

"Kristori—"

"Not alone." Kristori was firm. "You will nee' help."

"Are you positive? This is a 'volunteers only' type of job." Darame gave them both long looks in turn.

"Miners never do anything they do not want to do," Doc assured her. A sinewy arm reached out, and nimble fingers flipped the toggle switch.

Weird moaning reached their ears, swelling and dying rhythmically.

"Hop on, everyone. Next stop, 2194." Kristori tucked Doc behind the two seats and, with effort, got the cab door closed.

"On a mucker? How?"

"Nay! It woul' take hours on the ramps; we woul' run out of fuel long before reaching that level. No, we will go to Number two and call the inspection cage. It hol's three big men, so we shoul' fit easily, eh?" Throwing the engine open, Kristori roared off down the drift.

Darame considered the blur of jutting rock, and closed her eyes again.

MARE IMBRIUM, ENTRANCE GUARDHOUSE
LAUDS

Minutes seemed like hours. . . . Sheel had heard that phrase before, but had never fully appreciated it until now. Sometimes there was nothing to do but wait—wait for Zaide to report in, wait for Kilgore's meth to land, wait for Crow to reach shaft six and Mailan to reach the mouth of the ore train tunnel. Sliding his gaze to one side, Sheel watched as Livia graciously took charge of the tea tray which had just been delivered.

Her sudden words shattered the genteel image.

"Fortunate that your wife is so skilled in an emergency, or we would not have known our destination." Livia calmly handed him a mug of hot oaffra.

"She was able to leave a message?"

"Not exactly." Livia smiled without humor. "She almost gutted the warrior who seized her from behind—he will be for tunate if he lives, much less enjoy it. He was in the room when Rex gave his instructions to his captain, and it was a simple matter to extract the directions from him."

Sheel decided not to ask how she gained the information.

"*Yes!*" The manager at the RAM practically shrieked with rapture. "Finally, something in our favor!" Turning around, she said to Sheel: "Have you noticed the ripple in our screens, Atare?"

"I was afraid it was my eyes," Sheel admitted.

Smiling her agreement, the woman continued: "All of our screens update regularly, in intervals as brief as fifteen seconds or as long as several minutes. That is the ripple illusion—when the data changes. But I have found the original, dummy screens still in the system!"

"Dummy screens?" Livia repeated.

"The original sales tools which sold this system to the Mare Mines many years ago," the manager clarified. "We will contact Cole over at the main control room, and find out what screen the underground room is watching. Then, when the next update comes up—" She fluttered her fingers suggestively.

"You will put up the dummy screens? To what advantage?" Livia asked.

"Because the dummy screens will not react when strange things begin happening at the ore train level," Sheel whispered. "You can do this?"

"It will take a few moments, but yes, it can be done," she replied, her concentration on a line of jumbled numbers and letters. "Ah, Cole," she said into the mouthpiece of the earphones she had strapped on. "We have thought of a new way to confuse the enemy."

"But who is the enemy?" came a familiar, expressive voice.

Energy flowed into Sheel. Turning toward the door, the faintest of smiles momentarily crooked his mouth as he said: "I had begun to wonder if you were swimming up."

Nadine's crystals chimed as she threw back her head in silent mirth. "You have never tried to wheedle a platoon of soldiers out of my brother and sister," was her dry response. "It will go down in the annals as my greatest performance." Glancing at Livia, she said: "Ragāree."

The neutral greeting was acceptable. "Do sit down, serae," Livia said with a sweep of her hand toward a chair. "We must give thought to the discipline of this fool who calls himself—"

Sheel nearly dropped his mug as a siren wailed through the room. Immediately the second of the managers leaped toward a membrane, his plump hands cutting the volume by more than half.

"What is it?" Sheel said quickly.

"It . . . it is not good," was the reluctant response. "It is the siren code for an injured miner."

"Not exactly, Wald," the other said, her head cocked to one side. "Listen. It is still repeating."

"How?"

Swiftly she called up another screen. "Someone has set off the switch at 2366—no, 2372—" She broke off as a third box lit up.

Now he had someplace to center that core of energy. Standing, Sheel moved over to the screen. "I may be optimistic, but it smacks of my woman's meddling." He glanced at the managers. "How will those below react?"

"They will try to call in," Wald said. "If Dielaan is monitoring the wall boxes, his ears will be filled with annoyed miners wanting to know what in seven hells is going on."

"I know that code!" The woman looked briefly stupefied. "It is the 'Evacuate mine, fire/explosion danger' siren. The same as the injured signal, but repeated indefinitely!"

"What?"

"Think, Wald! When you first went in the hole! Remember that stupid list? I think I memorized the entire damn thing—your pardon, seraes," she said quickly, "before I found out they were archaic!"

Wald started laughing. "Well, someone is on their toes down there! With any luck, half the shift is on their way to Number six!"

A *guaard*'s whisper in his ear told Sheel the moment had arrived. "And now it is our turn. Did you not tell Dielaan you would inform him when the Atare reached the mine?" Sheel asked softly. "Well, the players are present, and the stage is set—" He gestured to the *guaard* behind him, who had just slipped in with communicator in hand. "We have reached both tunnels. Call over to your Cole, sir—we are ready to ask their terms." Giving the other manager a sharp look, Sheel added: "Can you place the dummy screens while we talk to Dielaan?"

"Keep him talking," was her grim reply.

MARE IMBRIUM, MAIN UNDERGROUND CONTROL ROOM   LAUDS

"Silence it!" Rex's fist shot out as he spoke, slamming into the supervisor's jaw.

Three of the present warriors immediately leaped to membranes, calling up various subheadings in an attempt to find out what was causing the siren. In the meantime, the mining supervisor was using the edge of a RAM to pull himself to his feet. Garth had to give the old fellow credit—he was tough. He did not so much as touch the side of his face.

"It is no good, Dielaan," the supervisor said slowly. "That alarm is an old one, in place long before the internal RAM was set. We might be able to close the switch on it, but—"

"Then close it."

Lucy moved almost imperceptibly closer to Garth's side. He resisted the temptation to slip an arm around her. It might be seen as criticism. . . .

Seated once more before the screen, the man punched in several codes. As he typed, his fingers hesitated.

"Do not waste—"

"Something is funny. That is not the injured code," Campbell muttered. A wiring diagram came up on the screen before him. "There—2366. Someone threw the switch back there . . ." Another box lit up as he spoke. "Now 2372. How many injuries do we have, for Mendülay's sake?" As he turned off 2366, a third box lit up. "That tears it to shreds—I cannot stop it, but we can turn it off in here." He gestured to the horn above the door; a warrior moved over and touched the button beneath it. Instantly the shriek diminished, the sound of the siren muffled by the control room door. "We are receiving a vid call, Dielaan." The Ataran waited for Rex to respond.

"Are there still guards on the cage and corridor intersections?" Rex asked aloud.

"No miners have been allowed into the area, Dielaan," a warrior bearing silver stripes replied.

Seating himself, Rex growled at Garth and Lucy: "Stop cringing." Settling his arms on the rests of the chair, Rex turned a three-quarter profile to the screen. "Bring up the vid."

The man with the copper-colored patrician face was once again on the screen. "You asked to be informed when The Atare arrived. He is at the guardhouse. We can feed you the outside vid line, when you are ready."

"Do we have infonet access yet?" Rex asked coolly.

"We can turn a camera on a screen with outside hookup."

"Not good enough." Rex bit off each word crisply. "Can we receive the vid?" he asked Campbell.

"Yes, Dielaan."

"Then do so."

Campbell sent the image to the large, center wall screen. It did not overpower—the lights in the guardhouse were set low, and starrise was far away. Only one person was visible, a man simply dressed except for the fine, ruby-studded trinium chain around his neck. Sheel Atare was actually leaning on one arm of his chair, his body relaxed.

"Welcome, Atare," Rex murmured, choosing Caesarean for the conversation. "I hope you are enjoying the entertainment."

Sheel Atare actually lifted one eyebrow. "If you wanted a tour of a trinium mine, Dielaan, you could have requested one any time in the past year."

Surely that would do it. No . . . Rex had better control of himself than Garth thought. Usually ridicule, even indirect ridicule, goaded him into indiscretion. Lucy's hand crept over to grip his cuff. He found the action oddly comforting . . . something was still recognizable.

"I have already seen enough for my purposes," was the soft response.

"You travel with a large entourage, Dielaan."

"And growing. Do you like the second cordon, around your own?" The words were very smooth.

"Do you like the fact that their captain just sent word that he will not take sides between Dielaans?" Sheel responded gently.

"There is only one Dielaan." Who would have thought Rex's face could look so harsh. Chiseled, even; it had always seemed soft to Garth, free of expression or impression.

"There are three undisputed heirs to the throne—or so it has been explained to me many times," Sheel corrected gently.

"Quen reb^Livia is not in a position to pursue a claim, and a child? The outkin are through with regents," was the retort.

Sheel Atare rotated his chair, his eyes shifting up and to his left. A slim, red-headed figure moved into the lens's view. At Garth's side, Lucy grew rigid. He drew her attention with a poke; making sure the others were watching the screen, Lucy mouthed the words: *His mother.*

Ah. The ragäree who was regent. Nicholas's Balls, he wished he and Lucy could talk! But Rex would allow no one to leave the area, except when Lucy stepped into the lunch room to tend The Atarae, and they certainly did not want to speak in front of him. Silas was sufficiently cowed that he had not spoken in at least an hour—the sight of his aunt seemed to visibly frighten him still further. Garth wondered what Rex's face looked like; he had swiveled the flexseat away from them.

"If necessary, the future Coll Dielaan would greatly mourn

the martyrdom of his brother Quen in our pursuit of continued peace and prosperity for the world of Nuala,'' the tiny woman said tonelessly.

A drawn breath, so soft Garth scarcely heard it, came from Lucy. Her black eyes were wide with shock, and her hand tightened on his sleeve. He did not have to ask what had just happened—Rex was going to have to move fast to heal this breach. Of its own will, Garth's gaze slid over to Quen. The young man looked calm; there was no longer any tension in his mouth.

A tilt of the flexseat; Rex Dielaan's expression was rigid, whether with shock or fury Garth was not sure. The sudden wild look in his eyes did not clarify matters. Flicking his attention back to the screen, Garth saw what had triggered the last response.

A third person had entered the scene, and was standing to Sheel Atare's right. A tall woman, with dark blond hair woven with purple glass or gems that matched her vivid irises. Her smile was thin-lipped, without teeth, almost but not quite a grimace. "If you three are done amusing yourselves, I would like to talk about the antimatter," she suggested crisply.

Rex Dielaan turned his face to Campbell. Whatever the man saw in it, his response was immediate—he disconnected the vid.

"What?" Garth heard himself whisper to Lucy.

Dazed, she made no attempt to modulate her voice. "We have lost."

"If you must speak like a fool, then be silent," Rex snapped, rising to his feet. Gesturing to his remaining officer, he said: "Bring in The Atarae." The warrior started toward the closed panel.

Lucy's hand tightened painfully on his wrist, and Garth felt a brief, irrational hope. *Fool—how could she have stood upright, much less put any distance between herself and her captors?* Suddenly Garth realized that Rex was still speaking.

"We are in control of the mine itself, and we have the antimatter. I fail to see why you should despair." His black gaze burned into them. Light blazed from the adjoining room, as the warrior turned on all the overhead lights. "Are you trying to blind us?" Rex yelled after him.

"Dielaan, she is not here!"

"What?" The whisper was incredulous. "Impossible. She would have had to have crawled to get out of there."

"That is exactly what it looks like she did," came a mystified mutter—the warrior was bent over and examining the far wall. "See, here—"

"I am not interested in how she got out, I want her back! Send every available man after her!" Whirling, he turned on Lucy and Garth.

"Rex, she could not even sit up!" Lucy shrieked, leaping to her feet.

"Dielaan, the main control room is calling back. Do you wish to talk to them?" This was devoid of emotion, but Garth had caught the glitter in the man's eye—he was enjoying the slow unraveling of Rex Dielaan.

"Why did you not tie her to a table?"

"With what? You did not tell me to—"

"Do I need to think for you?"

"This is not going to help," Garth started, relieved that Rex was so distracted he was apparently unaware that Lucy was telling he on top of lie.

The center screen flickered into life once again. Appalled silence descended upon the group. Instantly cold, forbidding, Rex turned toward the screen, remaining standing. This time the supervisor on the surface had not paused to intercede—already Sheel Atare and his "guests" were visible.

"It seems there was a technical difficulty, Dielaan," The Atare said pleasantly. "A pity we cannot speak face to face. As Nadine reb'Ursel Kilgore was saying, about the antimatter?" He paused, then added, casually, "And then there is the question of my wife."

Rex said evenly: "The antimatter is under the tender guardianship of my captain. If anything at all threatens us, he will activate the timer."

Sheel Atare actually looked mildly surprised. "Well, you must please yourself, of course," he said, "but personally I would not wish to be 800 meters below the surface sitting on top of an unstable trap of antimatter."

"If you do not wish to seriously discuss this," Rex started, carefully spacing the words, "I will merely tie the nuisance of a woman to the trap and have done with it."

Silence. Nadine of Kilgore smiled again; this time, her teeth showed.

"Excuse me," Lucy said clearly, stepping into the circumference of the surveillance camera. "As you suggested, this is difficult over a vid. Perhaps you both should simply state the starting point for the negotiations, and then Rex will send one of us up with his thoughts on the subject."

"The antimatter," Sheel said without hesitation, "and the hostages, returned in one piece."

"Reparations," Nadine went on, her teeth hidden once again. "For the burning of crops in Kilgore and Seedar. We *know* you are behind it, Dielaan. We caught one of your firebugs."

"You will forget all about this," Livia said simply. "You will contact Tsuga by satellite, you will order the ships home, and then we will talk about your trip to Caesarea."

"And about the warehouses in Amura, and my dead *guaard*," Sheel finished pleasantly, leaning forward. "The antimatter was insured, and the insurance company wishes to talk to you about the 'accident.' Wergild will be expected for the family of the *guaard*."

"Your turn, Dielaan." Nadine was no longer smiling at all.

"Only one offer. For half of the trinium hauled out of this mine in a calendar year, I will give you—intact—the antimatter trap, the mine, and all hostages. And shut off that misbegotten siren!" Gesturing sharply with his hand, Rex indicated that the conversation was over. The diagram of the entire working mine reappeared on the main screen. Rex's face relaxed. "I had completely forgotten they must have cameras!" Snapping his head in Campbell's direction, he said: "Give me the cage area on this level."

Campbell's face was grim, but he was undoubtedly grateful Rex had not lashed out for his "forgetting" about the cameras. Instantly the dim corridor outside was visible, a warrior standing by the folded doors.

"Can he hear us?" Garth heard himself ask.

"Perhaps if you shout," Campbell suggested.

"Any problems, warrior?" Rex said, raising his voice.

"None for some time, Dielaan," the man yelled back. "The miners were unruly, but I let them call the cage, and when they realized it would not come, they all retreated down the passage. Then the siren began."

"Remain at your post." In a softer voice, Rex said: "Can we see the cage area on the lowest level?"

Stoically Campbell punched up the appropriate screen. Garth felt his throat tighten as they viewed the beginning and end of it all, a one-hundred-kilogram Stanford trap of antimatter. Conserving fuel, the captain had turned off the puff packet beneath the pallet—the flat rested directly upon the stone floor. There was a peevish look on the warrior's face; as Campbell brought up the audio, they could hear the siren loud and clear.

"Why is it blowing down there? I thought no one goes to the train level?" Rex questioned.

"Rarely. The train is fully automated, and so is the sweep that catches the few loose pieces of ore that miss the cars. Maintenance checks the level every shift—just a walk past the panel, to be sure no yellows indicate something needs work. Easy enough for them to walk through, and it saves sending someone special, if an adjustment is needed." What might have happened to the maintenance worker this shift, Campbell did not volunteer.

"Check the surrounding tunnels for that woman," Rex finally said. Glancing at Lucy, he said mildly: "Whatever possessed you to interrupt?"

"You sounded like cats insulting one another," Lucy said shortly. "I thought to spare your dignity. It is of no matter; we have lost the toss."

"Stop saying that!"

"Do you not realize what your own eyes told you?" For the first time in days, Lucy seemed animated, in control. "That was Nadine, Rex—Nadine of *Kilgore*. And when she spoke of reparations, she included Seedar in her request. Seedar—included by a Kilgore!"

Lucy continued talking, but Garth suddenly could not hear her. Something tightened in his chest even as ringing swelled behind his ears. *Kilgore?* With Atare . . . and Dielaan present, instead of either backing Rex without question or stepping aside. *And Seedar is part of it, somehow* . . . "It was almost perfect, and you destroyed it," he whispered aloud.

Both Dielaaners stopped shouting at his words. "Garth?" Lucy whispered his name.

"You have undone everything you claimed you wanted," Garth said steadily, trying to ignore the numbness settling on him.

"Just what I said," Lucy snapped. "We had The Synod mere steps from each others' throats, Yang and Valdez about to walk out, Kilgore recalled—or so Captain Annich told me—then you decide to have a nice little war! Suddenly we have at least four and possibly more tribes working together in closer consort than ever before!" Once again, she was shouting. "So, our entire plan has been rendered useless, and we are left with the wergild on a death and an unstable container of antimatter!"

"There is no problem," Rex insisted. "Except we must recover the Atare woman. Other than that, we can come about! After the ransom is paid, the antimatter will be given over to them; if we do not allow them to stabilize it, they will deal all the sooner! And the hostages—" Here he shot Quen a venomous look. "Were merely taken to insure neither one of them had any clever ideas, both Quen and Atare's woman being known for that. Tsuga is nothing, I can deal with him, if I choose. As for the rest—people can be Dielaan citizens, can claim our immunity, but they cannot connect *us* with the fires or the death. That we will push aside as criminal intent, and do what we can to extradite the minions. Or the warehouse exploding—we stole antimatter, for a purpose—we are not terrorists! As for mother—"

"Poison did not work. What is your next step?" Lucy asked acidly.

Her words rang out without fear or apology, and every face in the room whitened. It took visible effort for Quen to remain seated.

Garth found himself past surprise. *Well, mother, father, what a fine monument I have erected to you—helping an idiot destroy the peace of a planet and try to kill his own mother*. Enough was enough. He was out—no more helping anyone, no more plots, no more brushes with free-trading. Even . . . momentarily he flinched away from the final step. *No more pursuing the wergild. At this rate, I will owe her as much as she owes me*. All this, and I am no closer to knowing the truth.

Or was he? . . .

"There are explosives on this level?"

That question snapped Garth back to the moment; he slowly stood.

"We could place small explosives," Rex muttered. Glancing over at Garth's movement, he said: "I will not give up a ransom.

Either they part with trinium, or they will spend all of it rebuilding this mine."

"I begin to think Atare would rather rebuild than give in." Garth folded his arms over his chest and gave Rex his pale, blank stare.

"His wife will tip the balance." Rex switched back to the ore train level. "Captain An—" He broke off abruptly.

The antimatter was gone. There was no evidence of how it had vanished, nor any sign of Annich. The cage, frozen in place, blinked its yellow warning message . . . the siren screamed on.

A hard, tight smile pulled over Rex's face, and he carefully read the Nualan code running along the bottom of the screen. Touching a square, he switched to the passage running west . . . then east. At the end of the eastern passage, at the double doors leading to the ore train platform, they could just see the bob of a hard hat light.

"Behind a puff pallet," Rex said simply.

"Where is Annich?" Lucy whispered, her quarrel with Rex momentarily set aside in confusion.

Rex turned and pointed a finger at Garth. "You." He gestured to his second-in-command, and still another warrior. "Accompany him, Sim. Recover the antimatter—and the Atare woman, if she is there." Glancing back at Garth, he said softly: "What do you think, Garth? Even odds that she is there."

A chill crept into Garth's numbness. *Ah, my mother—indeed, the horns of a dilemma! I know Lucy has been up to something, while I haven't been able to accomplish anything toward our goal of stopping this egoist. To let him think I have meddled is bad—but to shift his suspicions to Lucy would be worse.* "The antimatter is a bargaining chip," Garth said aloud.

"I am so glad we agree. Bring it back to this level."

It was not a good time to argue, but. . . . "Do you want it that close?"

"As Lucy pointed out while you were leagues away in thought, the brass chit system means that usually they *totally* clear the mine before blasting—any blasting. If we are still in the mine when this decides to blow, it will not matter where we are."

So. We may all die, and you have admitted the risk into your game. Garth did not look at Silas, who was alternating staring at the wall with sipping from a flask. He glanced at Lucy. "Shall we hunt?"

"No. I may need Lucy." Very final.

Garth flicked a glance at the two warriors. Both large, and carrying small side weapons of some kind. . . . He smiled faintly, and sketched a parody of the Axis Republic salute. Turning to Lucy, he considered what to say. Was there anything? Before he could open his mouth, she threw her arms around his neck, pulled him down and kissed him fiercely.

"Be careful," she admonished him, her dark eyes wide.

Grinning, he lightly caressed her jawbone. "Take care, love." *I hope you understand. Now you and Quen get yourselves out of here!* Nodding to the silent Quen, who had shrewdly kept out of the entire preceding conversation, Garth turned on his heel and headed for the cage.

Once on the ore train level, Garth understood why the shift boss in the changing room had wanted them to take miner's lights. Away from the cage, illumination diminished to the intersections . . . and in the distance, not even that. Through a window that had been set in the left side of the passage, Garth could see spotlights strategically placed in the rail area. Was there movement? . . . He was not going to mention it if the warriors did not.

Already they were on edge, the darkness, the increased warmth and the continuing siren only adding to their agitation. Twice the group had stopped at small rooms, seeking a portable torch of some kind. Nothing.

"I would bet gold there are light switches on that console," Sim said suddenly, gesturing through the window at the glowing dials of a control panel. "The doors are down here."

"Use caution, sir—this is the same door," the other whispered, indicating that Garth should move in front of him.

"Surely the miners do not carry weapons."

Garth smiled crookedly. Miners made their own rules; it was that kind of culture. He started looking for someplace to duck behind, if necessary.

Afterward Garth was never sure what provoked Sim. Without warning the officer pulled off his side weapon and fired toward the rails. White-orange light blazed a trail much less than a meter from what proved to be the antimatter trap. A crash indicated several bodies leaping for cover.

"Have you lost your mind?" Garth screamed, diving behind

the bulk of the control panel. The other warrior did not protest the criticism—he was burrowing in right behind Garth.

"We must have more light!" he hissed, and edged up over the top of the waist-high instrument box. A *crack* near his head brought him back next to Garth.

Reaching out, Garth's fingers closed over the object that had smacked into the wall. "A rock?" he said aloud.

Grinning idiotically, the warrior began to creep around the side of the control console.

Huh. Don't get over-confident. So, how do you change sides in the middle of a fight without getting bonked by a rock? A good throw, too, if he was any judge. A sharp-edged rock . . . ore. *A ton or so more, and you'll be rich.* Garth had a sudden urge to laugh. Leaning cautiously around the corner, he found he had a decent view of the platform. Before he could make any plans at all, he heard the sound of the ore train.

It had entered the cavern at a good clip, being empty, and was now slowing in response to what sounded like air brakes. Someone had tried to take advantage of the arrival—Sim's weapon flared once again, and a shout of protest rang in the upper regions of the rock.

It might have been a signal. Dark forms swarmed from the last three cars, diving over the side and disappearing like slugs into dirt. Garth decided that the reinforcements had arrived—it was everyone's tough luck that Sim was in a position to keep them pinned, at least until his "burn" was drained. Shivering in response to the memory of his one experience on the wrong end of a burn, Garth started crawling in the direction opposite the one taken by the Dielaan warrior. He needed the controller, and the person with the controller had jumped in this direction. They must have been planning on loading the antimatter onto a car—

More fire; someone was moving again. Now on his belly, Garth had reached the edge of the platform. No one was there . . . more room to either side of the rails than he had expected, but not much depth—

"Whoops!" came a male voice. A hard hat was briefly visible, then the individual dropped back out of sight.

"Do you have the controller?" Garth asked in Caesarean, hoping a normal tone of voice would carry through the siren. It was not quite as loud in the platform room; there was never a need to clear the rails. *Usually.* "Pass it over!"

"Would I want to give it to you?" was the understandable response.

"It would be easier to load that trap while looking at the car," Garth pointed out.

"Very true. Will the pallet lift that high?"

Damn. Good question. And if the trap fell over. . . . Closing his eyes against the thought, Garth considered the risk. "No one down here would purposely hit the antimatter," he said finally. "We must try."

"Sim, report!" The voice actually overwhelmed the siren. Even with distortion, Garth knew it—Rex thought they were taking too long.

"Is that another of the Dielaan kooks?" came the calm voice from the rail level.

"You could say that," Garth agreed. "He is on 2377—can he control anything down here?"

"If he understands the panels, he can control the train, the ore pass doors, the sweeps—#!!*!" The man appeared briefly, then vanished again. "And the lights, I fear. If he spots the screen for maintenance, we have problems."

"*He* must have a problem, since he hasn't found it yet." They could not trust in that for long. "What should we do?"

Silence from the rail level. Burn fire erupted over their heads in several directions, and a groan came from the depths before him. "Sweet Mendülay, I do not want a burn. Hey, boy—we need to make sure no one moves the train. There is a switch on that panel, in the second row from the right—a big switch. Throw it."

Now was not the time to ask for explanations. Garth let his fingers creep up the side of the control panel, waiting for a burn to lash out. There only seemed to be three of them firing—did that mean the others had no targets, or that they had no burns? Searching with his fingers for a large switch, Garth quickly looked around the area. A few dim red lights . . . cameras. So, soon the game would be over.

He bumped a switch, pulled it. A metallic groan competed with the siren and the burn fire, and suddenly ore began pouring into the car on the near side of their chosen receptacle. Somewhere a woman screamed.

"Hell, not that one!" The miner popped up higher this time before vanishing below the platform. A glance told Garth that the miner was actually only a handspan below his own level.

A second switch, larger to his fingers . . . desperate, Garth pulled it. A brief hum felt by the arm pressed to the instrument panel. . . .

"That was it; the rail shut down. All right, then—we have manual control of the train. Now we load this thing." Carefully a small rectangle rose above the poured edge of the walkway . . . settled itself as if it had a life of its own, then was abruptly slid toward Garth. "Catch."

Someone else had been waiting. Burn fire lit up the platform, revealing the tip of a hard hat and a worn, dusty hand, both of which quickly pulled back toward the ore cars. By some miracle, the shot missed the pallet controller. Garth closed his hand protectively around it.

Now what? He knew better than to ask if the man—a miner —was going to follow the controller up and over. At any rate, the antimatter trap was three cars down to the left. He might be more help right where he was.

"#**#!" Rustling indicated that the miner was moving again, but he was trying to keep low.

Something was causing him to move . . . no time to waste. A spotlight suddenly flashed out, illuminating the far end of the console panel. DAMN! Rex had finally found the correct subscreen! What if the pallet would not lift that high? What if it was too wide, or became wedged somehow? If it fell, and the controller was disconnected, how long would it stay cool enough to keep the superconducting rings working?

No choice. Pointing the controller around the corner, Garth activated it. As if by magic, unruffled by the burn fire, shouting, and rock throwing, the pallet rose serenely, vigorous air movement from the puff packet adding to the dust created by the falling ore. Using the outer ring of the spotlight, Garth quickly scanned the tiny box. An arrow pointed toward the top of the control . . . he pressed it. The pallet jerked up a notch. Touching it again, Garth held it down and watched the swirling air increase. Finally he averted his eyes from the wind. With agonizing slowness, the trap rose into the air.

The chute directly in front of him suddenly dumped a full load of ore into the appropriate car. Shielding his face from dust and fragments, Garth kept his finger on the button. *Having fun, Rex?* Fighting the urge to wave his arm at the dust cloud, Garth strained to see the trap pallet.

It was now higher than the ore car. *Sweet Peter, the Gate is before us!* Cautiously moving his thumb to the button below and to the immediate left, he prayed that Nualan controller patterns matched the republic norm.

Occasionally, prayer is answered. The pallet began to move —left, toward the ore car. And the trap began to rock.

By now, the cavern was a kaleidoscope of light, movement, and noise. Rex apparently was hitting everything on his screen, and machinery noise was actually louder than the siren. There was no time to worry about an ore shaft opening above the car—he had to keep his finger on the button. But if one of the supports had moved. . . .

Figures, hidden between the cars and below the platform, rose and reached for the trap. What they thought they could do to stop a hundred kilogram trap from—The support. They were wedging the support in place. And it was working—Garth threw up his arms as another burn blazed by, and one of the figures twitched and collapsed. The other, losing hard hat, silver hair askew, threw itself—herself—back between the edges of two cars—only a moment—then reached once more for the pallet.

It was more courage than he had. Garth honored it the only way he could, by gripping the controller until his thumb locked. Only a bit more. Just a bit—The figure stumbled, and now Garth had enough light to see that *something* was moving next to the rail, moving the still form of the fallen miner down the narrow trench between rail and platform. Standing again, reaching for the trap support, no time to watch the miner—

Using his other hand, Garth placed a thumb on the down button. A quick shift of the eyes told him that the fallen miner had completely disappeared. How—? A blur of dark clothing sprinted from between two cars, one hand held to a hard hat, and the stocky form dove behind the control panel even as Garth threw himself up against the side of the big control. Two burn beams arced in their direction. He could barely see for the dust; praise all saints the spotlight on the console had been shut off.

Rocks again, now coming from behind the console. If the other person was Silver—Still pushing on the pallet support, she was leaning against the ore car, straining to keep a hand on the trap, when another burn sizzled by. Contracting, collapsing into the trench—

The pallet support snapped. One hundred kilos of trap dropped like a boulder into the ore car. Heaving the controller into space, Garth rolled into the trench. *What are you doing, we are talking about antimatter!* The stocky miner was on his heels, creeping in the opposite direction.

How many tons of ore normally crashed into these cars? A solid kilo had caused scarcely a tremor. The trap was angled slightly, but as he wedged himself between the cars and peeked over the edge, Garth could see that the controller lights still showed green. Burn fire bounced off the edge of the car, and Garth threw himself back into the trench.

Only luck caused him to miss the sweep bar which had just passed. Something to pick up the precious ore that bounced— then where had that miner been swept? Garth started crawling down the trench, looking for Darame Daviddottir and an answer to his question.

Lights shut off completely, then flashed back on. Alone. How? Then he saw a glint of hair, and the curve of fingernails.

A silver lock was clamped under eight digits, which in turn wrapped around the lip of an opening a good meter across and easily high enough for a body to have passed through. The left hand suddenly released, and without thought Garth reached in and seized the remaining wrist.

Stone muffled the chaos considerably; the moment was almost intimate. Trying to find breath, Garth gasped: "We got it in the car."

Whatever surprise she might have felt, her voice did not reveal it. "The train—we must start the train."

"We switched—manual—"

"Start it." Although whispered, it was an order.

"Can't—reach—"

"Let go."

Silenced, Garth tried desperately to swallow. *Let go?* What was underneath, some kind of conveyor belt? "How . . . far . . ."

"Oh, no more than five meters."

One hysterical note escaped Garth before he bit his lip to still it. The dead weight was incredible, and she was making no move to reach back up with her other hand. *Can't reach—*

"Start the train." This time it was very gentle.

All options reduced to one . . . if they did not get the trap out of here, Rex would detonate it. Garth was sure of it. And she had already weighed all possibilities, chosen her path, *their* path—*And why not? Oh, my enemy, my friend; Gavrielians do so like to die well, and in good company: Whatever made me think I was Caesarean?* "Sweet Peter," he whispered aloud.

Her tone was almost humorous as she answered: "He is waiting for us."

Garth let go.

Throwing himself backward into the dust and noise of the cavern, he scrambled onto the platform and to the console. Which switch? How could he—He started by reversing the automation, which set off a new warning bell. Then he threw everything in the row. Grinding, sliding rock indicated movement, even as he dropped to the ground to avoid burn fire arcing in his direction. Another chute sent down a load, partially filling a car with ore and tossing fusillade over trench and platform as the train began to exit.

Impulse sent Garth sliding up the side of the console, groping for the one button that had to be there somewhere. Over by the chute controls, the ones with the levels—ah. By itself; it was even bright red. He slammed his hand on it.

A horn sounded, blaring a change in instructions. Overhead grates began to close. Two burn arcs crossed at the panel, blowing the back completely off, as Garth dove into the trench and swung himself legs first into the maw of an ore pass.

Rock and thunder followed him down into darkness.

Bloodwite: Recognized by most Nualan authorities, this descendant of Anglo-Saxon tradition is a fine or penalty for shedding blood payable to a government or ruler in compensation for violating the peace of the land. Compare *WERGILD*.

CHAPTER FOURTEEN

ATARE CITY   TWOHUNDRED TWODAY   TIERCE

There was no pain . . . she floated. Darame had expected none; in the course of her days she had considered many concepts of an afterlife, and none of her front-runners had contained suffering. *Surely there will be answers here,* she thought idly. *So many things left unfinished—a few answers would make up for it a bit.* Take care of my children, Avis . . . wrap them in your all-encompassing arms. Do not let Sheel grieve himself to death. . . .

Nonsense. He was stronger than that. . . .

On impulse, she decided to *see* the place where she floated, and her lids obediently slipped up. Diffused light, and pale blue . . . walls. Walls? *Hell's Bells. I am alive.* A thought of wonder and delight, except she knew that would mean pain, eventually, and there had already been so much pain. Who would have thought a burn could hurt so much? . . .

Forms moved in the diffused light. One wore the day uniform of a *guaard*. On duty . . . no. . . . Darame focused on the individual.

A rainbow of color swept across one side of her face, the

forehead marked by several cold torch lines, indicating mechanical healing. A light sling took the weight of one arm off a shoulder joint.

"Do I look as bad as you do?" she heard herself ask quietly.

"Worse, Atarae," Mailan assured her. "Worse."

"You are enjoying this." Darame closed her eyes again.

"I have something for you. You must not be careless with it." These words made Darame open her eyes again. In her free hand, Mailan held the worn hilt of the Cied cat knife.

"Praise Mendülay. I was almost as worried about that knife as I was about you." *That does not sound right.* Darame felt herself frown, but Mailan nodded graciously. *Guaard* to the core, she was greatly complimented.

A slight change of expression. . . . "I will keep it safe for you, Atarae," Mailan said suddenly, rising from her seat. "Rest easily."

Easily? After so much? As Mailan became a shadow in the room, someone else came forward. Without effort the frown eased, her mouth relaxing. In silence she watched him lower himself into the chair vacated by Mailan. Very drawn, his cheekbones jutting—

"I have been bad," Darame began humbly.

Sheel actually convulsed. For a moment Darame was terrified, then she realized he was laughing—silently, shading his eyes to hide the tears.

Never again. Together, or never again.

In a while he calmed himself, his shoulders settling into familiar stillness. Propping himself up on one elbow, he rested his cheek against two fingertips. "How do you feel?" Barely audible.

"I do not."

"Good."

"I imagine the alternative would not be pleasant," Darame agreed. "So, tell me everything."

"Where should I start?"

"Where would you like to start?"

His eyebrows twitched, as his gaze wandered off toward a pale, blue wall. "You should recover completely, although we must watch that burn carefully. Old Doc will be in bed for some time yet—he was not so lucky. Your concussion is mild, all things considered, and your skull not cracked. Why, I cannot imagine," he added acidly. Then his face lost expression, and he said: "We could not save the embryo."

So small a thing. . . . She felt the tears, trickling out to pool in her ears. With feather-light fingers, Sheel reached to catch the rest. What was there to say? To ask? Ten years ago she would have considered it but a momentary inconvenience . . . *I am too old for a baby, anyway.*

"If Mendülay wills, there will be others," Sheel said simply, pulling her from her thoughts. "Do you know," he went on, "you and those miners and that nuisance of a child Kristinsson saved nearly two hundred lives. Not a single fatality—not even that Dielaan warrior you hit with a rock."

"The antimatter?"

Sheel snapped his fingers in dismissal.

"Where?"

"A few kilometers into the tunnel. The *guaard* in the cavern had time to emulate your innovative idea and jump down the sweep chutes. Even the Dielaan warriors decided it was a good idea."

"Kristori?"

Sheel smiled. "She got on the conveyor room wall box and *demanded* somebody free up that cage and come help. She was the only one who went down that chute conscious and aware of where she would land."

"Good people, the miners of Mare Imbrium," Darame murmured. "Any idea why the antimatter blew?"

Relaxing slightly, Sheel settled back in his chair. "It was not Dielaan—we found out later that Lulani wrestled the timer remote away from him while Quen pounded him into the floor like a stake." At Darame's look of surprise, Sheel added: "Rex sent one too many warriors to the train level. All he had left were two innocents. Quen correctly deduced that, no matter what Rex was yelling about, as long as he was not being killed, those warriors were not going to use burns on two royal Dielaaners."

"Should have issued jabbers," Darame suggested.

Actually managing a faint smile, Sheel said: "Only one of his many mistakes. I think the transference reached a critical point, because Kristinsson swears the controller was still green when he last saw it."

"Do you feel up to guests?" That throaty voice was familiar. Sheel turned in response, and gave the entranceway a hard stare. Livia Ragärée walked gracefully into the room. "Your city is boring, Darame," Livia went on. "All I have seen is the hospice. You must heal faster."

"I thought you disliked the north," was all Darame could think to say.

"I do, but I needed to return your *guaard* and your knife, and retrieve a few Dielaan possessions." Livia looked equally as exhausted as Sheel, but her smile was full of warmth. Darame took in her attire; black with multicolored scattered threads. . . .

So, for better or worse, it is over. "Quen—and Lulani?" she asked.

"Quen is fine. As soon as mourning ends, I expect him to marry that merchant of his. One hopes for an introduction before then," Livia added archly. "He will be crowned at the new year, on his twenty-first birthday."

"And you will retire to Amura in leisure?" Sheel suggested.

"Mendülay, no! He has asked me to stay close by at first, and I am nothing if not obedient to the needs of the people." Livia's eyes were a bit too brilliant as she spoke, but her chin was lifted. Her gaze settled on Darame. "Do not worry about Lulani—her debt is so great right now, she will not sneeze without my permission for the next twenty years." She looked away. "Rex is dead. Yesterday morning. We had confined him to a suite of rooms, and . . . he cut his wrists." Her face became hard. "I think I could have forgiven him everything except cowardice."

Why—Darame knew it was quite likely they would have kept Rex on the throne. But . . . *He could not bear to be brought back to Dielaan, then shipped off-world like a whipped child, in hope that his people would forget his trespasses.* "Not a coward, Livia . . . consistent," Darame murmured. This won her an especially warm look from the ragärée.

"We must let you rest," Sheel said abruptly.

"Kristinsson," she whispered, stopping both of them in the act of rising. "Have you found out why he came?"

The two of them actually looked at each other, quickly, before Sheel answered. "He has spoken freely about their conspiracy —he no longer sees any point in disguising his part in it. But so far he will not reveal 'why,' and we have not forced the issue. He only says that you two 'are even.' "

"I want to talk to him." Sheel's face grew visibly harder. "You may take whatever precautions you wish, but I want to know why he spent a hundred years looking for me. Please, Sheel."

The "please" succeeded—she so rarely resorted to the actual word. "All right."

VESPERS

They made her sleep, first, before they would let her speak with Kristinsson. And they packed the room with *guaard*. Mailan escorted him into the room, her silence eloquent. Gesturing to the chair, the woman said evenly: "If you so much as lean forward, I will kill you."

Well, no one can ever accuse her of not speaking her mind, Darame thought wryly. "The last time I saw him, Mailan, he was trying to save my life." Bowing her head, the *guaard* leaned against the door, her free hand toying with the hilt of a cat knife. Darame let her gaze wander to Kristinsson.

Like a blank slate. There was nothing left—the fire that had burned within him had extinguished, and no other passion had risen to take its place. Almost colorless, his pale eyes bleak, he sat quietly, ignoring or unaware of the *guaard* in the room. A cold torch line extended past his collarbone to his throat . . . even he had not escaped injury.

"You got the train moving," she said simply. "Many lives were saved by that act." Did an ironic smile threaten? Nothing certain. . . . Well, then finish it. "You came a very long way in time and space to find me. I must assume you have a question. Would you like to ask it?"

That got his attention. Lifting his head, Garth stared at her for a long moment, then said: "In the year 2288, my father was involved in a scam with a man named Hank Edmonton and a woman named Silver Meath. Within forty-eight standard hours after 160 bars of gold were deposited in our family account at Traders' Trust, my father was reported dead, my mother committed suicide, and our savings account was emptied. The only thing left was a message . . . 'Aesir considers the debt to be paid.' " It was dry, a recital of facts. His face now revealed an absence of expression rather than a lack of it. "I was hoping you could tell me what happened."

"Kurt Eriksson . . . he was the third partner. Lisbet's husband—and I never knew." A sigh filtered through her. *So many things lost in the scramble of time.* There was something missing here, something Hank had known that he had not shared with her. . . . "You have asked more than one question."

"I have always thought of it as a piece." No emotion in that voice.

"The answer to my part of it . . . can be summed up in Hank's words to me when he returned to our base of operations." The words from the pentimento rose up in her mind. Her eyes unfocused as she repeated them. " 'He's dead; I don't know why. We'll leave his cut of the gold at Traders.' "

"Did Hank kill him?"

"Once I thought so . . . now, I think otherwise. He went to kill Kurt—we thought he had betrayed us, had taken the shipment and spirited it away. Someone killed Kurt before Hank caught up with him." Darame turned her head. "I begin to see. The Caesarean police never asked you about the condition of the body? Aesir usually leaves a sign." Garth shook his head negatively. "Caesarea must have been sure you knew nothing."

"If he betrayed you, why did you leave the gold?" Hard; he knew something of free-trader law, then.

"I was the junior member of the partnership. I . . . assumed . . . that Hank *had* found something that explained the irregularities. And we *had* recovered the metal. But. . . ." She smiled slightly, lost in a memory. *So, old man, you had a soft heart, after all.* Concentrating on Kristinsson once again, she continued: "I think he knew Aesir was involved, and knew your father had dependents . . . suspected your father had crossed us instead of coming to us for help. A desperate act. So Hank left the gold in an attempt to convince Aesir to spare the family. There was no way to know if it was enough, but . . . that was a *lot* of gold. Aesir's main business is loaning metal; there was a chance that a lump repayment would be enough."

"Then the message meant? . . ."

"Aesir's reply to your family . . . only there was no one left who knew what it meant. Lisbet could not have seen it, or she would not have killed herself."

"She killed herself . . . for nothing." A whisper.

"No, not nothing." Darame spoke quickly.

"Lowe said she did it for a reason—that there were things to gain by killing yourself." This was thrown at her, as if asking her to deny it.

Reluctantly, Darame said: "He was trying to spare you. Aesir has been known to cause entire families to disappear. Do you know the word 'thrall'?"

Garth shook his head impatiently.

"It is a type of bond servant, a slave for a contracted period. Gavrielian law is odd that way. As long as someone who signed the contract lived, Aesir could seize *assets* of the immediate family—including the persons of the immediate family. Lisbet must have put her name to the loan. She killed herself to cut the obligation . . . and the threat to the family. Aesir investigated, after either purposefully or accidentally killing your father, and found enough metal to satisfy them as to the debt. It was merely . . . bad timing . . . that they did not move faster, and that she did not have the courage to go to Hank and ask him for the gold."

"A farce from one end to the other," Garth said quietly. "No guts coming or going."

"No, it was not lack of courage. It was . . . the luck of the game."

Garth gave her a hard look. "A stupid way to make a living."

"To some," she agreed.

"I cannot see it."

"Of course not. You were not born to be a free-trader."

"You can tell?" Honest curiosity touched his words.

"Usually. You have a different type of courage."

They sat in silence for several minutes, Garth studying his hands, Darame looking at nothing. At length, he said: "Thank you for telling me. It seems I now owe you—"

"You owe me nothing," she said harshly. "You saved all our lives."

"But I—"

"Think of it," she continued briskly, "as tying up old business. That is how I see it."

A crooked smile touched his face as his gaze remained on his hands.

VESPERS

They had isolated him in a small but adequate room. Lucy came to him at starset, dressed in a somber dress of black, trickled with threads of red and gold. Her hair was mostly down, a blanket of polished copper down her back; she looked much younger than her years. Her face was free of cosmetics, and pale from crying. She did not wait for an invitation, but went to the window and sat down on a bench near it, just out of arms' reach.

"Did they tell you Rex killed himself?" she finally said.

Garth tried to find some interest in this, but it would have been a lie to express sympathy. He continued looking out the window. "Did he? So Quen will rule?"

"Eventually. He will be of age at the new year. Since he will marry Rebekah, he will not go off-world." She let the silence sit between them for a time, then said: "You were going to tell me why you came here."

Why not? So he told her—all of it, from the night his father died until his conversation with the woman he had called Silver. *Oh, my mother, my father . . . I hope I am not a disappointment to you.*

"And now she is letting it all go, as if it had never happened. I am still not sure I know why." This was a whisper. It bothered Garth; like a scab begging to be scratched.

"I am so sorry, Garth," she whispered in turn, and sounded as if she meant it.

"Even my attempts to wreak havoc end in failure," Garth said lightly.

"Was that what you wanted?"

"So I thought. In the end, all I wanted was to make it right, because I found my enemy worthier than my so-called friends. I don't think I accomplished that, either . . . But the Atarae seems to think it was enough." After a moment, he added: "Except for you."

"What?"

"My enemy was worthier than all but you." They studied each other's reflections in the glass. "You have been the only good thing about this trip. I hope you will not suffer too much for what Rex led you all i—"

"We chose to follow," she said sharply.

Garth shook his head. "Nualans offer oaths to their rulers,

and the rulers offer them to their people. You kept your oaths . . . even if I do not understand why. Rex broke his oaths to you. It is that simple."

"You kept your promise, too." Garth merely stared out the window. "You came for wergild. In the end, you found your answer and pulled down a tyrant . . . maybe set up a much better situation here. The Atarae seems to think her pain was worth it. Can you not think the same? It . . . it appears a much better wergild than gold—at least to me." This was hesitant.

"What have you learned, Lulani reb Carlotta, daughter of Tensar Dielaan?" Garth asked huskily. "Clever, how you never quite mentioned that the last Dielaan was your father."

"It does not mean anything . . . except that maybe I should have known better." Soft words. "I will leave politics to those with a head for it. I find there are things worth more than the hereditary rights of a ruler."

"There may be hope for you," came a weary voice. Lucy's head jerked up, but Garth looked at the window, watching the reflections mirrored in the glass. Sheel Atare had entered the room. His two black shadows trailed in his wake. "What am I going to do about you?" Sheel asked quietly.

Lucy decided he was talking to her. "Do you have the right to decide what to do about me?" The slightest bit belligerent. . . .

"What do you think? You were in Atare province threatening to blow up an occupied trinium mine. What should be the punishment for such a crime?"

Lucy looked away from him, the show of arrogance draining from her face. "If my aunt has her way, I will spend the next twenty years scrubbing floors in Dielaan Palace."

"Do you have one good reason why you should not?" The question was quite neutral in tone.

"I am terrible at scrubbing floors. There is an art to it; not a sophisticated one, but an art, nonetheless."

"I have a better idea. Your aunt intends to repay the debts . . . all of them. Wergild, antimatter, crops." Lucy literally went white at his words. "A great deal of wealth, which will be years in the repaying. I suggest you find occupation which will legally increase revenue, and pursue it."

"Surely you cannot simply forget about all this?" Lucy whispered.

"No. Silas and Malini will go off-planet with the next long-hauler. Their inheritance will be paying into the same reparation fund. You may either join them, or vanish in some other way —but no one is going to see you laughing at an Amuran dinner party for many, many long years . . . if ever." Sheel did not look directly at either of them; rather, his unnerving gaze wandered out past the rim of Atare's rocky shore. "I have plans for the tribes which do not need angering anyone over your punishment or lack of the same. So you will disappear."

"And Garth?" Again, almost defiant.

"Another problem, but of a different sort." Contemplative . . . "You managed to involve yourself with murder and localized treason, an impressive record for such a short visit. Have you any thoughts on the matter?"

"Not that you have not already heard," Garth said simply.

"We have talked to conspirators, underlings, spies, and observers, and it has come down to this: You did not intend to kill anyone, and you did not intend to start a war . . . or even to do anything patently illegal. More of a demonstration than anything else—that is correct?"

"Yes."

"We have the vial Rex Dielaan tried to blackmail you with, but we know that was a plant. Still, your fingerprint is on it."

"Atare?" He turned his head toward Lucy, meeting her eyes. She did not flinch. "The . . . Atarae. How is she?"

"Alive."

Lucy's face deflated visibly. "And . . . the baby?"

Sheel shook his head once.

Garth stirred at this, looking to Lucy for an explanation. Glancing quickly away, she would not speak. So he turned to Sheel Atare, and read his answers in the Nualan's face. *You may forgive that loss, but you will not forget. Ever.*

"I will not play with you," Sheel said abruptly. "My wife asks me to consider Gavrielian wergild in my decision—and we do not execute people for conspiracy against a cartel. Since Dielaan is paying the wergild for the *guaard*, I can take this upon myself. You may be deported to Caesarea as an undesirable, banned from ever returning here, or you may stay on Nuala as an immigrant—provided you find a sponsor, and that you stay out of my sight. I do not wish to see you again. My wife tells

me any danger from you is past. For your sake, I hope so."
And he was gone, as silently as he had arrived.

Stay? He did not have enough strength to laugh. But his fingers
gripped the pill packet in his side pocket. So little food in the
past few days . . . he had forgotten to eat. But he had taken the
pills when he had. . . .

"Where will you go? To your sister on Gavriel?" Lucy asked
quietly.

"Even with FOY, she would be 140 years and more," Garth
said listlessly. "No doubt she has forgotten my face. I did not
do well by her . . . but at the least I should send her children
this tale, so it is known what became of our parents . . . and
what became of me." That stirred an odd thought. He glanced
over at Lucy. "There is only one FOY office here, in Amura.
Nualans do not allow longevity treatments?"

She smiled wryly. "If you use FOY, you become sterile. We
do not tamper with the organism. Besides, Nualans who take
care of themselves live a long time . . . ninety or a hundred
Nualan, with wits and health." Thoughtfully, she added: "If
you live well, it is long enough."

"So where will you vanish?"

"The southern continent."

"Is there one?" he countered.

"Oh, yes—even hotter than up here, but very wet. All the
tribes have colonies down there. We have a great tea plantation
that needs a new manager. I think mother wanted Silas to go
down there, but . . . I thought of volunteering. Do you think
we could learn anything about growing tea?"

"Tea?" He realized he had meant to say "We?" For a moment
Garth drew a complete blank, then—"Would kona grow there?"

"Kona?" She looked puzzled. "On Nuala?"

He smiled. "I might even be able to find a backer, if he can
still separate business from personal affairs. Halsey."

At first her mouth dropped open . . . then the laughter burst
from her, her eyes narrowing slightly in the way he loved so
well.

"But who would sponsor the likes of me?" he went on, as if
they had never considered any other possibility for either of them.

Controlling her whoops with an effort, she replied: "I would
. . . but I am not of age."

They stared at each other for a long moment. Garth considered her seriously, who had followed her clan chief to war over a principle . . . and had betrayed him for a higher one he had never acknowledged.

"We have a problem."

"Not necessarily . . . I think we could convince my mother to sponsor you . . . or even Aunt Livia." At his stunned look, she smiled shyly. "Quen still thinks well of you; he says everyone is entitled to make mistakes and look foolish once in a while, and how can anyone preach to a man who offers his life to correct a wrong?" The smile broadened. "And what better tribe to keep an eye on a conspirator, hummm?"

Garth started to laugh—his first real laugh in a long time. There were no witnesses but wind and water, so he was able to say: "Lucy, do you know I love you?"

"Yes," she said serenely.

"I wish you had told me," he said. "It came as a shock."

"Life is full of surprises," she agreed. "You will get used to it."

"Never."

"But think of the fun recovering."

Garth only smiled. "Hope I make a better farmer than freetrader."

"You will," she assured him. "It is in your blood—loving the land."

That struck a chord somewhere. . . . Maybe she was right.

ATARE PALACE, ATARE CITY
TWOHUNDRED FIVEDAY   COMPLINE

It was dark beyond the windows of the fire room; tiny Eros, waxing once again, had yet to rise. Leaning back in the chair Sheel had placed her in, Darame breathed a sigh of relief. The vid had just been shut off—her first talk with her children since the "incident" had gone off rather well. They were not completely reassured—Ardal, especially, was suspicious of her condition—but they were content to see her face. With luck, they would never know of the layers of cosmetics which hid both scrapes and bruises.

Damn this weakness. Even talking to the children had been an effort. Sweet Magdalen, she missed them so much—

"Sheel says you may have wine, if you like," came Nadine of Kilgore's low voice. Since she had brought a glass with her, Darame did not refuse it. Dressed for once in pale colors, emphasizing the softness of her lace tunic, Nadine had actually chosen different crystals for her hair. Blue topaz, this time, which led her deep amethyst irises back through lavender touched with pale ruby. Whether this meant she was feeling sentimental or fierce, Darame had no idea. But it was good to have her present, for no special reason . . . just for the pleasure of it.

When are you coming back? Ardal had asked.

Actually, it is almost time to come home, she had answered. *Eighteenday from now is when we usually head north.*

Could Avis keep them calm and happy? Sheel was returning tomorrow, since Leah still had not delivered, but—

"You are far from us in thought." Her free hand was seized and kissed.

"Alasdair! How lovely!" Darame laid her hand against his cheek.

"How late," Nadine said, chuckling. "Did you row those things yourself, Alasdair?"

Snorting vigorously, the man accepted a glass of wine from her. "No mean trick to get up here in two days, my dear."

"Warships," Nadine pointed out, seating herself. "All you had was a merchant fleet."

"Potential profit always moves faster than a troop ship," Livia reminded them, strolling in on Sheel's arm. "But it must see the profit. Let us give credit to Mendülay's winds and call all efforts even."

"Ha! Until the fall, ragáree. Let us play at friends until the fall." Alasdair took a gulp of wine and sat on a stool at Darame's feet.

"Why, Alasdair, have you found a new fancy? Have my eyes grown common to you?" Darame asked sweetly.

Flushing slightly, Alasdair said: "You know better, Atarae. Wallace men dote on Atare women, I fear. But come fall is the harvest."

"Yes," Livia said tranquilly, accepting a glass of her favorite claret from the palace wine steward. Sipping slowly, Livia rearranged her black skirts and seated herself, waiting until the steward had left before continuing. "Come autumn, Dielaan must feed most of the continent."

"And if folk have different ideas on how it should be handled? According to the infonet, Andersen is already in a panic—hoarding food, threatening to storm granaries, demanding action from Andersen herself. What if you find their ships on your doorstep? Or Kilgore's? Or mine?" Alasdair's expression was intent; under his banter, he was serious.

"There are clouds in the west, Alasdair," Nadine said quietly. "Do not borrow trouble, we have enough as it is."

"Even if the rain comes now, we will be on short rations," he insisted.

"Yes," Livia agreed. "But we shall make amends to Kilgore and Seedar, for the money they shall lose—probably by giving them a percentage in grain. And new seed, of course. Perhaps even KTL-83," she added roguishly.

"And the price of bread quadruples, as we blackmail each other into submission," Alasdair finished, draining his glass.

"No one will go hungry," Sheel said briefly, moving over by the window.

"I wish I could be sure of that, Atare. And others will think the same . . . will consider hedging the bet." Alasdair set his glass down with precision on a cut crystal table top.

"No one will blackmail another clan, for food or reparations." Sheel flicked a brief glance at Alasdair. "Set your mind at ease."

"How can you be sure?"

"Because we will make sure," Livia said gently. "The whole of the harvest will be turned over to Sheel Atare."

"What?" Alasdair turned his entire body toward the window. Even Nadine sat up a bit straighter.

"The only way to make sure the harvest is fairly distributed is to have a neutral party handle it—one everyone can trust. So I found one." Livia gave him her frostiest look.

"Do you expect me to believe you asked your oldest enemy to—"

"The tribe of Atare is my enemy!" Livia said, flaring. "Sheel Atare is my friend." Her gaze was a direct challenge.

Darame made a production of reaching slowly for the nearby tray; Alasdair turned to help her set down her wine. Thanking him with a smile, her gaze slid in her husband's direction. So stern tonight . . . what—*Are you dreaming again?* As far as she knew, it had been more than a year since he had had a nightmare which had preceded some horror. Those wretched dreams, always bleak, always foreshadowing a probable future. . . .

A wintry little smile crossed Nadine's face; she bent quickly to her glass of wine. "There are those who will not like it," she pointed out, interrupting Darame's train of thought.

"There are those who care for no plan," Sheel responded.

"And if they choose to argue?" Nadine's eyes had grown darker, again . . . or was that a trick of her own eyes? Darame was not certain.

Sheel gave her a long look. "We will argue."

"With words?"

"With whatever it takes. No one will go hungry; no one will use food to break another clan. I will not allow this stupidity to continue any longer." His gaze traveled back to the rocky shoreline.

"*You* will not allow?" Alasdair was clearly astonished.

"He will not allow," Nadine agreed, her smile broad and inviting. "He is right, you know—The Synod will have to deal with this. Sheel is simply arranging things for The Synod."

"Oh."

"Or so it will seem at first." Nadine kept her eyes on the swirling liquid in her glass. "I imagine things will be well along before the others see where it is going. You will need help, of course. It would be even better if able people from other tribes agreed with your course of action. It might . . . avert the shedding of blood." She took a tiny sip of wine. "Although the people of this planet are rather sensible . . . and among clans with free infonet access, Sheel Atare is a respected name." Looking over at Darame, she asked: "Can he unite the tribes?"

"He must," was the answer. "I told him that when I first met him." Lowering her voice, Darame added: "Next time, Alasdair, we might not be so lucky. We are not allowed private quibbles among ourselves; we are a starfaring people, and we must present a united front. The Synod must be that front, unless we wish to start from scratch with something else."

"A committee cannot handle some of the types of decisions that must be made," Alasdair said stubbornly.

"No."

"What controls can be placed on such potential?" he demanded.

"Have you ever read the history and creed of the *guaard*,

Alasdair?'' Darame asked quietly, her eyes resting on Crow's silent mien. ''You should investigate it . . . you will find it very interesting.''

''And we will be in the thick of it,'' Nadine said with a delighted grin. ''Unless you have been recalled, Alasdair.''

''I thought you were?''

''Last we spoke, Klaas said to sit tight—the antimatter being a moot point. My husband is packing up the rest of the household and taking a ship north . . . he hates to fly,'' she added, her expression crinkling at the idea of an off-worlder disliking flight. Then her expression sombered. ''Better I have everything I can carry out of Kilgore, before the fireworks begin.''

Alasdair watched her quietly. ''I take it you do not refer to the new year festivities?'' They might have been alone in the room.

''I am farmer and fishwife, when I am not a diplomat, Alasdair,'' Nadine said gently, her expression distant. ''And I tell you, between friends, that we lost more crops than was announced. Even replanting cannot restore the amount lost, and then there is the cost of seed. . . .'' She looked over at him. ''The shift in the weather has also affected the fishing. You are right—we still face Rex Dielaan's war, although he is no longer around to either fight it or benefit from it. If we fight each other piecemeal, some tribes—Boone, for example—will not survive. The balance *will* be upended. Better to choose when and how we upend it.'' Giving Sheel a lazy look out of the corner of one eye, she added: ''Have you given thought to a new oath, or will the one your vassals have used for centuries suffice?''

Silence. The fire Sheel had ordered built for his wife had burned low, and the sizzle was barely audible, even with the lack of conversation. Turning toward the fireplace, Darame watched Alasdair in the mirror above . . . he was visibly taken aback. *Come, my friend; we never really believed your bluff baron act, though it was a good one. The war you fear is coming . . . and both Livia and Nadine have as good as told you straight out that they are backing Sheel. What will you do?*

Her black gaze shifted to Sheel—and found him almost as astonished as Alasdair. Composing himself, he had yet to turn back to face them.

You inspire this trust in your own people. Does it surprise you so much that others can feel that lure? As he turned, Darame instinctively caught his eye, warning him.

Warning him . . . old free-traders did not die, they merely changed the stakes. . . . Tactics, tactics—

"I think the current oath will suffice," Sheel said finally, lifting his glass to Nadine.

For now. Do you hear those words as clearly as I do? Darame wondered. In silence Livia and Nadine returned Sheel's gesture.

After a long moment, Alasdair grabbed his goblet and reached for the wine carafe.